THE LESSER BOHEMIANS

by the same author

A Girl Is a Half-formed Thing

EIMEAR McBRIDE

The Lesser Bohemians

FABER & FABER

First published in the UK in 2016
by Faber & Faber Limited
Bloomsbury House
74–77 Great Russell Street, London WC1B 3DA

Typeset by Faber & Faber Limited
Printed in the UK by CPI Group (UK) Ltd, Croydon, CR0 4YY

The right of Eimear McBride to be identified as author of this
work has been asserted in accordance with Section 77 of the
Copyright, Designs and Patents Act 1988

Lines quoted from the screenplay of *On the Waterfront* by Budd Schulberg
are included courtesy of Faber & Faber Ltd

A CIP record for this book
is available from the British Library

ISBN 978–0–571–32785–0

2 4 6 8 10 9 7 5 3 1

For my father
John McBride

THE AUDITION
Saturday 12 March 1994

I move. Cars move. Stock, it bends light. City opening itself behind. Here's to be for its life is the bite and would be start of mine.

Remember. Look up. Like the face of god was lighting me through those grilles above, through windows once a church this hall, and old men watch below. Come in. Please go straight to the stage. I snag my skirt on continents of paint chipped out black by toes and heels, by fingers picking clicking for years. I'd do too if I was here. When I'll be here. Will I be here? Take a moment, they say Then let's have your first piece. I. Suck antique air and. Go.

I don't know but it's done by some switch of the brain, this fooling off the girl I am. Giving tendril words to the dust-sunned air or twist from my mouth weeds of her until she's made her way through time from Arden, Greece or whoever wrote these lines of words learned in my head. Innocent to the work of balconies or beds, I let her talk run free in me and bring her for the age.

And after.

They bait me. Strip me a bit. Ask who and you're young, why not see the world first? Shouldn't actors see so many things? But I'm sure I have in the deep of my brain. Against my tick-tocking minus in life – books and films, fancied plays I'll be in, men surely meet, New York taxis maybe run for in elegant heels. Shouldn't these outweigh what dun school skirts there's been in this bud of life I own? And lower too, just left unsaid, time when life was something else but I've understood a whole world, all remaining is To Do. Can they not see this print on me? Ho ho, they flock You're all grown-up certainly but second speech, if you would?

Seated on the floor this, lino underfoot. Her giving out little thoughts, some simple things she's understood. This lady in her simple skirt, hands open to a gentle earth and though I'm close inside my voice fills wide into the calm. Beseeches but such a quiet way. And this time they are with me, know in her I've done my time. May hold her up for looking at and gently set her down. Then let chipped paint oceans roll me back to their shore, hopeful as a breeze. And they only Thank you we'll let you know. That's it? Letter next week in the post. Go on out through the canteen. So my audition's done and can't be undone now.

From their path I stroll to the City no city, I think to Camden Town. London unspooling itself behind. Traffic all gadding in the midday shine. So many people. So much stone. All at once and streets ahead. I'll bring it with. I will make myself of life here for life is this place and would be start of mine.

TERM ONE
Monday 19 September – Friday 9 December
1994

Lo lay London Liverpool Street I am getting to on the train. Legs fair jigged from halfway there. Dairy Milk on this Stansted Express and cannot care for stray sludge splinters in the face of England go by. Bishop's Stortford. Tottenham Hale. I could turn I could turn. I cannot. Too late for. London. Look. And a sky all shifts to brick. Working through its tunnels, now walking on its streets, a higher tide of people than I have ever seen and – any minute now – In. Goes. Me.

Worm in their wormholes. Versts of stairs. New eyes battling posters and escalators I find my way to Kentish Town – wind-slapped in the face as the tiles lead round. Up though, yes and to the house. Tall. Taller than I knew and an old Irish landlady with no T's by now. Maybe in time that'll be you? No. Maybe that'll be me. Her – on her top floor – rules, only one: Absolutely no strange men, show me no lies and I'll ask you no questions. Oh   yes   of course. But at the pad off of her slippers, I rattle at my lock. Then turn about to open wide and touch the room on either side. Three-foot bed of freedom. Beauty board walls of delight. Streaked nets of the escapee. Four floors below, a London street. Unpack knickers and unpack tapes. So the first weekend begins like this, here in the homesickless new. And later, under condensation drip from the wall, I still think here is for me. Even when auld langers row in the hall. Even incandescent piss on the toilet floor, even so. Here I am and here is for me.

Weekend then to Monday.

Nine brings the day. Dampened to fresh-cheeked I go up the

stone steps, in amid the already-belonged. Laughing and smoking they verve from the start. Darling! Coiffs flying. Surveying each other. One welcome enough to point the Registrar out. Alright there? I think I ushered the day you tried out. Lank silver streak down his hair rings true. Oh yes I remember   what year are you? Third, and pulls the door to, allowing me in for the start. His lassitude and longitude like rebuke to my nerves. Thanks. No worries, hey you'll be alright. One of them now just the same.

Hum walls of the well-known once I'm in. Is it only me? No. Must for everyone. Don't we all wonder whose head, hand touched there? After registering, which famous foot ground the grooves in these stairs winding up to the balcony? Up to this top. Costume racks and plank floor. Boys right. Girls left – some already stripping off to their lovely English skins. Upright in their bare bras with crisp-type speaking while I'm ducking in a locker to cover mine up. Ah, amn't I here to get over my body's stops. Well? Time and more to come.

Tss. Shhh. Get in quick. Don't be late or. Definitely don't take the piss. He can't be as bad as. That's what I heard. He is the most. He's like the dad – if your dad kicks the shit out of you.

Ten.

So if he laughs at me? So thinks I am young? He's the one offered my place into this room and ring of the mesmerised, ready to care. I do too and am impressed by his stalk across, and eventful stare, as he gees us towards books and plays not yet read. Wills us to fend off the swine philistines who'd have us all kept in the kitchens of life. If we let them. We won't let them – jobbing actors or stars – sat on paint that I pick at and click at with fingers. Yes I'll be fired glass where stray sand has been. Sifted and lit. Here you'll make what you'll be. Broken mirrors are waste in a broke society. Well there's not much I know about that. But straight off, envisaging strife For A Cause, turns running away into running towards. And horror-storifying prior life things lets the future be what London brings. So glory Bye to the left behind. Smiling right at me then, as though divined. No coming here wasted, he says That's strictly for the weekend and for those of you who've just left home, remember to use a condom. It gets like a hothouse in here and we don't want anything going around.

Jesus. Jesus he never. Jesus he really did. No teacher Never, nor anyone else. Bang out blatant about going permissive. Noting, I note another face laughing just like me. Trying not. To be mature. To keep the rict from boiling over. Of an age she also seems so I Hello when I'd not usually. Then she, sloe-eyed with slowest smiles, says Cuppa? In the canteen? And so wriggle in. Slip in. Remember people are blind to under your skin or. Under my skin now.

Vaudeville she, drawing all around. Funniest. And good to found a friendship. At least she's a side to go side by with to class. Vault the day then with its procession of self. What's your name? Whereabouts are you from? Live close? I hate the announcing but new futures demand new reckonings so I shuffle around what I have. Not much, not much, only me. Far from exotic when there's Spaniards and Greeks. And here the first Dane I've ever met. Australian girls. Not white or Irish. You mean English up North? I only crossed a sea. Speak French then? Amazing. Fluently? I'd love to slip my homogeneity but. On to the next class. Go.

On the night bed, I ache with foretelling the term through. Who to sit by? Or's bench to amble to? Where I am in the ranks or might belong? With the younger, yes. And if I'm youngest? So? I'm not of the glick-tongued university set. Nor those opting in as an out from office work. Not with the encyclopaedic-knowledged of every ever staged show. Or the paying rent by modelling. Or the money's all from home. No. I can't align myself. Odd one out, but intentions the best and I don't mind much because Fuck Off fitting in – not that I'd refuse a spate of more usual fun. At least here I'm in, rather than waiting on and. Fishes in the water fishes in the sea might we not jump up with a one two three?

In days:

In your mind's eye stand at Chalk Farm tube, then walk from there to here. This morning's walk. As it was. Recreating what you saw and heard. Traffic. Birdsong. Fumes from a bus. Notice every little thing and if you go blank, restart. Is it clear? Yes? Alright. Begin:

I fa. I. Step into. Ticket in my hand. Lift. Memory lifting. Concrete wet. Muck tiles. Memory lift to. Queue to. Bank machine. Roadside. To. Bus. Beggar. Back. No. Lift to 'No Begging' sign. Ears to the tussle traffic. Mini-cab rank. Cross I here. Salvation Army Hall and. Lift. Marlon Brando Guys and Dolls and. Pub called. Pub called. Turn to and see. Frill and I. See the. What? See the. City. City. Ah fuck. Fuck it blank. Start again.

So time moves, out in slow spins. To the first of life – keep your fingers in. And my head turns drowse in its lazy rings at the starting pull of gravity. Push me through to a different eye,

to this world of pearls polished up for I don't take for grant-
ed I. Not a single gasp of air. For here's the spot to cover my
tracks, where my butter-wouldn't-melt slams shutters down.
You're God so young. Youngest one. Youngest in our year. Like
the sinless one in Babylon despite hacking at my naïve. Free
to singe my wings though on others' likely tales – my own
knowing, knowing to stay well away – I do learn a little how to
be. Hithering out on fast Fridays. Go out go out whoever you
are. Slip in with the cliques – if estranged from their midst – at
the Enterprise, Crown, Fiddler's Elbow, I burnish myself on
their glut of chat, though mouse-trapped or snapped by snide
schoolboy rat-tat that I can't quite and cannot use – Wiggins,
we are the clever clogging clever while you are only you – but.
Even with, I dive into this. Gaudy myself with cigarettes. Daub
my soul with a good few pints til my mouth swings wide with
unutterable shite. Laughing lots too, like it's true. Worldening
maybe, I think. I hope. Certainly serving to get me bold and
fit for whatevers come. Truth or Dare then? She laughs Dare!
Show a nipple. Nipple? There! Unseen I ripen behind long
hair at her cool-eyed show and scoff. Now you Irish! Truth, I
cough, faithful to my fear of stripping off. Weighing, he waits
my cigarette stub then The first time   did you bleed much?
Ground butt ground. I bled enough. Like I bet you did, she
rescue laughs and my lie ate, they banter on. But come the hour
Back to mine, she says All of you.

And we're a forged crowd round hers, locked to the jaws,
rattled with chatter and choke on worse as the night undoes
its lace. I don't hold with the Fuck! Fancy digs you've got here!
and the What does your dad do? brigade. I am all for the spell
of her elegant room – white tulips in a vase. And the shop talk,
I can only half make, working place for itself in my brain. Swim

swim, maybe you'll find in to the life they apparently share. So my rule, when offered, is to partake. Tinkering ashes as spliff rounds the place. Tink too of beer bottles. Odd ends of wine. Music from her new cassette going riot to loose and loose the tongue. Float up of stories. Legs gone serene. Second years tattling You'll see what we mean; they'll kick you to bricks then desert to rebuild. Deconstruct you, they say It's no lie. My brain puckers with these, then – surprise – divides and the room begins to spin. Very like and nice verl. Easy now! Someone help her. Better step outside. Better I will and will someone with? Yes.

Topple out to her sill going chill against the stars. Take a deep breath. I do. That's right. Rub my fingers much tread-on this carpet-cooped night. Humful her room seems now, from outside. My flake throat ow but swirl's whirling down. Feeling any better? A bit. Goose bump our arms. Bit airless inside, he thumbs. I nod. But my chin's in his hand. I. Get my chin palmed. Pulled. Cheek palmed. Neck back scarlett o'h. Click! My mouth with a mouth on. My mouth by itself letting kiss and kiss draw in. Soft with the addle. Wine in the crease. Skitter I little and traitor knees. And knees. Touched. Knees. And kissed at more. Loddle of his tongue making flesh go No. Sorry and No and Shit! Slank my body. Are you alright? I am. I am Sorry. No I'm sorry, he says Just pissed and whatever. I go back on myself. I am I think I better go. Don't because of me. No no. I am no. On my heel. To the end of her road. Sorry, and 'Night, and can't.

What a stupid useless baulk. I curse to the traffic and its tooting horns. Why couldn't you? Jesus. He was barely there. Even now could you tell him from a privet hedge? A mouth and something to get across. And anyway you're dying to be a looser-limbed doll. Wrong at the first post. Ah there'll be again, claims mortification, re-attuning itself. Before long you'll diffuse in the city's fuzz and after all, I recall, footing traces of chips, tomorrow is another day.

Other Things.

Morning freeze. Market. Downed I at dawn. One foot in rubbish. One in Camden. Suckering up unctuous noodles now for lunch and no longer listening out for birds. It turns lonely though, shouldering in through the hordes. All the speculative friendships I, jealous, observe. It's just space but I have so much distance to make and this seems such a wilful world.

Glazed under bath water I go seven to eight. Drip moments remaking last night's puce mistake. Dream I am turned slender and high as an arch. Glibbing and joking, reserved and smart and faraway eyebrows – not soaking here, under scum. Not landlady screaming You've used my hot water up! along with How much washing does one person need? Depends, I shout back. Don't you 'depends' me. The rate you get through it you must be piggin. And I remem Shift. spit ert from slinged knees at dirt nursing finger hair grips clips and downdard spurtling clink through the byre floor don'
COME BACK.
MAKE back.
Here, from those votiveless margins of past.
Await await some blousier you and know her day will come.

Weeks.

Goes on time so. Every day. Hours spent opening lanes of ways on which I might set forth. These are your oysters, boys and girls. Here are your worlds of pearls. I remember it as I sit in dust. Put on tights. Stretch on mats. Lean with hot drinks

13

on stone steps where the throng pokes holes through shy. Her shoving up a bench Do you want a fag? Grateful, I arrange beside but wishing I was less flesh and much more air. Still, isn't here the right place to discover: don't wear knickers, always thongs, without a flat stomach all the world is poisoned and no serious actress will ever eat cheese. Really? Really, I mean Jesus reeeaaallly. No, I didn't know. At least I reek of new less and less. Now at night, uncurling stretch-sore self, I conjure farther futures from the ceiling cracks – in glorious technicolor – what this pleasant present lacks. I will it, hope and dream it. Fine my life'll be when it comes. When I am right. When I have made myself. When I have. When I

By morning I'm returned to day's black-and-white flick – flute-throated but learning to reach first for cigarettes. If the earthbound early clogs me in those dreams I'm soon enough back at a moderner me. Inhale. Blow. Lick splits on my lips. Permit cursory gawks at where my body's remiss. Relent a little sometimes. Recall I am here and think where can't I go? What else might I be? Besides, on the street, while the moth-life makes its way to bed, someone waits for me. She is my friend and this is Saturday.

Damp on the footpath in my furtive skin I slant at passers-by slipping in through Kentish Town. Like me, or natives? I can't yet tell. London's utterness making outers of us all – though this morning, mostly, elbows to be missed.

Morning! She's at the ticket machine, face frayed with smiles, our eyes already gossiping. What were you up to last night? Slow twirls her foot. I root out my purse, sorting coins from fluff. And clink. Ticket. Tell me? Roll of the eye Sommmeone staaayyyed oooverrr. Oh God! I die from my innocence and her

14

thrill lack of it. How much can I ask without without. Tick. Who? No. No? Train's in, quick! Off and through running down the steps. In the doors before they close. Pant collapse on seats. So now tell me? No names, but alright. Nipping auld nosiness I say Go on. Well he kissed her at the Fiddler's so she took him home and then and then. Eek. Details of fuck. The trip bed and kicked glass and her, throughout, left rubbing the wine stain with her foot. And worse – the shame – next door banging the wall. Her anticipating laughter. Her thinking I know. I do laugh too and do not say. Just play normal, pouring out cod-shocked He never dids! across the stations until we're halfway choked. Me hiding in her skitting all my basic don't knows. Even her So. So? You? Anyone yet? No. Me? No. Sharply I revert to her prior boyfriend woes that this new fella will surely not repeat. Once hedged past my innocence I keep straight on, wringing her for minutiae like He shouts Christ! when he Stop. This one's ours. Get out at Barbican.

Her first into the salient wind, fists of grasping hair. Me blinking the grit over the bridge and after her. Brick and towers. Lour and paint. Here's nowhere like any life I've learned. Even going under, it goes on up. She saying how it's ugly and I think not. I think it is Metropolis.

Still and so we're here for Art. She has the tickets while I have a heart that I hope art will burn. But her shrug au fait keeps my mouth shut and I map my gait on how she walks. Blasé with the sculptures. Stooping to the glass. Paintings mostly lingered at the same amount of time. So this is how I do it too and when the crowd gets hard for art to squeeze out through I chase after. Encourage it myself. Seek to feel but think instead and wonder if that's wrong –I'm a God's fair innocent after all when it comes to galleries too. Toe heel to her toe heel down the rows.

It's not til she's gone round the corner though that art inclines to quicken itself. First particles only – split seams in its side – making gateways into bodies that are not mine. Then gyring off to anarchic sublime. Then congealing to form some other eye I can't focus into use. Sharpen sharpen sharpen, it hisses I'll teach you how to look, then always be there to make your cupboards bare and breed you with loneliness. DON'T. Back my back to the picture. Too soon and far to see. It's only from lying alone in this body too long, I should get someone to lie in it with me. I will. My will. Something will be done. When? Oh for God's sake one thing at a time. She psssts me back, nudging That one's just like his dick. I inward groan and outward snicker. Come on come on, let's get a coffee, I'm dying for a cigarette.

So rosed we flee back to Camden, laughing on the air and pass again into where London roasts. Earthlier than its solemn-eyed Goths, livelier than its New Age Travellers too. Not cataclysmically friends but enough for now and plenty for the World's End.

Here's miles from other Saturdays I've had. Traipses to Kwik Save and Help the Aged. The market if I'm flush – Mc-Donald's if I'm bad. Speed line-learning running into smoking fags or dog-earing Solzhenitsyn on my bed. Landlady's lodger cabbage tea at half past five. Making free with her telly til she's back at nine. It's this or upstairs manhandling the time into stretching over itself – only so many times before you get depressed. That's the ledge too and dangerous. Gloam into staring at the net slide of lights. When the batteries go and my Walkman dies. Waiting, behind the distractible time, a little bit of pain. Just to tipple. Hardly a thing. Almost pretty pink petals cigarette burns on my skin. Bouquets exist, rosiest at the shin, contemplating though up my thigh. It's a pull rope, for the wade of hours on my own, and matches slice for slice all diversions I know. Tonight I'll not be at that garden though because Look at me, I'm out with a friend.

Five inch hours after and drink-ate bones, she's collecting men who woo. Eclipsed by the gilt of her toss-hither mane I smoke myself a pool, drawing only out to dip in their flames. Yes thanks, or It's lit! College together, she explains with a kind of liquid negligence I'd like to dab on the backs of my knees. Wheel they for her languor. Wheel I for it too and, if I were them, would easily choose her funny ha ha over my funny peculiar no real eye-opener there. Besides, my drunk eye's once again seeing itself but swooped back from art to more clay-ish complaints: unflat stomach v vociferous wants. Cheer up love, might never happen, one taunts. And what if it already has? God you! she says, so I do up a smile. Hidden depths, she repairs while I cross my mind to engage more aptly with the room. Success hits on Look. Where? Some lads from our school. Oh? Oh! and – well caulked – she signals them to. Nod they, up glasses and make their way through. Ladies. Gents. Jesus, above my ears though, every thought heads to sex. If I had to choose one which one would it be? Don't know but some galled-virgin loop in my body's going Pick so something might get done. Pick and begin to be a person who always gets to pick. Alright then, studious, choose your best. Him. From my audition. Wrong choice. Right away. But recognising why makes it okay, even interesting, to divine for from opposite ends of the table I see she and he at a cautious elide. Oblique refer-ring, offhand offered cigarettes. She intent with his friend but he stares at her neck. Palpable in this smoke-clod air a weft that neither can eschew. So it's he was last night and her mouth gone tight makes all earlier piss-taking undo. She likes him and he? I don't know. Sits in my blind spot, along with all men, I suppose. What did he take of her body? What's he like without clothes? In on their secret but out in the cold, me and my bodiless eye.

Hop out a swear. Fuck my leg's gone to sleep, and I start up going foot to foot. Have you to piss? No my leg is sore. Well stop it you're making me want to go. Sorry. Fuck's sake get off my toe. Fuck's sake yourself. Hey leave her alone. Never mind anyway, I'm going home. No don't go yet. No I'm wrecked. Then I will too. No you stay put. Ah look, a few of us were about to walk up so why don't we all make tracks?

Enslithered by pints I follow her lead. Sweet Ta ra! to the courtiers who do not leave. Then out in the mangling crowds on the street we make our clump move through. Four or six. I take their steer. Completed evening for me but not for her. More modest in her drunkness too with him here. Is that true? I wonder why? Seems with drink even pulling off panels of self, I can't escape the audience of one I make, so resign to my private view of their fun. Them still playing it friend-like. Still not touching. For why? If I had. If someone. Shut up, you're just much more drunk and can't carry it off like they do. At her gate I surrender. Night and kiss. What a nice day, did you enjoy it? Yes. He's just coming up so I can lend. Of course. Then they're off upstairs to her fully fledged bower while I and the remaining other turn ourselves to Kentish Town.

Shall I walk you home? No thanks I'm grand. You've had a few. So have you. And? And? Don't get jippy come on let's walk. First of the autumn. What are you on about? Really the chill, don't you think? I think you are really drunk. Well aren't you such a gent to say. I think you are really drunk, m'lady. That's more like it. True. Stocious so, but friendly, turn we up Anglers

Lane. Shop glass by my face making farce of my brain. Some boozed Alice going in through panes while he's at theatre chat chat chat. Oh! What a lovely not to be, just between ourselves like a birthday party. Crutch-kneed, stick-kneed. This way and yon. My eyes curbing upstream to well beyond the balance of body. Far as stars I see and let the world go sway. Whoa there now, don't bash your head. Wisha the night and wish this way of floundering could be every day. Is this your road? Yes. Hand on my waist. Gate grate. Handbag. Keys in my door. Somewhere gauging he's no worse than any other and all my nets go Twitch. Dividing the space. Dividing again. Do you want to come in? Thanks but not this time. I turn my eye back to sky. It stands me in good stead. Some other time maybe? he. No, I say Sure my landlady would kill me anyway I'm just too drunk to be thinking straight thanks for walking me home. No problem. Night. Intacta. He's off down the street. Were and am intacta yet. No problem. Don't panic. Intacta to bed. It'll be fine. It's not like men can see.

It's not like Sunday yet either and. Sunday is not worth the price.

Monday. Is every eye knowing? Hers, even in fun? Everyone now appraised of the edges I cannot make to round? Worst he says Are you alright? and How fucking drunk were you Saturday night? Lying by the sin of my teeth I'm fine, and Sorry, I'd forgotten to eat. No worries, you were hilarious, totally out of it, he says. And so I wish that he was dead. And I wish that I was dead but neither of these deep wishes come to be, or are true.

Pick a scene for two. Twentieth century's best. Two scenes per class so fifteen minutes max. Put a list on the board. We'll start in two weeks so you've no excuse for showing up unprepared.

She nods. I do. Any ideas? No. Will I ask my Him about it? Your who? You know – scutter us then down to the toilets for such squeals as required by a lovebit neck. God he's lovely and a Third Year too so he knows what's what and he didn't go home until this morning, imagine, I can hardly stand up! Lipstick on the tile and the wall above and Hussy! I know but oh I'm in love and I think he might be The One. Purple bang of left right in my chest. Good for the gossip but bad for the friendship. Now weekends'll be for giddy-up on her bed while I. Ah fuck. Ah so.

In the week though.

I smell the coffee, the gravy granule, always is to me. See it in its thick white cup, stub and quick to disappoint, a pleasure surely for only grown-ups? Ah. Concentrate everyone please. *Make its hot spread in my hand – tolerates thumb, intolerant palm – disdaining to demonstrate like others around who prick fingers and tssst tongue to teeth. Instead I bear – as I would in life, and maybe private too.* Good you're not faking but feel its weight. *Don't fake weigh so.* No. *See myself sat on her floor, cup in my hand, hoping my Drop of milk? didn't offend. Feeling it sag in its burn while I wait – careful now – mind her carpet. Her back from the kitchen saying Sorry it's finished, and the whole roasting load to down. Its smell in my face. Crick in my neck. What would I not do to please my new friend so.* Raise it to your mouth. *I suffer it up and.* Don't pretend to choke, that's the worst hamming up. *True too, for I swallowed it really.* Alright folks, let's call it a day.

And for some weeks.

I play a game of walk, up Lady Margaret Road. Still inside,

when the eyes reach focus. Here garden walls. Here starker trees. Adhering to my footfall but inured to the leaves and the rattle-tattle skip-up they suggest. It is forward and only. Nothing else. Thigh to ankle making tread in the light night, or the early day, no more in my body beyond its moving me. To have slipped it, purely. To go up so high. Witness all these windows from which I hide in my red coat. In my black boots. These are worth the going through of sirens and of rain. They torture me with comfort in these weekends on my own; spewing sheen on the matt of this longed-for life that's becoming lived alone. Why am I. Why am I not. Where's even the way to could? I'm not lost. Or not lost much. Lonely. It is that and   I don't know what to do.

So I move. Cars move. And it's almost life. City operating on my mind. Here's to be, even if not quite right. But not long before the fun begins.

Ninety I it, the afternoon we're set to rehearse. Necessity prising her Saturday to, for we've lines to learn but. He's moving flat too so. Come in and on to the neat peace of her room that soon dwindles to laze on her floor. Scripts and buns. Coffee. Tea. Lullish the sun through a scant cherry tree threading meek in and out of the blow. Her though, finickity. Is something wrong? We had a fight, he stormed off. What happened? Who knows? Some fucking man stuff. All I said was Should I expect you back this evening? Sounds reasonable. Well, so you'd think, but the next minute he's shouting You don't own me and slamming the door and. Fuck him, I say shit. Pause she, then Sally Bowles Yeah I already did! And I spit laugh. Cross-eyed, she adds, cross-eyed herself. Oh Jesus you're terrible. Well that's not what he said! Then I'm into the kink and she falls in too.

What a fuck-up. Which? Him or you? Both! Ah don't worry, he'll be back in the end. Probably something mournful between his legs, it's just, you know, don't be a dick. Or at least not until dick's appropriate. That's it! And laughing to the guts, floor, we stretch endly out. Cherry shadowing the ceiling, bowstrung then upright. I wish I could be more like you, she says You're so independent, especially about men. I let the nice lie slip settle against and wonder how I might make it fit? Or is it possible to say I don't work properly, without giving away anything else? Instead I sigh I don't know, I wouldn't mind more sex. She crack claps Well then, so you should! Let's get Piss Off by Chekhov done and dusted, then I'll do your make-up and we'll go for a dance down the Palace, what d'you think? That maybe your frilly valance put him off? Oh shut up, that's my mother, are you up for it? Alright, but these Beats first though? Yes. Hurray!

Drink time. She makes me. Curls my hair. Mascaras and sticks me but does say Nice dress while I smoke and feign how much I don't care that she thinks I could do with the help. It is us though, and exciting, setting off for Camden Town, clipping quick into the buzz around. We being young here and so we can. And fuck him for not calling. And who knows I. I might. But won't. But still. It's a tad early for the Palace now, let's stop here for a drink.

Old boy I'd say and awful Irish. Royal College Street. Space though and I'm not mad for the heave. She goes to the bar. I get us a seat. Marlboro Lights and lagers and we with some gossip. Not much of it kind. And after only one she's fidgeting over maybe she should call because, you know, perhaps he has and. Don't you dare, just wait him out. I'll get us another then we'll set off down. Weeeelllll, she reluctants Okay.

Squeeze at the bar thinking Don't let her call, give me the night out. Drum my fingers. And stop, so the barmaid won't think it's at her. Hurry up but. Then she does and I order and see, any moment, that cigarette will spill. On my hand too – if its smoker isn't careful – and that blink minute, very second, it does. Ow! I Ow! though really not hurt and its owner goes Shit! Are you alright? long fingers flick dusting ash into my coat while I – circumstantially too close – blush Fine. I didn't burn you? No. Good   sorry about that – and book indicating – Bit too engrossed. Ah you really shouldn't do that, you know. What, read? Fold it back, it'll break the spine. It was broke when I bought it, but he straightens it out and I go The Devils? That's right, just at the end. The confession? You know it? 'I killed God'. Impressive. Why? No reason, you just don't look the kind. Oh? Boobs too big? Hair too blonde? Jesus! his eyes wide and laughing Not at all, I only meant that you look kind of young. What does that mean? muttering a fuck at the puce I've gone. Nothing, I just thought all the kids were into lightness and being, I apologise, I didn't mean to offend. Well I've read that too and. Want a cigarette? No   I should get this back to my friend and. I'm going to finish off these last few pages, he says But after that, as reparation, can I buy you a drink? I doubt we'll still be here. But if you are? Well we'll see. Then we'll see, he smiles into his Penguin Dostoyevsky and I mortify my way back to her.

Oh my fucking God! she Oh my God what was that? Don't just don't   you won't believe what I said   Oh God I wish I was dead. She just kicks at me Tell? And friends are made this way so I spin it out, laced with plenty Don't stare's. Well he could buy me a drink, she smirks at the end He's older too which equals good in. Stop that, besides which, he's probably already forgot and even if he hasn't   anyway   what about your fella?

She nips up the bait and off we go, me careful ducking his eye-line until Hey Dostoyevsky girl? Same again? I ahhh yes. He points to her You as well? She shakes her head, I have to make a call. Don't, I Please? Begging ignored and the scruffy Devils stuffed into his pocket. It'll be all wrecked now, I think.

It'll be all wrecked now, I say. Library school is it? he asks. Drama school actually. Which one? Does it matter? It might. How come? I'm an actor. Oh. He long-angle lights a cigarette Are you always this bad-tempered? And my cheeks go shame So then what would I have seen you in? Now, now, you should never ask an actor that, he says. Why, in case you've mostly been 'resting'? Exactly. And have you? No, I've not. So what's the last thing you did? This month I started work on a script. That's not. Sorry to interrupt, but can I get my coat? No! Eye beg her as he sits forward to let. She tugs it up and while buttoning, merciless mouths Good luck! then gives the goading eyes Come round tomorrow alright? Alright. Left bereft so, I watch her now going   going   gone.

Irksome slowly, I turn back. Don't worry, he says You'll be alright, canines showing in his English smile. Eyes a little tired but features fine. God, to be a parrier not I know I, being all I can get through my lips. Him, tapping his own, takes pity I think, long legs eased out asking When did you read it? The Devils? Yes. Two years ago, three. Did you like it? I did. Why? Stavrogin. The child-molesting nihilist? He's not a nihilist, really. Smoke sheets from his mouth I'd say the child-molesting is the more concerning part. At least he acknowledges what he did wrong. What does that matter, once the irreparable's done? But he's sorry. Even if he is, so what? Forgiveness. He's not entitled to that. Why? Because the child's still dead. He didn't kill her. He nods his head But there are more ways than literally to make someone die. So then just waste another life? That life's already wasted. Is it? Isn't it? he says. Well he did something that he regrets and isn't needing forgiveness common to all of us? That's just being alive then being dead. Don't be cynical, I say What about hope then? Or love? And have you ever been in love? Not yet but   I will. Faith indeed, he smiles. So what about you? I pin him. Have I been in love? No, what do you believe in? The lifelong struggle to remain indifferent. That sounds sort of sad. Oh you think so? I nod. Just wait until you're my age, he sighs. Don't you patronise me, I say. Then don't patronise me, he replies. Silent us. I bite my lip. Oi mate! somewhere at a barman, and hot to the gills. This my worst by far and You know, he says, through his cigarette You're the only girl I've ever said that to and still wanted to keep chatting up. Are you chatting me up? I thought I might   how's it going so far? It's going alright. So if I go and get us another pint you'll still be here when I get back?

Turn turn the blood in my cheek. Eyes accumulate his universe, whatever he is. I daren't even guess at the cut he must see − unshaved leg and old bra on − while he's half a head up on the pub's other men and. What you thinking about? he asks, sitting again. Nothing and don't look at him strange are you from London? Up North, can't you tell? I don't know English accents well. Have you travelled much anywhere else? And I steal into her, what would she be? More than clay. Go on. It's only this evening, sure when will you see him again? Weirdly, more exotic places, I say. Naples, interrailing, boats stretched out in the bay. Age eight, with my father, foothills of the Himalayas. A friend's parents' house in Crete. Thailand, me and a boyfriend sneaked. Got caught and killed but. Was it worth it? Yes   for the sky burning in the night. And these lies like me, tear out of me, ring almost as fact. And they're pristine copies of someone's

25

truth, I'm fastidious about that. But he listens like I'd never lie and seems amused enough I cast shyness aside. Praises a boldness he doubts he'd have managed then charms away for more. And at some point I know if he asked, I would. What? he says. What? I say. What's that look? Don't be paranoid, nothing. He holds his hands up. I go red and so we carry on.

To flickering lights. Shouts of Time! How was the chatting-up in the end? Pretty good, well done. Thanks, he smiles Good enough to warrant taking me home? Here it is then. Here I am. Oh God I would but I'm up in Kentish Town in this bedsit and my landlady. Oh right, never mind. Sorry I'm sorry. Don't worry, it's fine. No it's the truth, it's not that I wouldn't like to and I. Okay, so come back to mine? Oh, I Nearby is it? ask, like distance is the thing. Yeah, five minutes up the road. I feign indecision but he is so easy in the wait, like he already knows. Alright, I say. Alright then, he says Come on, get your coat.

In the metal clang night talking films we walk. Fish my hand near his but he only smokes. Maybe he's a murderer? Fuck's sake. He's a fuck and, look at him, he's probably done this lots. But oh my body opts out and in. Flesh scraping fear against the Do of my brain. So slice my fingertips on every railing to keep by him up the Camden Road.

See not far, he says brushing round the hedge Just along, number five, with the broken gate. God! this is your house? I gasp. Floors high and white. Not mine, he laughs Where I rent a bedsit, up there, first floor. Have you lived here long? He mulls his keys Ten years, give or take. So since I was seven or eight. Jesus, don't tell me you're as young as that? Why? He shakes his head Never mind, then thumbs his fag end back down the cracked wild path.

No hall lights, sorry, follow me. I follow up the stairs. Silver key and Let me turn on a light first, just wait there. So I lull in a dark ocean of motely air as the traffic beyond here calms. Motorbike and lorry alike hold all I know about tonight. To do and then to be. Click and glow and It's a mess but you might as well come in, he says. Choose him. Choose this, and now.

Higher but smaller than Jesus what a state! Hence the suggestion of your place first – him down at the fake fire striking the gas – I wasn't expecting to bring anyone home. Sink in the corner. Bay window jammed with desk. Books going topple. I pick by old letters, ash saucers, scripts, half-filled mugs. Give me your coat. His single bed. Dumped on the armchair where I could've myself but. Politeness is polite. I'll just clear these plates. Goodbye dried mince. May the kissing go better for the Pinter beneath it. Will it? Orange peel on Valle-Inclán. What might have been a plaster on Howard Brenton stop it stopit. So   Let Love In? What? Do you like Nick Cave? I don't know, I say. Well let's find out. Dum. Devils tossed and his long coat slung. And I see it then, quiet tense in his mouth, how now's getting past time for more. Come here. But the nerves make a faff of my own Actually it's not that bad a room how much is it a month? About two hundred. That's pretty good but   the way you treat your books. Bollocks to the books, he says touching my face. It is the first time we have and I go quick to the thrillpleasuredread. Terrible mouth though, keeps on saying Is it annoying   always having to bend to kiss   unless she's as tall as you which I'm obviously not and. He is so tall he must bend a lot. But he does, saying No, then kissing me.

Fright I. He holds to. The make of his lip, turning into my own, turn until I kiss back. I think he is smiling but means it the same. Kisses to bit breaths and touch of his tongue making fast me, does he notice? Doesn't say or doesn't care. Just amuses his mouth and flips all my blood over. So here's how grown men kiss and this one knows how. I know it's a fine kiss but gird for what follows as, in the depths of his curtain, some dying fly sings. Hear it go against the glass and. Put your bag down, he says stripping it, tossing it, kissing again. Gone fuck to forbearance. Mouth on my neck. Then deep with mine. Open. Working out something else like under his worn shirt his whole body is. And his skin is so live and likes being touched – even my barest morsel of palm on his stomach. My skin shifting too, if not quite there, scares to his search for a zip on my dress. There isn't one either, he gets that quick. Instead ups the dress, up my thighs, past my tights. Up my back. Arms up, he says, pulling it off and I am I'm. Getting bare. Bra. My old bra, the red marks it makes and. Oh God I am blood thud at the hand on my breast. Beg off the moment he might want to look. Undoes his shirt though. Thanks reprieve. Shrugs it off and swings far with kissing. Lovely. But getting precise with his hands. My grey straps simple tugged down. Then where he slides one of mine so I Jesus! I eyes wide. This isn't a game. This is already well underway. And I'd like to look at his body but he doesn't know that and I am miles too shy to ask, for now the kissing's more biting. Now it's Show me your breasts, and the bra's off like Voilà! He steps back. I fold up. Too late for modesty, he laughs, yanking my wrist. I can't though. Just clench in. He tries again. I double over. Hey, is something wrong? I don't reply. Are you sick? Shake my head. Have I hurt you somehow? No I, eyes pricking wet. His voice turning anxious What's just happened? What's wrong? And I know I must any minute NOW say I'm sorry   I'm sorry   I'm shy.

Silence in the courtyard. Silence in the street. His low laugh. Don't laugh. Well don't be shy with me! Jokes won't go for now though, not with ignominy to the eyes. I'm not laughing at you, sorry, he solemnifies, then hides me with his body. Touches my hair. Whispers You don't have to be shy with me, pulling up his duvet. But Oh my God, I just Oh God, exhale. Ah now Ireland too much shame. And he covers as much of me as I'll let. You know, we don't have to if you don't want, right? I do want   I really do it's just   Alright then, he says Let me have a think. So the fly and Nick Cave get their wicked way as he ponders my state, and I cringe.

Okay, he rouses Here's the plan: I strip off while you look on. One good gawp at my skinny white hide should cure all that shy, don't you think? Hot-faced I imagine what I might see, and he gets smile-narrow eyes Alright, sit. So I do, clamped in duvet. Now look up at me, he says That's all you have to do. I force my eyes up, though not to his. To his slim shoulders. His pale chest. The curve of his arm and strings of veins. Ribs showing a little through. Darker hair on his stomach than his head. More? I nod. Trousers pushed down long legs. Thin, not skinny. Sorry really old pants, and he flaps at his shorts Still with me? Yes. Excellent, because this next bit's the best! And he inches the waistband to his pubic hair. Fuck go my guts and squirl. He bends. I. Oh. Rips a sock off instead. Ah ha! Caught in the act! he says What a filthy mind! No I just. Then he just takes them down and

I've never seen a whole naked man.
Bits only, in isolation
but
that's not the same and
Here you go, he says doing a turn and
the thrill of him goes right down my leg.

29

Stop catching flies, he says, then – air-hostessing himself – Time for the guided tour. Head with own hair. Face. Neck. Collarbone, once broken. Shoulder dislocated – painful that. Chest. Left arm broken. Right, intact. A few fucked fingers. Ribs cracked, three. Stomach. Legs. Left foot fractured. Jesus, what happened you? I fell off a roof. Ow! I say. Ow is right but   it was a long time ago. And this – presented in finger and thumb – is my penis, at half-mast now but I can promise better later on, circumcised too, for your delight. Are you Jewish? No it was too tight or something when I was young. Why 'for my delight'? Women like that sort of thing, he says Or so I've heard. And I don't know if it's planned but all his chat feeds time to familiarise. So, feeling less shy or more sure I'm a freak? as he hunkers down in front. Both! Well no pleasing some people, then he leans in and kisses me again. Soft this time. Like coax with his tongue. Persuading though that what he wants, I want. Implicating me in first incursions to my breasts. Then in his suggestion I open the duvet to let his mouth touch as well. And I do, just enough to admit him in and for me, not him, to see. Plenty though for me to. Fuck. Neck clicking back at the little of his teeth and I must red nod when he asks Nice? It is. Good! Now how about the knickers and tights? And my fingers unprise from the cliff.

First – Duvet from between my knees.

Second – Mid kiss, his proposed I'd like if you touched me.

Third – My quick Oh! That's big! Great news, he laughs But it's about average, mind if I touch yours?

Fourth – So if I let him?

Fifth – Enjoying that?

Sixth – Yes   a lot

Seventh – Then you know what's next. No! I'm not taking

this duvet off! Come on, sex through a sheet, maybe, but a duvet? Anatomically no way and besides, it's freezing out here.

Eighth finger – Fucking hell, you came here for this.

Ninth – His thumb runs the length of my face. Listen, I think I know what the answer is but is this your first time? Oh God! I look away. Don't worry, he says We all have one. Why don't you lie back?

Tenth – And let's just get it done.

So here we are. Here I am. Naked, in bed with a naked man. Under his body. Matching his kiss. Tangled legs. Parted lips and daring myself to the furthest furthest til What are you doing? Going down on you. No! No! I'm not doing that! Well, technically you wouldn't be, I would. No. Come on, you'll like it. I would not! Just try me, I've been told I'm pretty good. Thanks, I say I'll do without. Might help, he says. How? With the getting wet. Oh Jesus – I sit bolt up, crucified – That's it! I'm going home. Don't go, he says, plying me back. No, this is a disaster. Don't say that, I'm actually having a weirdly good time. Really? Really and if you don't want to that's fine I'll just do something else. Like what? Well you'll have to stay and see.

So tempted enough and shame defied, I let him elaborate where he's allowed. And he gets me as ready as anyone might, almost to wishing he would. If this game's touch he knows it well and where to find what of me understands. Getting breath getting quick against his mouth. Sync timing hip til I'm gripping his side. God I could really be inside you now, ready to have a go? And his fingers and going and Alright, yes. That's the spirit, I'll just get a thing, he says, patting a hand about under the bed. Finds. Rips and rolls it down on himself. Oh God it's really now isn't it? And he's so ready it's true. You know this

31

might hurt a bit? I know. Just say if it's too much. My eyes go open at this, to his. Close up I think they're grey. Flecked with concentrating on mine as he finds to the place. Little spit on his fingers – Just in case. Kissing then sloping me, shifting his weight Ready? Yes. And he. Jesus Christ! No don't pull away. It hurts. I know but it's not quite in yet. I can't. You can, just let me, he says It'll never be as bad again. How do you fucking know? Educated guess. Then Oh fuck, he goes That's it. And he is all against me. And he is inside. Attempting to kiss through a pain running wild from his body far into mine. I bite my own lip and stare above. Ceiling swirls there. Cracks. Worlds beyond the pain not improving. Now. Or now. Or yet. I wish I hadn't. I'd never done this. I wish he didn't know. Oh God. Hey, look at me, he says. I don't. I'm being gentle as I can, do you want me to stop? No. He tries to kiss again but I won't. Come on, don't make it like I'm here on my own. Humiliation immaculata though sprouts its own tongue. Just get yourself off, isn't that what you want? Don't be like that, he says Do you want me to stop? Just stop fucking talking and come and be done. The look in his eye then, what does that mean? Fine, he says – voice all turned down – What the fuck is it to me? And he does it then. Jesus. And again. And again. Until I cry but now he's not asking how I am. Just fucks like I said. His breath showing work and some gratification at what he does, in and to me but only for himself. I can't tell how long until – so far in – the gritting and fucking starts becoming every sex sound I've ever heard, all at once in my ear, while his body works through every single thing it wants. And mine, in his best moment, silent, accepts the mess it's made.

There you go, he says breathing hard and, quicker than I expect, pulls himself out. Straight off the bed and condom. Snap.

Tossed at the bin. Bit of blood there, he says showing a streak on his palm. Then, all lank impassive, lifts an old bathrobe and goes on out the door.

I lie in the pain. Climb his cities of books. Hand between my legs. The wet, true, blood. So that's done and something wrecked, what should I do next?

Where's your toilet? I ask. End of the hall. Here take this, and he slips the robe off You never know who you'll meet down there. No looking at me either, just for his underwear, and not finding, takes his trousers instead. And the toilet roll, you better take that too.

Murderous landing. TV lights on the floor. Go in. Hover. Piss and blood in the dark and wish I'd never have to face him again. Clothes though. Bag and girl aren't you a woman – sore woman – now? But still.

I knock. Just come in. He is cigarette lit. Tap in a kettle. I couldn't find the sink. No there isn't one, use this, let me get out of your way. Strangers were and strangers again. He's only over there but we are back in his wild room and I am vanished punished. My blood on his bed that he kicks the duvet over before making tea. Wash my face. I'd like to more but not so near. Redd out my knickers with the tights rolled in. Quick unpick and put them on. Bra. Dress. Thanks for the dressing gown. No problem, sugar? Actually, I'm going to head. And this the what turns him Do you know your way back? Sort of, I'll find it. No I'll walk you   it's late. You don't need to. It's not a big deal, I'll get dressed. No, no, I Irish insist. Fuck's sake, he says It's after one and this is Saturday night in Camden. I'm not leaving you to wander about on your own, have the tea then we'll go. And calm again as quick as he wasn't but has kicked all the spit from my row. Alright. So clear off those books and sit, sugar?

Please. Milk? Yes. Strindberg hits the floor and me his chair. He passes the tea, sits on the bed, lights then offers a cigarette and stares at the smoke between. All in the air though, new music What's that? Schoenberg, he says Transfigured Night. Are you taking the piss? Certainly not, he laughs. But laughs. It's beautiful, I say. Yeah I think it is, I often play it here when I'm by myself. So sit we. Separate. Years apart while the night turns itself, in his forty watt, into waste and into past. I tip tongue to questions but he is closed eyes and I know what I did. Here's the room though, where done though. Remember everything. And I do not expect his Just stay – at the end – It's so late you might as well. Hmm in my manners, and really still for a flee but it's knackeredness overrules any thoughts of my blood on his sheet. Alright, I say. Standing up and lamp off.

He at the wall. I the edge. Back to. Sheet damp. Far light bleeds on the litter floor alongside. Gas bud glow. How long until he sleeps I wonder? And if he wonders that about me too? Him that done – stranger of a man who perfectly knows I have failed the perfect game. Where was stoicism? That much I'd relied upon but had not, in the end. Useless you are useless. Sting the eye and fill it up. He shifts. Don't notice. Please not that. Then I abandon my eyes to keep heaves from my back. I almost hear his eyes scanning above. It's alright, he says touching my arm. Adds no more or else to that, for which I am grateful, as soon after for his gentle snore.

Sometimes this night I sleep as well. Sometimes contrast my Was that usual? with I'm only the latest after all and maybe next time? Shut up. I'd turn but can't because he lies there and how deep is his deep? So hours rise heeding curtains and the roustabout street below. Heels clacking, laughing You tight cunt! So if I am? I'm still waiting. Well you'll wait a long time!

Shrieking now, then laughing until wee wee all the way home. And sirens belting to, or speeding fro, like London's alive in another time of its own. On towards five, banging at his door. Next one mate, he shouts until they go. Fucking Saturdays, he says back asleep before the weed smells or bottles bash in the street. But all this cheers me, picks me up. Slips me to my new world. If sleep would only come and against me, the long thin man. Alive. A-sleeping. In. And I drift in under where
She walks the tongue of the world, narrow as a road.
Far below where earth is and where fire goes.
Unrippled now.
Weeds.
Dry and frei.
But the weight of.
Banished poor famished eyes
lake music
Fuck!
Morning.

Fuck! he wakes like a scare. What? Sorry, I forgot you were there. And I lie by him. Shy by him. Sorry, he repeats but in-gentle, unpersonal, prying himself cock from bottom, toe from sole. Sweat where he's laid against me although the room burns cold. Christ I ache, he yawns This bed's too fucking small for one never mind about two. Can I use your toilet? I ask. Yeah, you know the drill.

He is lovely indifferent when I come in. Leant on his desk. Steam and smoke wreathing. Cigarette? No thanks. Tea there, hot mind. Thanks. Sit and slurp. Are you alright? Fine. No, I meant   after last night? Fine, I maintain for what can he want? Bulletins on bruising or how there's still blood? I just, he says God I'm wrecked. Yawns it. Shears it. Bye to the night. I stare at his Chekhov but can't help asking Who's that? Who? The photo on your desk. That's m   my daughter. Oh, I say Are you married then? Does it look like I'm married? he laughs, offering the room. No   but   were you? No, what's the time? Half eight. Shit! I've a meeting in town   sorry to rush you but. Don't worry I'll just get dressed. He picks up the towel I used last night then makes on out the door. And I steal a look at his daughter up close. Like him I think. Eyes and mouth. Three? Four? Who knows how old children are? Sneak a drag on his fag. No. Get dressed before he's back and you'll be. shy. So to the end. Clothes again. Uncover his underpants but it was last night he looked for them. No matter. Old fag smoke against the new, I race my clothes back on.

Do you need the sink? No. Then I'll have a shave. Dripping hair. Towel round his waist reaching for his fag in such one-track haste I'm an emptiness fastening her shoes. Button my coat. He lathers up. Well, good luck with your audition. Just a meeting – to the glass – But thanks   and also   for last night. You're welcome, I say. He smiles to my reflection then starts to shave. And I wish that I was someone else, a girl with words behind her face, not this one done up like a stone in herself. You won't see him ever again. Fuck it, this, and all anyway. Before I can't, I go wrap my arms round his waist and say, nose into his damp shoulder blades Thank you for not being a bastard last night   for being kind to me. Silence. He and. I. Have I bad chanced? Peek round his shoulder but in the mirror his eyes take up mine, most surprised. Gentle of day forgetting the night. That's alright, he says, touching my fingers to his mouth Thank you for choosing me. Then, self-disgust over-running my everything else, I grab my bag and leave.

Into the world from out of his room I blink in the light of day. Will I look back at his window? No. That's done. If I turned around even the house might be gone. Let his soap kiss devolve into scum on my hand. Relinquish. Extinct it. Go. Hedge again. Road. Schools and railings. Train up on a rail bridge ahead. Cheap second-hand fridges lining the path. That turn's where we were. My turn is right – so I would have found my way back, mid kebab salad gossamering to puke. Sun of the morning. London day. The banjaxed exhuming themselves from doorways. Buses and music. Spivs and Goths. New Age Travellers and leather coats and too-tight jeans and diamond whites. Everywhere heaves of fighting in the streets. This is the finest city I think and, no matter how awkward or bloodily, I am in it now too.

I go straight to hers. Good morning. Good night? Come in come in, we're just woken up. Into her room and her fella stretched out asking So did you shag him or what? She Tea? and Sit! indicating the bed. I plomp back, maybe on his legs, and tell my tale. Well not all. Well some. Well anyway the bit about sleeping with him. She going I knew it! Him going Fuck! You do know who he is, right? And I don't, but he does, so rings him in. Theatre mostly. The occasional film until that one last year had everyone raving! Now he's the dog's bollocks. Oh, is he? Yes! God you're such a div! Then follows various smart-aleckings before tinkering for truths. What was he like in bed? What did he do? These I proffer as Transfigured Night, The Devils and filthy dishevel of bedsit. Incredulous they but sniff my palm for his soap. And I can still smell him on me under my clothes. Seeing him again? Probably not, no. Why? she says. I chuck forth an embroider and love my shape in its light: Why

37

ruin a perfect night? Bravo! he bravo's offering his joint which I slide down with, saying This is the life. Knowing that Yes it is.

Do you have to use my hot water up? I have to wash. Every day? Too much lady, too much. Get a shower, I think but keep to myself and wash my expedition away. Fare thee well purple foothills of sex. I clean a man off my body. I clean a man off my face. Lick from breasts. Spit between legs. The sweat and. Where mouths. Thigh dry blood what's he. What? What is he doing now?

Up Lady Margaret Road in the wintering air. The trees and distance and closeness, the same. Evening, to you, town. Evening, to me. A little light think amid bus staunched breeze and he's really only streets away. Somewhere over maybe there. Did he wash his sheets? Is he with someone else? Or his daughter? How he smoked his cigarettes. Three or four draws down to the tip, is that a telling thing? Back in my room I practise it. And smoke far on into the dark, until dawn goes white over Kentish Town Road, the Assembly House, the Forum and beyond to? Don't know. All London then, I suppose.

We are rat tat pull and snigger. We are drinks and draggeldy home. I am chips and she's pickled egg. Always for the tale and tale again. And it gets heavy with the lies I make but I like them. She does too. Thrown on the bed type three times come. Interlocked fingers or wrists held down. Why she doesn't notice the new every time is beyond me. But I lie well. But not inside. That, unhitched, goes flail about. Wheedles its sticks into You let me down. Sorry, Mind says to Flesh. No matter no matter, get over — though Camden stays shoulder checked. Revoke that memory. Forget the face. Just be in on the joke. Part of the tease. These are not things barred to me any more. These are me as well. And the. But the. Fleadh wears down. Knees from kneeling. The time on my own, until my once becomes like not at all. This the lamest fun of lonely that she can drip feed to her Him. So the cigarette gets to like the leg. The arm wonders what it should do with itself. Nicks with a razor but then gets a band-aid for for fuck's sake what are you at?

River run running to a northern sea. Thames. Needle skin brisk and the eyefuls of concrete. Lead by the. Strip for the. National Theatre. Go on. Get a ticket. Go in.

Here the vault and not Hawk's Well. Smacks of the hell-less or at least of the sensible. I'd be. What I'd be. Is this the Olivier? Yeah, on upstairs for you. Through and oh to its canyon. I never saw so many chairs. On beyond uncurtained stage – You may take and have me, please. But Saturday matinee. Sole in my row. Where is everyone else?

In the dark comes spiders out of art and first I'm sleuthed away. Measuring up the vying worlds. Meandering into the emphasised words but under neat speeches are oceanous platitudes and so I slide and slide. Up. Don't sleep. Don't. You do not. Settle my head back on my neck but the veining of boring expands and contracts until I'm left to myself. And soon I'm judging a hupped toupee. Then predicting a spit trajectory. Right down, I'd say, to that redhead asleep. Too far from here though. Over there would be Over there   ov is it? With black specs on? Really?   such a dead cert knit, and for London. Him. Of course it is.

                  And the air makes whistles.
                  And my brain makes hay.
Guts to gorge. Look at him. Be sure? It is. oh god. But if I sit

39

still. Live for the stage. Focus on the actors and glorious fake and. Look again is he looking at me? Read at the programme.

Then he definitely isn't.

Then it's the interval. Look again. He gets up pray for poise. More as he excuses himself across. Yet more at my aisle. Please poise at my step. Hello, I thought it was you, he says and I remember and I remember and make some word like Hi. Enjoying it? Yes I. Really? he says I thought I saw you nodding off? I wasn't   it's just my first time   I mean   you know   I was looking around. He solemn nods but somewhere smiles So how have you been? I scald-cheek Fine   and you? Fine, he says Coming out for a smoke? an unlit in his fingers. No, I No thanks, and go at reading biogs. like War and Peace. He loiters further but I am shame sealed. Well, I'll leave you to it, he says Nice to see you again. You too, I say and don't look up. Do not watch him climb the steps. Nor think at all Why were you rude? Only Bladder, why have you forsaken me now? Just wait til he's gone, then go.

Right, stick on that nonchalant smile don't buy an ice cream like a child and get what urbane I possess into line as I go back in. But at the bottom of the steps he's all chat to some girl. Close and smiling. She giving laughs. Him too, or thoughtful, pushing his hair back. Gets kissed on the mouth too at the bell, and offered permutations of See you soon then, before he heads back to his row. And so what of it? What do I care? I am here for the Art.

And the dark swims over. And the play winds on.

In twenty minutes, he's up again. Maybe leaving? Should I wave? No. Oh here. He crosses aisles instead, comes up to my row then drops in the seat beside. You pissed off with me? he asks, leaning his long self in. No, why would I be? Don't know, that's why I'm asking. Well I'm not, and glare at the stage. I had a good time the other night, he says I know it got a bit weird at the end but Don't, I say Just don't. Alright, with his eyes wandering down my face So let's go. What? Let's go, this show is shit and it's not going to improve. It isn't. It is, you liar, he says Come on, then gets up and leaves and I, for only trouble it seems, get up and go as well.

On the stairs down he says The designer's a mate so I have to say a quick hello backstage but I won't be long. Won't he be offended you left? No, I made the effort, besides he said it was bad.

Bang out. Sky gone to winter but still fanfares of sun. I'll just have a look at the books while you're gone. Don't wander off, he says. I shrug. No, I'll be five minutes that's all   I mean it, don't go home. But I turn on my heel. Into the book stalls and the so many books. What is he after? What am I up to? I think it's called adventuring. So shuffle on in with the shufflers then lose myself in spines.

And tick on the moment he reappears where I pretend not to see. His friend as tall as, not as thin, dark-skinned, older, earnestly discussing, the pair of them. His fingers negotiating something imaginary but stops with a loud Yeah, anyway. Then he looks up for me into the end of the sun. Pick me. There she is, over there so   til next weekend. There's a form of an arms round and his friend laugh calls to me Watch yourself with this one, sheep in wolf's clothing my dear! Terrible English! he shouts, walking backwards from him After all these years, you should be ashamed! then turning around warns Ignore him! with the concrete halving under his feet.

Anything good? he asks. Lots, I say. So what do you want to do? What? You're the one who wanted to leave, what do you want to do? He hmms at the river, casts about Okay   ever

41

walked across the Hungerford bridge to Embankment? Not yet. Then I'll show you my favourite view of London, he says as we go into the weeding dark. Where's your friend from? Algeria, and France. Do you know him from work? That, and he was with my oldest friend. Not any more? No   he died. What happened? Cancer, he lights up Pancreas. Like my father. Really? When was that? He died when I was eight. Horrible thing to see, he says and I nod because it is.

Up to the walkway under hulkish sky. Breeze licked and nerves cracking fissures inside as he points out Big Ben. Parliament there – look through the grating. At halfway he says Here's London spread out for you. In the murk cold Thames still curling away. Lights just beginning across the city. All the stone world of it. Its stone face. Showing its towers and flanks and shapes, purplish in this light, and grey. And I stand, strick, by its great space, watching the boats til St Paul's there, he says the Oxo Tower. Barbican. Pointing out places I cannot see, then can, because he stands behind Look along my arm. No there. No. There. Do you see? When I still don't, he bends to see it how I see and I see all of it then. This is the most beautiful view I've ever seen, I say. Really? Better than Naples with those boats stretched out across the bay? Ah fuck. He remembers my lies. Sorry, those were all lies, I say I've never been there, or anywhere else. His elbow on the rail Well you're a surprise, what did you make all that up for? I don't know   to be interesting I suppose. How very calculating, he laughs And I thought you believed in love? I do but   love isn't what that was. True, he says But what if I'd been a lonely soul looking for it? Are you? No, I'm not, and you're not much of a liar – I guessed. This I concede, I've never been. Oh well, that means you're probably quite good at the acting. I quick look up to see if he's joking.

He's only watching though and in a moment says So, you just used me for your sexual gratification then? Well, I say It didn't turn out to be that gratifying so perhaps I got what I deserved. Didn't you get what you wanted? Didn't you? I say. Sort of   it started out well enough but. You were hurting me, I whisper. You were a virgin, he whispers back I'm not responsible for the laws of nature. I know that but   I thought at least I wouldn't have to see you again. Ah, well you shouldn't have shagged an actor then – but by now he is laughing and I almost am, over my chasing brain. So throw my breath to the Thames and the strange of the day as we strangers stand looking out on the city. Quiet then but for its sound – that noise it must make for its life to go round. Slow aftershave smell of some passing man. Loud of the train as it clanks behind. Me watching the river. Him watching me. What? I ask. You know well what, he says and stoops and kisses me. Fresh inclination and the blood goes up   Bends me like a body   puts inside   into my mouth   and we   deep and open   where is no mistake, where are only runs of thoughts of next   of kissing him in that short past, naked and   He stops   I stumble forward in perfect dazed unfurl his breath on my hot cheek   then kissing me further. And I might fall over but he has my arm and we kiss like he drags me live from under the Thames and where was allthiswant when I needed it? I don't care I don't and I could do   Enough! he says This is getting ridiculous now, do you fancy getting something to eat? There now legs but disgraceful knees. All his impulses working inside out too, it seems, for even as I nod, see him almost go again for me. And I am all for that. But he turns instead, wiping his mouth on his hand, leaving me tapping the prickle of mine, to trail him over the bridge.

We walk up the Embankment by Charing Cross Oh God

please take my hand. But deaf to petition he on the Strand asks Do you like Chinese? I do but. But what? I've no money. You're a student, he laughs Don't worry, dinner's on me. By St Martin-in-the-Fields I'm lagging his gait Could you slow down? I can't walk as quick. Sorry, he says Sometimes I forget, how's this? Better, and is. Soon walking gives — bus-lunged — to staring at the road-load of bookshops and that. God there's so many, I could live on this street! Up twitch of his mouth. Are you laughing at me? No! I wouldn't dare! I'm just enjoying the wonder, he says. When I Oh Les Mis! though, he tilts his head Musicals? Really? It's not that, I say It's the being here. Thank fuck for that, he says Chinatown's this way.

And the smell comes out to get me as I follow into Gerrard Street. Look at the ducks in the window! Look! Do you like duck then? I've never eaten it. Okay, well go on in there to Harbour City and let's try to rectify that.

He picks a table by the window so I can see out. Beer or wine? What goes with Chinese food? I wasn't allowed to drink at home. Jesus, are you really only eighteen? I am, I say How old are you? Mmmm, he swallows Older than that   I'm actually thirty-eight. Twice as old as me. And then some, he says Fuck   so a beer I think and quick. Feeling like a dirty old man now? A bit   actually   quite a lot   yeah   thanks.

Still. He eats prawn crackers and smokes in chains twisting quotes from my first term play. 'Hell hath no limits, nor is circumscrib'd in one self place, for where we are is hell and where hell is there must we ever be.' Cheery! I chew Have you done it? Not yet but I live in hope, I've a few more years before I'm too old. What did you do last? 'Tis Pity. Where was that on? Here, in the West End. Did it go well? Think so, he says But can I ask you about something else? If your father died when you were eight   how well do you remember him? Pretty well, better than people expect, are your parents alive? My father is, much married and living in Bradford. Is that where you're from then? No, Sheffield. And your mother? Dead, a long time dead. How long? Don't know   I was in my early twenties. I'm sorry. I'm not, do you want another drink? Alright, I say Thanks. And the food goes over and I watch him eat, liking long fingers manoeuvring chopsticks thinking God I fancy him something wicked. What? he asks. Nothing, I say.

Once he's paid we go to the street, salt dark now but hot with seething. Tube? he asks Or a bit more walking? I could walk a bit. So he's off and I'm after. Charing Cross Road. On it me saying My friend's boyfriend knows you. Oh right, does he? What's his name? No I mean, from the stage. Small pool, he shrugs. So are you famous? Well am I famous to you? No, I say. Then there you go, let's make a stop in Foyles.

Upstairs in second-hand, he finds it – I knew I'd seen it here. I'm going to get this for you. What is it? I ask. Book about Marlowe, you'll like it, it'll help with your play. You shouldn't, I fluster Anyway, isn't there some weird paying thing? Yeah, Soviet three-queue system, I'll be right back. So I follow him with the track of my eye, cheek to the shelf and tired by the weight of all I don't know.

You alright? he asks, handing it over. I Thanks, go to kiss his cheek. But there it is in the turning dust. Oh no, he warns No kissing in Foyles. Maybe though, just because I am already close, he kisses me anyway. And more, until Excuse me, we're closing up! I Anthony Burgess over my mouth. He offers the intruder a grave Of course, me a significant eyebrow and Alright jailbait, let's go.

Quick down the stairwell together and out. Cross between

traffic on Oxford Street. Past the Virgin Megastore. Up the Tottenham Court Road. Past sex shops. Electric shops. Let's cut down. So Torrington Place then. Across Gower Street. I went there, he points back. Posh! Not really, scholarship. Nips into Dillon's for a new Time Out. Over Malet Street. Byng Place. Gordon Square. Out by Wellcome building to the Euston Road. And we go across it, glittering, in buses, cabs and the race of things. Night upon us and I must quick to keep with his long legs. As he lights up on Eversholt Street, I ask Will you tell me what your script's about? It's about someone falling off a roof. Is it based on you? Ah! he says You remember that? Is it? A little. How come you did? The usual, a problem of balance, and drugs. So because you were high? No, because I usually was and things a little got out of hand when I stopped. When was that? I ask. Oh years ago – probably when you were two. Do you miss them? The drugs? I nod. Sometimes but not enough – Royal Mail depot – to go back. And won't you miss acting while you're writing? He says I might, acting's been a lot of my life but it's time now for something else. Walk quieter then – quick took looks at him. Tall and straight. Proverbial thin. His face showing different in the light and dark. What? he asks. Nothing, I shrug as the drunks go fight up Oakley Square.

By Mornington Crescent, legs wore from wear, I ask Can we get the tube? Sorry, eternally closed for repairs. The Palace pumps to our right though won't get going until late. Oh we're in Camden, I see. High road spilling up for the night. So weave we through serious clouds of spliff. If you're tired we could stop at the Liberties for a drink? I'm alright, I say, divining junctions ahead and the hope in me wanting him to be explicit. He, oblivious, only moves us through so by the World's End I stop. In here? he says It'll be a meat market tonight. No,

I point to the Kentish Town Road sign. Oh right, you going home? Guess me guess me with your grey eyes. Shame, he says I was hoping you'd want another go on me tonight. There it is, on a plate, and he only giving smallest smile. I suppose I owe you for dinner, I say. You don't really think that   do you? And what if I did? If you were that stupid I'd make sure I got my money's worth, he laughs. I don't owe you for dinner. I know, he says Come back anyway.

No this one, he grabs me as I go the wrong gate. Careful on the stairs too, still no light. Here again for what new night? Were you expecting to bring someone back? Why do you say that? It's all tidy. I tidy sometimes, he says. Yeah but there're also clean sheets on your bed. I get a look but continue anyway So, if we hadn't met would you have gone to the World's End to-night? Might have done, he says Pass me your coat. As I pass it to him If you think it's a meat market, isn't that a bit grim? Well not liking it and not doing it are two different things, aren't they Nancy Drew? And he kneels at the fire letting the air go thin. I scrabble back What're the boxes for? Keeping my stuff in. I never noticed them last time. Well you were some-what preoccupied, he says With what you wanted to achieve. Quiet bite. How wrong's my foot? So – he leans back on his desk – What now? Sorry   how do you mean? Well we're both here for sex aren't we? I just thought, given your insightful-ness, maybe you'd like to get things going this time? And his eyes say nothing so I die inside. Don't make me make the first move. Why, would that be unkind? I mumble I think it would. So you see, he says – surveying his shoes – I also have insight and, if I wanted, could be unkind as well. Sorry I   it was a stupid thing to say. No, it was a clever thing to see but I don't need to be caught out so what exactly would you like to know?

47

Nothing. Really? Nothing. Adversaries it seems but I don't look away and he is the first to smile. Well, in that case, he says I think we should get back to the kissing now.

From which, on to mischief. By the time of the bra he's joking Still coping without the duvet? And wrangling the waves of myself rolling through I let him cramp up the small space between. Good that the smell of his body's not new. Helps he remembers small what's of mine also like God those freckly shoulders again or. Laughing Your tights are the bane of mankind. Kissing to strip off, to lick of my palm then sliding it sliding it down. God! I God! Do you mind? he says. No but I don't want to make a mistake. You won't, just do whatever you want, if I don't like it I'll say. So, and pact made, fall in with his mouth but what is it he wouldn't allow? And I let him do all sorts now, modesty flying everywhere. It's only him backing me back to the bed, suffering Fuck you do that well, that re-catches me old sight of myself and opens the anxious eye. Wrestle. Be easy with this stuff said – not as if it never has. But this is not that, here with him. He kisses like he means it, like he's with some person who can be liked and kissed. Who is not bits of body, floating parts, there for a finger in the mouth or What? You know what things. In the atom though his fancying must be a lie and I go so far from my body now. Left, from his skin to the switching off. Turn it down. Turn it Stop! I Stop Please Stop. And bolt my arms across until the air goes lock. Why? he asks. No reason, just stop. He stands back Whatever you want, but his eyes stay right on mine. Shy again? I shake my head. Something I did? No. Something I said? but rathering chaos than answering questions I panic Stop talking, shut up! He drops his eyes Okay, let's not have this again, this is when it stopped being fun last time, remember? And I see he

48

is now calm annoyed, showing only to the carpet, but I am Oh God filled with remorse. I'm sorry, I say I don't know what's wrong. He, as though I'm lying, shrugs Never mind, some other time, stooping down for his shirt. Don't do that, I say. No? Why not? There and has me on the spot decide decide on him. So turn I braille eights on his long hand. Prise the shirt from him, tug and down. Please don't put your clothes back on. I won't if you won't, he says. I won't. Promise me that! Why? Because, he laughs I nearly had to take you back to the Gents at the Festival Hall before. Really? Really and as for Foyles well. But then. Then he. And he makes it so easy for me. I'm glad he wants to, still.

Elbows and laugh stumble bed again. His body – it seems – liking everything while mine still doesn't know what's going on but tries so hard to please. Catch it watching him follow the pleasure though, then – where he expects – starts finding its own. That's it, he says and farther goes than I would think to give. Straight to manhandled knickers and every inch he can. Can I go down on you? No! Little baby Jesus won't mind. Oh my God no! That's a shame, how about? haAh. Oh you like that then? Likes it himself when I Yes. And get close now so close with him. All the clicks and licks and, by the time he says Do you want to fuck me? Yeah, I say I do.

Best day night life. I am all for this – him getting in a condom like one-handed trick – and wanting to. Wanting it. Free for the fucking til he puts it in and Fuck it hurts. Fuck it. Why again? No. I refuse that. You alright? he says. I counterfeit Fine, while silent abjuring whatever part of my body hasn't yet learned how. And instead breathe the pain across his back to spare him more of my trouble enough so do you owe him, after all? Just take it. Fake. You you can. Replay revive Betty Blue for sounds, for how they went at it he I am. But But. Duse myself undone. Are you faking? No. Is that a lie? A little bit. He leans up Why? It's still hurting me. Fuck's sake you should have just said, him getting straight from me, then the bed. Where're you going? To sit in this chair so we can try something else. Like what? Get on me and find out. No, my God, I'm too fat. What? No you're fucking not, get over here. Do then, covering myself up. Ribs enfolded. Pubic skimped. Him yanking me onto and in between kissing saying Now you put me in and let's find out what works.

He tries to, but can't quite, disinterest himself. Just as well though for my mule body won't – inciting itself only at his obliging my hips. Bit harder? he wonders. I. I. But the mouth on my breasts then – tickle and strange delight of being seen – surprises me, if not to everything, to something. Like first foot inveigle toward what this could be. With the look in his eye. With his body in me. Going and going and harder until Oh fuck, he says Hold still, I'm way too close, any chance you are? Not this time no. Can I help you? and his hand sliding down. No, I like it but   I won't tonight   I want you to though. Just as well, he says, body going tight. Going barely barely. Can't bear to shift. Go on, I say. Then his legs go and. Lights he. Pain turning white inside me. But. Even in this moment, even as he takes, he is the one getting killed.

That was really fucking good, he says still kissing and not like on the afters of sex. You're so warm inside. Is that weird? No, it feels great. His blood slowing under my hand. Sorry it was all interrupted and that. Don't worry, it's good not to be a lazy bastard. What does that mean but he asks instead So how did you find it this time? Much better   the second way. Well, that's a start. I say I think that's a lot. He Hmms, unconvinced, but Does that count as my second or third time having sex? Second, why do you ask? Because we did it two ways. No I think that's still second, he says Unless there's been someone else since? There hasn't been, has there for you? Don't think so, he says. Ow! I Ow! My leg's gone asleep! Hang on, let me get hold of the condom first or all the good work is for nowt. Slide off him. Pins and. Hop and Don't look. Bit late for that, he laughs – standing up – Right I'm off for a piss. Bin goes the condom. Swats my arse on the pass, all naked unbothered getting into his bathrobe. And how I envy him that; the looks and not giving a shit.

Silent in his room. Cigarette. Sit or shift? I halfly dress. Stay or leave? What do men expect? What would I like? To know exactly what he considers to be the right what now.

Dressed already? Yeah   it's getting late. You off then? Suppose so. Oh right, he says Don't you want a tea or? Well   if you don't mind? Why would I? I don't know, does that usually happen? Usually? Afterwards. That depends. On what? Whether or not she fancies another round. Do you fancy one? Yeah, I reckon could. I'm kind of sore. Well then, we should probably leave you be. So I should go? Do you want to go? Not really. Oh my God! and him laughing now Just fucking stay and I'll think of something else to do with you, alright?

Barefoot I then, through his lamp lit room. Tip touching his boxes Is it clothes in them? More books and scripts, that sort of thing. Why don't you get some shelves? I should, just never get round to it. But it's been ten years. Actually   more like   Jesus, is that true? – his eyes calculating above – Fuck! Fourteen years and I don't even like it here. So then why've you stayed? At first it was all I could afford. After that I   I don't know   I stopped thinking about it I suppose. And passing the

51

tea. Such blue in his wrist. Mouth shifting his fag and an intricate quiet he crashes with Anyway let me lend you this, and he's into a box, elbow deep. Black Snow? It'll make you laugh and, by all accounts, where you're studying, you're going to need that. What do you know about it? What everyone does; that they love to kill people up there. Oh thanks very much. Pleasure, he says then Wait, isn't that Dennis Potter thing on tonight? I shrug but he's already down on his knees hauling an old portable Kayvision out. Untacking dust and used tissues Sorry about that. Up on the drawers and aerial twitched, he lies down on the bed and offers me in beside him. So I, head by the tamp saucer on his chest, lie soon yawning while he stays rapt. Fine though, all of this I think, and like it, before falling right off to sleep.

Two-ish wake, bursting. Roll out of bed. You leaving? No, toilet, I say. Mm, him, sleeping again.

Eyes pull in what light there is and someone backing the door. Is there a queue? There is, she drunk. I, hopping the hop Are you Irish? And? Nothing   just   me too. Oh? How long're you over? Two months, about. Well let me give you a word of advice, never read the Irish Times. Why not? On the tube. Why's that? Why? I'll fucking tell you why. I was at Warren Street the other night, minding my business, reading my Times when the train gets held, only five minutes like, and this fella starts going I know what this is, fucking bomb scare, fucking IRA. I said nothing, no one did, everyone was like Just shut up, in their head. Then oh my God, he starts going Do you know what it is? I bet you fucking do. Don't bother starting on me, I said which was the wrong thing because Jesus fuck he went apeshit, roaring Paddy bitch and your Paddy rag. We're all stuck here 'cause of you lot. I said There's a ceasefire, which you'd know if ever opened a paper yourself. Anyways, the train started then but he kept going Thick Paddy tick Mick, all that. Eventually this wee Paki lad says Enough mate, enough. You've had your say. Soon as we got to Euston though I just legged it. I was shaking, you know the way, when you're fit to be tied? Twenty years I been living here, paying my tax. The toilet door opens so she swaps the man sliding out. Anyway, for what it's worth, that's my advice. Thanks, I say and let it dander my brain as she pukes away, suffocatingly.

Back from the world in the stuff of his room, I strip down to knickers and no bra. Slip off his glasses too. Him waking just enough to help me back into the warm space of his sleep. But maybe later, passing three, I wake to, in the long deep, him. Sat at his window. Smoking like breath. Staring off into the street.

Morning. Light. Him asleep on my hair, legs patterned to mine. I search hurts out and where, new laying his print on his print from before. Each pass brings clearer. Turned out more right. Is that sex or him? Which would I like? Be glad for the night and the what next I. It's not everyone you're not lonely with.

Hair caught under Ow, as he sucks the air Morning   are you awake? Yes, did you sleep alright? I did, you're like having a hot water bottle in the bed. Stretch and click. Are you wiping your nose on me? Itching only itching, he laughs And you smell so good   fancy making it the best of three?

Last relics of old pain work down to his up. Sparse though, palled by his damp on my back. Thigh pinned. Reached. He has me every which way but still it circles just beyond my body. Where I see and want. Where it's certainly him. Where his long fingers perform while I long to give in, way, gratify. But the skin and what's in it can't let yet. When I tell him so Fuck it, he says Really? What can I do? Nothing, I like it, bit sore, that's all. He goes Mmm, in the grip of his qualmless own, making its way to the well-traversed close. Even where and how he touches me in the moment seems re- and re-rehearsed. Many times I'd say. All but the bite. Back of my neck. Sorry, don't know what that was about – he says after – Luckily I didn't break the skin. War wound, I say. Now that's more like it! as he lets himself slip out of me.

And he opens the curtains in the spiral of day. Body white in the light with his cigarette. Have you work to do? he asks as I blind in the dazzle. A scene to learn from Richard III. 'Was ever woman in this humour woo'd'? Yes, I shade my eyes. Shall I be on the book for you? he offers. Oh, okay.

Stare up for concentration instead of at him. He knows it already better than I do. Makes tea and prompts from all round the room while I stumble and untether text. What about your RP? I can't do that. Have to learn, he warns Might as well from the start. So I hide in the pillow but the words make blocks, hard, with no movement in them. Despair-ING, he corrects Not Despair-EEN. I think it sounds exactly the same. He repeats in my accent 'And by despaireen shalt thou stand excused' Great accent, I say. Irish mother, he mumbles. From where? No, you can't distract me – but consoles with his own student tales of Mercutios sounding like Hepburn Doolittles and the slaggings he got for that. Eventually though I am saved by the Toast? And hang over the bed, over his shoulder as he passes back triangles to chew.

I love that play, he yawns into Time Out. You love lots of plays. Don't you? I suppose, dot dotting my crumbs from his shoulder and neck. So fancy a film or are you in a rush? No I'd love to, if it doesn't interrupt? Interrupt what? he asks. I don't know, your writing? Family stuff   are you seeing your daughter this weekend? No I'm not. Will you next weekend then? No, she doesn't live here. In London? In England   she's in Canada with her mother. Oh   you must miss her, I Fuck! he gets up I can't believe I nearly forgot, Nostalgia's on in Belsize Park we'll make it if we run.

Coffee smelt cinema no kissing here. Long limbs crooked to fit. Balled coats kicked under. Darkening. Music there. Quiet here. Then it comes, in its light and white-light. From the start, it has me. I am unprepared. Paralyse in its image. Forward to breathe as birds fleer from the Virgin's dress. The stamp of it. Weight in me. All down my neck. Going farther than I know how to be. Rain. Pool and bottles. Soft book in flames. You want to be happy but there are more important things. I'm not only lost though. I'm unmade by the intent. Scalded by the too beautiful eye of it. How the far side of despair is reached by faith but not life. And there, beneath its great cathedral arc, let its loneliness be all of me. Relinquish the bounds of myself to become just a girl, another person in this world, who life is running out of now. He, letting my hand slip into his hand, says nothing but looks also burned now. So in this – belief or no belief – find we two are the same.

Still and stay it, as all the others drain. Each in our own life but palm to palm. I do miss her, he says then lets go of me and gets up.

Silenter walking down Haverstock Hill. Hands in my pockets. Cigarette on his lips. Me growing pink-faced in the chill while he stays white and fine, staring off into the winter light, higher and further than I can see. Looking up, I'd like to ask him things but he hasn't the face for it now.

At the Steele's he says How about a drink?

55

Thanks, I say as he puts down the pints. Sip and smoke til the tongue unwinds. How many times have you seen it? I ask. Four or five maybe. Do you like it a lot? Yeah, he says I like how it takes a while to adjust but once you shift yourself into his time Jesus   what you get to see, was that your first time? Yes. What did you think? It's beautiful but   do you think there are more important things than happiness? Yeah, of course there are, he says But it's pretty hard to do without   or face not having again. And his life opens a little to let me look in. I want to ask more so badly but say I'm glad you took me. Thanks for coming with, he smiles.

And it's almost five when I say So   I've got to go not cool enough for any Ask for my number, won't you? Well, if you have to. I don't have to but   you know   I should probably wash. You smell alright to me, he says. That's because I smell of you, and I catch his eye but he only goes Yeah well   I smell of you too. Will he ever ask? Ask. I – reluctant – get up. He also goes to with I'll walk you back. No, no, you stay put and Irish myself from what I most want   thanks for a lovely weekend. Yeah, he looks into his pint It was great. Jesus Christ. Well   bye then. He stands up now, to give me a Shit! You're bleeding! What? You have a nosebleed. He dabs and Fuck I haven't had one in years. Sit down, I Put your head back. He obedient does and quiet wiping ensues with what I find in my pockets. He is so white though and dark under the eyes Should we go across to the? No no I'll be fine, he says and God how stupid is this? But it's a bad one. It takes an age to clot. On both our fingers by the time he says Look, if I promise not to haemorrhage all over you would you like to do this sometime again? Jesus, I thought you'd never ask! Slow starter, he grins Always was, but showing the blood on his teeth. I write my number on a beermat and one for the school. Go on then, he says I'll give you a call, and we try not to kiss goodbye too much because of the blood. Beyond the door though my bottom lip licks of rust. So lick it out into the chill on Haverstock. And that is the end of the day.

Who's been doing the mauling? she asks, in the changing room, as I don everything unedifying for ballet. No one, I say but with hair up high a fine dog of teeth marks are plain and press the blistered memory of his room. I'd give her all of it later but, for now, have it mine – just as lustre on bad pliés or lepping about like fake Fonteyn. She'll have it now though and I knew its! loudly when I say who. Didn't I tell you you'd see him again? Then Where? When? How long did you stay? Which film was it and is he dirty in bed? Remember, brief, him licking my palm but cannot think of one dirty thing. Giving to what she means though, I say He knows what he's at. She, mad for a mystery though, plagues for Origin of the Bite? Kitsching now I When he came! hand fanning myself. The Bounder! she adds. But I like of his upon me, whatever marks he's made. So smoke away and drink my tea and read Black Snow, this Monday after him.

Just one moment Lady! the landlady calls up the stairs. Yes? You were seen, she says. I was what? One of my working gentlemen saw you in Belsize Park with a man, an older one at that, apparently. I burn but a lie comes quick That was my Acting teacher. He was also at the film. London's awful godless, she says I may not be your mother but I feel responsible so I hope to God you're telling the truth. English men have no morals, you bear that in mind. I will, I mumble, scarfing the embarrassment down, then legging it upstairs soon as I can, for relentless reliving. And godlessness notwithstanding, the rest of the week is the same.

And I wait. But there's nothing. A long silence on the phone. Any messages? No. She asks after? No. Why doesn't he so and hasn't he called? One week slides to fortnight and reliving palls amid tints of my mistakes. Then dawn of thinking about who he is. How easily he can get hold of someone else. And this I see. It claws itself in my brain. Some glossy real actress, bones in her back on display. They'll speak interestingly of the Royal Court at some elegant restaurant where he'll footsie her up. Then go back to her flat. Pet her Siamese cat and spend the night inside because he's the type knows what's good for him – women who give men what they want. Not me, with a band-aid on the hook of my bra, unable even to fake it and no idea. All the women he must've slept with. Why would he call? And my own gullibility galls. But then. Then again. Didn't I get what I wanted? Bloody virginity banished, and more. There, you see? Rise and fall. Party this Saturday at mine, she says Come, it'll cheer you up.

Slop riot here. Music. Drinking. Passing things around. Cheque guarantee cards chop unwrapped talcs. Ponytails like tidal waves slap tabletops and nostrils butterfly. This is new but I am fixed and press his memory to some hard place. Just smoke whatever I am passed. Getting stoned and stoneder. Getting much more stoned and stretch myself beyond myself out into the crowd. Smirking. Snarking. Little jig. Up in her room Here have some of this. She and me and the back of my Jesus. Yow it burns. But not too long before it turns my brain. Bright and dark at the self-same time. And the night, it seems, begins again. To the sitting room! she cries. Running through hours like water then. Losing track of everything. Drink, lines, blood in my brain. Talk to him or her. People I know, or not, the same. Fine to be out of my brushed-off skin. Anyone can dance with me and I can dance with anyone. Saying only sometimes This fella I knew   And who cares anyway now? Hither me, thither me. Smoke on that. Drinking drinker. Vodka. More of. Gone to play and such distance made that when some fella says Sit on my lap, I do.

Numb mouth mirror and roaring eyes, we go reeling down her path. Take my hand, he offers. You a funny guy. What're you on? he asks. Lots of miles an hour. Better than drunk I'd say and quicker and faster for the sharper world I see. Trees black under a blacked-out sky. Cutting cut out stars over black bits white. The grass and wind. Has my hand now. My heart going go go go. I can't tell though, stop from go. Just this big fella with new smelling hair. I'll see his Pericles Prince of Tyre. I know I know his name. Sure he's all lips and muscles – what more do I want? Where're we going? To get a night bus. I'm whirling. Slip. He catches me. Sit down, no sit down there. I a-seat myself. I agree with his kiss. I love an Irish redhead. Can you see I'm not? Well, and were you raised by nuns? Convent girls are best. Best what? Conquests, apparently. Go on with your conquering, but fall in with his way. See me. Skirt high on Adelaide Road. That's a party. The way I want. Taste this man, but see the. No. Come down you sweet little roses, I sing Come down you little rose in the garden. Bus stops. I slip. He pulls me up. Transfigured night ahead. Wild one convent girl, come on. The tug of him and the brawl in my mind. Don't, I say Leave me alone. Sister, I know what's to be done.

England? Camden? Kentish Town? Turn like someone's snapped my twangs. A man's blond hair. His broader back.

Mouth raw. Jaw stiff. Hey, wake up! Was I snoring? No, fucking hell! Relax, he yawns It's only me. Blinks of dancing. Where is this? Finchley. Really? Jesus Christ. Nothing either of any sex though pretty sure there's been. In fact, none of the night I see. Just being there, being here and empty in between. Fuck! What happened? What do you think? Where'd I get these bruises? You fell on the bus. Really? Several times. I don't remember. That's weird, he frowns But then, all that vodka when we got in. You were a right laugh though. How'd you mean? Well the guided tour. Oh God! No, he laughs It was good, especially all the 'head, own hair' part. Scan for iotas but all that's blinded out and the nothing's rushing fast. Then like playing Dallas, I sheet my breasts Did we use   something, at least? He picks at a tissue Yep we did. Not as handsome. Not as tall. Relief but laying itself across what's certainly, seriously disappeared. I should go. Bra skirt shoe shoes knickers top. And when I'm dressed, he says Cheers for that. Yeah, I say You too.

Out to the out. Bang the front door. City blast in my ears. Pigeon shit on sycamores. Don't panic. I already am. Panic like a mad one the whole way home. London crossing before me, preoccupied with itself. Content I'm the girl who does this for a laugh, but later, alone, bats an eye.

Good party? the landlady asks. I offer my best occluded self and Didn't get much sleep on her sofa though. Oh, she guiles I'm sure the drink didn't help. I smile to let her in and keep her out. Any nice boys? No, not at all. Ah, time enough for that. Exactly. Go on so – I am dismissed – have yourself a little lie down.

Still. I can. I make myself still until I hear her leave. And into the bath to scrape skin off. Rubbed under bubbles til I'm pure gold butter dripping from my tongue. No. Never that again. But everything else? I might have. I can just about guess by the aches and pains where his larking was. Think. Don't. Think of. Him. Just go to my room and as the day goes down, light a cigarette. Then let it find its own information, for pain knows what it is. Better there where I can see. Better than his mystical fading. Landlady later screaming You used my hot water again!

Sunday

Door opens on the scrat of party debris and her howling at the sink. What is it? I got here quick as I could. She Did you see him on his way out? Who? She means me. You duplicitous shit! He lights his rollie Anyway I'm off. Wait, I say What's going on? But he's already out the door. Oh God, pink marigolds hit the floor. Her sliding after them down on her arse. Come here, I say Tell me what's wrong? as hicks and kinks go mad. Pick by bit though it comes out He just told me   only now   that after Christmas after Christmas. What? He's marrying some Czech-oslovakian bitch – shrouds of crying and sheets of snot – It's a visa thing. It's a what? So she can stay. So it's not for real? He's really marrying her alright. Is she paying him or something? It's for his fees! Well that means it's only the money. Oh come on, she says We all need that but I'm not marrying strangers for a few thousand quid. I touch her lovely haircut But. Don't defend him to me. I'm not, he's a gobshite. He is   whatever that means. Another rumple of awful tears. Ah don't, I say Sit up here, I'll make you a cup of tea.

Weeks roll over to December. Room and school the same. A month of holiday meeting every eye and today is the last day.

There's a message for you on the notice board. Just a number and 'Please ring him' below it. It's got to be your Him, she says Who else would it be? Will I? Or Fuck him! It must be five weeks, never mind what else I've been at. She says Forget about that, he has no right to know.

Hello? Hello there, how are you? Fine. What are you up to? I'm off to Ireland tomorrow. For good? No, for the Christmas break. So   are you around tonight? Actually this afternoon's our Showing, then we're all going for a drink. Right, Doctor Faustus, I remember well break a leg maybe catch up in the But I could do later on? Okay, Prince Albert again? Round nine? Half past, I say – to be the final word.

Clearly none of you have a clue what this play is about. Do you know how it feels to be in the grip of evil? To have a desire for which you'd sell your soul? To have sold your soul and owe the devil? The Principal waits, pacing, until it's clear we don't and then he really starts. Guts spill and – though it's no surprise – we flinch against the music of our own tear-ing sound. Bloodless. Sexless. Stick insect. Blank card. Beat to low by the end. But afterwards, shoving flats back into the furniture dock, hanging costumes on rails, packing, we laugh and think of drinks ahead. One or another peel and pick off to the Fiddler's Elbow or Barnacle Bill's for chips. I, slow and almost last, love the dust of the day closing off. No more Song Exercises. Drums. Madding about. Night show-ing itself beyond the canteen light and forgotten water bot-tles on its floor. Past cutlery dumped by the serving hatch door. Tide-marked jockstraps on the sofa. Scripts. London's Calling fliers ripped for a roach. Spotlights with our favourite actors' pictures torn out and mugs on the tile tabletops. One white sheet on the notice board reads: School reopens 10 am 9 January 1995. And I choose these months – for everything – as the very best of my life, so far.

Later

Breath of winter on me, brain crawling little from drink, I sit where he was with The Devils that night and read my book like pub doors are quiet and will not look up for him. Then at my shoulder Women in Love? – stoops to my cheek but gets an earlobe – Thought you'd be long past the Lawrence phase. Well, hello to you too, I lifting my eyes to him, damp and cold-faced from the wind. Have a few in you already? I do. Better catch up, and to the barmaid – rubbing heat into his hands – Two, when you're ready, and a salt and vinegar please. Come on, that table's free.

Stretching his legs out When are you off? Tomorrow afternoon. And when are you back? Sixth, I say So what have you been up to since? Writing mostly, he smokes I got into a jag – which is why I haven't called   sorry about that. Oh right any more nosebleeds? No touch wood, and leans to kiss at my lips. Oh God. Terrible, how pleased he is to see me when I did what he did to make hard things easy with someone else, for a laugh. Alright? he asks. Why? Funny look in your eye. I close them There is something I. Okay   go on. I   well I   slept with someone else. Out in the innocent world a cash register dings and a woman whinges I asked for change. Oh I see, and how was it? he says. I don't remember, I was a bit out of it. Probably not the best idea that. Then why are you smiling? No reason, he smiles You're lovely when you're feeling guilty is all. Aren't you angry? No, why would I be? I'm not your boyfriend and you're eighteen, what else would you do with yourself? So this

63

is the way of the world it seems. Catch up. Quick shed my guilt to match worldly with him Does that mean you've also slept with someone else since? The cigarette rolls in his mouth. Nod. How was it? Fine. Are you going out with her? No. Are you seeing her again? No. Why not? He shrugs Why would I? Now, another round?

Watch him pass a tenner and the barmaid take. Laughing together. Skitting I'd call it. She knows him and knows him better than me. I see that all over them. And the devil shifts. Don't say it. Don't say. But the drink running through me has its own vocation so when he comes back, I ask straightaway Was it her? Peanuts down. No. Pints too. You have though, haven't you? Why are you asking that? You know those things about me, what do I know about? Alright, once, ages ago, happy now? And the girl at the National? His frown goes scowl. Come on, let's not start this. I'm only asking. His narrow eyes Okay I did, now let's leave it at that. But the drink has grips that make questions of their own How many people have you slept with? He Jesus Fucking Christ! quite loud. I shrink from his temper and he's immediately calm Sorry   I didn't mean   it's just. He opens and empties the peanuts out, lining them up one by one. Time crucifying me on the mark I've hit. Stupid girl stupid fucking eejit. Ignore me, I say It's not my business and. The answer is a lot, he says. Sliver. More than twenty? Not this year, but it's been unusually quiet for me so   Trail of it trailing off and I watch him, cool-mouthed but   his eyes   at the edge. Sorry, I mutter. Don't be, he says What does it matter? It's not something I'm proud of but   it is what it is. Then he sits back. Lights up. Shifts himself. Shifts again to find more comfort but can't. And I know in this moment he would make me laugh but I am not funny or clever enough to prise this weird weight off.

64

Unprompted then, and into this Friday night, he says It's just
there was a time in my life when I didn't behave very well that
way. What that sort of thing makes you isn't great so   I try
not to be it any more. Problem is   was   it gets like a game   like
everyone's possible, like nothing will ever stay and, once you've
got that knack   it's so fucking easy to do   which is not a good
thing to know. His face, so silent with these words coming out,
becoming completely strange to me now and, although I still
don't ask, he goes on There was this time   No   I was killing
time, in town, when this woman in a shop asked me to reach
something down   but   the way she said it   it was just
like I could see inside   and I knew exactly what it would
take. Not much   but the right thing   and five minutes later we
were up in the Ladies in the Lamb and Flag. Twenty minutes
after that I was walking down the Strand and couldn't even
remember her face   Sorry   I don't know why I've
told you that   it's horrible. Not really, I say Not if she wanted to. She did, he says I've never done anything I wasn't let. I
wouldn't want you to think it's like that but   Fuck – he shakes
his head – The things people let you do. And there's something
in this story I've not understood, I know, but don't know how
to get to it. He though just lights a cigarette then swipes the
peanuts onto the floor. And I'm left swimming and drowning
here. Nowhere for feet. Too far from shore. Seems I can only
hold onto him now and go wherever he goes. So I stand up. Are
you leaving? he says. No, and wrap my arms around his neck.
I'm sorry for all those things I asked. It's okay, he says – taken
aback – Hang on, you're strangling me. I don't stop either, so
he gives in. Puts his arms around me too and I'm so glad to see
you, I say kissing him with all the weeks of waiting rising. And
too bad too if the barmaid's watching – until I see she is. Is she

65

jealous? I whisper. Married, he says. Was she then? Enough, he begs – shovelling me back onto my chair – I could do with a real drink now.

So the rest of the evening goes into the drink. Him smiling and fooling my fingertips. Talk now kept to decent amounts of Why's there greasepaint in your hair? or How do you find working out dialogue? or My friend's boyfriend's getting married because. Spin and chat and flickering lights by the time he asks Coming back to mine? Depends, are you behaving badly with me? I am yes, he nods Absolutely, but not at all in that way. I'll come, I say though langer-kneed. Him getting hold of me Right then drunk arse, let's us two go home.

Coat and coat. Shirt shoes caught hem. Rolling in under the weight of him. Back bare to the grit on his rug. Gas fire scorching my thigh a little as he kneels up to unlace my boots. Laughing Those were a mission. Belly flat to the curve of mine. Long fingers encouraging half-taken breaths. Mingle struggle the last of underwear off while he kisses me, that way he does, til we are only mouths. Then all over each other in this red dark. Salt of his skin. Bruise on his neck. Did she do that? I don't know, I suppose. Did you bring her back here? No. Where did you go? Leave it, he says – tearing open the condom – I don't want to talk about her. So defer to the body, unlocked from shy. Falling together. Ready? I am. And he climbs me. Goes to go inside. Goes. Doesn't. Tries. Can't. Tries again. Fuck! Sits back. Fuck! What's wrong? Jameson's mixed with the twenty questions, he says. Can I? No, leave it. And I'm disappointed. I thought tonight would be the one. Instead I'm lying in all my new-found want, watching him peel the condom off. Right, he says Time for you know what. No! Yes, and don't bother being squeamish about it. I stare at the stains on his ceiling and suffer but   the twirl of his fingers. Let me, I really want to. I really want to too, so I do. And he does. Soft first. Kissing it. Opening it up. Touching. All gently. Then he opens his mouth and I   I understand what all the fuss is about   if I let it   I let it. And my body corrupts. Pangs of it going to every part. Don't do that! Really? No actually, do. Or Or Where did you just put your tongue? His barely raised eyebrows. You're filthy, I complain. Yeah, that's one advantage, he says. And whatever he is, he's so complete with me now. His tongue finding feeling until I cannot avoid where I am. Late restraint ebbing. Him saying Go on. I try to not but, in the work and rise, in the mad of it then, I do. Shame biting my lip down to blood   and all the pleasure rushing through.

Straight after. Jesus. I cover my face. Sift through surprise for the way my blood beats. Fragile in the wither. How should I be as he – tidily – wipes his mouth on me and asks So how was that? It was   it was good – trying to arrange back into a body that only wants his close. Then let's go to bed, he says Before you get cross. Why do you say that? I've met you before, he laughs Vulnerability isn't your thing. So I let him lead. Lie with him in his bed and whisper in his ear Don't say that, I won't be cross. Good, he says and strokes my hair til he sleeps. I should but can't and for the vaulting night listen to the city outside.

City sound makes morning too. Post hitting the floor downstairs. He moans I should never drink whiskey, then crawls over me out of bed. Where're you going? Shower, it's the only way. So alone I lie reliving events and solving how I'll ever look him in the face again.

He faces me though, saying Get in before the hordes, without a trace of strange. And when I don't move, pulls the covers off laughing Go on, this is all the time we have, lazy bones.

So, under the drip of his shower, I wash my hair with his shampoo. The rest of my body with his soap and, in his towel, make my way back to his room through his wet footprints in the hall.

Tall and shaving in the early light. Bit better? he asks. Bit, I nod. Well, come put your arms around me, like you did that first time. I do and. The smell of him then, damp shivering against his damp back. I don't want to go to Ireland. He says I really liked last night. I say I liked it too. Can I do it again? What now? Why not? I won't be able to for another month. While he rinses his face, I prevaricate but what need here for No? Turn and tug his towel then get myself dragged to bed. And soon I'm rolling back through the pleasure again as though it is brand new. Cold drops from his wet hair trickle my thighs. Mint from his toothpaste mouth tingles nice and long fingers locking through mine. I give in to him. Resign to his tongue, to every single thing he does, for it's good to have this thing we do as the hangover breaks my heart. And take his lips on my stomach   breast. Biting my shoulder. Into my neck. Kissing completely until   I look up What is it? I want to be inside you, he says and I am ready, surely ready for him So Yes. No   I mean without anything on. What? Just for a bit. I won't come in you and I'm completely clean. What? Nerves hitting lungs with the thought of what it is. But not come? Not come, I promise you that. So and watching each other I say Alright. Jesus, he says as I, for surprise, cannot even think to say how it feels. Just open myself to his body in mine. Stretching to the want of him all over me now. This is it and I am   like normal like. Like that? I do. I know, he says I can tell. Given over to him and the creak of his bed, racket of both until Close? he. Yes. Well do, I can hold on. And far beyond shame my body longs. And him doing all he can to drag it down. So I hide against him. In his neck. Let it go through. Like a burst. Like a hurt. Clung to him clinging to gritting his teeth. Tiding me, though pulling out after so quick to sit on the edge of his bed. Leaving me in a body clicking inside like it never has.

I curl in to hide my delight. Blushed with it, or shower and no face cream for after. Come lie with me. But first water's splashed down his front. Getting a condom. Lighting up. Kneeling beside to offer a drag That was bad but, fuck, you feel good inside. And I think Am I not my own self now? Can't I do too what I want? I can. So. I take his hand. Lead him across like it's my turn now. His long legs naked and my knees shake. What's this? Sit in the armchair, I say and when he does, kneel down. You sure? he asks. I'd like to   if you would? Well I'll just lie back and think of England. Any tips? Nope, far as I'm concerned you can do no wrong except bite and you won't do that, will you? I hope not. Jesus, that makes two of us, he says as I put him in my mouth.

Fuck, his whole body goes to it and I wait for the impatient Open it wider. Instead he takes what I give and only strokes my wrist. Concentrates on the ceiling. Sometimes holds his breath. Sometimes pushes my hair back to watch but I like how he looks at me. Easier this than I thought until. His breath catches in his throat. The only sound I rrr. Not here. Not this now. Don't freeze. Make your way through. Talk, I say. What? Say something. What about? Whatever   a poem   anything. Him looking down strange at me now. I'm nervous, I say Please   it would really help. He puts his head back Alright   well Now is the winter of our discontent   how's that? Better, I almost laugh Go on. Mmm   made glorious summer by this son of York. And all the

clouds that loured upon our house in the   deep bosom of
the ocean buried   Jesus   now are our brows bound with victo-
rious wreaths our stern alarums no   our bruisèd arms hung
up Fuck   more? Yes, I say. Ah   what the fuck is it?   Our
stern alarums changed to merry meetings our dreadful visaged
war hath smoothed   fuck I forget   Grim-visaged war hath
smoothed his wrinkled front   I don't I You're a bit distract-
ing, you know? Then goes to go silent but I cannot. Please
keep talking and don't stop. Alright. He wets his lips then goes
to the words at a similar lick Nowisthewinterofourdisconte
ntmadeglorioussummerbythissonofyork and allthecloudsthat-
loured upon our house inthedeepbosomofthe ocean   burr-
rrieeeed nowareourbrowsboundwithvictoriouswreaths   right
I'm right I'm there I'm. I pull back quick. He presses it onto
me as his body gives up. Wet on my chest, ends of my hair and
my breast and the heat. Goes everywhere and him smearing it
all down me as I, touching the threat of bruise on my lip, lay
my head on his knee.

   He eases himself off with my hand a while. That was lovely
Thanks for that. Sorry, I say For not letting you you know   in
my mouth. Don't be, he says I think it's rude to expect. And I
look all about at the mess made by our versions of sex. I've been
naked, embarrassed, touched and kissed and brought the whole
way like any woman might. So after that what is it to say When
I was little someone used to and   now I don't think I can any
more. And the past sits forward and the cold comes pouring in.
He looks down at me What did you say? I do not say it again.
And he. Slides down beside me then. Takes me in to the lean of
his chest that rises and falls in time with my pulse. The tight
of his grip keeping me safe until I am calm and recalled to the
smell of his neck. Until my soul re-finds its place. Listen to me,

fuck him, he says He's nothing to you now. And it is as if he always knows the very best thing to say.

I'd like a cigarette. I bet you would. He lights one for us both. Lies on the rug. His damp hair resting on my thighs and blowing smoke rings to make me laugh. I do too, dipping them, twisting about. Do other shapes. Rings not enough for you? Stretch yourself! He laughs but only stretches his legs. Fancy a walk to Regent's Park? Some fresh air might do us good.

So we go down through Camden. Market now under way. Slack queue for cash at the Midland bank, though it's early in the day. He gets sandwiches in Cullen's. Bag of Minstrels for me. I watch for agitation but he doesn't do a thing. Just eats his like a hungry dog then has a bite of mine. Somehow light with all that's in us now the night has rolled away. Only tired from drinking – and other things – treading up Parkway to Gloucester Gate. And this the first morning I can see my breath clear as smoke from his Marlboro Red.

Regent's Park is freezing but we walk on and on. My arm dandling in through his. He even takes my hand. Eventually settle on a bench. Cigarette? Please. He lights. I take and there we sit, breathing smoke across all dead flowerbeds. You alright? he asks. Fine, I say Was it a bit much, that? On contrary, it's good to keep your speeches up to scratch. I scrape my heel through the gravel and nudge No   really   do you mind? No, why would I mind about that? I'm not sure but instinct backs all those secret years when it burned down holes through me. Soiled goods maybe? Wow Holy Catholic Ireland, he laughs I've been soiled goods too long myself to care about that old crap. He watches me though, with those eyes of his. I can't see in or past the grey until he smiles Just as well you're off today, I'll need a month to recuperate. You're just hungover and shagged out, I say Can't be easy at your age. You shut up, he says, beginning a kiss and he is cold to the lips but quick with smile and soft too from his shave. Remember this moment. I will remember this because, even though this morning's not much of his life, it's very much of mine. Whatever happens, nothing will be the same after and nothing will be like it again. Right, he says It's getting late. We should go or you'll miss your train.

Christmas Holidays 1994

In the cold and dark of Ireland, I burn my month away. Tell
friends about London. What wonders seen. Where I've gone.
The fame in the street. The way we're learning to make the
world make. Art and all of that. But he is a secret worn down
deep in the seams and thought. Does he think about me? Or is
he away to the next? Real life's not all romance and I should remember that. Still I send him a postcard to gentle note when
I'm back, and hope he's doing well. Fairly nonchalant tone I've
struck, if rewritten again and again. While, on the other side of
myself, think of him all the time. All he said. What he did and I
did, to reciprocate Not that. Go to sleep.

She floats face down. The world can do anything to her. Under
here she is fingers and the weight of water piled up over her
head. Under here with the empty torch of her breath she opens
an eye and a quick fish I
Open mine to the bright, bright day. And the land and the life
comes in.

Letters too, from her. Exclamation mark mazed! Did you see
your man's in a film next week Oh My God Channel 4!!!

Smoke cigarettes round the gable then. Eat many Minstrels, in
honour of him. Read some books. Try to see that film and wait
for January.

TERM TWO

Monday 9 January–Sunday 2 April 1995

By the crushed tin bin. At the 5 on his door. He must be there. His light is, so press the bell. Press again. All afloat with the. Clang keys. Then him just filling my eye. Barefoot. Shiver. Bathrobe slack tied. Hello there, he says. Hello, I light, tip-toe-ing up to How come you're back? he asks. I'm supposed to be, it's the sixth. Oh right, he crosses the threshold to kiss my cheek making everything in me go but Look   it's lovely to see you but   I'm sorry   I can't ask you in. Oh God, I Sorry, are you working? I'm not, he says, going quiet-eyed. Oh. I stare at the step and the phlegm there, spat. That's disgusting, I say. Well I didn't do it   listen   if I'd known you were back to-night   You'd have done it yesterday? Sorry, bad timing that's all but I'm really glad to see you. So tell her to go. I can't do that, he says Not now. Fuck you, I say backing down the path. Wait – him quick checking up behind – How about tomorrow? We could meet in the morning and have the day. I turn sharp though and hurt his gate by the looks of rust crumbs fly. Come back, he loud whispers Wait, hang on! But when I don't the front door shuts and from across his street I look up. There. His room. The lowliest bulb. Skewed curtain light stream-ing and what beyond? Then even it goes out. You bollocks! I scream I feel like screaming but mostly that I'm such a child as the rain comes roaring down.

So happy home to London. Rain-haired unpack my case. Hailstone-eyed smoke cigarettes, despising these last thirty nights spent liking the thought of his body on mine. There for you now with your worthless wiles. Singed myself already when my landlady shouts Phone, and you can tell your friend it's too late to call, I'm half an hour in bed.

Hello? You're Falkland Road, aren't you? he says Which number? You can't come here. Come on, just tell me? No way. Please? he says. So I tell him it. For what? For trouble   again.

Stooped against the drizzle he comes then. Neat though. Clean. Hair wet from showering, now from rain. Stands on my step with my front door barely opened What? is all I say. He tosses his fag Can I come in? No. I won't stay long. No. But it's raining. I'm not allowed men in. I'll be so quiet, he says Please let me in — raising a look that runs over the wound — I'm sorry about before. I. So. Relent. Alright. You fool.

Blink noughts from her oven. Almost all the rest dark. Can I smoke? No. There's an ashtray there. So? And put the kettle on, for something. Come here, he says. I ignore that. Will you look at me? I don't but Did you get my postcard? I did, yes, thanks. And when I meet his eyes now he knows. But those weeks of waiting, for them I hold out. Let him flex his long fingers until they Alright   I did know you were back tonight. And still did it? Yes. On purpose? No   for no good reason   I just   I'm sorry   it was a shitty thing to do. The kettle rises to the boil. Will you forgive me? I won't. I'm so sorry. I see he means it but You better go before someone comes. Instead he reaches for me but I won't let him touch. Just turn my face and, when he kisses it, relive Lights Out on his street so that's where all the feeling goes. And when he kisses to my lips I stay close-mouthed. Cross. Immune to his every practised pass, even to the most of myself that wants. Stop doing that, he maddens at last Let me kiss you properly. You've been having it off with someone else! There. At last it crosses his face, a sign he is   ashamed. I know, he says — stepping back — I know I have and that was poor and

78

I'm a piece of shit, which is historically pretty accurate, but   I really am sorry and   you're quite right   I should go so   I'll go. And I give him an eye. Taste of smile. His turn to calculate me now Well, bye bye. But as he turns I think fuck all those other things and close my hand around his wet wrist. And even that, just that touch swings both bodies to.

He kisses me in the best way then. Back banged to the sideboard and Watch the kettle! God and a month is too long to wait for being kissed this way. From here, so quick us, to badly behaved. My pyjamas unbuttoned. His long coat the same. Eye on the door. Ear to the ceiling. If we're quiet, can we manage a quick one here? he says. Is she not waiting for you? No, once you left I told her I had an early start. Jesus Christ! Well   you asked. Have you no shame? That cup over-runneth believe me, he laughs But I've been thinking about you for a month.

Slow suffering eek then up the creep-proof stairs. Pointing my landlady's room out with Shush. Slapping at him for his hand up my leg and wanting it to all the more.

Fuck your room's tiny. And the walls are thin. Wet coat shed and quick caught me. Osip Mandelstam digging in the back of my knees as the kissing gets me pinned. But laugh we in the struggle to strip and not bump. Stilling into statues at the landlady's coughs. I trample too on his new-pressed shirt, just a little just. Just for her. Worse though the mattress when he inches me there. Shush, I shush. Shush yourself. I am so for him now and yet What traces has she left? What did they do? How did they kiss? Did she do this to you? He considers – I see it – telling a lie. Did she? Yes, he says. What do I say to that? Like a stone on his back. Like a stone on mine. Have you protection with you? Of course I have. And, for all my want, I could kick myself for so easily giving in to his charms. When he's ready though, I lift to him. Kiss him as he's about to, then it's just us two again, finding how we creaklessly can and we mostly do – mostly he finds – while I hold to him, shaking in the silence. He makes me and waits. Lets himself once I have   and and   The weight of him on me. Christ. But all things between us made new.

In the after, I listen to the rain. His breath on my shoulder That was great. And this is how I'd like the night to be – hours of lying here with him – but Don't sleep, I say You have to leave. Don't send me back out there. Consider it punishment for your sins! But I'll get up so early. No. An hour? No. Half? No. Five minutes more? Those five he gets but after them Up. You're a hard woman, he says getting off, all reluctant. And so I am, watching him dress now in the dark. We kiss a good while though before my door shuts and I listen to no sound on the stairs. Practice makes perfect. But I go to my window. Heavy rain beyond and him coming out into that. Tugging up his collar. Lighting a cigarette. Look up look up. He looks up. I show a hand. In turn, he bows then goes out to the footpath. I follow him to the end of the street where he disappears round Our Lady Help of Christians. Then slip back into the smell of him on my sheet. Search out the last of his taste on my lips. Imagine that I'd kept him here. Then think of him, in the rain, out there. That could – if I wanted – make my heart a little break. But I don't want it to, so it does not.

Drift steam in the bath. Early morning. Thread his name through the bubbles and pop. Counting last night that's six times I've had sex. If he was still here he'd make it seven. If he was still here   if he was still here   what would we not do?

Before leaving, I wrap up the condom – if she found it she'd kill me stone dead. But at the bin on Leighton Road   that

80

little bit of him with Andrex wrapped round. Put it back in my pocket. Does he wish he had something of me? Even his sheets smell of someone else. No. Remember us there in the dark. I hang onto it so, until the bin at the top of Anglers Lane.

She stands smoking by the gate. Happy New Year! Her eyes are red. What's wrong? He stayed over. He was collecting his stuff and   you know how it is. I ended up begging him not to do it but she's going to pay off his fees. And inside her distress, I see a little of mine. They won't be 'married married' though, couldn't you still go out? How could I trust him? He kept it secret all this time   I mean   it's happening Friday afternoon. Sorry, I say – pushing my own glee down – Why don't we go out that night? You're on, she says And fuck him anyway.

Congregate in the Church first for Acting. Welcome back. I hope you had a good break. This term we'll work on the Private Moment exercise. So choose something you really only do in private, something you'd never do around anyone else and No – before you ask – no kind of masturbation. There's enough of that going on around here as it is.

Go.

Plays read. Cigarettes on the step. Ballet gear re-squeezed into cursing Quality Street. A laugh at lunch with some of the lads. Meet our new director. Sleep heavy every night and every day wait for his call. It comes How about Saturday, I'll get us tickets for something? Yes! Great, meet for a drink first at the Prince Albert at six? Poor her though. Her week drags. Thinner and thinner. Him avoiding her now. By Friday afternoon, I'm pleading Please eat something or. That fucker's already been married an hour, time for a drink, she says.

We are installed. We are impinted. Somewhere in the West End. She has a brief whimper, then the real drinking begins.

Come on, she hisses, hours later – hammered completely and fuckeringly now. Staggering brothelly-haired outside. In the mucklight, the starlight, we are on the town. Fuck him the fucker I knew he fucked around   have you? No. Why NO? Just no. Ah   you probably swill. Nah! I laugh. But he's good, your one? she offers the bottle. It hits my throat, rascally sweet – we are in the tooth-rinse stage, fine, but gone to the dogs. Do you know what he know what he did? I cough. What did he? Shagged some other one the night I came back. In the room. In the very bed. Bastard! she Wankers all. Cat-headed and slurry-mouthed mewlers on the tiles. Eating a kebab she scorns Dick on a stick. Disgusting. But we have it, slocked on a bench, eyed by some fella who's surely pissed his pants. There's no one suffered like the poor of east London, he says Do you hear me? Do you know that? Sure I'm not English. She is. What? Come on girls   give us some change. Fuck right off, she says. Jesus chilli sauce my friend. Queens and cockroaches. But you got your oats? Certainly cerealisation, I agree. Men are bastards, she shouts scattering the paper around. On we go – langered for heaven, or under it tonight. And apparently, girls are Here Here Here. Men making kissy suck sounds as we gawk in the door. Are you lookin' at me? – when they gawk back – Tell your sister get her knickers off you scum bum-ming pig. Me sliding on the Soho muck of shed human skin, jizz, piss chips spilt lager rain onion rings. Out to the cobbles, licking sauce from her hair. What for money though? What for geld? Nun on me Not twenty of the pence. Pounds, she finds. We've started so we'll finish. Bitch of a baby still this night. Come on. What are you staring for? I never saw men hold hands. They'll think you hate them and you'll be a homophobic then. I don't. I'm not. But she's fallen off the path. Hobblety when I haul her up. One blue high heel snapped and now I am not looking. Where to? Leicester Square. I've never seen it after dark so many nevers. No Toto, woof, you're not in Ireland any more. On Shaftesbury Avenue laughing 'Tis Pity she's a Fiona Pshaw! You wish you were! And swaying around lamp posts. Singing in the rain. Heave through the heave. There. Arse on the bit of stone. Flicking chips at the tourists gets her laughing a lot, while drink makes me tired and foolish work. What do you think he's doing now with Frankenbitch? Taking her roughly from behind. Cake mashed in her dress. Talking Czechoslovakian. Let's toast him. Them both! To his clap and her burning pants. A pox on his penis. Minimus! Egg! Dwarf! Can I have a chip? some man asks. No, I say. She says Yes. Are you Irish? Oh for fuck's fucking sake! but make that chat Irish people must. Do. Where are you from? Do you know my cousin? Yah. Nah. Yah. Nah. Sure I'll buy ye a drink. No, I say. She says Yes. So up on our trotters we go off again. Slithering through Chinatown. Glitter ducks and squids and all. There were I with. Lonely for him now. Up yet another street. In there. A bar. A new kind of glamorous for – under wigs I long to pull – are men in white dresses with blue satin sashes, and him saying I'll get the cockstails in. What's his name? Who cares? What's the harm? It's only pink drinks from a Connemara man. Get that down you, he says. I drink and try not to burp. He talks. Strokes my hair but the room starts to twirl as he's finger flicking Another round, more. She sliding down the pvc telling fuck all men. So this is how we drink, dribble kiss and   go to bed? No. No. Not with him even if I let a kiss with the tongue. Whoo! she says Look at you, and I

am   I am   Got to go to the loo. But the toilet's a maze, now
I'm drink undone. Far drunker than I know how to be. Wee.
Wash my hands. Stare. Is she really me? The sad of her. Her
sad eyes ponder. Ow! Smack on the cheek. Ow! Sorry, I didn't
expect someone there   that'll bruise sorry. Don't worry   I'm
perfect, and stagger out into crashed light. There's him, but
where's her? Ah her, slumped. Hey! I say. He doesn't look.
Reaches over for my hand. His other up her top and   Hey!
Stop that! Let go! Hey! Wake up! She, head swings. Sees. Hits
him a thump. Fucking slut. I pull her Please be able to get up. Sit
down, he orders I bought you drinks. Fuck you, you fucking
pervert! then slipping between tables of men going Who are
you calling pervert, love? No, not you not you HIM!

   Wake up, wake up I think I'm going to puke. I call Stop, on
the bus, and she stumbles off. Does. Me holding her hair back,
trying not to myself. Oh Jack's Sore Asshole   how'd we get to
the Heath? I don't know   I don't know where we are, and as
the two-ten disappears What are we going to do? She points to
the park Kentish Town's the other side. No way! Are you mad?
There could be rapists or anything. More like men having it off.
And, in all our drinks, that's enough. So down we go. In. Sobering under tree creak. Terrified to holding hands. At least the
wind doesn't whip as we trudge, smoking, regretting our liv-
ers' work. Do you know where we are? No   I've not been here
in the dark. Some rustle sets us running out to the open and
up. Look! Look at that. Night London. God it's ugly, she says.
But no no no I take its side. Somewhere below he is sleeping I
hope on his own. And her beloved lies married down there while
we, above, wait, enumerating our grass stains and watching til
dawn lifts through the morning sky. Froze to the bones and
organs tired, making our ways down. Well, that's all folks! See

you Monday, she says at the gate and knight us it Skank Night for immemorial ahead.

Six thirty-five and him pulling me out to Royal College Street.
   Jesus, fucking Hellcat, what's wrong with you? You heard him. I heard him but that's no excuse, he could've fucking killed you, he could've killed me – he was easily taller and four times the width! I barely touched him. That's not the fucking point. I bet you're glad you bombed Warrington, you heard what he said. I know and it was out of order and I told him that but you shouldn't have hit him. Yes I should   anyway   you got him to stay back. That was only luck and him being far too drunk to realise he could've snapped me like a twig. Well   fuck him. Yeah fuck him but I have to tell you something   I'm not much good in a fight any more so let's not do that again.
   After, I lie across him, all licked and kissed, lifting odd drags from his cigarette. Warm in the gaslight. Half under the clothes. My hair being wound his thumb while I smoke and So much for Blasted, he says. Sorry, maybe we shouldn't have stopped for a drink first. Yeah   I can now see that. But I'm frisk and careless, tracing his ribs So tell me which ones broke? Left   lower   those three. Which arm? Left too press there   feel that? Poor arm – I kiss the spot. Well, it was years ago, he says. Was it a high roof? Three-storey house. You could have been killed then. Ah   I fell in a bush. What were you doing up there? The Book of Revelation, I think, with asides from the man Himself. And what did he say? Not much   not enough   anyway I soon fell off and that was the end of that but listen   the other night   I know why you were upset and it was shitty but   I wouldn't want you to think I expect   I just think that, after everything, you know,

85

in your past   now is the moment to   let yourself have a good time. I am, I say Here. Yeah and me   but if you met someone else – maybe more your own age – you should feel   that you have no obligations here. Why do you say that? Because   because this is great but   there's twenty years between us so this is all there is. And I could let that ice slide down my neck or refute with Have you been watching Manhattan or what? That I choose. Oh you're a wit, he says I just thought I'd mention it. And I don't really believe him but   is it the thought that counts? So   I'm not your girlfriend then? I'm not up on that stuff. In what way? It's just a long time since   I've been with someone more than once or twice. How long? Oh long, he smoke exhales. Why's that? I like it that way and   it didn't end too well with my daughter's   with her mother and that. What happened? Oh, you know. No I don't. Well   just the usual   I suppose. What does that mean? Nothing   anyway that story's too long for tonight. But I see a world turning around him then, usually invisible to the eye except for every so often when something slips out, like now. So ask. Would you like to get married one day? What, he laughs When I grow up? Nip him. Ow! No, I can't imagine it. Do you have other children? Not that I know of so I really hope not! Would you like to have more? Oh, he says   I think all that's done for me. Don't you like being a father? That's not what I said. And his face suddenly   then just as quickly blanks so his eyes let nothing out. But something grows heavy, fastening him down while I stiffen to dull like told off. Sorry. It's fine   it's just a subject best left. He's away though and what have I by way of recompense? Sit up. Take his cigarette. Look at him down through the gap in my legs. Can I touch your penis? Which he does not expect Why? It looks so sleepy now. Well, before it was busy enough. So can I? I never refuse that request, as a rule. So I take it and touch it. And watch him watch. Aren't you shy about me doing that? No. What's the scar? Where my foreskin was. I like them better like yours. Him laughing again then I'm glad to hear that! His knowitall smile and my mouth on his stomach. Sharp bone of his hip. Ruck quilt and go to lower. Hey, you don't have to do that, he says. I know, but I like shifting his lank body up into life as my own learns to forget. Airlessness helps. The slight sweat on his skin. It is a new way, made for him. I like even how he lets me and how much he likes me to. Come back here, he says I want to be inside you now. So I get up on him and do. Tangle then in the twisting play. Mix sorting what to where and when. Ignoring him saying Let me get something on, because   because I can. Him liking that too, I can see. Follow though his instructions of You go   I'll wait. The pleasure then, side of my face to his face. Surprised by how much and Fuck I feel that, he says then quickly Fuck! again and pulls me up. Pulls out. Springing straight to the wet, sticking him to my stomach. I don't care. Or when he's done. Or when he says That's why we shouldn't do that, you know. But he divil-smile smears it and I divil laugh. Glop it up on my finger I'll try if you try. He solemn assesses then abruptly licks Tastes like chicken, he says. I lick No   tastes like come. Well come here pretty girl and let me sweeten it up. Then he kisses me until I'm grand. Until I'm airy in fact. Can be. Full of sex and dare. Stretching and letting him do the mop up himself. When he clicks off the lamp though I ask Can I just ask? Absolutely not, he says. Have you ever had sex with a man? Excuse me? You heard. Sex Ed. for the under twenties, is it? he laughs. But have you? Why? Just wondering. Well then, yes, I have. Did you like it? I did. So you go both ways? I wouldn't say that. Then what would you say? That I was young and fucked up and he helped me so   when he wanted to I didn't object   no   actually that's not quite right   I was very happy to oblige. And my fingers run round the seam of his lips. First to the past, then forward to Could we try it, like that? Not tonight Josephine! Another time then? No and, before you ask, the list of my achievements in life doesn't need to extend to sodomising teenage girls, alright? But? Shush now, go to sleep. And soon as his eyes close he's off into it, leaving me fluttering there.

I sleep so safe here, far from the world. Rousing only when I'm stirred by him, climbing across. Go back to sleep   I'm just making some notes, tucking the duvet round. Then through til morning. Light and smoke. Drowse-eyed watch him push his glasses up, stretch, light another cigarette, itching to run my hands down his back. And what can want mean? Something in here. So tumble out to kiss his messed hair with a Morning – then a mis-angled Love. Morning, he says still writing though, in his loping old-fashioned longhand. Do you want to come back to bed? He kisses my wrist Do you mind if I don't? I'm just   Fine – but a little put out – Tea? Yeah   that'd be nice. Then Actually, would you go get some breakfast in? Like what? Eggs, bread, butter – not that spread shit – and whatever you want yourself, any cash in my wallet? I check Receipts. Take my switch card then and get out fifty quid. The number's three six seven eight.

Ambling Camden, before Sunday breaks loose, I divine this money thing means trust, so take it out, get what he wants, make sure of receipts. Check his balance? No. Don't. Be better than you'd like to be.

Here's your wallet, the receipt and your change. Chuck it anywhere. Oh   okay   scrambled eggs? Please, he says and while I make it, boxes get dragged out. What're you looking for? Old records   might just remind me of stuff. Strew. Some I've heard of. Most, I've not. A player and speakers dug from a box filled with postcards of the sea. Before I ask, he asks Know this? No, I don't. Wild World it is then. Hey!

It plays as we eat. Repeat. Repeat. He cleans his plate and makes the tea but with all his other self listens until I can see old weather in his eyes. You like The Birthday Party? I did, he says. So why are the records put away? I don't remember maybe   I got too keen. What? But he's back to the desk. Repeat and repeat. On he writes so I read and, in a little, sleep.

Don't move. What? Don't open your eyes yet. Why? You look so peaceful   and you get so pink. Shut up! Lazy lapse to a kiss. But. I've got homework, I better head. Still, there's wrestling before I persuade off the bed and only then permitted by letting him walk me back.

Light, this winter wander. Kentish Town. High on the night and eyeing his hand but Don't take it. Kissing at the gate. Devil don't care for the London Irish social's today, meaning she and all the rest should be out til six. So   sneak in with me? And I don't have to ask twice.

Up! Slam my door. Kiss like slaps. Bang against the wall with me fiddling flies. Stripping to stumble. Down on the bed. Pulling me under. Him inside. Ow! Sorry. No don't stop. Between us though, and irk of the mattress, it's rowdy enou What's going on up there? Oh Jesus! Oh fuck! She mustn't have gone out. What're we going to do? Bollocks to her, keep going, he says but she's on the stairs, shouting Stop that! Panic What'll we do? It quicker? he suggests. No, stop it, shush. Stop that fornicating! she yells and he tips, laughing, into my neck. No, don't laugh, stop! I'm trying, he pleads. It jumps him though and kicks me off too. Ripping us, the pair of us, to cracking ribs. I hear that laughing Lady, stop it! He rolls off me For God's sake woman, have mercy! Don't cheek me, she shrieks Get out of my house! I'm going, he says. Right now! Or you may take that hussy with. As it is, Madam, you have your two weeks! Shit, shit, what'll I do? Don't worry, he says We'll find somewhere for you in Loot, minus the landlady interruptus, how does that sound? Good, I say, hurrying to help his shirt on. Dressed though, he lingers Come back to mine? No   I better not. Will you be alright? I'll be fine. I'll head off then   sorry about all this. But before I reply he's away out into Yes off you slink! You're a disgrace and that girl is a tramp! Don't, he warns. Don't you 'Don't' me, young man, you should be ashamed! Doubtless, he sighs going on down. And pressed to the window I watch him come out, hoping he'll look up, willing him to see that I am all for him. But he doesn't. He goes and does not look back.

What are you like? she chokes. I thump her back She called me Jezebel this morning. You are too, she laughs But is he worth it? All the faff? Ah he is, I'm mad about him. We stamp our feet on the froze stone steps. So did you catch his film at Christmas? Yeah, I started it but there was so much sex my mother had a fit so then I tried to tape it but recorded something else, was he good? He was amazing, you should ask him if he taped it himself. I couldn't, he never talks about work and he might think you know. True, it'll be out on video soon enough but   don't you think it's weird with the TV leads and West End stuff that he still lives in some crappy bedsit? No, he's not fussed, his mind's on higher things. Or lower! she cackles Speaking of which, Don Giovanni might have a room going in the marital flat. Oh really? That'd be handy, thanks, I'll ask.

That'd be yours, he yawns, nudging open the door It's only a bed, but bills included. When do you want move in? Week after next? Perfect but, one thing, will she be over a lot? No more than she has to. Then it's a deal. Which is just as well, because a few days later Listen I have to go to Scotland tonight. They've been dicking about with these film dates for a while. Now suddenly they're ready so I have to go but I was thinking, if you need somewhere to Don't worry, I've sorted it out. Great, that's a relief, I'll see you in a couple of weeks.

On that said Saturday she helps me move into the flat. Tired white walls. No curtains or blinds. But perfect. Landlady free. The I hope you're proud of yourself, ringing in my ears as I lug my stuff from the Safeway's trolley I nicked and pushed down to Patshull Road. I think I'll blank him, she decides. Fair enough, I say, blu-tacking Betty Blue up. I pity you, he's such an asshole! Keep it down, I live here now. I bet he shags you before the term is out. I wouldn't. You will, I know what he's like. Give me some credit, shall we go for a pint? Sorry, I've got a date. And when she's gone I sit mapping this weekend alone. Coast clear? he shouts. Yes. Then come meet the wife and her boyfriend, we're getting a take-out. So.

New again opens to me. Girl I've been, woman I'll be. This weekend becoming the first of many video-watching nights on the sitting-room floor. Spliffs and parties. Self-pitying Sundays, hungover. And this tides me across his away, on into February when A certain northern gentleman rang, asking you to meet him in the Prince Albert tonight. Blind again with delight for it's been long long long. First though, this morning, Private Moment exercise.

*Baited in Room Two and the dust light there. Prokofiev tape. Cig-
arette. I put my father's jacket on. This an only when I'm alone. Its
yellowed tweed still smells of him though it's getting hard to tell. But
here, beneath analytical eyes, I remember when he wore it last. Me
reading on his knee. Nineteen eighty-five and not knowing it was
the final night we'd ever spend that way. Next. A letter I've read
once before – written from the hospital after he'd been told. Printed
in block capitals because I was so small, and opening it slowly now.*
Concentrate, the teacher says And – trying to remain by yourself – start to read aloud. *IIIIII put tongue to words but the sound
is none.* The reason is, he interrupts We can see you're having
an emotional reaction to it and, when that happens on stage,
your speech needs to be clear for the audience's sake, do you
understand? *Yes. Wish I'd never chosen this and just leapt around
naked like everyone else but I don't do that when I'm alone. It was this
or the clipped breath of burns and.* Be brave, the teacher says. *So
I open. Open it. Make myself by myself and read MY DEAREST*

Fine again, nine and in my coat, I make my way down Prince of
Wales Road. Weaving the dark and rain of it. Frail for a friendly face, and warmth, and going back to his.

Hey there! He looks up Hi. You're tired, I say. No   I'm
drunk. How long are you here? Since three o'clock. Why's that?
He shrugs. Is something wrong? No   I'll get you a drink, but
even standing up's an ordeal. His walk there an intricate maze
of wheels. At the bar, he orders pints and a shot. Sure? I see her
ask. He nods. Tosses it. Manages back. Thanks, I anxious How
was the shoot? Ffffffff, he shakes his head Waste of fucking
time   the fucking director   I fucking hate his kind   shit and
sweat confidence but   you know all the time there's nothing
else going on. So why did you do it? Producer's a mate, and he

92

wipes the spit from his lip then resurrects Jesus! and 'Beautiful ingénue' my arse. Fifteen years too old for the part and that full of plastic if you fucked her she'd bounce but   she's the 'name' so we're left hanging around in the freezing fucking cold while they sew her face on it's bullshit   it's just   And it's a shock to see, like he's gone deaf inside. Just pulling words over whatever's behind. Suddenly though taking my hand Sorry for ranting, how's your new place? But the temper still going up and down in his eyes. It's above Blockbuster   sharing with my friend's ex   listen   did something happen today? He drags his cigarette to the quick I wanted to apologise   for you getting kicked out of your place I should have   I should   sorry for that   I'm such a fucking arsehole sometimes. You're not, I say. I hope you don't mind me calling   I   I know they rehearse you late up there   I just thought some company might   I'm glad you called. Really? Of course, I say. So ready for another then?

Soon we are in the fet night. I and him. Drinking like savages. Smoke every breath in. Another? And Another? If that's okay? Yeah, what isn't with me, he says Every single fucking thing. Pints retired for the lash of Jameson's until tempting the welt of his strangeness, I press Won't you tell me what's wrong? I can't. But something is? Oh well, isn't it always? The way he speaks though, some unknowable voice. And I've never seen anyone get drunk this hard, like hammering nails down into his head. Stoops to kiss though in his drunken elegance. Long kiss. Good, first. But quick switched to rough. Hand between my legs. I push him back Stop! Why? You never complained before? But not in public. Who the fuck cares? Please don't. Fuck this! he says, then seems to see himself Sorry   I am   I'm very   I think I'd better be off. Wait! I get my coat. No, don't come, he says, and reels on out to the filthy night. But

I follow – if only as crutch – except Get the fuck off I can walk by myself. And though he falls again in the London muck, I tow behind to under the bridge. His face in the streetlight, in the sockets of his eyes. Something gnawing. Wheedles open his fly. Don't, hang on, we'll be home in a sec. I-have-to-take-a-leak, he says. Pisses right there, while I, mortified, wait. What is going on tonight? Mortification interrupted by another kiss and in the midst of, my skirt hiked up. Let's have a fuck. For God's sake, not here! Don't you want me? Stop! You do. You're wet. And I do want him. I always want but I am not at all drunk enough. Let's go back to yours. I don't want to, he says I hate that fucking place. I yank away. What's the fucking problem? Hey! I'm not going back there, do you hear? I walk on, leaving him to stagger in circles and then slowly roll after me.

Up the stairs. Into the room. Take your knickers off, he says. Slams the door and Oh God the state of the place. I missed you, I say. It's nice that you care but you're here to fuck aren't you   or why are you here? Don't be like that. He drops his coat You can take your knickers off or you can go, either is fine by me. So there'll be nothing like kindness between us tonight. Acquiescing the bargain, I tug at my tights, shy with his watching. Him, much tightened, gripping hold. Kissing full on but kissing cold. He's off into this, I think, on his own, just with my body too. And it's stripped impatiently like I'm a bold child. Fingers in til That hurts. Get on the bed. So I lie down to become bits of girl for him and one who's going to have it bad. The fear of it though, what it will spoil. I switch from myself into her and he knows. Don't fucking look at me that way, turn on your front. Then a rage at his belt. Fucking come on. Let me do it. Shut the fuck up. What? Just be quiet, and he gets it. Kneels down and Turn over, I said. So I give him the body,

94

hope it is the trick but he takes it so hard and Christ you're tight! Light streaking across the ceiling from the cars in the street as I struggle. Don't you like it? You're scaring me now. I'm just fucking you, he says No need for alarm. Something though. He eases off then. Lies himself down on my back. Does things with his mouth – which may or may not be a bite – but how he touches me makes my whole body soft, collapsing me onto my front. What's wrong? I ask. Don't, he says You ask so much. Then far again and hard as he can. Too much, I Too much you're hurting me. Well now you know how it feels. What? Do you think this is easy? What is? Shut up, he says Shut up shut up, until I gasp with the take. How long will this be? Can I manage? Please not so deep. But the way he is. He. Fuck! and he comes. No! I NO! Ripping free. Him insisting at it as I claw from beneath. Turn, chaos-blind, and slap him in the face. Like woke, he Fuck! I hit him again How fucking dare you do that! He slumps against the wall, dick in his hand. He knows what he did and won't meet my eye or look at his come making trails down my thigh. Race. Run. Get it out.

Now the lightless hall sings sanctuary from the frenzy left in there. But crouched in the loo I start to cry – no fucking toilet roll either. Don't. Be grown-up now. Hunt the dressing-gown pocket. Used tissue there. Wipe it out. Take a breath, and myself, right back in.

Gloom. Him. Thin and long cat limbs stretched wrong-way on the bed. Limp in the aftermath. Head to the side. Wash between my legs. The anger though. He is not allowed and I can trespass too. So in the black, sit. Asleep or awake? Run a hand up him and take hold of it. Damp shrunk back in its bad self but I begin the graft. Soon there's life and rub until – despite the drink – it's hard. Flicker his lids up and What are you at?

almost scared then Fuck! he knows what. Don't you speak to me, I say and silent so, he lies. Only once reaches across and sounding like his old self asks Can I touch you too? No. I no to whatever he wants. Avoid his grasp. Still, he strokes my wrist. More tenderness in that caress than anything else this night. Although drink holds him off, I keep on until he does. Little, this time. Fragile almost. Spilt on me. I don't care. Mess it into that dark hair. Gentle, he says but I do what I want and when it's over, neither blinks. Or knows what to think about what's gone on in here tonight. Just sit dishevelled, sore and drunk. At last, he says I'm going to sleep. Then go to fucking sleep, I say. But watch him fall off, far from me. Brush the hair back from his cheek. Its fine bones. His open lips. Beautiful for a man, I think, and know, I am afraid. If he was awake, I'd lie on his chest. Make him tell me it's alright, even if it's probably not. Not for me. Not for him. A half-way though is take his hand and in his sleep he squeezes mine. It is the best that can be done.

Later on, he climbs across. Naked, goes out. There's throwing up. Under lowered lashes watch him falter back. Rinse in the sink. Mirror stare. No relief in water from what he sees there. You awake? he asks. I pretend I'm not as he slips in by again. Then warm and drunk, tired and scared, fall asleep together.

Rise up to morning from hours of dead. I open my eyes. You were snoring, he says. Sorry. I examine his face. Him examining mine. Quiet and grave as close we lie, shattered by the night. Its afters spread in the early light but link our hands beneath the quilt. Palm to palm like silent prayer. Soft and with more feeling, I think, than we know how to say. Soon enough though it's too bright to hide. You came in me. He closes his eyes I know   I'm sorry   for everything last night   will I take you to the. No   tell me what happened? What does it matter now?

96

I should never have called. Tell me? I sit up but following me he goes Fuck! What? He backs from the bed. Oh fuck oh fuck look what I did. I look and all down my arms skin pushes forth purple bruise. Oh. Jesus fucking Christ, he says I'm so sorry I'm so sorry. I forgive you, I say. Well you shouldn't   get dressed. Why? Because this isn't right. I can't be at this with you. You scared me, I say But   No, I can't see you again. You can. I can't. So you're throwing me away? I'm not. You fucking bastard! Agreed, he says starting to pass my clothes. I start to dress and I am so   I am so   after everything. Not to have or be with him. Please, I say. He shakes his head. Well if you don't want me there'll be someone else who'll want me and want me. It's not that, he says It isn't that at all. Then why is it over? He hides his face. Because   oh God   I can't manage this   it's fucking pathetic but I can't and   I don't want something bad to happen. Something bad already has. Yes   so nothing worse. And how he looks at me then. I know it's done. And I am so crushed I walk straight out, hoping he will call me back then hear his door go BANG.

I find the smallest part of my life and crawl in there. I have no faith in the night or the morning either and cannot believe how this day dares glow all up to Kentish Town. Past Kwik Save. The steps off Patshull to where I live. To where I live. I live there and know that now. Every bit of you lives here. No bit of you lives anywhere else.

And my flatmate's ejecting some girl at the door. She doesn't seem to mind. He is sweet enough. When I squeeze by though he goes What the fuck? You look like shit on toast. Thanks.

If I could I'd lie under the bed but it's only a mattress so the sheet instead. Minutes later he knocks, I ignore it. Then there's a wallop outside on the glass. When I look up, he's pressed to it You alright? I just want to be by myself. Okay, he says I'll catch you later on. All later ons though I avoid, knowing what I should do. Get the morning after pill but   that needs a face to look at me, which needs me being there. And I am busy in the smallest part of my life. I have crawled in here. It's made for abstaining. A box of breath. Blood pumping and limbs shifting over pages of the A–Z. A couple of days and its good stead should have me flesh again. Nice again. Back on, though hoarse. Go get the morning after no, I don't want. Cannot go. No volition to bring. I would rather lie here, make a face of my palm and listen to the traffic outside.

Bollocks. Cup of tea. Pizza. Spliff. That's what you need so you're in luck, the Missus brought all the leftovers from her work. I'm tired. Every part of me is broke. You've been in this bed for a week and if you don't quit skiving they'll turf you out so come on, we're all in the sitting room. Blast of Withnail will do you good.

Key. Key. I do see it but don't care about making it turn.

Lazy bint, get up! I made you a coffee. Thanks   I just. Drink it. Hop in the shower. There's toast if you want and in half an hour you can walk in with me.

Work.
Work work work work work.

Look out at Camden from a bus and the Oh God oh god ohmygodthefuckingpainofthis

Three minutes.

We are only on the first.

Why didn't you tell me? How late is late? Late enough. Too late, aren't all lates that? And I'm always late   so   it's just to check. You should've gone on the pill. I know I should but You should go on it now. I will. Imagine if you were though, she says Pregnant with a famous actor's child, how romantic would that be? making moustaches with her hair.

Second minute.

Would you tell him? I'd have to. He'd have to pay for the operation. So, you wouldn't have it? How could I have it? Yeah, you're probably right. Plus he doesn't want any more children himself.

Third minute.

Well he should have thought of that first. It was an accident, so. Happens to everyone I suppose. Does it? Yes, how could it not, is this really your first ever test? Ever. I had mine at fifteen. Positive but negative on the next three, thank God! Beginner's luck, I say. And may it extend to thee now. Thanks. So, she says Want to have a look?

Yes.

Check it.

And again.

All hooks offed.

Oh

No blue.

Pill. I say Good girl, to myself. That's the spirit. When there's war be ready for it. Have it. But I don't start it. I might though. I will though, soon.

Black ceiling above. Somewhere there's stars. Music soaks down. The first coming up and rolling out. Feeling the love? Flatmate laughs, ducking around me Come on! Let's dance! Giddy and led so, I give to the trance. Where the bodies are greeting, beckoning mine. Where the heat is. Joy lives. Swapped smiles and mixed hands. Inside me opening as the room begins to go. All turned to heartbeat and all I am is all hope. You're beautiful, he says. You too, I shout. Kiss like we're meant. Memory wiped. This night the finest yet. Freer than I've ever been and we're all here dancing so free. Dancing in the absence of my body. Weight or look or pain. As though I am perfection moving against the sweat of strange men. Him. Her. The strange sweat of women. I find and lose, the very same. I relinquish my best self to them. Sometimes he dances where I am. What he offers, I take from him. And who wants my love has it, for we're a unit of life. More. In this dark we are a unit of light.

Great night. Another night. One more dance? One more pill. And the night bus. Grand. Feeling any better these days? I am. I really love you man. I really love you back. And laugh into each other as London gallivants in its circus of lights.

I really feel like shit. Me too, he on my bed Missus? Hey! Missus? Make us a brew? which she actually does What time back? Five or so. Her hairy boyfriend, in her dressing gown, smirking asides. She translates You are together now? No. He was cheering me up. Your broken heart? Stays broken but   I am up for the odd chemical whirl. Pure selfishness on my part, Flatmate says Couldn't stomach another month of her lying in bed!

I'm glad that month is over too. In it I thought I'd die. I thought about you every day. I think about you all the time. Missing more as the bruises greened – which wasn't long because they were gripping not hitting – and when they faded I started burning again. It didn't work. It didn't hurt enough. And I should hate you for what you were. And I do want to hurt you but can't manage either, for how's that done to the closed-over door? Look for ways though, sleeping beside your Black Snow. Just so much feeling left behind. It wishes you'd tell me you want me again and tells itself it would turn you down.

'Nother? Please. Lounge between the flatmate's legs. He pours over my shoulder Coming out tomorrow night? Where? Camden. Few drinks with mates – men – you should come. Okay.

Skite over the hours until we're drunk. Last glugs of vermouth. Mound of fag butts with gall-guts and gall-eyes from watching Reservoir Dogs. After that Bound and Gagged. After that Your Missus is nice. Isn't she though? After that How's married life treating you? Brilliant. So   tell me   what upsets men? What, like Spurs losing? No   like your ex   what would she have to do? She couldn't, I don't fancy her any more. But if you did? Seeing her with someone else I suppose. And cat out on the carpet to ponder that. Low to play jealousy but I'm all tats and Would you ever give me a love bite? Why? Just because. So he, too trashed for incompliance, does. Ow! Me kicking That fucking hurts! Yep, you'll need a load of toothpaste on that, he showboats. And there, touching my throat on the pain he's made I Look outside, it's light. Pull myself up Time for bed. Wait! What? Do you want to sleep with me? he asks. In blear-gratified vacuum I say Yes   do you want to sleep with me? Yeah, let's go to bed – which is back on the floor, him on top, kissing to rubbish truck squeal beyond.

101

He kisses well too, without remorse but no iota in me stirs. Still, I just have his jeans off when the front door creaks. Sssh it's your wife! Mithered by giggling we freeze where we are. Czechoslovakian-sounding words. Wait. Ssssh. Her bedroom door. Right, your place or mine? Follow, I instruct, stumbling into the hall. Dawn spidering across my mattress now. Still no curtains! No one's around to see. Slide down the wall and he slides down on me. Kiss. Stripping. Different. Why shouldn't it be? Though he's tall, not as tall. Thin, not as thin. Further unnerving the not smelling the same. Still, it's friendly to wriggle about, touch in those ways. And, despite the drunkness, I like this something like sex, even though it only seems its cousin twice removed when compared with. Don't. Don't think about him. Too quick, he says after Sorry about that. But sprawling I offer the comfort of females Don't worry about it, happens to everyone. Go to sleep then knowing I've made the first step towards rubbing him out.

Bit weird that, Flatmate says around three. Yeah, I eating my bowl of rice crispies Let's not repeat it. Yeah, nice love bite though   why did you want it again? I forget I haven't. It's the best thought I've ever had. Could I though? Dwell on him. Pick at the scab of missing him. Just to see him. Even to hurt him, that's something. He's the one closed the door. Got to say it, Flatmate says lifting my hair to inspect Damn fine work there on my part.

Six hours later. Come the fuck on! I'm coming but I have to drop this book off. Where? The Prince Albert, it's on the way. Hurry up then! Okay, I'm just doing my hair.

Feast of the crowd. Pub. Saturday night. Rites of laughter. Crisps. Fags. Pint. Flatmate declares he's off for a slash, deserting me to the boots and bag straps I. He's probably not here anyway. He's probably at the World's End. He's not. He's in the corner, lighting a cigarette. Two girls beside him of course he has. No. Look harder. They're just there as well. Then all I can do is look at him, burning with what's left of not burnt down. Tired, he seems but hair been cut. Little more grey, maybe. Don't see me. Please don't. Palming the bite mark I make to retreat. Flicking a match though he catches sight and Shit! Drops it. Stands. Paperback swatting it off while my inside life shows whatever it wants. Hello, he says, once fully extinguished. You shouldn't dog-ear it, I say. Oh God, spare me the books, he says then It's nice to see you. And you. But I can't meet his eyes so stare at his fingers instead. He's a better trier So how've you been? Fine, you? Fine   here for a drink? But suddenly remembering I came to be cold I fish out his book Just returning Black Snow. Oh   did you read it? Yes   it was good. I'm glad you enjoyed it. I really did.   Listen – quick his hand goes for my hand but WHACK from the flatmate hits my arse right then with Awight darlin'? Ready or what? So here it is, the flower of my plot. Them face to face, with him – for just a second – off guard. Perfect in every way except   I don't feel so vindictive now. Oh God   you did this so you have to now. This is my new flatmate   Oh right, he says Nice to meet you, and he shakes his hand. You too mate, the flatmate says impressed then, for the moment's a bit crippled, adds I saw you in 'Tis Pity last year   you were great! Cheers, he says It worked out alright, but his eyes move back across my face and down my neck. I see him see it then by just the tiniest flick that he covers by itching at his lip. So, Flatmate soldiers We're meeting up with some mates, you're very welcome to come along if? Thanks but   I'm just out for a quiet pint. How he looks at him though, gauging what might be the thing. Fair enough, Flatmate says Well   I better head out   nice to meet you – and to me – don't be long, then disappears into the crowd.

He seems like a nice lad. Yeah, he is. Well   I'll let you get off, and he stoops to kiss my cheek but the chaste peck turns to kiss, half-kiss, between us. I'd go all but he says up close I'm so sorry for what I did and I want you to know I've regretted it every day since. I know, I say the pain of this What upset you though? Won't you tell me that? He steps back, but then just says I spoke to my daughter on the phone and it had been so long I didn't recognise her voice I had to ask her who she was which   wasn't great   I suppose. And the bareness of him, down to the bone. What I'd give to ask him more but Anyway that set me off   and it's not an excuse but you're owed the truth so, poor as it is, that's it. Quiet world again. Thank you, I say. He just nods so I   If you want   if you'd like   I could stay for a pint? Don't be silly, besides your bloke'll be freezing his arse off outside. I'm not with him, you know. He says Oh right. So and because there's nothing else for it, I say Goodbye, and leave.

You sneaky fucking cow! You made me look a right twat! I cool my face on the tile What does it matter? It matters because he's fucking great and now he thinks I'm shagging his bird. I'm not his bird and he doesn't care. Are you crying? No. Stop crying. I'm not. Fuck's sake, you'll be alright, look, take one of these.

In. Under the hot and dark. Waterfall pictures. Plastic flowers. Doner turning. Seven Skol. Chippy fingers. Back room. Smoke. Some girl going It's like a vision in my head. Some lad's hand sitting welcome on my leg. Me to Flatmate passing the joint. The laugh of it all on this good night. Mix compound found and herb-induced free. Hours of drinking over the E. But gathered together. Brain working loose. Belonging to London. Safe from the world. Three o'clock. Four, before they start picking off. Got to get the last night bus. Him. Then her. Then Flatmate with the some girl staggers out to the breeze. Coming? Not yet. My accomplices lads, saying You're very welcome to our floor. Sure? Sure. So, caning, stay until we're turfed to the dawn.

We three here. Thy will be done. Satan under every skin. Skinful under all our skin. Skitter bedraggled laughing in the streets. Linking arms. Split cigarettes. Steps and stairs and to the room. Copies of Loaded. Dirty tissues. Cramped. Drink more? Shall, I think – bottle of vodka that stinks of fridge. First, more drugs? Jesus, please. Snuffed off a Dog Man Star. Kick away boots. Tights the bane of mankind. Better off with young men, amn't I? Chin, my dears. Chin chin to you. Hum in the lungs and the spine and the gullet. Everything cancelling everything out. Dance lazy loose like playing trust. Safe they rock me about, between. Kind hands helping air to my skin. Draughty strip. More! More! they complain and I lay, am laid down. Still, I have laid on beds before. Who objects? Answer – No one. No one in here ever does to a speed quick kiss from two drink thick mouths. Sure ye're nice lads. Decent lads. Nestled in my neck. What are ye at? Well, what would you like? To be dead no that's not right. Twine me round. More kisses perhaps? A mouth finds mine. A mouth finds my back. Smell of hair on a pillow. Bra unclasped. Devil at my navel. Devil at my breast. Right hand in tight jeans, doing its work. Whoever they are though, they're good to me. Good at pointing out my sovereignty. And why shouldn't I reject my scum-rid history and wherever I'm wanted, go? So I touch. Am touched by both. If it's more than I bargained for it's only life. Fine to the moment of Suck us off? Then No, I won't do that. We thought you were up for it? I thought I was. Quick one? No. Please? Listen lads, maybe it's time I head for the wilds. Don't. Stay. We'll have a good time. Plenty condoms. Plenty drink. But I can leave if I want. We know that. We just hope you won't. So now as I chose him can I choose them? If I let it this will happen. If it happens, who would care? Not all girls have fathers who get upset. Not all men hurt girls for their daughter's sake. And how much do I already know I can take. To spite myself, for him. To hurt myself. I open my thighs saying Lads, do anything. Nothing matters. And it is nothing. Empty vessels making most sound. Stretch her. She deserves it. The well-trained mouth. Just go where she treads herself underfoot. Beneath unwashed bodies. She chooses this. This time she chooses what she is. Beyond the fright, even disgust, she passes her body on to their want and only when they have fucked enough goes down to the sleep where no dream penetrates.

I wake up. Again there's life. I wake up. It is daylight. Their trousers off. In my skin. Find my clothes. They stay asleep. Got to go. Monsters approach and the morning knows what you did.

I push outside to the night that's day. To the street where I was before I became what I've become – a form of thing. What does it mean? Look into the sun and want   and want   to be safe. Down Chalk Farm Road. The Marathon. If I could step back there, I'd choose to go home. But it's in me, forever. The Roundhouse here. Safeway's. Offstage. The Monarch. Moon under Water. The Fusilier. Under railway. Over canal. The Elephant's Head. Market stalls. Round the tube to the Camden Road. Canal again. Cross beneath the overground. Again over

Royal College Street. Further up. Turn right. The hedge. The house. His door and ring his bell. Ring it and listen and ring.

Steps. Unlatch locked opened. There. Him, light-wincing, half-asleep Hey   it's barely seven   what are you doing here? I only stand. Then his eyes catch up Jesus, what happened? But she is silent, spring-snapped. What's the matter? What happened? I   did something bad. What did you do? I went back to this fella's   with him and his friend. Why are you telling me this? Can I come in? No, go home. Please. No. Please   I'm frightened. His fingers in his sleep-flat hair Alright, go on upstairs.

Lair early, old cigarettes and sleep. The stuffiness, comfort. Even the mess. Oblivious to its magic he leans on the desk Right, what is it you want? Can I say what I want is to lie on his bed, in his crease on his sheets until my body forgets what it's done and where it's been? By the cool of his eye I don't think I can. Instead I stare at floor. He takes a deep breath From the beginning then, did they make you? No. Did they hurt you? Shake again. Use protection? I look up – he looks away – Yes. Well that's something at least so   why are you frightened? Because of what I did. And what exactly was that, do you remember? Everything I did everything   with the both of them. For fuck's sake! he says. It was only a good time but then I woke up and how can he not see what it took to make myself do that? So what is it you want me to do? Let me stay here. No, go home, sleep it off. But fright goes everywhere like losing blood. Don't look at me like that, he says What am I supposed to say? If you're upset by what you did don't do it again   you know   these things happen   you'll be fine. I nod. Do you hear me? Yes. Then why don't you go? But Sorry's all that comes. Don't apologise to me, he shouts I don't give a fuck what you did. Why are you shouting at me

107

then? He just shakes his head and seeing now he won't be kind, I shut my eyes. Shame fuses to silence letting the night maraud, killing bit by useless hope of not being this girl I was. Am. She is. Don't fucking cry, he says Do you think I don't understand? I know all about having a good time. Having it and having it until a good time's all there is, until it's not a good time, until it's everything turned to shit and you can't believe the things you've done, look at me, is that what you want? I look and   I think   I'm going to puke. Ah fuck it! he grabs me, drags me by the arm out. Half carrying by the toilet. Holding hair back and me forward Just try to aim. Drugs, drink, chewed chips spittle bile. Again. Again until That everything? Yes. Go wash your mouth in the shower then. Brain whacks with spun though and balance off. Hand out to the nowhere. Knuckles the lock but. He catches me. Hikes me under his arm over each nail in the floor. Past blue telly flicker. Click. Green mirror mould and. Puke stain all down my top. There's the. What's she? Just get in it, he says so I try to but   seize up.

Cold drizzle it spits as he strips me then, detouring his eyes to the crust-scaled screen. Get in. Slip. Oh! It's freezing! Take this, he says – beige bar of soap I rotate, rotate, drop. Fuck it, he fishes for it, finds. I drop it again. Come on, stop fucking around. I'm trying. But in the froze water and distress turn myself to wall, to the thousands of cells of the thousands of bodies who have cleaned themselves off by these cracks. And I'd be one. Any of which, any, to slip this being this. Back scratched by some two. Flatmate neck bit. And him there, seeing all of it. Knees give in. Give. Slide to the shower floor with the greasy ingrains of one thousand soles and cry like I am ripped. I'm afraid I'm afraid   of everything   please don't be angry with me   I don't know what to do. Sssh water down. Sssh. Step and he steps in. Pulls me up

108

by the arm. Wangles me round to him. I know, he says I know, I'm sorry for   I'll switch on the hot water now.

He scrubs me then. Forehead to feet. In between my fingers. Everything. When he's done reaches No towel. Shit! Rolls me in his bathrobe instead and, shorts sodden to see-through, limps me back to his room. Dries my skin to the smell of frayed towel mildew. No hairdryer, sorry. I'll just wrap it up. Here, drink this tea while it's hot then have a lie down. Such witchment for me in that unwashed sheet. He'd laugh if I said but, still, there is. Get some sleep now but I grip until he must slip fingers free Close your eyes, I've got lines to go through.

Down down I down to the last flakes in. Dreaming for hours I think in my dream. Over over. Day white tongue teeth. Quickness and slowness. Stilts pander to streets and their up down their. I don't know what I've yet. Wander where no notion wanders in amongst the dust of. Devil may Slip. Then wake up.

Where? Here. Light on my leg. Four fingers. Lift. Another place. Five tips pressing. Flutter open my eyes. Him, smoking and carefully matching his fingers to the prints they left behind. Calculating their progress. Mapping their night. What time is it? Five-ish how are you feeling now? Ashamed. That'll pass   it always does. Always? Mostly, it's cumulative though so as long as that's a once-off in a few days you'll be normal. And now he, smallest fragment, smiles Come on lie down here. So lay my head on his legs. He picks the hair from my eyes and lets me curl in there, be fragile with him. Lets me cry and be a little girl again although that wipes nothing out.

Later. Hungry? Famished. What do you fancy? Chinese. Alright, up you get, I'll find you a T-shirt and we'll see what we can see.

It is the evening and the last of bright. Streets still Saturday

109

tawdry but up for the night. And lurch along we, like after the twelfth. Step syncing though. Side by side.

I watch him in the glass as he watches the street, lolled on his shoulder. His hand on my knee and the quiet inside moves between as he picks at the last of my plate. How much of your term's left? About four weeks. Off to Ireland for Easter? Yeah, for the month. So when are you back? Beginning of May. It'll be summer by then, he says I think you'll love that. What? London in the summer, especially at night. The smell of the trees and the heat of the streets – it's always hot because the concrete holds it in. When I came down here first it was sum- mertime. When was that? Seventy-two   I'd just gone sixteen god   to think I was so young then. I can't imagine you as younger than me, I say. And yet   once upon a time. Was it amazing? It was   and a mess   and violent but incredible as well   the clothes women wore down here drove me mad. And the music. I didn't know what was going on but that was also it, like not being alright was alright   was fine   was how it should be. And I was so shy then, hanging around, smoking fags in the street. Wanting to be part of things but not know- ing what. Not knowing anyone or anything. But even when I was lonely or when it was going bad and I was scared, I was still always so glad to be here. Safe in London. Even if I was all fucked up in myself. How were you fucked up? Let me count the ways! Will I ever get a bigger answer? Not tonight but   maybe one day. I bet you were lovely, I say. I bet I wasn't, he laughs In those days a girl like you wouldn't have given me a second glance. But the streetlights glitter on then so he hauls himself up Come on, I'll get the bill, you get on your coat.

We spend the evening lying on his bed, watching his old Kayvision black and white. News, sport, some crappy film.

Later he packs an old duffel bag. Can I stay over? Yeah alright, but I have an early start. Is that the truth? It's a half-seven train. How long are you away this time? Two weeks. Same film? Luckily, not. Was it really that bad? It really was. And this? Week in Prague, a week up North. Will you go see your family? No. No time? No, I don't, anyway, how are you? A lot better now, thanks. Good, shove up, I'll turn out the light and let's get some kip. So we do, as if everything's simple for us and, in the dark, it is.

And where the eye goes, an ocean. No. Overcast sea. In with the hiss of it. In with eyes wetting breeze like sea does, hair goes, strands across tongue. Far off, in pewterish clouds and rain. The rolling unseen where whales might be and under-neath does not even bear thinking of. Does not bear there but bears me up. On a skillet pallet small boat. Where I am stood strid and balanced, but for the swell. Over small roilers. Over the place like unreasonable same. Hidden from a shore. Tir na. From nowhere then comes iron and stain. Up close a harbour wall. And a man, just as the rain. Just as it comes he. Knowing who I am and waiting for me to know him, know that he is an again. His eye makes my eye and I kno ww ho you are. How many ways to, and know you, and can know you still. Do you know how much I suffered when you went away? Or how now my heart grows large with pain? That longing for you running over everything else. Was all I ever knew a trick and you were always coming back? I touch the stone. I find the step. I climb to the highest. Why are you further off? Turn around. Let me see you. Turn around. Wait. If you leave again now my heart will break. And he does. And it does and Wake up! Wake up! Wake up love, it's only a dream.

Back in the. Back in It's alright, he says Don't cry, I have you.

111

My father was like I've never seen like he's always been somewhere. That's a rough kind of dream, he says, smoothing my
hair You must miss him. But that miss is already making chain
with the weight of my heart, then the body it hates. Blind in
revulsion at what it did. On a floor. In a half thought. It should
spit itself out not to mingle with memory or become what I
might. I hate it, I fucking hate it. What? All of myself. Take
it easy, he says. All my fucking skin. I'd rip it off if I could. I'd
start again. I wouldn't be this. Stop! him wrestling my hands.
Stop it, you'll hurt yourself. I want to. Lie down! Lie down, and
him pinning me best as feral permits. But what worthless limbs
can't, my mouth invites Hit me, I want you to hit me or fuck me
til I bleed. You can do anything you want to me, until he's shaking me Stop saying those things, like I'm only half wild when I
really, all am. Would he hate me? Would he hate me? Would I
make him sick? Your father? My father. No, he'd never feel that.
How do you know? Because because   You don't know. I do.
How? Because I have loved a child and   I'd never feel like that
about her. Then I try to kiss him but he won't. Do I make you
sick now? No, you couldn't, what do I care about those things?
Then he does kiss me and sear go the weeks. Keep kissing me,
I say I missed you too much. So he does and we kiss to   No,
he says Not tonight. Why not? Don't you want to? I do but not
like this. I sit up Well fuck you. No, don't be offended, and he
kisses my back I really want to but   not when you're this upset. Humiliated I look at the litter of his room. Buckle of boxes.
Piles of books. Scripts on his desk. Tore. Overfilled bin. All still
here and now I am, again. Lie down with me, he says. Instead
I turn to look. Study each other but his mouth gives first. So I
lie down and we kiss like innocents with disco nerves. Enough
and not too much and let fingers fold. Just to be with him. This

112

isn't the last time though, is it? Don't know, he says What do you think? I don't want it to be, I say What do you want? Well I don't have much right to want anything but   you've been pretty hard to do without.

Morning lovely daylight early I get out of bed. Tie up all my hair. Put his dressing gown on. Kettle too. He sleeps deep on his front. I light a cigarette then watch the sunlight inch up to his face. Young-looking despite the lines that show deeper when he laughs around his eyes. In a little they open. He rolls onto his side What time is it? Half six. Come here. I sit by and he takes my hand Some woman's yellow hair has maddened every mother's son, he smiles. Impressive, I say, softly itching his chin. Then you better go put your clothes on before I make both of us late.

Partly patched so I go back to the world. Blue of the day and Monday round making my way along the Prince of Wales Road eating a Belgian bun.

Where the fuck have you been? Flatmate shouts from the steps I thought you'd been murdered, I nearly called the cops. Out, I say. Doing what? I haven't seen you since Saturday night! Just stuff. What fucking stuff? he says Oh wait, I can see.

In the changing room I catch sight of myself. Mischief bruised. Slightly proud. It's a long enough way to here from Ireland. But there is one more bad thing.

Ho ho harlot! What have you been at? Couldn't take my eyes off it all Character Analysis class. Did someone try to suck your blood? It was a mad weekend. Well bring your tea out onto the step and tell me EVERYTHING! Who? Where? All the pork. Mmmm I Mmmm I. Mmmm.

It was terrible. I feel terrible. She was so upset. So what did you tell her for, you fucking idiot? I had to, besides, she guessed. I'm a terrible liar and now she's going to hate me forever. Yeah well, join the club.

Dubious this, and awkward – from here now unto then on. Such sufferous vistas of eye-rolled ignoring I had not thought possible. Allegiance-mad others crowd in too with You know the rules – though I perhaps didn't. Take it all, as my due. But it's a mercy to get cast in the Third Year play. Maid. And why not? The Director says The Irish sort. Raw-boned you know, I want you to play that. Raw-boned. Okay. Still, to be sitting in with them from six o'clock to nine every evening helps cut to the last of the term. Finding a little more out all the time. Making something of nothing's easier said than done but – oh – once it gets done is when the fun begins. Solving the search for that idle moment when the own eye loses touch. When slipping the focus allows it to reach elbow-deep into other, and else. Additional. Extra. Hinted at. Imagined. Imbibed. Made possible because of. Bent to the will by. Smothered at the breast. Left for the wolves. No. Thrown to is best. For it's finding to there that finds to where pure is indivisible from its reverse.

Hold on and suck in! the Wardrobe Mistress instructs, rib cracking corset as I suffer gulp. Now hike them up and, as if by magic, Jacobean boobs. So starts Tech Week. First I've had. Costume fittings. Running lines. Keyed-up Third Years. Lighting and sound designers keeping us on set til late. Home from rehearsal and the Missus's pizza box No help yourself, they give me so much. Flatmate Here, have a look at my contact sheets. This one's for Spotlight but maybe that with CVs? What do you think? I don't know, they all look nice to me. Yeah but which says Just some nice guy. Not too good-looking or serial killer mad. Ordinary bloke. Some guy you would. Jesus maybe this? And as for the phone. Drilled to the drill. If an agent calls TAKE ALL HIS DETAILS and you, don't be a twat – to the Missus's boyfriend whose skittering English often makes him hang up.

And one Sunday morning phone Morning. Are you back? Just. How was it? It was alright, very early to very late. No buxom extras to cheer you up? No, they were all a bit grumpy for that, anyway, you around tonight? Later on. Later when? We're supposed to be teching at least until ten. After then, want to come back to mine? Or you could come here? Aaaaaaalright, what's your new address?

Only onto the couch when knocks a knock. Flatmate goes out. I should have but, devil loves bait and can't resist the straitened Oh   alright mate? Alright   she in? Yeah   follow me. Eyes from the flatmate like Fucking Jesus! Placated though by the bag of beers and For the fridge, help yourself. Flatmate takes to the kitchen as I swing round his neck. Kiss, then a quiet Didn't expect to see your mate. Why not? Just thought it would be us, why don't we head to your room? No I haven't eaten yet, sit down, slice of pizza? Okay, thanks, stretching long legs out. Can? Flatmate calls through. Please, but accepts it cautious-like and eyes him sitting down by my left side. So   how goes the tech? Fine. You in this too? I'm playing Vindice. Great. How was Prague? So and tides until our small chat sticks and Flatmate mines his stack of tapes. How about The Italian Job? Why not. On. Mystified me but both of them, right off, doing their Michael Caines like easiest segue for English males. Reminding each other of The Swarm or Ever seen his Acting on Film? Making this weirdest couch weirdly alright before Flatmate reaches for his. Do not, I kick. What? Just making a spliff. No, put it away. What the fuck? She's looking out for me I think, he says But it's okay, there's no need. Come again? I think she's concerned, he says Because I have a history of problems with various substances, am I right? I nod and my hand gets squeezed. Like how? Flatmate asks. Like a junkie, he says. Like shooting up and shit? Yeah, at the end   mostly other stuff but, really, weed was never a problem so feel free to roll away. And so Flatmate does brazen asking How long are you clean? Sixteen years. Fair play mate. Thanks, he thanks him, though wrestling a smile off his face. What did it? He yawns up at the artex Let's just say life's rich buffet signalled it was time for a change. Anyway, look at this, she's wrecked, come on you, let's go to bed.

In the dark he says Leave off the light, so instead we shine in the moon and car light. He sits on the mattress while I undress. You need some curtains. I do. You alright with all that chat? Were you really a junkie? I really was, does it bother you? No but   I just can't imagine it. Well   that's good   I suppose. It was another kind of life and one I don't plan on returning to so   have you slept with him? Yes. And are you still? I'm not. You can, you know, as far as I'm concerned. I know but it's not like that. Okay, he says. Kicking off my knickers so, I sink onto his lap. He kisses me then and I kiss him back. Too long, he says pulling up the duvet to hide us. Far too long, I agree.

And night. And us, sleeping nose to nose warm. Waking each other up for more. Until we're alone in the world. Half four. Naked in the kitchen, drinking glasses of water, looking down on the High road below. I'm knackered now. And me, I say. Him tipping drips on my elbow. Me kneeing his knee. Black cab go. To the drips on my breast. Night bus. Touching the drips on his chest. Two cars. Three. Kissing my neck. Come on, and I lead him back to my bed. For what is the night for? Lovers, that's what and how I will think of him now.

Jam. Yeah? I think. Raspberry or strawberry? Check the fridge, second shelf is mine. Missus's head round my door Who is the man? HIM. Oh, I see, I'll go talk. Then hear her in the kitchen finding him a knife. Don't forget tea, I shout as excuse to come down. She pointing and mouthing Very handsome, while he pretends not to see. Only stopping his spreading to kiss my cheek. Telling her about Prague and asking things. Her boyfriend stumbling out to demand Czech-sounding Coffee and be, friendly enough, introduced. Translations too then. Turn the radio on. Fuck off Take That. Flatmate roaring KEEP IT DOWN, some of us have an all-day tech. Him laughing through his cigarette Better let Vindice get his beauty sleep. Jammy thumb lick turned to jammy quick kiss until chat, slice, pour gets the better of quiet and rowdier feels just fine. We in my kitchen. Eat toast in my kitchen, for anyone to see.

And hard to kiss goodbye at the corner of Prince of Wales Road with the flatmate's Come the fuck on, we're already late for the call! Him calling after Have a good run! And See you Saturday night!

Mad so, the plummet and hell breaks loose. Opening Night. Tech unfinished. Lighting board crashed. Director panicked. Designer in a huff. Wardrobe Mistress's weary It's always like this, and abdicating pell for its mell. In the dressing room Flatmate drops a card in my lap From the pigeon hole. Rip it open – though scarce half made-up. Postcard of the sea and on its back Hope it all goes well tonight, break a leg!

Starched and parched I jit in the wings. Flatmate, most dashing, has remembered his lines and all those hours spent chanting seem to have paid off. Don't drop the tray. Mouth my own and Please God don't let me drop the tray. Cue. DSM Go. Go into the light. *Yes sir and no sirs present and correct. Recalling raw-boned, recreating the life of the country girl who's fled. Here in the city with the Dukes and Dames. I am impressed and think of what I will say in the letter I'll write by candlelight tonight while the bootblack stomps the corridor beneath. Three sisters at home I will tell about silk. The fine perfumes of the fine and handsome gents. How there's one has stole my heart but I'll not give him more, yet. Yes, there he is across the room, deep in conversation but as I pour tea imagine he might look at me so tuck a stray lock back in my cap. I'm not a vain maid and raw-boned means a little obvious too   perhaps. True-hearted though. So hide my hands behind my back because they're probably red from skivvying because the skivvy's off and I'm last in so it's my job but I wouldn't want him to see. Too soon though and long before getting his gaze I'm signalled out. Yes madam bob my knees. One last bit of longing as I exit stage left but, poor maid, her heart stays broke.* Over the cables and out behind flats. Three sets of pressed bosoms pushing past How's the house? Good I think, more than three quarters full. Great!

And for all my five lines, goes a good run for me. A little stare at the brink of how life might be. Loneliness loves camaraderie, the fun, fuss, even the fright. Then our relief-giddy traipse out to bow and get clap-salved end of every night. Learn the ritual of cards – mine tight wedged in the mirror by the flatmate's greasepainted Break a leg Slutty Maid! X. Flowers for some or My Mum's in tonight, let's make it a good one! Or the fortunates – quiet – whispering how they've had a call from some agent but keeping it low so the miscast won't feel bad. Under house lights after, notes on the stage from the Director, Voice teacher, Movement analyst. And in the day, the Principal letting it be known who'll pay for bad work with bad casting next term.

In my free second half I'm usually up smoking in Wardrobe with its Mistress's cough and great gossip from her stack of life in the theatre, this way or that. Tales of the school from when it first begun and all the young Turks out for revolution. Dreadful tales of famous who she knew back when that I love to hear and again. When I tell her about him, she knows who he is. Fantastic Oswald in Ghosts must be ten years ago now and that 'Tis Pity, my God he was good. So how old must he be? And how old are you? Tut tut, though I can't say blame you and that voice of his ffffff like a cave.

Terrible nerves but, Saturday night, knowing he'll be in. If he thinks I'm useless. You've got five lines, besides – her strapping me down – Your cups over-runneth so I doubt he'll see much beyond! Oh no, don't say that! Why? she laughs Or have men suddenly stopped being men?

Crane in the wings but can't see a thing. Even sneak looks at the audience during. Only at the end though, spot him there at the back, giving us all the good clap so I drop my best bow his way.

Third Years hug in the dressing room, whooping relief and cracking open champagne some rich one's aunt sent. Unloosing me from my dress, the Wardrobe Mistress says I was in the foyer before when your man walked past. How'd you like the maid? I said. He said Why do you ask? I said She was nervous. Ah, she was great, he laughed Lovely presence, don't you think? She has, I said, giving him a wink. You didn't? Oh God, but I'm shame-delight red. Well done all, yells the Director across the mayhem Now let's go get very drunk.

Unringing ringlets, I weave the canteen. Not in the foyer. Sideways out through the throng and there he is, by the fence beyond, smoking a cigarette. Hey curly! But in my hop down get a fly in the eye Ow! Rub it to watering. Let me see it, he licking a finger, preparing to poke. Careful careful. Look right up   there I've got it   now   try not to rub   there – tiny dead midge that he flicks. You were great by the way, but Hello stranger, and he. Straightens abruptly. Turns around. Standing behind, a woman in white. Older, beautiful, elegant and Oh God, I tongue-tie at her fame. Hello, he says offering a hand but she rolls her eyes so he must kiss her instead. I haven't seen you since the funeral, she says Let me look at you. And she looks at him like she's looking, then touches his face. You look tired. I'm fine, he says Been away on location, you know how it gets   so   what are you doing here? Oh they want me on the Board   you know, ever since   it's like I'm made of gold and everybody wants a piece. You'll manage all the adulation, he says. Yes, I expect I will. Both go Anyway, then laugh and she But what brings you up to these wilds? When steps he to show me No! she says No! It's not! No! My God! I can't believe it! and I am caught in her arms. No wait! he cuts sharp across but I'm rich perfume up close now, delicate crow's feet and kissed, thrill-bewildered. Oh my darling, she's saying You're all grown up, your father must be so   Don't, he says Stop, this isn't her. Oh? she says, setting me down I'm sorry, my mistake, and there I was about to launch down memory lane about you bringing her to the dressing room but of course that was only   well   how many years since that Seagull now? Fifteen, he says. Fifteen. And his quiet face. As many as that? Yes I suppose you're right – and releases me completely – But you were in the play, that's why you seem familiar, what a charming performance you gave, how do you know each other? I look over to but he's looking away. W we're friends, I say. Yes I'm sure you are well I think I've embarrassed myself enough for one night. Lovely to meet you – like kiss of the signet – and you my love should get some rest and, as usual, take better care of yourself, speaking of which – manicure drumming his chest – how's all of that? Fine, thanks. Truly? Yes. I know you hate a fuss so I won't press but really, my darling, I have to tell you, this protracted bachelorhood is making you odd. Yes, he says That's something you've mentioned before. I mean, how old is this jacket? she mock-exasperates his cuffs Time for another trip to Harvey Nick's, no now don't pull that face, was that or was that not a beautiful suit? Beautiful, he mollifies but fond sounding too of whatever this memory is. Well then give me another kiss and let's not keep leaving it to chance to meet. So he kisses her again Give everyone my best. I'll be sure to and, I mean it, take care of yourself – turns she then, then turns again – And little girl? Good luck!

Spell and probably waft of Chanel, people part for her path. Out to the car waiting. Knees in then heels up. Slam and immaculate exit. Ignore her, he says dropping his cigarette as, laid bare, I uncoil at curls and rankle. Did you bring your case? Yeah, I'll get it from inside. But my legs make pools all the way back in, perhaps from the wade and wade.

He shoulders it Coming? We make onto the street. A chiller night than planned to be. Preoccupied silences pushing between, part buffeted by others racing down to the Crown. Coming for a drink? No do. No come. No. Okay, see you next term. Until we're at Malden Road. You hungry? crossing to Barnacle Bill's. Starving. Come on then, and he steps in Two large, open please, anything else? No, that's fine.

Chip smells close the distance as we trek on down. You were great tonight. Really? I had five lines. Not many lines but so much soul and that dress had a vivid inner life of its own! Oh that doesn't sound pervy at all   what about him? Vindice? Not bad actually. He had a lot to carry and I thought he managed it pretty well. The trick with   How old is your little girl? Fuck, he says This bag of yours weighs a ton, how about stopping here til we're fed? Alright, and sit on a bench in the damp. Ta-lacre gardens opening empty behind but, across, the Grafton Arms making plenty of life. He eats his chips though like dis-placing quiet. Head down. One by one. So I eat and bide but he eats on. I know you don't like talking about her but   Nothing. Chews til his mouth is clear and only at wiping his hand on the paper says I was twenty-two when she came so   she's sixteen, seventeen in June. And it falls through the air like the starting of rain. Put my hand out into, trying to grasp what it means but can't. Or don't, so say You must find it strange   I do find it strange, he says. Is it strange though? Yes it is   why do you think I didn't call you all those weeks before Christmas? I didn't know. No   how could you   I suppose. Why didn't you tell me before? I don't know   it was never the right time   the day you asked about her picture it wasn't like I thought I'd see you again   after that we were always   well   There were plenty of times you could've   Maybe but   this wasn't sup-posed to be   More the sex? You know what I mean. And now it is? He nods So here comes the fucking mess. Why's that? You're practically the same age as my daughter   what do you think that makes me? I don't know. Well I do, he says. Really? I make you that ashamed? Yes   no   not you   myself   I mean   what the fuck am I playing at? I mean   if you were thirty-eight, even twenty-eight, twenty-five   What? I don't

122

know. Well I don't know either. And the truth is all I can see is this is harder for him than it is for me. Would be again for her, though isn't, I'm sure. Does she know about me? Does she fuck! I would never discuss sex with her. I don't mean sex I just   No, she's my daughter and I   can't even see her that way. What way? Being older   being nearly seventeen and   I know she is but   I haven't seen her since she was eight and I haven't really been her father since she was younger than that and, despite the hours of staring at photographs, I can't seem to make my head make up the time. Which makes So how much do you love her? go all around mine. To not ask I light a cigarette. Smoke and pass. He smokes it and. I. He. I. Then back. Lay my head on his shoulder. He allows that and both breathe out the breeze. I can't stop thinking about Sunday night. Me too, he says. Do you wish we hadn't? No, I don't. Do you want me to go back to my own tonight? No but   I can't think this is normal, can I? Why not? Can't you think what you want? That's not how it works, there's right and wrong. And I'm wrong? You're not. But being with me is? Yes. Fuck you. I get up. No! Wait! he catches my wrist It's not as simple as that and   there's just   there's a lot that you don't know. I want you anyway, I say Do you still want me? I do. Well that seems pretty simple so   let's just go back to yours. Jesus, he – eyes supplicating the sky, cross to the Grafton, down to mine – and breathes out Alright   let's go.

    Maybe against his will I hold his hand. He lets me though, now and then swaps the bag but also indulges my Tell me one thing, what's the story with her? Nothing   she's always like that. We did The Seagull together. It was my first proper job. She played Arkadina. I was Konstantin. One thing led to an-other. There was some carry-on. Not more serious? No, not for me, but enough for her to wreck something I should have been more careful of anyway any chance that'll do? For tonight, I grant and at last he laughs. Then we're fine walking through the scurf streets side by side. My back moulding to the bridge under Kentish Town West where I persuade him to lean and chippy-kiss. Later I'll ask more. Further from this. After. Once we've made our way home.

Up out of the world back into his realm. All tidied and hoovered. Expecting someone? Maybe, he smiles but subdued for him. Get that bottle from the fridge. I do. Is this champagne? For you, for the last night of your play. Thank and kiss him and sit on his desk. Open his shirt while he opens the cork. Turn from the pop, then swallow the fizz. Drip bottle mouth to mouth. Kiss. And make what I want, my own normal with him. Belt first. Next his fly. Both now falling back into time where all the past waits outside. It doesn't matter to me, I say. Then it doesn't matter tonight, he says Now take off your clothes and show me yourself, I want to remember every freckle when you're gone. And I. And bra. Kneels down to my breasts. I. Watch his mouth there. Teeth making twitch running right up to my scalp. How he knows me – and all of me – so much. Kiss. Touch. Already damp his. Slip down where he knelt to. Lick. To put. Oh Fuck, he says, gone so hard in there and now neither us care for she's away to the back of him. Let her. Let her. His hand in my hair God I love how you do that but lie back on the floor. So do and wait for you on me. In me. This is my father. What? Mine. Just beyond. Little girl in a photo who looks like him. He made me doing this, what he'll do with you. He made you with it but did he mean to? And after, did they know they had? In that other life? On that far-off bed? This is my father. So? What of it? He's taken care of me. And me, from the first.

But he is my father. And your father taught me this, showed me how until I love to and know him like you never can. This is my father. Taking my knickers down. Putting his fingers. Putting his mouth. This is my father. The want he makes and I have no father. Who cares? Who cares? You can never do what he and I can. So sayeth the latest in the longest line. How many have gone before? I am the kingdom. I shine above because he is my father. Do I ever shine? Let me just get a, he says   You don't have to. Why? I'm on the pill. But Sunday. Wasn't safe, now it is. Are you sure? Yes. And. All him in me. The work of it. God that's lovely, you're so wet. He is my father. I prefer him this to that. My father. I choose your father over the dead. Choose to kiss and touch and fuck so it hurts. And good to be hurt by him in ways you never will. Good to be hurt by him in ways no one else has. Kissing each other so deep in our mouths like forgetting now who is in who. He is my father. Not now. Always is. Not where I allow every journey he wants to make across my body. It is for him so get back from it to where you belong in the usual world, in the distantest time as slow he, slow. Kisses back down to wait. His beautiful eyes on me and his beautiful body pacing inside, asking Are you with me? I am. Kissing and. Then we hardly can for There it. I. He I am. All my body, lighting, all over his. I could say anything, anything. Just feeling and heat as and. Wet from inside him so far up inside me. Stings from the rough of. One atom in tiny wishing that the pill was a lie. Wishing for risk or being that moment in his past. Being closest to. Making life with No   do not even   anything and
     wild sky and

                 he is   really don't really   I
  really me

              him and

          my whole body breathes
Fuck, he by my ear Fuck   you beautiful girl   I thought that
was never going stop   godthatwas wh wwww I can hardly speak. So kiss me and kisses me. Be off all that stuff. Just
take the pleasure of being young under his hands. Safe in his
knowledge. Full of his heat. Forgetting time passing and the
sleep that we'll need. Separation ahead. Touch. Breathe how
he breathes and try keeping him, try keeping him inside. Still
though he slips from but whispering Stay. I can't. I know, and
he rolls away That's just the sex talking now. But pretty good
sex. Yeah, not bad. Curl I into then kiss at his hair Oh, getting
a bit grey in there. Tell me about it, he says Any more fucking
like that and I'll be white by dawn.

    Sit side by side, smiling down, almost shy. He kisses my
shoulder every once in a while. Drinking more, now warm,
champagne. Who needs glasses? and laugh as our legs shake
from the effort of what they've been through. Elbows slit carpet burns and where they'll bruise. He'll have bite marks tomorrow for I was bad. Such straight teeth! he observes and
examines. But stay close these last hours. Fall asleep. Wake.
Repeat. Sleep. Do again. All the night wrapped in his quilt on
his floor. Eventually him saying No white yet but it's dawn
and we should try to sleep. Don't. And instead sit the far side
of his desk. Pull open his curtains to watch the sun together
rise slowly through the Camden sky. Help itself to chimneys.
Across bins and bikes. Between footpaths and hedges. Up our
naked legs' swing. His reach to the window ledge. Mine not as
long. Take the light on our bodies and not caring who might
see from the street. Besides, they'd be lucky to witness. Finish
off the bottle. Smoke cigarettes and. White will be the day.
Later on, maybe blue. What you'll do once I'm gone? Sleep and

not think about you, what'll you do in Ireland? Walk. Where? By the lake. Nice lake? Has its moments. Just a month, isn't it? Yes. But we kiss long to stave it off and shiver in our tiredness until he says Come on. It's time to get dressed. I'll take you to the train.

Through quiet Liverpool Street he carries my bag. Quiet concourse. Stansted Express. Quietest platform. Loneliest journey I know. I'll miss you, I say Will you write? If you want. Or you want. Then I'll want, if you will. All I want though is to tell him how much I   No, go, or you'll miss your train. Just one quiet kiss more so before taking my bag and going. And. What if he just disappears? Has already gone as utterly utterly as before he came? Snatched look back. No. There he is. Tall in his long coat and glasses. Waving to my wave. Watching me to my carriage. Wave again. Get on and all doors slam. Then the train pulls away.

Easter Holidays 1995

Ireland is what it is. Sealed in itself, like me. I miss London, with my fondness for ignoring in the street opposing endless Howaya's from impenetrable people to whom I am blood belonged. But I can do that talk. To mind myself, do, for the more vocabulary managed the farther between you. And into that revel space instead open ways of considering aspects of him. The delve deep burn of body. Done, told, and the gap between.

And I write notes about walks. Books. Trips to the flicks then try not to pang for the longed reciprocate. He said he would but he might not, which would be no surprise. Such a plain brown envelope enveloping it when he does, neat in his lovely long-hand. Sketch of fraught meetings about his script, a Duchess of Malfi he thought was alright and a chance bump into the Missus on the street – her Easter lunch shopping and pity invite. Nice of her but he probably won't, though perhaps, if I don't object? I don't. So by the next he has. Says my flatmate – and several Czechs – send their regards. He supposes he finds him decent enough despite the way too many drugs – which he knows he is in no position to judge – and the Missus can cook pretty well. Later he tells me to prepare for the change in the trees. How, once it's warmer, we'll go lie up on the Heath, read books whose spines we won't spoil and drink cold beers. That in Regent's Park the first fat men without shirts have been seen so summer is surely on its way. And I study his chose punctuation for leaks of hide or tell. But do not find so do not ask. Especially about the little girl who is not. And this greater swathe that she cuts through his life, what is its   what can it mean?

As for his years? What hides in them? Her in almost all my eighteen, then the twenty before I was born?

And something else, though this I don't tell. It or its resultant fag out on my leg. Choose to recount how my mother instead – at the sight of such obviously male handwriting – said Missy I hope you're not up to anything over there that would make me feel ashamed! He replies Her concern's well and truly out of date but, if I'm inclining to make a clean breast, I should mention how those bite marks I gave him have only just healed up.

TERM THREE
Tuesday 2 May–Friday 21 July 1995

Come on to fuck. Will the bag never come? Skate a concourse and lugging for the five o'clock. If I miss it will he wait at Liverpool Street but it is it in old jeans T-shirt, rubbing beneath his glasses' frames? Trolley guiding to, then from again. Is. With his film cut now all grown in I Hey! Hey, the smile of his see and following down to the end of rail, me. You're here. Why are you here? I was early so I thought I might as well. And. These are for you, I don't what they're called but they smell pretty good so Kiss him. Kiss his lips. On the tip of my toes. But crowds insisting on their inroads push our mouths out of place. Go to again but Give me your bag, he says If we're quick we might still make the five. And knot his fingers back through mine, to pull me through with Jesus Christ, what's in your bag? The fucking Good News?

But blessed to a lone lift we indecently kiss. Backs pressing buttons. Mine first. Then his. If the door doesn't open Opens. He palms his mouth but crushed petals fall all down my front. Platform Two. Come on! Quick! Dash it. Make it. Just to the back. Sit. Go. Kiss and Tickets? I. Don't worry, I bought two. Clip. Fuck my shoulder! as the conductor aways. Show me? Pull his T-shirt. All bruise broken veins. Sorry, my bag did that. Don't worry, he nosing mouth to mine and. Kiss, ineloquently, to make up time and. His hand up my bare back and I climb across his lap and. Him over my shoulder, quick checking the carriage If we're quiet. Never mind quiet we're almost at Bishop's Stortford be quick! Yeah quick won't be problem I've not had sex in a month. Really? Really. Me either.

133

You could have though Why? Because you said? No I just that's not what I meant Don't spoil it Alright I just I meant Ssssh Okay, he says and Fuck that's good.

All mess walk back through Liverpool Street. He leads through the throng and the want is unspeakable but the tube rub of sweating from infinite people slowly nulls off his smell from my hair. Slung so close in the crush though I could bite his neck. I think to but don't do. I'm watching you, he says like he knows and he does know, well. And although he's too old for kissing on trains, he's considering it. I see that on him and exacerbate by letting each jolt jab me in. Just relief then in the breeze at Kentish Town.

Fuck I'm fit to keel over, he says up the steps. Rubs at his shoulder and hall dumps my stuff. But lopes to the sitting room like he belongs. Oh hello! from the Missus. Quick kissing sound. Find him hugged across her ironing You are so happy now. Ah well, he concedes dropping onto the couch. Lighting up while I go fill a vase. As soon though, I grab him Time to unpack! No rest for the wicked, he laughs following back to my room.

There, reach and kiss. Hang on, he says opening my window to chuck his cigarette. Right, let's have that again. Then kiss like the night is come. Bang but. Bang! Startle back to the world. Other side of the glass the flatmate lurks, faking camera snaps. One for the Sun, you nymphos, welcome back! Piss off! But he finds himself hilarious a while before going on inside. We really need to get you some curtains. In the meantime though he pulls over my duvet to spread just below. Then we lie on its dust and occasionally sneeze in the stripping and sex that ensues. For there's hours of catching up. Hours of making new. So quiet remembering but noisy too, for even old dears there out on the walkway must understand how long a month can be.

And after, watch the light go down across my wall. Hear the Missus's boyfriend come in. Stink of spliff and stewed spuds. When he goes for water hear the flatmate smirk Whatever can you two be up to in there??? Never you fucking mind, you nosey git. And sit we together. Pass a cigarette. You let your hair grow. He tugs at the back Didn't get round to it. I like it like that. Then I'll leave it, for now.

And the sleeping is great in my bed this night. Soft his eyelids. Holding hands, if we want. While I fall off. While I fall under. Into the
Glass she stirs in me.
Stirs into the water and what can she not see?
Fingertips too white to bleed.
Moving in last advance on breathing but moving all the same.
Where she hurts or galls. In the name of
What?
His whole length warm against me in the earliness that becomes Monday morning too soon.

Empty flat, only for us. Loll at the window studying buses, guessing what ages Blustons has seen. Hang those dresses for a hundred years. On the sofa, he flicks through the flatmate's Stage that's been circled, re-circled for telemarketing jobs but peace in the bright, bright sun. And this will be us for the next three months. Any minute I might go lay my head on his knee or ask if he fancies another tea. When I look round though he's looking at me Going to tell me what happened to your leg? Turn back to a woman pushing a pram. Shopping maybe? Or towel rolled up for the baths? I'm not blind   why've you been doing that? Watch her walk on past the Owl bookshop but he waits for my answer so   I saw him again. Who? The man who. Where? In the street. He walked up to me, could walk up to me.

Kissed my mother on the cheek and Long time no see, she said. Then he kissed me   and took my hand and   I let him because he looked so innocent like   he'd forgotten and   maybe he had I was five so long ago. He said My God, look at her, she's all grown up. A fine-looking girl, she does you credit. Never be as good-looking as her mother though, my mother laughed. Well now, he said I don't want to cause a fight. But all this time still holding my hand, talking about his girls – when we were small, we were friends. Pop in if you're ever passing, he said We'd all love to see ye again. Give them our best, my mother said and he said he would. He petted my face. Why did I let him? Like I couldn't not. As he walked away my mother said Why are you always so offish? Who do you think you are? Lady Muck?

Behind me, in London, I hear him stand but does not cross or touch and he's right. You never told her? No, what would I have said? When you gave me to him to take to the lambing shed, I did the first thing in my life I wished I could forget? He didn't forget about it though, want to, or try. For months and years after with no patience for panic. Come here I want to show you this. Put out your hand and see what God gives you. Lifted up from the bed beside his daughters at night, knelt on the blue black tiles, convinced, as his wife lay snoring through the wall, that he was only wearing human skin for show. That house in the wilds so far from the world and being at the mercy of someone with none. What am I now because of him? How do I know what it'll make me become? You don't, he says You never can but you're at no one's mercy any more. It's there though, isn't it? I can't see it but   can you? Should I make myself forgive him? I don't think I can. Listen to me, he says You had to survive what he did all by yourself. You don't have to forgive him as well. And that is enough. I don't need more to make back to

136

the silence that served me so well before. Re-refuse the past. I will not have it here. Mouth or bed or in the air. I'll show you what I see, he says Let's go out today.

Ice creams in Trafalgar Square? Not the significant part, he explains. So lick and laugh at tourist pestering pigeons. Then the National Gallery, up the steps. Going to show me a picture? Yes. What? Guess. Rembrandt? No. Hieronymus Bosch? No through here   there. In the dark. Virgin with Infant. John the Baptist beside. It's beautiful, I say. I knew you'd like it but   it's the Angel makes it, don't you think? The light of her. I look at him. And know this is the edge. The instant. The very last point before the fall. That it will come soon now I'm sure but when it does   what then?

Back to in and world of mine. Hello-ing. Scabbing a fag. Check-ing notices on the canteen wall. Shakespeare this term. Sun-bathed bench coffee. Her showing up with a spanking new man. We nod but at almost ten it's Acting class first thing.

Off into it so. Time rushing through days. Crucify lazy flesh. Defy lazy brain. And the much and much of delight, of make. Turning the body. Converting the self into flecks of form and re-form. Her. Into her. Into someone else. This one. Long for Juliet and get cast it. Jubilate back at his. Good for you, he says Gallop apace! Rehearse most nights and when it's not my scene, craftily smoke in the study room, doing the back forth of speed running lines. Or sacking the costume rails for her perfect nightgown. Find the what that makes me she. Help the not far imaginative leap to touching lovers, windows, dawn. In all, I think, I might make her fine, but for the nicotine stains on my hand. Now oftener too with him these nights. So much he buys bowls and Weetabix. True, when he doesn't call, me and the flatmate smoke spliffs. He's a certain of happiness though, far side of a month where my past had inveigled its foot. And succumb to the normal of finding him there, lounging in my kitchen, cooker sparking cigarette or telling me to Shove up the bed or mocking what the flatmate's dragged in. So it just sits, that maw I've seen. Close to my tongue but kept silently like those still waters of his past that, whenever I dare ask, he presents as glass. He sees more than me though, or better because, when it's at me, he does it rough and fucks the anger free. Complains only once after You split my lip. Takes my kissing it as kindness he doesn't expect. And the feeling for each other is a much-changed subject. An always Right I better head, if I keep staying over I'll never finish this script. But I know and know he must. It shows all over me and he tastes of it. He won't say it though, being hindrance mad. That, occasionally, drives me astray in the head but then. But then. Life makes itself with little heed for the appropriate, whatever he thinks that might be.

And we are the week. We are Thursday night. He's not here, so in – sloven stoned – with the flatmate. Smoking only I. Him, on all else, leaping about shouting Feats of strength! Trying out pull-ups on a curtain rail that gives and Shit! Snaps. Gangle and drops the spliff in my hair so I am Fuck fuck you set me on fire! Hopping. Him tackling me onto the floor to wallop with cushions until I scream Get off. Ingratitude! I saved your life. Plus my many split ends. Oh! I see! That's how it is! Pinning me under. Tickling my legs. Both so locked to within an inch of our lives that neither hear the door, or the suffering Missus get. Just shrieking, clawing with hair going feral then – against the doorframe – him. Evening all. Hey! I say endeavouring quick exit from under the flatmate. What's going on? Keeping her warm for you mate. Ignore him, I He's off his head. Yeah, he says through his cigarette, offering a hand I try to take but Flatmate impeding No way! No way! holding me down. Come on, get off her, he says, brooking no further games and, pulled up then, I wend into his arms. Nice to see you. Did you miss me? I ask. I did. How come you're here? Just passing, saw the light. And when he sits down, I sit beside. Kiss some. Smoke his cigarette. Get a room, the flatmate yucks. Jealousy, jealousy. Nudging my toe into his roots but he grabs it and bites. Ow! Drags me back onto the floor bellowing Feats of the Warrior! Stop it! Ow! Help me! I yelp. Get off her, he says Come on you, let's go to bed. I'm pretty fucking shattered. Old age, yawns the flatmate, settling his head on my knee. His eyes drifting down across the clump of Flatmate and me You must think I'm very evolved, get yourself off her. Flatmate laughs Fuck off, I was here first. He was, I join in laughing before seeing he does not. No you weren't, he says kicking at him a bit. He's an eejit, I say Leave him be. Leave him to what? Or do you want me to leave? Of course not. But the flatmate sprawls triumphantly I saved her life, she's mine. So are you trying to get her into bed? What? You're all over her, it's a reasonable question. No, I say You know he's not. I know he did, he says. Flatmate howling And she loved it! No I did not love it, shut up! But this opens something, a disarmed spot where his reticence might get caught and all the feeling for him in me can't resist Besides, aren't you always saying I should sleep with who I want? Not now, he says Let's go to bed. Here though my spliff-loosed stitch knits sense. Admit you don't want me to see anyone else. But he refuses the bait Why would I? You're free to do whatever you want. Oh mate, Flatmate chokes That *is* evolved. And I get such a land from being hand-washed of that Then you won't mind me

139

doing this – near dislocating a shoulder to kiss the flatmate's lips. What do you want, a round of applause? he asks. I'm clapping, claps the flatmate. Mind your own fucking business, he says. The weed though making me cat and mouse so kiss the flatmate again. Alright, he stands up I've had enough. Fuck him, don't fuck him, do whatever you want. Maybe I will, I say What do you care? Relents he, a little Just come to bed before you do something we'll both regret. Only if I can bring him, I insist. Ho ho, roars the flatmate. Are you being serious? Yes. Don't seem to remember you liking threesomes that much, he says. But stubborn shrugs I liked it well enough. So you up for that? he asks the flatmate. Yeah, it's all good – and, apparently bombed clear of hero-worship, adds – Thought you'd be more up for it mate! You must get asked to join in all the time. Fine! he says, catching my wrist If that's what you both fancy, then what's it to me? Easy mate, Flatmate wavers I don't think No, you picked the wrong fucking man to play chicken with so it's too late for 'Easy mate' now. And I'm dragged into the corridor. Shoved the length of it up. Him, all the while, calling Come on, you too 'mate'. Then Come the fuck on I said.

Go on, get in. Bangs the bedroom door. Flings me around and I. I am stagger, confused. Struck with outrage and filled with but. He is so angry. Worse than I've ever seen. Unbuttoning my top, losing patience then. Tears it. Throws it at the floor. Whoa mate, goes the flatmate. Don't worry, I've done this plenty before, bit of drama just adds to the fun so – unless you're here to talk about your fucking feelings – it's getting time for pants down mate. Unthumbing his own. Everything. What have I? Going wrong. Too late to dig heels against the moment's momentum with Flatmate, all sheen-eyed unzipping his fly. Him, half-naked now, catching my eye Still sure about this? And prodded perverse I insist I am! Okay, skirt off next and – don't fret – I'll help you work all the geometry out. Then pacing off to arbitrate What, not hard yet mate? Must be the drugs. Need a hand? Flatmate scares back Keep your hands to yourself! Well now, that's a bit off. I don't care, I'm not fucking gay. So it's only her who gets fucked? That hardly seems fair but, I'm – obviously – a very understanding guy so if it's that you're feeling shy, you can kiss her first. When Flatmate still prevaricates he gets a shove Go on, get on with it. Yeah, I am, fuck off – taking up my face and kissing my mouth. Great start! he congratulates, slapping the wall Now let's find out what she really wants. Me? Yes, just say the word and   Kiss him, I say like the devil would. He laughs but Flatmate goes No way! No way! I'm not fucking gay! Yeah yeah so you keep saying but – given what she's about to share – it would be pretty fucking rude to refuse. No! Yes and, come on, be up for it. Then puts his mouth onto the flatmate's, who squirms and wriggles until he admonishes Stop it, give her what she wants. And something in that makes the flatmate succumb, a while. While, like watching TV, I watch. Strange to my skin, him kissing someone else. Stranger to be on the outside, recreating its taste and. If it's all just bodies I still only want his, so go wrap my arms round his waist. Lay my head against his back and, wait. Then, like long ago, feel him take my hand. Alright, he says You win. Get off, says the flatmate, from the wall where he's pinned. He steps back But you're pretty hard mate, best go ask yourself what that means. Go fuck yourself, poof! He just points to the door Out. With pleasure, Flatmate says – almost crying now – You two are fucking fucked.

And listen to him cursing us right down the hall. Then he lets go my hand, starts putting his pants on. What are you doing? Heading home. Don't, I say kissing him. Pulling him onto, down on the bed. Stay with me, stay with me. I'm sick of this, he says Do you know how I was before we met? How were you? I was fucking fine. Then go home without me and be fine again. But we kiss instead and he puts himself in and the world closes round us. And I look at him. Let him. Hide in him when it comes, like he'll help me through it. And he does. And I mind him. I hold him while he lets himself, tracing rivers in the sweat on his back. And, when he lies down on me after, say in his ear Stay   every night   if you want with me. I don't want to fuck this about any more, he says But there are things I should probably tell   KNOCK What? Flatmate opens the door a crack I think I'm having some kind of attack. He sits up and I expect Fuck off, but Yeah, he says You don't look so great. Thanks to you, Flatmate complains, fragile, freaked and, before I prevent it, sits down next to me. I think something I took went bad. He reaches for his wrist. Get off! Hey, relax, I'm just taking your pulse, your virtue's safe with me. Any pain in your chest? No. Arm? No. Stomach? Bit. What have you taken? Litany. Well, go drink something sweet then get into your bed. No don't make me, Flatmate begs There's something weird in my room. And even he laughs. Alright, lie down there. Only a while, I add, filled with what might he say? Thanks thanks, Flatmate stretching the very edge while he turns to the wall, reprieved of himself and I lie in, against his back, knowing that's it for the lee of the night. Still, I stay awake nearly half of it in this weird bed of unsettled men.

Banging banging. Wake up! What? Men at the door! Missus at mine Wake up! Wake up! Coming to, he sits up. You all? she says. Long story, he yawns And only slightly what you think.

Another batter scaring Flatmate around What the fuck? Will I answer? she worries. What's going on? I ask into his hip. He nods to my window. Light. Men gawking in. Oh! I cover. But, already there, he passes my knickers asking Missus who they are? Don't know, she But so so loud. Well, Flatmate says Let's find out, unkinking into the corridor. No don't! he calls after Wait! Too late. Opens the door then rotate some exchanges the rest of us can't quite hear. Voices raise. When Fucking cunt! rings out, he hops from the bed and pulls his jeans on. Buttoning, steps out into the fray. More talking and. What's going on? Served, he says You're being evicted I think. Flatmate arguing We paid our rent! It's not that, it's the mortgage, didn't you get the letters? Our landlord doesn't live here. Then you've been had mate. Hall wall punched and Turkish cunt! Calm down, the voice soothes. Fuck you! Flatmate shouts. No need for that mate, we're just doing our job. Well we're not leaving, so take your job and fuck off. Sorry mate but that's going to be you if I have to drag you out myself. Fucking bring it. Hey, take it easy, he says Why don't you go tell the girls to get dressed? Flatmate effing blinding, bundled back to my room. Don't fucking need it, the voice grumbles If we get any shit. You won't, you won't, you just gave him a fright. What? Worse than waking up next to a naked bloke? causing hilarity in the crowd beyond my window and a forest of Phwoars and thumbs up. He takes it – easy-goingly – I'm sure that didn't help but seriously, you can see we're not at fault, can you give us a couple of days? No can do, sorry mate, my hands are tied. A few hours then? No mate I would but I can't – sounding apologetic enough though for him to try We've got a couple of girls in here – you know what they're like – give me an hour to get them organised and I'll make sure everyone leaves without a fight. Somehow won,

the voice says Alright but after that   We'll be gone, I appreci-
ate it, mate. As they troop down the walkway someone shouts
in Nice tits! He looks round my door Sorry, can't do much once
they're already here, so get your stuff together. You can always
come back later, change the locks and you've probably got a few
weeks before the electricity goes off. Squat, Flatmate nods Nice
one mate, and wanders off to his room, tailed by the Missus
asking What squat is? Never a dull fucking moment with you,
he laughs Come on, you can stay at mine.

On the hour, walk out into the early sun. Kiss the Missus goodbye See you soon, and her boyfriend. Flatmate bag hefting with
him and me. After he's turned Prince of Wales Road we continue
silently into the morning tide. Taking breaks to rest our hands.
Snatch looks at each other. Smile. Look down. Last night working cringes of so many kinds and yet, still, we are here.

Dark his room, after the light. Bed rumpled and desk spread,
all ready for work. I sip a glass of water with dust. Thanks for
letting me stay. It's alright, he says Nice having you here   so
listen   I was thinking   it's my birthday tomorrow and   Is
it? You never said. Well   remember my set-designer friend?
He'd like us to come over   and   what do you think? Okay, I
say despite the fright. Alright, I'll tell him and   tonight   let's
well   sorry I'm making you late. Yeah, I better head and. Yeah,
see you later on.

Shame succeeds, on the school steps, in shredding through my
skin. Alert and naked conscience blinking red in its machine.
But back on course too, somehow, as if I'd had a plan. Stitches
seeming my terrain – the making and dropping them. Lucky
last night he caught those few. How or why, I can't tell. Meaning though he must want to. I go alive with thoughts of it. And

long for this day to be over, to get running back across streets. Yet when I do – in the crook of night – linger by the bin staring up at his light, shying from the meanings of Should probably tell, until the waiting makes the wanting more. Then ring the bell, catch the keys dropped and go on up his stairs.

Ah ha! Over the threshold. Into his room. Look, I've tidied, even cooked! Jesus, I say Even hoovered! What's the occasion? Early birthday, he says setting me aside to pootle with pans, cigarette kept and skilfully managed in the corner of his mouth. Then chicken flipped. Hiss and spit. Are you annoyed about last night? No, you made your point   a little dramatically perhaps but   well. I kiss relief to his shirt and slide a hand up his leg. Brief he lets, then No! Dinner first, we're being normal tonight. A quick one? Go on, he shoos My culinary skills are virtually nil. So catting a little, I wander across to push back the curtain and look into his road. Crown-flowered chestnut. Weed-cracked path. A livelier wreck than last winter implied. Nobly crumbling. Time has passed and it's long since I first came here. I like your street. Changed a lot, he says All of those houses were bedsits once. It won't be long before this one goes for luxury flats too. Not yet though, I say shutting out the streetlight. Well, he agrees Not tonight. Then the room becomes Here, and Mind it's hot. At his desk – set as table – we use new plates, knives and forks, drink wine from new glasses. Make out civilised. Pretending nothing separates this night from its lineage of before.

Soon lax, dinner-sated, dissolving desiccated peas we nift through the tidy of scrape rinsing clean. Wet hands wiping. Pass to dry. Stack. Flop on his bed, top to tail, sipping wine. And I toe smooth wrinkles from his duvet, from his jeans, right to his No! No! socks yanked off Have Mercy! Mercy only if you

145

sit up here on me. So I take the chance. Make playful. Lacing fingers. Kissing palms and I am light bright to the glint in his eye. I've been thinking about you all day, he says Sitting here writing by myself. What were you thinking? About how you smell just like the right thing. I stroke his hair. Its neat parting. Odd ribs of grey. Watch him arranging mine, so precisely as to invite a Why're you doing that? Reminds me of   What? Some girl from your wicked past? Rush to his face Yes   no   the first. Oh my God, you're shy! Yeah well, he says Even I was a virgin once. Trace his chest. Kiss his collarbone. Were you mad about her? I really was, she was beautiful and   good to me when I was a mess. And although the eyes close, making hard to read, I already know the word Mess is why we're here so clumsy on into where it leads. Was it your mother who did that, made you a mess? Why do you say that? You once said you weren't sorry she was dead. But then a thing I don't expect, a click, like a tic, at the side of his mouth. Fuck, he says You going in for the kill tonight? then – trying to hide it – What the fuck must I look like. You look fine, I touch it You look perfect to me. Well, he says If I'm going to tell you those things I'm going to need some help. Anything, what? Take off your top. Done. I don't think that'll be enough. Take off your bra as well, and helps undo the clasp You have really beautiful breasts, and bringing to his mouth the tic dies away. Catch his eyes, and we begin again. Gets his jeans off. Opens me with his tongue. Every muscle in him relaxing and tensing. Getting to and going in. As though kissing can barely hold the line. You're my beautiful you're my   A helpless smile like he knows I know what's happening to him inside. And I do. Me too and I. Keep with him. Like as we have always been struggling to find the find the Come with me, he says and I, holding on as it rises, the high tide. Him and. live words I can't make out. Cracking with the. Slam. other. Let each other. Out. Just being together. Being so fucking close. And I feel so much love for him in this moment I can't imagine ever feeling anything else.

But.

Soon.

It's the past again.

Pity the finished. We do and lie quiet remembering which body's his, which is mine. Well, I've never experienced anything quite like that, he says and laugh as our legs twitch in time. Only part of each other for such a short while and move no more than have to. Until he slips out. Settles beside. Damp and this is how we try, listening to each other now and someone coughing in the road. Toilet flushing. Cars cars. Music above. Blood going round us. His vein like my own. But sooner than I'd like he gets from bed and lighting up smiles That did help, so   what was the question again?

Do you have brothers and sisters? Why do you ask? Nosiness, do you? He refills my glass Halves on both sides but I don't know most of them or even how many there are. Really? Really. Make a guess. Two boys on my mother's, that's easy enough. My father though, eleven? Twelve? Could be twenty. Might be more! Do you see him much? He occasionally comes scrounging when I'm up North on tour but not if I can help it, no. And your mother's dead. He nods but rubs at his lip. And she was? Irish. What was she like? Difficult. Strange. Fucking nightmare actually – the tic again and he so conscious of it – Sure you want to know all of this? Yes, everything. Alright – he lights up and sits back opposite – So tomorrow, but in nineteen fifty-six, they had me.

And the long night begins.

Well, you know where she was from. The family came over after the war. Her mother died soon afterwards and the father was a doctor. Well off, I think, but I don't know much. They were traditional Catholics. Pretty strict. There was a younger sister I never knew because she didn't keep in touch. Or with her father who she always said was very tough. Then in her late teens she met mine, which was really terrible luck. He was older, twenty-two, twenty-three. From there, Sheffield, originally. I'm not sure what he did back then – being a man of mystery – but I think some kind of salesman. Apparently it was love at first sight, followed by a great deal of sneaking about because her father regarded the English as immoral, especially the men. An opinion somewhat justified by my father taking off with someone else the minute my mother got pregnant.

So they weren't married then? Hmmm, he says

She was hazy about that, sometimes said they were but mostly avoided it. I did ask him directly once but he was uncharacteristically tight-lipped and rambled on instead about her sainted memory or some shit. By the time I was two though, they'd both 'remarried' so I'd say probably not. Whatever the truth, she never forgave him. I think she married my stepfather for spite – that said, back then, in the late fifties, she can't have had much choice. He was a lot older – fifteen, sixteen years. Factory floor who'd worked himself up, a bit. And he was an alright bloke I suppose. I mean he took me on as part of the deal but the marriage went shitwardly fairly quick. Not rowing or violent. Nothing like that, just people living together, disliking in quiet. Certainly there was never any sign of love and the children she had with him she didn't like much. Both boys,

148

three and four years younger than me. We all shared a room and got on fairly well but   we had to stick together back then.

When I ask What was she like? he gives a weird smile.

Intelligent   and   very angry. Those were the poles she ran between. The intelligence covered what the anger did but the anger did so many things the intelligence had to work very hard and ever harder as the years went by. The trouble for us was never knowing which way she'd go. Perfectly rational one moment then screaming, breaking things. It made getting through the fucking day a process of inching. Don't say that. Go there. Mention, you know. I suppose the problem was this life she never wanted but couldn't escape, the man she'd married and didn't love, place she hated living and couldn't leave, two children she'd no interest in yet was expected to rear. Then somewhere in the middle of all that was me who she did want and did love but couldn't stop punishing for whatever my father had done. And all of that led to some very interesting behaviour as time went on.

I was quite small when I realised things weren't as they should be. After her third was born there was some kind of breakdown, I think. The word was never used but that's what it was like. She was definitely very unwell. Maybe it was having three little boys running amok, I don't know but I remember that time having a very particular ritual. She'd get us up early, dressed and fed, then her sister-in-law would take the younger boys for the day. After that she'd have her pills then sit at the table a while. Everything would slow down, then she'd take me to her room. Shut the curtains. Take her dressing gown off and lie on the bed. I'd have to lie beside and she'd get me to whisper prayers or recite the alphabet or go through numbers. We'd lie that way all morning. Sometimes she'd cry. At lunch she'd make me a sandwich and I was allowed out for a while. After that more pills again and bed. I must only have been four so the staying still was dreadful but I'd get a slapped face if I didn't or put outside the door. I hated that. I'd panic almost. I couldn't be without her and she'd always wait until I was all worked up before calling me back in. Then she'd spend ages setting me right, wiping my face, wiping my eyes. I don't really know what it was about. That whole period was pretty odd. Just me and her for long hours in the dark, like we were on another planet or the only people left in the world.

Anyway, it passed eventually and she began to get up again. Next, the other two stopped getting packed off but she stayed very highly strung. Lots of rules were introduced to help her cope. Everything from the volume you spoke at to not kicking a ball. They got very precise too and more every day. By the time we were at school it was like a military inspection. Couldn't think of leaving the house without being immaculate. She'd sometimes keep you washing and re-washing your hands until you'd be late. We'd just stand there, every morning, hoping to make the grade because if you didn't, fucking hell, she was quick with whatever came to hand: dustpan, poker, heel of a shoe. It got much worse over the years and I got the brunt because the other two were their father's sons while I was hers alone. And she beat the shit out of me. He almost never interfered. Certainly never raised a hand to me himself − not that I ever gave him cause. I wouldn't have said boo to a goose between those four walls. Though sometimes he'd come home from the pub to find me out on the step in the rain. That would piss him off so he'd bring me in. Then there'd be all kinds of shouting and screaming. She didn't like to be told what she could or couldn't do to me. So I got used to having my lip split for nothing reasons and soon learned to say it was my brothers' fault which – considering they never had a fucking mark – wasn't all that great. Mostly though the stepfather didn't notice me. If he ever remarked on a bruise or black eye, it was usually just Annoying your mother again? Good lad! which was weirdly comforting.

But almost worse were the gaps of time when she'd blank me. Completely freeze me out. She'd just seethe around, nursing some imagined slight – like shouting an answer from the hall or forgetting to switch off a light – then suddenly, without warning, all fucking hell would break loose. I'd be accused of everything bar the invasion of Poland and belted until I cried – later on I learned how not to, which had its own reward. Of course the next day was like nothing happened. Everyone played along. Over time I think she actually made herself forget. I remember once mentioning her chipping my tooth and she started roaring I never did that, my God, it scares the things you invent! Her denials were always so extreme that I'd end up wondering if she was mad, or me?

And he checks my eyes. And I check his. I do not cry. I would not do that to him. That much I know for sure.

This'll probably sound strange but, even after all these years, I still think there was something of love in those beatings. Like, when she hit me, she really felt it – and she can't have felt much because there always was a lot of medication sloshing around. Plus I know she felt guilt. If it had been very bad, if she'd cut me or   burned me   she'd come upstairs that night with cake. And lie into the bed with me telling stories while I ate. I always

felt better after it but   I did eat a lot of cake as a child. Still
have a very sweet tooth.

Then he smooths a canine with his tongue, as if naming it the
one, some treacherous left behind. The tic again. I love his
mouth even as he presses on it now.

The most difficult thing though, as a child, was the food. It's
hard to describe how bad that was. I don't know if she was anor-
exic, or phobic, or what but, when I was seven or eight, she
started this   starving herself and   really   down to nothing
at all   and as it got worse – whatever it was – the rest of us
as well. It seemed to come out of nowhere because   she was
beautiful, my mother. At least I always thought she was and
then, this thing began and it turned her into   I can't explain
but   you could almost see through her in the end   it must've
been the anger that kept her alive. It started with just not eating, herself. Then not being able to watch us at it. Then cooking
it, handling it – especially meat – and that was bad news for us.
That was very bad. I spent years dreading going home for tea
– all three of us did – because you wouldn't know what would
be waiting when you got in. We'd hang around out the back until she'd call us. Then we'd troop in, starving, but steeling ourselves against the inevitable slop and it always was   you know
mince burned to a crisp   or chicken that looked like it could
defend itself   fucking mouldy peas and her going off on these
crazy tirades   Jesus the number of times I got smacked round
the head for just sitting there trying to swallow that awful shit.
The fucking anxiety of it   every fucking meal. The only thing
she could bear to make was cake and that was only once a week.
We'd have our tongues hanging out for it by Sunday evening

152

but one little piece, that was it. I just remember being hungry every day, sneaking down in the middle of the night to fill up on stale bread. We were all so underweight there were letters home from school. Even the boys got whacked for that and I got the ruler until my knuckles bled. Apparently it was my fault we were these perfectly turned-out but half-starved boys.

I touch his foot and his eyes come back to smile at that. I think he's only finding light though for my benefit. Everything else in him seems growing still. Just watch, I promise Wait with him. Don't let him be alone.

It wasn't all bad though. Fridays were good because he'd arrive home with fish and chips. Then they'd go out and leave us with the wireless, or later TV and sweets. Plus, every summer we had a week at the seaside – ice cream, running on the beach, all that. She was so lovely then and so easy to be with. You'd wish you never had to leave. It was the only time she ever smiled. Also, she read like anything so there were books all over our house. She taught me to when I was pretty small. She was patient like that and with homework and stuff. She'd probably have made a good teacher if she hadn't been so fucked up. But then, maybe if she'd done that instead of having me she'd never have had those problems at all.

And what about your father? I say. He shakes his head, like mock and disgust. Another cigarette. Easier though, like these waters are clear and he can see him somewhere far away.

Ahh, my father   where to begin? He's a useless bastard at the very best of times. Five or six marriages I know of. Countless kids. Never understood the point of all the marrying myself but   he seems to like it and – not that I'm one to talk – he could never keep it to himself so I'm probably related to most of the North. I'm the eldest I think although that only means I've never heard of one older than me. Can't say much about the rest. Now and then one of them pitches up here and it's weird to open your door to versions of your father wanting answers to stuff you don't know anything about, like Why was he in prison? Is he a bigamist? Nothing would surprise me but   I don't know, I never saw him, growing up. There were only a few months when I was about ten and some wife wanted to 'heal the rift'. Some kind of hippy or something. There was a letter one day. My mother lost her reason of course but was, somehow, persuaded because, from nothing at all, I was suddenly in Liverpool once a month. At first I was excited because he was 'Oh my son' and 'These are the lessons life's taught me' but that didn't last very long. By the third round, he was slinking off down the pub, leaving the wife to instruct me on how miraculous he was but – as the bottle went down – that he was a cunt. So I preferred going out with him, even if it was my job to get him home. Even when he'd pick someone up and talk himself back to hers. Good luck on those days consisted of sitting outside her bedroom door. Bad luck was on the bonnet with them in the back seat. Really bad luck was rain and me in the front desperately turning the radio up. Don't tell – whoever she was – he'd say after   especially if he'd paid. I didn't give a shit. She got sick of me anyway soon enough, or he got sick of her. Either way the visits soon stopped and he never bothered after that except for birthday cards – mostly one month late. Wedding invites now and then, very much dependent upon my being owned or not. I went once or twice but all I'll say is that, after my mother, he liked them good and thick. So I didn't miss him, except in the abstract or when the stepfather'd take his to the Wednesday matches and I'd be left at home. That was kind of shit. Still hate the fucking football now.

That's sad, I say. Not really, he shrugs And the lack of a father turned out to be the least of my worries. She was always the one.

Over the years I'd worked out ways to avoid the rage. How to calm her down, get her to laugh instead – she didn't have a bad sense of humour when she wasn't being insane. And when I was twelve things really changed. We moved to a bigger house on a nicer street. She was delighted with that. Going up in the world. Bought a piano. I got a room of my own and, for a while, life became very normal. I hardly knew myself. Even the food thing improved. Anyway, it was all looking up until I hit four-teen. Started getting tall. She said Like him – I never saw it myself. It was just that I was growing up really but enough to set her off again. The paranoid rages and the ritual amends – bed and her slice of cake but getting different now, wanting to talk about him. The strange thing is, it didn't seem strange because I was interested I suppose. I wanted to know about him. I mean, I was the only evidence that life had existed and it wasn't great always being the odd one out. Besides, it started off as harmless enough. Things you wouldn't mind. How the first time they met she'd sneaked out to a dance. He was so drunk he spilled something all down her dress but he was the best-looking man there so it didn't matter. The next week he was at the school gates to walk her home after and all very cov-ert because of her father. To go away together, she'd faked some pilgrimage with something like the Legion of Mary. Ingenious really but I can't help wondering how that ended, probably with me. It was love though, she always said, which apparently made up for everything else. Some nights she'd tell me about what he was interested in: boxing, racing, anything with an engine. I liked hearing all that because I still hadn't grasped what an utterly worthless fucker he was. It began to feed on itself though, all that talking. Opened some door that should have stayed shut. Started extending itself into what I had no business knowing about. About marrying my stepfather. How she'd done it for me, how she hadn't wanted more children but he was a pig. Then the stories about my father becoming more involved. More explicit and the way they were told, over and over, as if I hadn't understood. As if she wanted a reaction I didn't know how to give. And she got and it got I dreaded her coming in. I'd pretend I was asleep and when she hit me I'd pretend it didn't hurt just so she'd leave me be. It was so bizarre, like she was   pouring herself into me, trying to stop my brain making the difference between   and I got so con- fused and it got so hard to breathe   the fucking weight of all the talk, all the paranoid shit, all the memories and   like she was creeping all over me. Then one night, after she'd already been and gone, I was doing what you do when you're a four- teen-year-old boy. I was pretty practised by then so I'm sure I took care but when I opened my eyes   after   she was there. Watching. I nearly died of fright. I thought she'd kill me but she didn't say anything. Just turned and went and   After that it got different again. The way she was with me. The way she'd lie in the bed and I'd be completely still, trying not to touch. Saying anything I could think of to get her out but   God even to remember it now makes me feel sick.

We are down in the down in the. Hold myself rigid and do not fail to meet his eyes. But now the busy tic's got so bad he has to pause and rub at it.

Alright   alright – still calming it – Alright then   here it is. I put it off for as long as I was able to. I kept out of its way for as long as I could but   I realise now it was always going to happen. At the time I thought it was my fault. Because of my mistake. I walked a girl home from school – first and only time I ever did. I remember being all pleased with myself because there'd been no awkward silences and I'd made her laugh. When I got in though, the other two legged it pretty quick so I knew I was in the shit. I just started with Sorry, sorry, straightaway, you know, trying to placate. She was just shouting Where were you? Where were you? so I panicked and lied about seeing some dog get hit in the road. She screamed Don't lie! Where have you been? When I stuck with the dog, I got belted round the kitchen but I kept to it until she started on my face. Then I told because   I liked that girl and I didn't want a bruise to explain. I walked a girl home from school, I said. The next thing I remember is blood on my teeth and thinking she'd broken my nose.

I was just useless and sore and went straight up to bed, cursing her for a fucking bitch under my breath. Hoping by some miracle not to bruise or that the stepfather would take her out, which he didn't. And once they'd all gone to bed, there she was I brought you some cake. I pretended to be asleep but she wasn't having any of it. Got in beside, saying all the stuff – I wish you wouldn't make me treat you like that but you're too young for fooling around with girls yet and   putting her hands into my pyjama top. I just lay there, pretending, hoping she'd give up but. I love you, she said You know that, don't you, son? You know you're my favourite. You know I've always loved you best, just tell me you still love me and let that be an end to it. I wouldn't though. I hated saying it but she wouldn't stop so eventually I said I love you. And then Is your face sore? she asked. No, I said. Is your face sore, darling? No, it's not. But when she asked the third time, I knew I had to give up. A bit, I said. She said A bit what? A bit sore   Mum. She said I can see that and I know what will make it better, love.

She was up and out after, saying Goodnight, like she'd been tucking me in. I just turned on my stomach thinking Did that really just happen? Was it some kind of mistake? She couldn't have meant to but there was the stain and   I remember getting out of bed, eating the cake, fucking stuffing it down, trying to get myself straight, but it was like my eyes wouldn't adjust and I had to go puke it all back up. I must've sat for an hour on the bathroom floor, listening to her roam around below – closing doors, checking plugs. The taste of the chocolate sick in my mouth and when I went back to bed, I couldn't sleep   I had another wank to knock myself out, fucking crying all the while. I remember that   so clearly and   just not knowing what was going on.

The next morning was like I'd been blasted. None of me was right. I kept checking the mirror and – bruise aside – everything looked fine except   I didn't know how to use my body. I remember clunking downstairs touching the woodchip that I could hardly feel and my weird fucking legs. She was pretty manic in the kitchen – maybe she had shocked herself. She didn't acknowledge me though, just raced about hurling dishes in the sink. Even one of the boys got a clip round the ear for laughing when something smashed.

For the whole week after she ignored me and I had a month of nights on my own. But after that, she got herself organised. Picked up where she'd left off. I don't know why the delay or what was the spur, only that it became fairly regular then, once a week, sometimes more.

At first it was all pretending she was doing something else. Eyes averted. Under the sheet. As if not looking at each other made it less real. That was only the beginning though, of the very very bad. I remember trying so hard not to get hard but what can you do at fourteen? Now I know it's a mechanical thing but, back then, I thought it was me. I couldn't understand why I would. Sometimes I'd imagine she was testing, that I was about to be hauled off to some hospital where they'd fix me up people like me, whatever that was. Later, when she got more confident she'd imply she was the victim   of me   that I was the   I made her do those things to me   and all the time it was getting worse. Further from what you could pretend it wasn't making it more like   wanting responses and   not the whole way   not kissing or that but   almost everything else   all under the guise of her fucking caring and love, how she under-stood I couldn't help myself. But I never cried about it again. Went into my body to get out of my head. There was no way to think about it so I didn't. And I stopped feeling everything pretty soon. Just let her do what she wanted and did what she asked in return.

He looks around the room but not at me. Lights another cigar-ette. Pours another drink. Then, pressing his knuckles to the pitiless tic, continues on.

Once she was done, she'd get up and walk out and I'd just lie there getting back to blank. Sometimes I'd throw up. As it progressed, I started dropping lit matches on my stomach, or legs. Not to feel, just to revive some self that could act normally in my skin – I know you know about that. I'd wait to see how long I could take it and, as time went on, for fucking ages. By the end they could burn themselves out.

I should have said No, I know that. I should've known to push her off   and it sounds ridiculous but   the way she had me   I couldn't go against her at all. For years after I left I kept wondering if the real truth was that I'd enjoyed or invited it because physically I did you know   do you know what I mean? She always made sure I did and   and once that happens it's like you're implicated, like you're the accomplice somehow. But   it wasn't what I wanted and I know that because of what I ended up doing to myself to get over it.

All of him shivering now, like a dog in the rain, but still You alright with this? he says I know we both have it so   is it too much? And I am   I feel   so distraught. This is not my story though or time for upset. I'm fine, you tell me whatever you want. The tic gone so bad his mouth can hardly hold his smoke. Okay, but if you change your mind   I say I won't, please don't worry about me.

Well, at some point, she started slipping me sleeping pills after – maybe the throwing up was disturbing the peace. At least it meant a dreamless sleep and started me considering when else I'd like that – which was already most of the time. So I began helping myself. Just the sleeping pills first but – once I started to search – there were prescription bottles stashed all over the

160

house. I used to lift so many at a time she must've guessed but she never mentioned it and, as she was only getting worse, there wasn't much incentive to stop. I can see now though I was getting depressed. I'd come in from school and just lie on my bed so exhausted I could hardly move. I was sick all the time. Every flu. Nosebleeds a lot. Then the tic started too and that frightened her, I think. She used to beg me to stop it – as if I could. It was that bad sometimes I couldn't speak. They used to excuse me from class to go sit in the bog just to get it under control – like school wasn't already nightmare enough. I hated it. Kept getting into fights which, actually, cheered me up. It was almost as if they solidified me. Gave me somewhere to be angry and feel like I wasn't queer because, once she started, I lost all interest in girls – that poor one I walked home, don't know what she must've thought, I never even looked at her again. My mother'd go mad though, at the bloody nose, ripped shirt, so I'd get another hiding and I always let her. Never even considered not. Whenever she wanted. Whatever she grabbed. Bottles, brushes, tin of paint once – had to get stitches after that one. I mean, by the end I was nearly twice her height but – same as the fights – I almost got to like it. Seeing how much I could take. Because the less it looked like it hurt, the angrier she'd get, then the further she'd go and that was revenge. She'd feel so bad after and I'd feel like I'd won. But also I was wolfing down pills by then so I didn't know what the fuck was going on. What I remember most was just finding it hard, really hard, to be alive.

So did you ever tell anyone? Did anyone know? He shakes his head.

I never told and   no one ever walked in but, that in itself, considering how long   she was very careful though, about the pretence. Always Morning love! like nothing had happened. Never asked about the burn marks or mentioned the throwing up. No one did. Towards the end though, the stepfather'd sometimes shout through my door Get out of his room, he's too old for that now. Or make jokes about her being cracked because of all the pills and we'd laugh about that, me and him. But I don't think he really knew and I probably wouldn't have wanted him to. Either way, when I left I never saw him again.

More wine? and he stands up without looking at me. Yes please. So he goes to the fridge. Gets another bottle. Opens. Fills my glass. Fills his own then sits back opposite. And when did you? I say.

By the time I was fifteen it was very bad, so I wrote to my father – he was in Newcastle by then – asking if he'd put me up until I got a job and a place. Only fucking thing I'd ever asked. Three months I waited for his reply. Barely legible when it arrived and full with fine phrases about the responsibilities of fatherhood he'd obviously nicked from something he hadn't understood. The gist of it being Of course I could but – unfortunately – I could not. I was so desperate by then though I decided to hitch up. He didn't recognise me at the door and, when I explained who I was, he nearly had a stroke. Fucker wouldn't even ask me in, said his marriage was hanging by a thread and I was old enough to take care of myself. I begged him but he wouldn't. In the end I said Please don't make me go back, she's fucking doing things to me. He just hit me a slap and said Don't be such a pervert! then slammed the door in my face. I didn't know what to do so   I hitched back again   in the dark and   let me tell you, that was one long fucking night.

She was pretty hysterical when I got in. Been up all night. Called the police. The stepfather had already gone to work so it was only her and the other two, hiding in their room. I didn't want to say where I'd been but she kept on and on so, eventually, I just said I went to see my dad. I had to but, even as I was, I knew what came next would be   well

She went completely off her head. Shouting how I'd betrayed her. Was an ungrateful piece of shit and just like him, slinking off into the night. That she wished she'd never had me. That I'd ruined her life. None of which was unexpected but   then I realised   she was only working up. And my heart just started to pound. Then it really began. Throwing things first. From the sideboard. Plates. Cups. Screaming You're in for a hiding, my boy, you'll never forget. And I thought Alright, get on with it. You can take it, whatever it is. So I leaned against the table, like she said – arms out to support myself and I was prepared for a lot. I had faith in my pain threshold. It had always stood me in good stead before   but   this time   she told me to pull my shirt up   then she beat me with the buckle end of the stepfather's belt   hard as she could   again and again   I thought I was going to pass out   and she just kept on and   probably would've but   I couldn't   I couldn't manage the pain. It got so bad I couldn't move and then   there was all this mystery blood so   I stopped her   I turned   I took it away. She went for me then, like a wild animal really, and I was so panicked I could hardly defend myself. When she said Get upstairs, it was a relief. I don't even remember how I did   but then she followed me up. The other two must've been listening because when she called them out they wouldn't come. So she went in and belted them out of the room. I want you to watch this, she said A lesson about what ingratitude gets. Then she started ripping my clothes, destroying my things – not that there was much but Where can you go if you're naked, son? Why didn't I get rid of you at the start and have a life of my own? And me just going I'm sorry Mum, please don't. But she wouldn't   just   fucking   out of control. Whacking me round the head with bits of books. Blood pouring out my nose. I couldn't even see my back but when the younger two did they started screaming with fright so then she started really knocking them round. That's what finally woke me up. I knew I had to do something before she killed one of us. So I got hold of her, best I could, and half dragged, half carried her back to her room. Her thrashing about, screeching Don't you touch your mother! Fucking biting but I didn't notice that until later. All I could think of was shutting her in and I only managed to, just. Stood there holding the door handle begging Lie down Mum. Please Mum. Please take one of your pills. Which she must've done because, after a while, the ranting died down and when I let go, the door stayed shut. Then everything went quiet and we went down to the sitting room.

I remember mopping the boys up. At some point making them lunch – meat paste sandwiches as I recall – but having no real thoughts, which must've been the shock. Then I remember just being sat forward on the couch hoping my back would scab soon. When the stepfather came home he couldn't believe the state of the place, or me – bite marks all down my arm and neck. Bloodstains from my back on the leatherette and no energy for pretending left. When he asked Where're your brothers? I just pointed up. And he raced up the stairs, of course he did. There was a bit of consoling, then he went in to her and What the

164

fuck did you do? You know, usually, if he put his foot down that was it. But not that night. She went for him – which must've been quite a surprise. He certainly looked pretty alarmed, coming back down, mumbling I don't think your mother's very well like that was fucking news. Anyway, she passed out again then he went out for fish and chips.

Luckily when she came round the next day she was calm. Spent it in bed. Darkened room, all that. The following day she materialised at breakfast, apologising Poor little boys. Mummy's just had a bad turn. Promised to see the doctor about her nerves. But to me Go to your room. I'll speak to you later young man.

She got him to take them to the pictures, to make it up. I had to stay in because   well   I couldn't go out   looking like that. And she waited until they had before coming up for me.

I listened to every step. I knew it would be bad. But it was still daylight so I kept hoping for a yelling at   Of course   it wasn't that   it was the other thing. And she took the blanket off so there'd be no mistake. The fucking fear of it. Lying there. Waiting. I didn't want to but   I was already half wrecked and she already knew how to make me go against myself. And she was so   she had no   knickers on when she got on me and I   He dry retches into his hand but when I   waves me back Will you let me? if you can?   I've never told anyone and I   I say Alright.

Breathe and watch him breathe.

I think she thought once she did that I'd never leave   be able to   or I'd be ruined at least. And in some ways I was. I was never the same again. But at the time I begged til I started to choke   and I tried sitting up but my back and   she   kept pushing me down   trying to get me to   and my brain fucking

165

jumping. Fucking gagging and panicking and then   you know
    it was too late and

        all of a sudden, I was that   became
    a person who has done the worst thing
    is that even a person any more?

If she'd left at that moment I would have gone out the window but she   she didn't. She kept going on so the pain   it started to do something else

    all those fucking bruises and cuts   wouldn't let out of myself.

And she hadn't counted on that   that there, in the fucked-up body getting fucked, was a person starting to come to life, starting to want to hurt her and do all the things to her body that she'd done to his. Do worse. Wanting to fucking fling her on the floor and stamp on her face and   I could tell I was starting to go off my head. That if it wasn't over soon I definitely would. So I went through to the end. Finished it, like she said. And when she got up to go clean   He dry retches again. Are you alright? He nods but the grey eyes black and the wall they stare through into that past is gone so eerily thin I can almost see her too.

When she got up off me, I said If you ever fucking do that again I'm going to kill you and then I'll kill myself and everyone will know you for what you are. It was the first time either of us had referred to it aloud. First time I ever saw her like that. Knocked off herself, you know? But, of course, the clever kicked in. Cogs going round. I could almost see it, her working out how to handle me, which trick might be best. She chose guilt. Falling down, crying I should never have let you do that but I love you so much. You're all I have. But the shock at myself had me out of the bed. Getting my clothes. Dressing quick.

Her following me, holding onto me and all the fucking talk. If only you could understand how lonely I am. All these years without your father but I love you son. Just shit pouring out but I'd gone completely beyond. I knew this was the only chance I'd get. If I didn't go now, I'd never have the nerve and then she would have me for good. So I   what was left of me   prised her off   and   took her by the hair   and I was just shouting it, I remember, repeating the same thing   If you ever fucking lay a finger on me again I will kill you and then I will kill myself and everyone will know. And I dragged her to the door. Still fucking hanging on. Clawing into me screaming Don't son! Don't! Then I threw her out. And I slammed the fucking door on her hand and   she fell. I heard her. On the stairs. Like fucking comedy bumping and   I shouted through the door I hope you're fucking dead. I hope you've broken your fucking neck. And she lay there screeching, pleading up for help. I just kept shouting I fucking hate you and I always have. Over and over. But she didn't stop. So I ripped up the bedsheets, all covered in fucking stuff, and I took them out to the landing and just threw them over the banister. Then I watched them tumble down and land all over her. Go wash those fucking sheets, I said. And she stopped screaming then. Stopped crying. Everything went still. Then she got up. Picked the sheets up. Went on down to the kitchen and   How fucking banal is that? Unworthy of her, I think, not to reappear with a knife. So maybe my father taught me something after all, because although I threw up with fear, it was sorted. That was the last time I ever saw her and, by the time the others were back, my whole life had changed.

The rest of the day I stayed in my room. At teatime I heard her tell one of the boys to fetch me down. Him running up the stairs saying Mum says come and eat. But I didn't. Him trying to persuade me but I wouldn't. So he went back down saying He won't come. Poor little bastard sounded so nervous but she only said Never mind, eat your own.

Unsurprisingly I didn't sleep. Just sat there trying to get myself together really. By the morning I'd turned sixteen and I'd made my plan – which involved lifting all the money and pills I could find. Once I'd done that, I left. Bought myself a bacon sandwich and a cup of tea. Then I walked out of Sheffield and that was it. Happy Birthday to me! Fuck! My leg's gone to sleep! And he stands up to limp. Twenty-three years ago to-morrow? And twenty-three years ago today. Oh God, I say. He nods but then goes on

I hitched down to London. Most of the way with this lorry driver who picked me up just outside Sheffield and asked if I'd been hit by a bus? But a fucking fortuitous meeting, that was. He gave me the address of some mate in Camberwell so I'd a floor to kip on that night. And that mate got me the first of many shitty jobs – Smithfield the first one was, I think, packing meat – the irony wasn't lost on me but it really set me up. For the next few years I lived in lots of dives. Fucked up lots of other jobs and had a great fucking time. No one at me. No one entitled. The drug thing was already well under way but – compared to later on – pretty harmless, actually. In fact I'd say it helped. Helped with meeting people and making friends and getting over what had happened. It gave me a bit of space in my head which was exactly what I needed then. But now I need to take a leak.

Then he just walks out, leaving me in the midst of this half-unpacked life, letting me look at it and I   what can I do but wait?

When he comes back he washes his hands and, on reflection,

his face. So far so horrible, right? But not you, I say It. Well, he says Not yet. There's so much I want to ask but I know to not. Let him. Let him say what he wants. But let me tell you something nice now, he says and sits back on the bed again.

Obviously I never had a girlfriend or anything when I was at home. I was pretty sure everyone could see I wasn't normal and wherever I went it was like she was watching me, which was a bit of a turnoff too. So coming to London got rid of that and, much sooner than you'd have thought, all this sexual feeling started to reappear. Nothing unusual I suppose for a sixteen-year-old boy but   completely new to me – noticing girls, fancying them. Even recognising it came as a shock and the first time something happened I couldn't believe I was so up for it. I mean   I was still bruised but   there was this girl at the hostel I'd moved to – she worked in the kitchen there. Older than me. Eighteen, nineteen. Curly hair. Big brown eyes and a fucking tongue you wouldn't believe. Everyone was scared of her but for me she was It. I couldn't think about anything else. I was always hanging around where she was, all lanky and shy, holding open doors, offering to carry the mop. I was no good at coy so whenever I saw her I ticced. Badly. And she'd take the piss but then feed me scraps, which was further than most men got. I'm sure she knew I'd never make a move and if she hadn't I'd probably still be a virgin now. Anyway, one night she took pity on me. Towed me into the women's dorm and said Do you want to kiss me? I went bright red but managed to indicate that I did. Well, tonight's your lucky night, she laughed then kissed me and   Fuck   it was good. I remember trying to work out what I should do with my hands and just putting them on her shoulders. She must've thought This is a right one, but   all she said was Come lie on the bed, and, when I did, she put my

169

hand on her breast and ffffffffff. We kissed some more. Then she told me open her top and I got that hard I thought I was going to pass out. It was the first time I'd ever felt properly turned on, from the inside of myself, you know? But, just as suddenly, she sat back up and said That's enough, off you go!

The next morning I couldn't stop smiling at her. The whole canteen must have seen. She kept saying Stop giving me those puppy eyes, you! but most nights that week we did the same. Each time a little further, always at her behest. First time she put her hand in my pants I freaked out a bit but   Don't you want me to? she asked and soon as I said I did I could let her and it was great. I still felt strange about coming though and coughed a lot to cover it up. She wasn't fooled but she was good about it and just put my hand up her skirt. I didn't want to get naked because I was ashamed of my scars. She had a way with her though and, a few days later, it only took Want me to put it in my mouth? to get my pants on the floor. And I saw her see them but she never asked, which I was grateful for. Harder was returning the favour. I'd always found it   particularly   you know   not great   but the next night I took a couple of pills and Jesus, the reaction from her. Suddenly all I could think about was making her come and what it would feel like to put it in, which meant − by the time she suggested it − I was sort of prepared, in my head. The body though wasn't much help. Couldn't get it in, didn't know what to do once I had. She was instructive, thankfully, and patient. Let me keep trying until I got it right − she probably thought I'd better come or he'll never get off. But the memory of that first time − real time − and after it, both of us sleeping in her bed with the smell of her hair and the smell of the sex. It was like starting the clock again but, this time, right way round. Like getting clean for the first time in my life. She was the very best thing that could have happened and I knew that, even then.

I crawl up the bed and offer my mouth. He kisses it too. Lets me put my arms round and find he is a bit like glass. But I want him to know I think he's such a fine man. He won't though. He'll never think that. And once I've settled back he just carries on.

She was a bad girl too. She'd flirt mercilessly with me. I'd go so red the drunks would roar Forget it lad, she'd tear you limb from limb! But I loved that, the ordinariness, being part of a joke. I used to run back from work just to watch her peel spuds. She'd pretend to be annoyed but kiss me up against the door, then throw me back out shouting Behave yourself youngster! Before long we were getting wasted together, usually with her mates in their half-empty dorm. End up shagging away while they'd complain, chucking pillows or moaning along. The occasional glass of water thrown over us, after which there'd be scream-ing and chasing about. She encouraged all that and would dare us to kiss. Then I'll-show-mine-if-you'll-show-yours and on to the next until I ended up getting passed around between them all. I think it became their mission to teach me how to do the filthiest stuff – which I now realise they didn't know anything about – but, after everything, you can imagine how I took to being fussed on by four pretty girls. It was all very harmless though. And I've done that kind of thing plenty since but it's never the same, just drink and drugs and athletics. Fairly grim really. Not like those nights. We were only young and had all had our innocence kicked out of us. Pretending to be grown up but, really, just being friends. Nothing heavy. No demands. The confidence it gave me, I hardly knew myself. And, more importantly, because of those girls I liked women again –which could have easily gone the other way because there was so much anger – but instead they set me on my feet. Little-brothered me too. Taught me how to smoke. Made me grow my hair out. Get some decent clothes. And somehow in that room I got to decide who I wanted to be. They seemed to like this boy who was getting a little cocky, took too many drugs but had a laugh and I liked him too so I put him on. From the moment I did the tic was gone and that terrified boy got locked away. I didn't want him any more and no one needed to know he'd ever been. And that new persona got me through the next few years. So I owe a lot to those girls and, to this very day, the sight of a pink candlewick bedspread – oh my fucking God!

What happened to them? Did you all stay friends?

We didn't. It just petered out in the end. Someone moved away. She got a different job. I went to drama school. We met up at first. Then less. Then lost touch. Everything was like that in those days. Drifting about. No one making proper plans. Years later I did, once, see her again. She came to the stage door after a show I was in. She looked exactly the same. We couldn't say very much though because she'd brought her son along. But she said she was glad things had worked out for me because I'd always looked like such a stray. When she was leaving she kissed me on the cheek and said how fondly she remembered that life. And I was really glad she said so because I do as well.

I press my sole to his. How come drama school then?

Working on a stage door with a mate – bit less nasty than stacking meat – then hanging round with the actors, seeing other shows they did. Don't know why I thought I could but when someone suggested drama school, I decided to give it a go. Auditioned. Got in. Got a scholarship. And that started a really good time. Acting just seemed to offer me another life for free. A way of exploring all the things I wanted to be without trawling through all the shit you'd have to if it was real. And all that anger and confusion, the stories I could never tell, finally had a place to breathe because there has to be a logic on stage that normal life doesn't often have. Whatever I was I was safe in the part and everyone was safe from the mess I was. Once the show was over, that was it. Like living without consequence – all of which turned out to be bullshit but that's how I thought of it at the time. Anyway, those years I was freed from myself. Not having to check which bruises to cover up or lie to people who knew what I was. And getting wasted. And having sex. Boys. Girls. I didn't care. It was all part of being free and imagining good things could happen for me. I worked like a dog and when it turned out I was good, people said so and that helped a lot – a little confidence is a great thing to get hold of when you've lived for years with none. And all this time she didn't know where I was   until I needed my birth certificate. She wrote back My Darling Son. Left messages at the school saying she'd be down and I was to call to arrange. That happened a couple of times. But I never did and she never appeared. I heard less and less and I got less scared. Then nothing at all. I left her behind and I started again.

So had you a girlfriend then? That's the next bit, he says.

She was the year above but two years older – twenty-one to my nineteen. Nice nails. Nice dresses. Completely out of my league but once I set eyes on her that was it. I was already pretty good

173

with women by then but she wouldn't give an inch. When I'd ask her out – which was a lot – she'd say Where are you going to take me? Down the dogs? But after seeing me in an end-of-term play she got a lot more flirtatious suddenly. Nothing was said directly but I saw it and played along. Whenever I was about to leave a party with some other girl, I'd always go say You've got first call love, if you want to make a man of me. I was terrible around women I suppose – never met one I couldn't find something to fancy about. So I had a bad reputation for that and she was   very straight but I could see she got a kick out of how direct I was about it, and playing shocked. Soon she started letting me over   to borrow books. As soon as I'd try to kiss her – which I always did – she'd turf me back out but then I'd catch her watching me all the way down the road. Being constantly broke meant I had to be more inventive than most. So I'd arrive to take her for midnight walks bringing bunches of roses I'd stripped from someone's hedge. I once got arrested in St James's Park for – while completely off my head – trying to swim out and steal her a duck egg. But it was the end-of-year party did it – reciting all of Goblin Market kneeling at her feet. It was her favourite poem and the grand gesture made her laugh, sitting there with all her friends checking each verse off. Worked though. She said Alright, you've earned your stripes, and took me home. We spent the next week in bed and she wasn't so fussy about my reputation after that. So we were together then for the next three years during which every single thing that'd made her wary about getting involved I did to her, and worse.

Was she who you had your daughter with? Yeah, he says That was her.

I was crazy about her in the beginning. Kept asking her to

marry me all the time – thank God she had the sense to refuse. But we were happy and it was easy at first. Lots of sex. Going out. Staying in. She even introduced me to her parents – I've never seen two people look more appalled. I'd borrowed a tie and everything but   it really was no use   I had an accent you could've cut with a knife. She liked that though, slumming it. And all the drugs fascinated her at first. I was happy then though so I wasn't too bad. Well   actually   that's not true   I was but they were still helping me to be a nice guy so the problem didn't really show itself then.

So, she graduated that summer. I had another year to go. By the time I did, she was starting to want more and I didn't know what more meant. What more could you want than getting trashed, having great sex and rolling around London having a laugh? But it was me she wanted more out of and I wasn't able for that. She didn't like my being closed about family. Whenever she asked I'd say we didn't speak or sometimes that they were all dead. If she really pushed I'd end up losing my rag and fucking off for a few days. She wouldn't bring it up for ages after that. I suppose I just didn't know how   how to be with someone, close to someone, or what it would entail. So I'd mostly agree to whatever she said – which is how we ended up moving in together, even though I'd no interest in that. We got a tiny flat in Finsbury Park. I remember being summoned to her father's club. Roundly informed of her mother's shame and warned if I got her pregnant I'd be in more trouble than I'd ever been. Of course, by the time I did I already was so it didn't matter anyway. Nothing would dissuade her though. She said she was in love and to be honest I didn't give a shit about what anyone's mother thought.

Anyway, by the time I graduated too she was already well on her way. Plenty of small, but good, parts and good in them – RSC, Royal Court, that kind of thing – whereas I auditioned a lot but couldn't land anything and, without the routine of school, I started to go down. All the confidence just began leaking away. As the months passed and I still got nothing I started spreading the weekend. Began needing a pick-me-up before going in. Same again when I came out. A whole lot more when I didn't get the part, then forgetting it's not the best idea to go auditioning off your face. It was like not feeling real any more. Disconnected despite all the talking. Watching the self I'd built up over four or five years just crack and fall off me like paint. People kept saying It's only a matter of time so I persevered in the hope they weren't lying. At the same time, beginning to think I might've been lying to myself. Wasting everyone's time with fantasies of this career I couldn't have. The person I could never be. There was just so much rejection and not enough of me. So I got afraid. And I lost my nerve – which is really fucking fatal in this line of work. By a year I was falling. Just breaking apart. Taking whatever I could to feel normal again. To get out of bed. To get back in. And I'd be a real cunt to her sometimes and not because I begrudged her, I just wanted something for myself. And she was always trying to help. Introduce me to people. So I'd get bits here and there but not enough to fix what was going wrong, as if anything could have been.

Then I cheated on her. It wasn't the first time, just the first time I got caught, and I knew I should feel guilty but, really, I didn't understand all the fuss. For me it was only a drunken fuck. She was shattered though, wouldn't see me for weeks. And when she did take me back it was different because it obviously meant more to her than me. So rows began ending more frequently with me fucking off for days and not telling her where. I stopped hiding the extent of my habit as well. I didn't care how much she begged or how much I spent. She started tagging along everywhere I went, mostly to get me home safe or drag me off someone else. I made her do that, take control and I didn't make it easy at all. I think we spent a year getting kicked off buses and out of cabs because of the way I'd carry on, picking fights with strangers and being a twat. I'd wake up with black eyes or cracked ribs and no fucking memory of how I did it, which brought shedloads of older memories in so I'd have to up the dosages to push those away again. And I'd have the odd moment of thinking What are you playing at? But they always came to nothing because I couldn't stop. I just didn't know how.

Did you still love her? As much as I was able, he says Which probably wasn't as much as she deserved. She just wanted so much and it suffocated me. I didn't want to talk about or hear about things. It was the intimacy I suppose. I just couldn't, I mean, my position was, if you feel down, down a few of these and spare me all the fucking chat.

By halfway through our third year together I was merci-lessly fucking around, hardly bothering to hide at all. When she'd threaten to leave I'd beg her to stay and she always would. Then I'd get that buzz in my head and be off to find someone else. And if I didn't wake up with a stranger's skin under my nails it was in bed with one of her friends, some girl from her play. She'd be so humiliated and I'd know I was a piece of shit but   I had no real conscience about sex. Just wanted it and wanted it. Always pestering her for it too until she stopped wanting to. Then we'd row because I wasn't able to touch her without it becoming that. Sometimes she'd just lie there and let me and   I still would. I fucking knew I shouldn't do that but   then it was another excuse. Say she was cold so I fucked someone else. I know I hurt her over and over   like I was looking up ways in a book. The worst part was, she couldn't hurt me back. Once or twice she was unfaithful and flaunted it. For appearances' sake I ranted and raved but I didn't really care. I think I got her to believe that it was all her fault. That if only she could make me happy I would stop   and that was a lie. It must have made her so lonely, all that fucking addiction, because even when I was with her she was on her own.

Then one day she told me she was pregnant and things would have to change. For some reason she was happy and I'd like to say I was but, honestly, I just thought Oh shit! How could I want a child with the state I was in, never mind the childhood I'd had? But she wanted me to be happy so I pretended I was. Swore I'd get clean. Swore I'd get a proper job – don't know what either of us thought that might be but that was what she wanted to hear so that was what I said. If I hadn't been con-tinually wasted I would have been terrified. I mean, I had no idea what a father should be. Mine – shagging everything in sight? Hers – breathing fire down my neck about having to marry her now? – to which I agreed and never got round to. Or maybe my stepfather, never walking through the wrong door? Then to top it off, there was her, my mother. What if? What if that was me? And the fucking horror of that thought I could not manage at all. So after a few weeks clinging to sobriety by my fingernails I let it go again. The drinking got worse. And everything else. Fucking nosebleeds every night. Going to the clap clinic all the time. Then my Big Break arrived, unexpect-edly, and about two years too late.

Juv lead in a film. Big Hollywood thing. To be shot out at

Elstree. She was thrilled because I cheered the fuck up and it meant plenty of cash. Promise of work. Future blossoming like the may. But by then it freaked me out more than anything else – the thought of having to succeed, knowing how badly she wanted me to, to justify all I'd put her through. And I couldn't. Couldn't work out what I was supposed to do. And couldn't sleep. Or relax. Weighed nothing at all. Of course there were also plenty of people happy to sort me out on set. Whatever I wanted to take. Whoever I wanted to fuck. It was so easy. I closed my eyes and just   dived into everything. Bottle of vodka by lunch. Coke after that. Speed. Uppers. Anything to get me up on my feet and running around, behaving like I was still capable which – it must've been clear – I wasn't. I remember one of the older actors taking me aside, advising me to sort myself out, even giving me some doctor friend's number. I swore I'd call then went out and swallowed everything I could get my hands on. But no one sacked me or said You're fucking up so I just kept running and running until it all came running back.

How do you mean?

Literally, I was running across the soundstage floor and I couldn't get my breath. The doctor took one look then called an ambulance. When it arrived I was able to walk to it – fingers tingling but   nothing bad. We were almost at the hospital, they said, when my mouth turned blue and I collapsed   and died. And, if I hadn't been there, I would've stayed that way too. I don't remember any of that, or for ages afterwards. Only black and void for days. Then lights. Noises. Shaking awake. Her, crying, beside the bed. Some doctor saying You've had a cardiac arrest, you're lucky to be alive. I remember saying But I'm only twenty-two. And he said I know, it's because of what you've been at.

I was in hospital for a while – I'd been in a coma a week – and there's nothing like being checked for brain damage to make you realise you've had a lucky escape. The worst part though was dealing with her. It was terrible. All she did was cry and the way she looked at me I   I think I'd almost prefer to have died than face that look. The complete disappointment. The being so crushed. Knowing I'd done that to her. Four months pregnant and it was   it was   I was so ashamed. I don't know what else to say. I can't really think about it even now anyway   anyway

A few weeks later she told me my mother was dead. She'd hunted down a home address. The stepfather told her. I said I didn't care but what I really thought was Now I'm done for. My head was so fucked up. I didn't know how to deal with it and started convincing myself not to sleep, in case she'd come for me. That I could never sleep again and I'd lie at night picking skin off my leg in an effort to stay awake. In the end they caught me – blood all over the sheets. But soon as they bandaged me up I started somewhere else.

How did she die? Supposedly cancer, he says But I thought then, and still do, that she starved herself to death. It would have been so like her – martyrdom as revenge. Not that it matters either way. He lights a cigarette and I don't know if I should agree. Instead I prod into an easier silence And what happened with the film?

I got fired. No surprises there. After leaving hospital all I was fit for was the sofa. She kept crying What will we do? We're going to have a baby in June. I listened patiently and said lots of useful things about borrowing cash until I was back on my feet and within a week I was shooting up.

Jesus! I say. I know, he agrees You alright hearing this? When I nod, he goes on Well, I went to see this mate. Just to get out, you understand. She could trust me, I said and it didn't matter that I could hardly walk because five minutes on his couch he was tying me off. And it was new to me, the needle. I'd smoked it a few times in the past but mostly stayed away. Not so particular now though! The anxiety was killing me. I told myself once would calm me down, that I'd go home after, change my life then and no one would ever know. My mate agreed. Of course he did – he was already going in between his toes.

Some friend! I say. Yeah but   it was what I wanted, he shrugs Whenever you fancy going into the dark someone will always turn out the light but it wasn't long before she cottoned on to it – aided by the disappearance of Grandma's wedding ring. She didn't make a scene that last time, just said she'd had enough. That the baby deserved a better father than a junkie like me and I didn't argue because I fucking agreed. The next morning hers came to collect her things and made the most of his chance to call me Worthless Scum, to my face while I floundered about clutching one of her shoes begging her not to leave. Amazingly, she still did.

So I moved into my mate's Holloway squat and   I was relieved. I was rid of the last thing that held me to life. The well of self-pity opened its arms and I was ready to be done. Stopped going for check-ups and any pretence of taking any care of myself. Sometimes I'd lie on the floor with my hand on my chest waiting to feel my heart go wrong. Willing it to. I still don't know why it didn't, with all that junk riding round in my veins. Then one day while I was – doubtless – pondering the mysteries of life, my mate appeared with his girlfriend, saying Alright

Little Boy Blue? When I said What? That's what you're called, she laughed For the colour your lips go when you're on the nod like you're OD'ing, but you're not are you? It's just your heart is fucked! And the way she said it gave me such a fright. I could see exactly what I must look like and I understood why that was. I think it was the first time I had or, at least, believed it was true. That I'd already died, could again, more easily than anyone else in the room. That I'd died and it wasn't a game. The two of them laughing but I felt like someone was pulling off the top of my head. Sunlight went in for the first time in years and the big surprise was realising I wasn't ready to be done. So what the fuck am I doing here? I thought and walked out of the room.

On the street I remembered a doctor saying walking could help with staying clean so I began to but not anywhere or to anyone. Which was fine for a while but meant when things started going wrong there was no one around to notice. Like seeing my younger self in flashes, actually on the street. That boy, looking beat to shit. After a couple of hours God began to explain. Remember this? Yourself? No? Can't see? Prise back those hoardings. Or empty those bins. Or wander around talking loudly about Sheffield. Or kick in that car window. Now escape. Then go drink tea in some greasy spoon while suspecting you're not quite right. In the end I went three nights without sleep going increasingly off my head. The comfort though, of that voice. To not just be me by myself walking barefoot through Archway, raving away at the boy I'd been. It was almost alright I had once been him but then God pushed at being him again and   not even being completely deranged could persuade me of the wisdom of that. But God insisted so I tried to understand. By that stage I really wasn't very well at all.

Starving from the puking but I climbed onto the roof of a dere-lict house – somewhere on St John's Way I think – and stood there trying to know what I should do. Up there. Close to God, I'd be sure, very sure, of whatever he said next. But I was also getting tired. Soaked. I started to think What the fuck has this all been for? This fucking awful life? Why didn't you let me die in peace on the floor? Or die in the ambulance? Or so many deserving times before? What is it anyway you've bothered to save? All these bits that can never be remade. Can you ever make a dead person visible again? Force all the pieces back to one? Do I even care? I asked God. I begged him to say but God went very silent then. And after so much noise, I couldn't man-age that so I decided on an Act of Faith. Divinely un-ignorable. Great. More than enough to make God respond. So – with a flair for the dramatic – I waited for dawn, then walked down the slates. Took a long look out on the city that had saved me before. The trees and cars parked up on the kerb and lamps switching off all down the road. I said to God Here we go. And then stepped off the roof.

Jesus! I say You could have died. Should have, he says So when I opened my eyes in the hospital I was euphoric, what were the chances of that? Brain still in my skull. Spinal cord still intact. Quite a few other breaks but my heart hadn't stopped. Even the doctors thought it was miraculous. For me, my survival was proof and at first that kept my spirits up – manoeuvring the heavens to point directly at me. But I wasn't that euphoric after a couple of weeks of lying plastered to the eyeballs. I realised God didn't exist and I was just another raving lunatic so I just let myself be that. It was easier than I thought. Then all that panic the drugs had held in check started unravelling all over the place. I just remember being constantly afraid and having panic attacks and hallucinations which meant by June – when the baby arrived – I was up in Friern Barnet strapped to a bed.

What's that? A psychiatric hospital, he says But I was all worn out anyway so I was glad of the rest.

When they contacted her, she didn't want to know and because I didn't have anyone else I was mostly alone. Then a week or so after the baby was born there was a letter from her mother wishing to inform me I had a daughter and should have the decency to stay away. That kind of brought me round, reminded me to be ashamed, reminded me I was lonely and – once they let me – I called. Who do you think you are? she said You clearly don't understand, I wish you were dead, that you had died, so I'd never have to tell my daughter what you're like or the awful things you've done. And before I could even start to apologise she slammed the receiver down. After that I just sat staring at the wall, wishing I could get high, then realising it wasn't that, it was also wishing I had died. But I was already beyond doing anything like that. Instead I thought If I stay where I am, and keep very still for the rest of my life, maybe everything will be fine. So that's what I did. Wouldn't talk. Wouldn't eat. Lost more weight than I could afford to and became filled with the hope I'd stop waking up. And it should have ended there really, with a quiet starve to the death.

Why didn't it? I ask, wrestling with how passive his face has become now. A visitor, he says Which was wondrous in itself. I mean, any mates I had were in much the same state. Then out of the blue there was this director I'd worked with in my final year. Big Scottish guy in his fifties. I'd liked working with him but he never let me get away with a thing. I thought he thought I was a tosser really but, one afternoon, there he was. I assumed it was for someone else so I slid down my chair and covered my face. But when he spoke to the nurse, she pointed me out so, as he approached, I slid further again. My God, is that really you? he said What the fuck have you done to yourself? And suddenly there were tears rolling down his face and   that he wasn't the crying type made me realise how far gone I must be. Anyway. Once he'd blown his nose we got a cup of tea. He said he'd seen in the paper about the film and tracked me down through a lad in my year. I think he could tell I was on the edge so he didn't press and spent the hour talking about his work instead. When he got up to go he   put his arms round me and   it'd been so long since anyone had touched me like that   I started to get upset. He didn't make a thing out of it though, just patted my back and said You're doing alright, I'll be in again.

And he was good as his word, came back three times a week. Brought me newspapers. Books. Sweets. Started telling me about shows he'd seen, what was going on in the world and, honestly, to have the company was great. I began looking for-ward to his visits and they began thawing me out.

Then one day he said he'd seen my ex. My daughter too. How beautiful she was. How much he thought she looked like me. I wasn't really able for it but suddenly she stopped existing in the abstract. I still couldn't think of myself as someone's Dad – the word itself just made no impact – but I began to wonder what she was like. Soon I was thinking about her all the time. He was a cunning bastard really. Scheherazaded me back to life. And by the time he offered me a room in his house, I was keen enough for out.

After a little wrangling I was released into his care and his amazing house up in St John's Wood. Loveliest place I've ever lived. Packed to the ceiling with interesting paintings and books. But that first month he spent every day trying to keep me clean because, on leaving Friern, that's all I was interested in. I gave him a pretty terrible time. Ate the contents of the medicine cabinet on the first day out. Found the drink on the next. Eventually he said Look, I'm not willing to spend my whole life at this so I'm going to tell you something – and not to make you feel like shit – but NO ONE is going to hire you again after what you did. You're twenty-three now so think about what that means. Either you go back to frying your brains, finish off what's left of your health, waste your talent, fuck your daughter up more than you already have – because even if she's reared to think you're a cunt, once you're dead, that's in stone. Or you can stay here and I'll pay for a shrink. In six months' time – IF you're still clean – when I direct The Seagull in Manchester I'll cast you as Konstantin. If you're not though, I won't, I promise you that. And believe me, if you don't get this job – and do it fucking well – you'll never work anywhere again. Then you can drink as much cough syrup as you like because no one – including me – will give a damn. What happens next is up to you. What do you want that to be?

So I went to the psychiatrist. And I stayed clean. Six months later he cast me as Konstantin and that gave me some life back again.

Getting up, he stretches. I'm going for a slash, and – with a kiss to the top of my head – Sorry, it's turned into an epic night. I'm not, I say, wanting to touch him but knowing to wait. Instead go rummage in my bag.

When he comes back, he offers More wine? Drains the bottle between. It's after midnight, I say Happy Birthday now!

Thirty-nine years fucked, he laughs. But takes the present and kisses my hand. Sits to open it beside. This is great, he says Will you put it on? So I do, explaining I knew you had their first one but this one has the same name so I wasn't sure but then I asked and I love it, he says Thank you, you shouldn't have. Then swings his legs back on the bed. As the music starts, lights up, exhales. I drop the cover in between and ask When did you first see your daughter then?

About five months later, just before rehearsals began. He spoke to my ex – I couldn't even get her on the phone – and after much persuasion she agreed to an hour once a month.

That first Sunday her father dropped her off, I hid, watching her come up the path. She looked different – still beautiful, elegant but   all the spark was gone and   whose fault was that? I almost went out the back door but A child needs a father, he said For better or worse you're what she has so go open the door, and smile. When I did my ex wouldn't look at me. Instead passed him the carry-cot with the baby, saying Tell him that's his and I don't want to see his face. He just placed it on the sitting-room table, then took her off to the kitchen for tea.

So I stood there, thinking I was about to have another cardiac arrest. I didn't know what to do with a child. I could hardly look at her, never mind take her up. Mercifully she was asleep though so I inched the blanket back but   she started to wake up and, suddenly, there were these big eyes wandering over me and   I just   froze. She was   real and   right there. Not just an idea or knowing she existed somewhere. But right in front of me and   I   just stood there   trying not to leave.

After about fifteen minutes, he came in to check. Come on pick her up, he said You have to hold her. She's your little girl. And I couldn't. But I touched her   on the hand. The little fingers went round mine and   luckily then she closed her eyes and went back to sleep.

Fifteen minutes later again he said For fuck's sake, pick her up. I just looked at him and said I can't   I'm scared. So he sat me on the sofa and put her into my arms. We just looked at each other, me and her, and I can't describe it, the feeling   I just started to cry   it was   awful   and wonderful   having her there on my lap and the smell of her   I just knew she was mine. That a little part of me had escaped into the good world at last and was part of her. Part of her life. You know, until that day, I still thought I'd find an excuse to use again. I missed it   and   never really believed I might manage without but suddenly   I understood why it was right I'd gotten clean. And nothing as grandiose as all that fucking act of faith roof-diving. Just   that I had to be her father – whatever that was – and take care of her. And I wanted that, for her but   even more for me. To be a man who would. So sitting there, with her on my knee, I finally began to be a person again.

That's the way I remember most of the visits now. In that big cold white room with this tiny girl. And I was terrified of her but it was as if she knew. She never did anything to scare me. She hardly made a sound. Sometimes I'd hear her scream-ing like the devil all the way up to the house and I'd start to panic but   once I'd wiped her face off she'd just sit looking up at me, hiccuping a bit. Sometimes she'd pull my hair or have a go at my specs. Once she was walking   well   that was some-thing else but   after such a long time of feeling nothing, and trying to keep it that way, it was overwhelming but that feeling for her   love for her accepted none of that. I think I cried sol-idly through the first six visits. And once those visits started, I couldn't get enough. When I'd learned to play with her, I'd

have to keep tickling her just to have more of her laugh. I'd
never heard anyone so happy before. But if she cried, I'd hear
her mother shouting What's he doing to her? Go in and see!
And he'd come in to ask if we were alright? Or put his arms
around us and whisper It's fine, she's just a little wound up,
then go reassure her but I'd sit there, getting scared again. I
was afraid she'd think I was doing something – you know what
I mean. But over the months she calmed down too, would hand
her to me herself. Taught me how to change and feed her. Tell
me things she liked. Then an hour became two. Became twice a
month. Then every week. Finishing up at all of most weekends.

Did you ever think of getting back together with her?

God no, that ship had well and truly sailed. Even to have
asked would have been an insult. I suppose, as things improved
between us, I'd occasionally wonder what it would've been like,
the two of us together bringing her up. Being a family. But I
also knew what had happened came from so far off it could
hardly have ended any other way. I tried to talk to her about it
once, to apologise. She just said I'll never forgive you, accept
it and we can be polite. So I respected that and concentrated
on trying to prove I was reliable now. She didn't think so, how
could she? Once you've kicked all the trust out of somebody
you can't ever get that back. She wouldn't even take money at
first, although he won her round eventually. I don't know what
I'd have done without him. I'd never have managed those early
days by myself.

And why did he help you so much? Hmmm, he says I knew
you'd ask that. Pity, initially, didn't want me to waste my life.
Over time it became more complicated. Of course it did.

So, maybe three months after he'd taken me in – before I met my daughter – we were eating dinner in the kitchen. Just talking about this and that when he suddenly said Listen, I'm out of practice so I'm just going to come straight out with it. I love you living here, it's been great, and I think I'm in love with you. I just stared. Don't look so scared, he said If it's not for you, I never mentioned it and we'll carry on as before. I didn't know what to say   or what I felt – about anything, never mind about that – but   I was grateful for all he'd done. I wanted to give him something he'd want and I had nothing but myself. So I kissed him and   it felt kind of right. He asked if I was sure. I said I was, so   he took me to bed.

It was the first time I'd had sex since I'd been sick. Probably the first time I'd ever had it without being wasted and   being touched like that   by someone who mattered to me   even if I wasn't   it wasn't easy and   I got a bit freaked out. But he was good to me in it   helped me relax until I was able to let myself. And it was nice. And the comfort of having someone there in the dark really couldn't be overestimated then.

We were together after that. He moved me into his room. It was a relationship, of sorts. He hadn't been in one for years so maybe I helped shake off the dust. But we liked spending time together. Enjoyed lots of things the same. He was pretty ferocious and I learned a lot from him. For me it wasn't love but it was warmth and affection. And all that sexual part of me was kind of dead anyway. I mean the sensation was there. The urge – at times overwhelmingly. But it didn't really connect to anything, hardly even myself. I could have slept with anyone and it would have been the same. I mean I enjoyed being with him, never had trouble getting turned on – nowhere near the way I would with a woman – but there was more than enough companionship to make up for that. Or so I thought.

And then came The Seagull. Lot of pressure about that. Being the director's younger boyfriend didn't help but once everyone realised I wasn't just, it was fine. Arkadina was already a big theatre star so most of us younger ones were nervous about working with her. End of the first read-through though, she handed me what was left of the fig rolls and said All you need is to gain a few pounds. After that she took me under her wing – I think he'd told her the story so she'd decided to look out for me. Taught me everything I know about behaving professionally and she was very unselfish work-wise too. Any little thing I couldn't crack she'd skip lunch or stay late until I was happy. Never treated me like the beginner I was or as though I was wasting her time. And we got fond of each other. She had a teenage daughter at home so she was always fussing over me, even then. You know, weird ointments when I had a bad chest. Helping me sort out a suit for the first night. And had me up for tea in her dressing room after the show every night so I'd unwind from it soberly. But being part of that company, and getting to work, was a life-saver. At last I was doing something I was good at. And I couldn't have had better casting than Konstantin. All that lostness and suffocation. I could practically nail every bit of him onto myself. Even down to the mother who was incapable of it – although he was parched where I was drowned. When we were rehearsing she'd often ask about mine – and quickly realised something there had gone very awry – but that relationship still informed the internal dynamic. And getting to be this boy every night, who becomes so destroyed by life, was very good for me, because I'd gone to that same brink but survived. Now here I was, working, hitting my stride, starting to make a life with my little girl in it too. Konstantin and I were blood-related but there was just enough distance between to let me properly give in to the part. Afterwards I'd be exhausted but feel so alive. It was a pretty extraordinary time.

It was a big success too. Transferred to the West End. Career-wise he'd needed that, so he was over the moon. Of course I needed it too. And once we were back in London he took me around town, introduced me to lots of useful people, made sure they knew I was now dependable. And we hobbled along in our sort-of relationship. Happy enough but

I was up in her dressing room after a show. We'd all been celebrating because she'd won some award. Everyone had had a few, except me – I didn't those first couple of years. As usual though, I was last to leave. Leant down for the goodbye peck on her cheek but – for reasons best known to herself – she took hold of me and kissed me on the mouth and. Fuck. My whole body ticced. Suddenly I was kissing her like she was everything I'd missed. Like I'd been starving for her. The taste of   Just the thought of her breasts. So this is how you made your daughter! she said You don't really like boys, do you? I tried to protest but   I couldn't even stop touching her face. Let's find out then, shall we? she said and   we didn't make it as far as the settee.

It was a Damascene moment that but I didn't want it to be and afterwards I was consumed with guilt. I mean, the fucking ingratitude. I went straight home intending to confess. Halfway there I remembered he loved me and I'd never leave, no matter what, so telling was only unburdening myself. Just live with it, I thought And don't do it again. Not bad advice really. For a while it even worked. I avoided her and wouldn't when she'd ask me up. Told myself it was unnatural to be with a woman in her forties! I couldn't stop thinking about her though, how it felt. Every time she touched me on stage I'd get a jolt. Luckily that works quite well for Konstantin, although she knew too and took her revenge – sitting way too close for the bandaging scene, lingering on kisses that little too long. Eventually the stress started fucking me up. I just wanted her so badly it made my teeth hurt. So one night, at the curtain call, I said in her ear I don't like boys. She said Follow me. Which I did. Back to her dressing room. Waited until she'd turned the key and   we went for each other then. She kept saying that she loved me and must've completely lost her head. I'm pretty sure I said it too because in that moment, I did. I was so fucking desperate for her. And, apparently, for another mistake.

Even in the midst of it the irony wasn't completely lost – normal Konstantins bang Ninas and it was Arkadina I wanted. But it was easy for us to get away with – we'd been working together so long and everyone knew we were close. I didn't even have to lie to him much. When I'd get in he'd always ask how she was and   she was pretty insatiable. I was too I suppose. I just wanted her all the time, and that she let me lead helped me feel I was no one's by right any more. And maybe because she was older – or maybe because of her child – it was important I be a man in that room, not a little boy.

The whole affair became incredibly intense and, in a lot of ways, it was great but I didn't feel very good about the lying and started getting down about it. Started hating myself for doing it and her, for tempting me. To make it worse he worried about me getting depressed and kept encouraging me to do whatever might help, but he must have had some inkling because we stopped having sex.

Finally I couldn't any more and told her we were done. She

took it much worse than I'd expected because, despite all the I love you's, I never thought she actually did. I mean, she was twenty years married. I assumed I was a fling. But when I said It's over, she said It's not. I love and I won't let you go. Of course hearing that I completely lost my rag. We had an almighty row. Traded lots of vicious insults. It got all melodramatic. She slapped me in the face and I stormed off. But in bed with him that night I was relieved and we had sex for the first time in weeks.

The following day was a Sunday so I went for the papers while he stayed in bed. When I came back though he was stood in the hall. When I asked what was the matter, he said Guess who's just called? and I fucking knew. She'd told him everything. I thought I was going to be sick. She'd said, most particularly, not to kid himself I was anything but straight. I started to apologise, got really upset. He, though, was very calm. Listen, he said I'm a romantic so I know you don't love me the way I love you. I'd hoped, in time, but you're not going to and a gratitude fuck's only good for so much, so let's just part ways now. I couldn't conceive of it. Couldn't imagine life without him. I tried to persuade him it wasn't like that, she was a mistake I wouldn't repeat but he said The problem is I think she's right. I don't think you really like men either, do you? Be honest with me. And then I couldn't lie. I did care about him, loved him even, and he knew that, just not the right way. Not enough. He deserved better than what I could offer – certainly better than what I'd done. So I went upstairs and packed up my things.

When I left he said he didn't want to see me again. The Seagull was winding down so that wasn't a problem. But I didn't know what to do. So I sat a while in a greasy spoon then thought Fuck this! And I took a bus to Hampstead – right to the wasp's nest. Soon as she opened the door, I said I'm about to do to you what you've just done to me, unless you fancy putting me up for a couple of weeks? With her husband and their fifteen-year-old daughter indoors, she really couldn't make a fuss. So that's where I stayed, in her spare room, for the two weeks left to the end of the run. Her husband was no fool. He knew. The first night I overheard her swearing I was a rampant homosexual so he should stop being paranoid – oh how I fucking laughed at that! And I didn't care how awkward it was. He and I kept it polite but her daughter got a crush. Used to follow me around, reading me her poems, asking me up to her room to listen to records. I always made my excuses but her irate mama repeatedly warned me off. That was never my thing though so she needn't have bothered. Besides which, she spent most weekday afternoons fucking me all over her sitting-room floor – in the noble spirit of Let's see the run out – so who'd have kept up with that?

Anyway, the guy playing Trigorin was leaving his room and it was pretty cheap. I kind of dreaded being alone but, at least, I was getting work. The loss of desperation was standing me in good stead and almost everything I went up for now, I got. So the week The Seagull closed I moved out of hers and   I moved in here.

Funnily enough, things immediately improved with my ex – she and our daughter were in her parents' Chelsea flat – and she began letting me have her overnight, would even drop her off at the theatre if she was going out. And I'd be so excited all day. Wanted everyone to see her. Loved getting to say This is my daughter. This is my little girl. If I wasn't going to be off in time I'd beg some poor understudy or baby-mad wardrobe girl to babysit until I was. And it was amazing to have her there in the best part of my life, rubbing greasepaint off my cheek, saying Daddy your face smells strange! Well worth the fortune spent on thank-you flowers and boxes of Milk Tray. I'd just sit her on the dressing table while I got changed, then tuck her up under my arm and get the bus back here.

Those early months though I was often scared of having her here by myself. I did get used to it and it got easier in time but those first nights   were hard.

Why?

My mother, he says The fear she was in me and would come out in ways I didn't notice. So I kept a strict check on myself. Never lost my temper. Never said a cross word – even when she was driving me mad – but it was the overnights took a lot to get right. I just wanted to be a normal dad but the first time she slept over I was paralysed. She must've been nearly two by then. I remember getting her ready for bed. The feeding and washing and dressing was alright. Story. Turned out the light and then   she wouldn't go to sleep. Kept wanting me to get in with her and I didn't know what to do, couldn't cope with it. I sat up in that chair the whole night, staring out that window, not looking at her.

Why?

In case

In case of what?

I'd get turned on

You really thought you might?

I don't know

my mother did.

When my mother looked at me she felt like that   so

                        was that because of her or because of me?
Back then   I wasn't sure.

All I knew was if I did I'd call my ex and never let myself see
her again and   I really didn't want that.

In the end it was time that sorted it. And tricks. Reading
until she fell asleep in my lap, then I'd put her down and get my
sleeping bag and then that was fine. I still remember looking
up at her little foot hanging over the bed and feeling so overcome, so filled with love. And that helped, and her being so
innocent. You know, sitting here, hearing her sing to herself,
I'd think How could you hit a child that size until they bled?
Or tear out handfuls of their hair? Or let them starve? It was
the first time I realised I couldn't have caused that, or in any
realistic way deserved it and that, actually, my mother had been
completely fucking mad.

But another problem was the affection, her expecting it of
me. She was always wanting a hug or something. It's not that
I minded the touching and I was fine with functional things.
It was just a total lack of instinct. She'd be reaching for me
and I'd just stand there. I could see she needed it though, so I
had to teach myself to. And I did. I was awkward at first but
I got the hang and before long liked nothing more than being
hugged to within an inch of my life. Picking her up. Kissing
her freckly cheeks. Eventually not even thinking first. Then
one night she had a nightmare, lying here. She was crying and
wanting me in the bed and I was freaking out when I suddenly

thought You fucking idiot. You're the adult here, be it, enough of your nonsense now. So I got in beside her and held her until she went back to sleep and that was the end of worrying about those things. I suppose the desire to protect her helped. Being very aware of my own inadequacy as well. I'd often watch other parents with theirs in the street and when I'd see them do something that'd taken me ages to work out, I'd get such a lift. Stupid things really. Obvious, perhaps. Asking instead of just in with a slap. Knowing they have their own likes and dislikes. Not shouting them down every time they open their mouth, or just wanting them to have fun. Simple, I think, if you've known some kindness yourself. Harder if you haven't.

She was so small and warm and full of chat and stuff she had to know. I love it. I loved it. I've still got tapes of her voice and I've probably never slept less in my life but   I didn't want to miss a moment of watching her unfold. When she starting talking I wasn't there. Her first steps though, were to me. It's ridiculous what you'll do to make your child smile but there's nothing I wouldn't have done for that hearty little laugh. Even at five a.m. getting my eyelids prised up with Daddy no more sleeping! I loved walking with her on my shoulders. Feeding ducks in Regent's Park – then having to quack all the way home. Swimming lengths with her strangling round my neck, screaming with excitement and knocking my glasses off. I remember taking her to Brighton, just to see the sea. It was a perfect day. Paddle. Fish and chips. She wanted to take the ocean home and wouldn't budge. So I ended up carrying a bucket of salt water back to London on the train. Stubborn as a mule she was and prone to a screech when she didn't get what she wanted. But I never once raised my hand. I'd sit her on that desk until I got Sorry Daddy, big kiss, then jumping off and back to playing birds. I was always trying to think what I'd show her next. I wanted to give her experiences because I'd no money for buying stuff. I wanted her to see the world and learn not to be scared like I'd been. To know she was the best person in it because she really was.

He smiles into the memory like warm inside. And what about the director? I ask Did you ever see him again? I did, he says Thank God!

Occasionally I'd get a note at the stage door to say he'd been in, hoping I was taking care of myself. That went on for well over a year. Then out of the blue he called and said It's time, come for Sunday lunch. So I went, nervously, but I needn't have been. He welcomed me at the door like the prodigal son and introduced the man he'd met – who you'll meet tomorrow night, and they were together for the rest of his life. We all had dinner. I stayed late, talking, catching up. Them about each other and work. Me too and my daughter, my health. That he was obviously happy relieved a lot of my guilt and that evening began the friendships that've been the closest of my life. They were   are   my family – what I imagine family should be. I still stay over there a lot. Often go to their house in France. And they were mad about my little girl, adopted her as a kind of grandchild, I suppose. Laughed off her yoghurt paintings on their Persian rugs. Made her doll houses from model boxes and bought the toys I couldn't afford back then. It certainly didn't do me any harm either, being around people in love.

Those were a few fine years for me and I was very well. Not up to anything destructive. Getting better at taking care of myself. If I struggled with the guilt towards my ex or felt low handing the baby back, I did nothing bad to shake it off. Just worked hard and tried to stay in London as much as I could. I saw a few girls on and off. Nothing serious because my attention was all for her but   I used to imagine I might meet someone one day, get married, have more kids. I liked the idea my life might be normal after all. Jesus, what a fucking idiot! I can't believe it now.

Why? I ask. Oh, he says, unwinding himself and closing his eyes.

One Sunday evening, when she was four, my ex came to pick her up. She said I have to talk to you, so we left her in here, asleep, and stepped into the hall, out there. You know I'm getting married, she said. I do, I agreed. The thing is he's Canadian and   we've decided to move back. Who? I said. All of us. And leave her with me? No, I'll be taking her with. But you can't take her to Canada, I said. Why not? she said Or don't you think you owe me this? You can't just take her away, I said I'm her father, I have rights as well. And whose side do you think a court would take? Do you really want it to get to that? No, I said But I won't let her go. You have to, she said You've already ruined my life once, you're not going to ruin hers as well. I said I'm not going to ruin anything ever again. If you don't let her go, you will, she said This is her chance for a normal life, to have a good man as a father, responsible, grown up. He'll take care of her as his own. He already has a house there and a good job lined up. But I'm her father, I said You can't change that. You're a broke ex-junkie actor who lives in a bedsit and can't keep his dick to himself. Do you think that's good for her? Does she deserve to live like that? But I love her, I said. So choose what's right − for her instead of yourself − because what do you think your love will be worth when she's stuck on some north London council estate? We'll give her a good education, a stable home, brothers and sisters, ballet classes, whatever she wants or would you prefer her to grow up to be poor and alone? And like you? Do you want her to have your life? Is that really what you want? Is that the best you imagine for her? Don't you want better for your daughter? And then I knew she had me. I had nothing to say. Nothing to offer in place of those things. Nothing except my broken-down self and how could that ever be enough? I just looked at her and   she knew she'd won. In the end it took so little but   she had it all. Alright, I said What's going to happen now?

So she got out the papers and made promises. You'll see her often, she said Every summer for at least a month. I'll send our number once we're settled and I'll make sure she calls. You can visit too. I'll write, of course. But I was so in shock I kept saying I can't. I can't. I can't let her go, until she lost her rag and started saying You'll upset her. Stop it. Is this how you want to say goodbye? What do you mean 'Goodbye'? I said. We have a morning flight. That's when I just started to beg Oh God don't do this, please don't take her away. But she couldn't be moved. My telling you at all, she said Shows more consideration than you ever did. And I could see she was enjoying it but I didn't care. All I could think of was how to persuade her. How will I send you money? I asked What about her stuff? Keep your money, she said And your junk. We don't want anything from you and stop deluding yourself that she's ever needed you in any way. What use are you? What use have you ever been? You, with your filthy, poisoned life and you know exactly what I mean. Just spare us both the pointless snivelling and go in and say your goodbyes. But I couldn't. I kept thinking This must be a game. Do it, she said Or I'll take her away and this'll be one more important moment you've fucked up in her life. So I signed the papers and I went inside to her. In here. Still asleep on the bed. Thumb in her mouth. All pink with sleep and   I had to wake her up to do it   say it   goodbye   and I did.

Eyes closed he asks Pass a cigarette? Lights and

She understood it was bad. She screamed for me all the way out. I can't really tell you any more about that night. It was the very worst moment of my life and after it, everything soft in me slowly turned to bone.

And, sure enough, even as I watch, all the light drains from him.

I often think if I'd been a few years further on there might have been enough of me to refuse and stand my ground. At the time though, the past still dragged me around, the shame at what I'd done. Feeling I could never get it right. Not knowing that keeping hold of my child wasn't just selfishness on my part. But I did what she wanted because I was ashamed and I've regretted it every day since.

So she took her away that night and   it was two years before she made contact. Two years of nothing and I mean nothing at all. I didn't know if my daughter was alive or dead. No one did, apparently. Her parents wouldn't say no matter how much I begged. I chased down everyone I could think of but no one knew   or would tell. I went to the police but I'd agreed to it so I'd only myself to blame. It was   a very bad time. I lost the run of myself, almost entirely. Somehow I didn't use again but drank myself back to the hospital instead and   a lot of other things started going on too.

What kind of things? I ask. Oh you know, he says Starving myself. Getting very fucking funny about what I'd put in my mouth. Like a test, or penance. I don't know what it was. I just remember it causing almost physical pain to eat. How about a cup of tea?

And making he wades through the lamplight, pale, thinking far inside himself. But once it's done, poured and passed, he sits back down again. What other things? The fucking around, he says. Like with your ex? No, not even a bit. Industrial this time. Will you tell me about it? Oh Jesus, he says   Okay.

Since The Seagull debacle I'd really worked on keeping my dick to myself – not that I'd ever miss a chance but I didn't chase around after it the way I had. I didn't want to be that man or for her to have a father like mine. Five minutes after losing her though I was bad as I'd ever been. Worse. Couldn't see the point of not being and, God knows, I should have but   you see what you want and all I could see was a life without my little girl in it. The fucking chasm in the centre of myself where she'd been and   I couldn't face it   not at all. So   off I went.

What does that mean? I ask, feeling the cold and his eyes doing nothing to dispel.

Remember that story I told you about the Lamb and Flag? Well, that happened three days afterwards – before I even knew that worse was on its way. I was beside myself. Had already had a bit to drink. I don't even know what I was doing in that shop, I hate fucking Covent Garden but   there was this little boy skidding about on the knees of his pants. I got talking to him, swapping sliding techniques. When his mother came along we fell into the chat. How old is he? They grow up so fast. Got any of your own? All the while she was giving me the eye. I could see she was drunk too so   it was easy to mouth Fancy a fuck? over the child's head because   I knew what the answer would be. So we went to the Ladies at the Lamb and Flag. Me, her and her son. And I fucked her against the toilet door with the little boy sat just beyond – drinking a Coke I'd bought. Jesus Christ. What was that? Even at the time I thought What the fuck are you doing? But of course   I didn't stop. I did not stop myself. Instead I really shagged her hard – so much it hurt and she was loud. After, getting her knickers back on she kept mumbling Oh fuck! Oh God! When I tried to help her she said Fuck off! I saw myself then, through all her disgust, really saw myself and knew this could go exactly like the drugs. You doing this again then, are you? I thought and, because I wanted to let myself off the hook, the answer was How many things have you had to learn to live without? Poor you. Poor you. You can't give up anything else. So Fuck you, I said to her and out I went. See you son, to hers and gave him a quid. Then I closed my eyes and I did what I wanted and I closed my eyes for years.

That was the real start of the sleeping around. Just picking women up at first, in bars, parks, at the shops. Women I worked with, met at parties. Friends' girlfriends. Wives. Daughters. Girls working on counters. Sat at desks. Handing out fliers in the street. Clap clinic doctor in an epic move. Cyclist who fell off her bike outside. Singer-songwriter who'd only do it with her guitar on the bed then lay around afterwards putting out fags on herself. Single mothers. Solicitors. Estate agents, Christ! You know, anyone who would. And if there was too much chasing I'd ask Yes or No love? I don't mind either way. I could always tell though. It was like a sixth fucking sense, like looking at a stranger but smelling myself. Did a second round with Arkadina too after walking into her on the street.

We were both polite, asked about each other's children. I lied. Then I phoned her later that night to say how much I still hated her and that I'd booked a room. More fool her, all she said was Where? So every Saturday for the next two years we went at it again. After the first time, she asked What's happened to you? I said Same time next week? There wasn't an inch of feeling left in my body and if there had been I'd have cut it out with a knife. So there was no talking or teasing. None of that wanting her there'd been. Just into the room. How are you? Fine. Fuck. Out again. I'd nothing to prove and there were no more games about who was in charge. When she pried I was cold, eventually she was cold in return. No matter how awful I was though, she kept showing up. But maybe she wouldn't if she'd known about all the other stuff   I mean   there was a lot of void to fill so   clubs of course and all of that. Places you could watch the worst fucking stuff but more often just depressing shit. Still had to look though, no matter how grim. Still had to fuck if I could manage it. There are places for everything, if you have time to look. Sometimes I'd appear at rehearsal so bruised I had to lie about fights – that familiarity breeding yet more contempt. Pornography helped a while until it started sexualising everything right back at the optic nerve. And the sex party bullshit. They were the worst. All the fucking away in packs. Women looking like they wanted to kill you, not knowing if they tried you'd probably only laugh. Half of them not even wanting to be there. Girls trying to show their dim boyfriends what nymphos they were. Couples giving their marriages a shot in the arm. Men who'd rather be with their families – if only they'd ever had one. Or men feeling guilty because they had but needed this all the same. And then the ones like me, circling all those ordinary people, working out how far down they would go. Taking advantage of their delusions. But never looking too close in case you caught sight of what lay behind. Jesus! The loneliness. And all the shit lies topped only by the shit lies I told. I'll ring you. I love you. No, I will meet you at Morden. I'm not late because for the fourth time this month I woke up not knowing where the fuck I was or what I did last night. I just did it until I couldn't feel, until it didn't even matter. Christ. People. What they'll let you do. But I did, and would have done anything, to keep that grief at the back.

And his face.

What else? I ask.

You know   don't make me say.

So I don't. Let the silence fill. Let his fingers curl. But the hair in his eyes won't hide it for long, or the blood working under his skin.

Paying, he says.

I knew that would be it. Same as I know I'd rather think of him as only lost instead of finding what he wanted inside some woman he bought.

First through some mate of a mate, he says I know this house, kind of thing and that didn't seem too bad because we were all getting what we wanted, weren't we? But there're only so many times you can watch somebody fake before realising you'd rather do without the charade. So then somewhere a bit grimmer. Eventually just off the street because down there you really are what you are. Don't care about teeth or clean underwear and because they're so much more fucked than you are you hardly smell the fear.

And when you did? I ask.

I tipped. And it never once stopped me. Junkies mostly – how fitting was that? I think I preferred it. I felt at home. No words, just up against the wall behind King's Cross. Or over the way in some derelict house, knee deep in shit and needles and dogs that died because their owners forgot to keep them alive and not caring either. Not giving a shit about the look or the smell or the state she was in or you were after. Just trying to clean up and calm down before going to the mate's who's invited you round – that you've kept waiting for over an hour because you just couldn't do without. I remember having dinner once, at this couple's house I knew. I was late because   I'd needed to and, on this occasion, I'd nearly got nicked – only just managed to talk my way out – and by the time I arrived I was pretty tightly wound. But I opened with lies about seeing a dog knocked down, then made all this effort to be funny and charming, to prove my innocence. Because you carry it just behind the eyes, so you always think people can see it there inside   and, whoever she was, she was with me all the while. The clammy body. The sore on her arm that wouldn't close. I had to keep saying Sorry, what? to the woman sat beside. I couldn't stop wondering if she could tell? The shame was so live I felt almost transparent. But the more I tuned into her, the more I got lulled by her talk. She was so gentle about the kids in her class and her Down's syndrome son that I caught myself thinking If I asked you   could you make me stop? I just wanted someone to, so badly. I must have looked a right state because she asked What's the matter? and I   didn't say. I think I went to throw up instead. After that evening though it started happening a lot, feeling suddenly desperate for help but so shamed by why I needed it. And I never did ask. I always forced it back down then took some other remedy home instead. Anyway   that's enough.

And for the first time tonight, he doesn't look ashamed. He just looks away.

Quiet we go, studying it. He stares at his own hand on the sheet. I watch his eyelashes blink to the twitch of his cheek. That's horrible, I say. I know, he agrees. Quiet again. Then he gets off the bed. Walks around like ridding himself. Lights another cigarette while someone from the night beyond comes lumping up the stairs. Smoke hid, we wait as they find their key, go in and switch on their TV but, once they're settled, he says If you want to leave I'll sort you out a room in a hotel. And I imagine myself falling asleep on some clean white bed, safe from this but Still? I ask. Still? he says. Prostitutes? No! Jesus! Not for years. It was a short-lived thing, a year in the worst and if I could take it back I would   here – he passes his cigarette but shuts his eyes to the light while I smoke. It scares me, I say. I know, I can see. It was a terrible way to behave and way to be in. But looking down on me now, he also looks young and frightened. Together at least in the fear of it. Hedging round the light. Can I touch you? he says then and I cannot think of anything I want more. So go put myself against him. Feel him all round me. I'm sorry, I'm so sorry, he says I can't imagine what it's like for you to hear these things. And what it's like is I've pushed my fingers right through his skin, caught hold of his ribs and must now fall with him. Down through the world while he grasps at everything. But we make the same rattling

208

sound I think. And so keep close together until we are calm. Can let go, finger by finger. Then sit back down. Person looking at person. Like shy and new again.

Did your friends know? The drinking, he says Not really the sex. They tried helping, feeding, sobering me up but he eventually said One day she'll be back and what use will you be to her dead? Your body can't take this drinking, love, knock it on the head. So I gave it up, for the next few years. Instead I tried to focus on work and   the other thing occupied me a great deal.

Then one day an envelope arrived for me at their house. Three photos and an address. No explanation or news of her but it was my first gasp of air in years. I nearly collapsed. It changed everything because now I knew she was still there, somewhere, and I would see her again and I didn't want her to know what I'd become. So I said to them I have to tell you something. Then I told them what I'd done. They both sat and listened. I kept nothing back. They were upset. Really upset. He yelled I was too old to be at that stupid shit and didn't I know there were consequences to that kind of carry-on? Once he'd calmed down though he said Well, this is what you've been but you don't have to be it any more, you know what you need to do next.

So I got myself back to the shrink. Threw out all the porn. Stopped answering calls from people I shouldn't. Had a good going over at the clap clinic. And cancelled the Saturday hotel.

She was probably the hardest to face. I was so broken open by getting those pictures I didn't know if I could handle a scene but   she was owed.

I was waiting when she came in. Usually it was the other way round. Soon as she saw me she said Is this the last time? When I nodded she came sat by me on the bed and took my hand. We sat for a bit. What happened? she said. I said I lost my little girl. My ex took her away two years ago and didn't tell me where until this week. Then I started to cry and she put my head on her knee. My poor boy, she said Why didn't you say? But I could only keep repeating that I was sorry. You know I love you, she said Despite how this has been, I've never stopped and, if you ask me I'll leave my husband, even now and we could start again. But I already knew how it would have to be for me so I said Don't do that. She stood up then saying Well, I'd better go home. Take care of yourself my love. She kissed me goodbye with more feeling than I deserved. Then she left. And I left. And that was the last semblance of a relationship I've had. Once she was gone that chapter closed and I didn't have sex again for two years.

Life without was difficult – all that energy and time. I didn't know what to do with myself so I went back to walking and I spent hours walking, all over London, every night. I liked it. I still do – the time to think and how it wears me out. I can't tell you how much better it was to be clean of all that, to feel sane again. I'll always be inclined to be promiscuous I suppose but I pretty much keep it under control. I've had a few lapses over the years but I usually manage to sort it out before it gets out of hand – which is why the video gets intermittently packed away, you know, things like that. Nowadays it's not so bad. Not a daily struggle at all.

And writing to my daughter helped. They never let me speak to her so that's how I kept contact. Every Sunday night. It was something to look forward to. Occasionally I'd get a note from her mother saying how she was. Then, at Christmas and her birthday two, three photographs. I'd study them for hours to work out how she'd changed so that I'd always know her, so she'd never seem strange and I'd send her passport pictures of me. A few years later her own letters began. Great scrawly things with crayon drawings on or paintings she'd made, telling me all about her school, her toys, her friends. At first only once or twice a year then more than that, then asking Did I have other little girls? About my job? Did I have a wife?

Didn't you go to see her? I ask. I tried to, he says Right away, right from the start.

I'd ask to visit or for her to come here but there was never a good time for it. Either her mother was pregnant and didn't need the stress or someone was recovering from whooping cough, chicken pox. There was always something and I soon realised there always would be. So the summer she turned eight, I just went ahead and bought a ticket. When I arrived in Vancouver I went straight to the house. Her mother answered the door and immediately slammed it. I just kept banging on it, shouting I'm not leaving until I see her. I'm her fucking father and this is not what we agreed. After about ten minutes, she showed me in. I kept looking to see if I could see her in the yard behind but got shown into the sitting room. I heard her called down and Jesus, the nerves. My chest. Then the door opened. She was ushered in and my ex said Two hours, no more.

And suddenly there I was again, trying not to cry. Just the sight of her. The first sight of her after all that time. She'd grown so tall. My solemn-eyed eight-year-old. New front teeth all uneven and so beautiful. I just wanted to grab hold of her but I knew not to touch by the way she stood there, watching me. Taking it all in. So I fished about in my bag until I was together enough to get out the presents I'd brought – some books and one of those Sylvanian animal things Hamleys swore all the little girls loved. Do you like them? I asked, holding them out. She nodded and took them and was very polite. They're from England, I said. She said Me too. I know that, I said I used to take care of you. She doesn't know me, I thought and my heart started to break but   then she just said it Are you my English Dad? I am, I said Any chance of a hug? And she did, came over, sat herself on my knee, wrapped her arms around and squeezed the life out of me, like she always had. I can't describe how it was, after those four years, to suddenly have her there in my arms. I just kept saying I loved her and missed her, and fucking crying of course. Eventually she said Dad, can I open these now? Oh right, I said Of course, and put her down. Then she got on with the serious business of ripping the boxes apart. Getting me to assemble the various structures. Soon enough, she was all talk. Her school. Her ballet class. Her dog. How she was going to camp and when did I think nail varnish was allowed? Would I like her to dance? Of course I would but I couldn't sing the tune right so that was no good and, Jesus Christ, that laugh! I kept inventing knock-knock jokes just to hear it again. But two hours doesn't last very long. Bang to the second her stepfather walked in and told her to say goodbye, then go upstairs and wash her hands. So she hugged me and off she went. I remember promising See you soon, as she went on up. Then standing there, with his son in his arms, he said You are never to come here again. My wife and I will not tolerate your being around our children. I only want to see her, I said I don't want to interfere. You made your choice, he said You have to live with it. No, I said I never chose this and I'm still her father, whatever you think. I'm her father, he said I'm the one she cries for at night. I'm the one who picks her up from school. I'm the one who buys her shoes and. Please, I said I'm not asking much. Her mother promised me and for years there was nothing. If you were me could you give up on your son? How dare you, he said We are not the same. I would never have put my child's mother through what you did and if you ever come here again we'll call the police. If you even phone this house there'll be no more letters, or anything else.

So I went home and relapsed over every woman I could. It was a bad one. Went on for months. Then I got someone pregnant and that snapped me back to myself pretty quick. She didn't want to have it. Just wanted me to help. Drive her there. Pick her up. Which I did. And I know she probably made the right choice – what other choice could she have made? – but I left that clinic knowing it was time to get hold of myself because I really didn't want to do that again. Which meant facing that my daughter was going to grow up without me and I was going to have to learn how to live without her.

I've had more than a few furious phone calls with my ex over the years. They always end with contact threatened or how she'll tell her The Stories. I couldn't bear for her to hear those and I can't lose her again so I've tried to be satisfied with what I have and   it's become easier with time. I write my letters and wait for hers. They've only become more frequent over the years. Twice a month without fail now. I love seeing them on the mat, even when they're hard to read. In her early teens she got so angry with me and wanted to know why I gave her up? Didn't I love her? Didn't I want her? Said she didn't care if my letters stopped. But I never stopped writing. Sometimes she'd ignore me for weeks then, out of the blue, reply and I'd be so relieved. She doesn't seem to be angry any more. I think we get on well. It's hard though, knowing how much to say about what happened between her mother and me. What's too much? How do I know when she's ready? I mostly just answer what

213

she asks. But this last while she's been asking about her grand-parents a lot and   I don't know about that. How could I tell her those things? And, really, why would I? Besides, I prefer hearing about her life. She wants to be an actress now. I don't think that's such a great idea but   anyway. When she's old enough she can do whatever she wants and I've enough money put by for her to be independent. She could go travelling. Buy a flat. Spend it on a PhD or dresses or whatever she'd like. It's de-pressing how money's turned out to be what I can most easily give but   I hope it will be useful and   that it won't be all. In the meantime I just stare at the photographs she sends – those same grey eyes looking out at me though she's almost grown up these days. They keep me going while I wait until she can choose for herself. I'm hopeful though. She always writes Dear Daddy or Dad, and that's what I've always signed. No one can take that away. That word is mine alone.

    And that's how it was for her and me until she phoned that day. Her mother didn't know, she said and I didn't recognise her voice. I thought it was you taking the piss, putting an accent on. No Dad it's really me, she said. I nearly dropped the phone. Just knowing she wanted to speak to me, that she knew I'd want to hear. I kept saying It's so lovely to hear your voice. But she was straight into When can I visit? Any day, I said. I'd book her a ticket and, whenever she was ready, just to say. I said I'd show her all London, that I couldn't wait. Me neither Dad, she said and it sounded so nice and   for me. She had to go but then she just slipped in I know why she doesn't let me see you Dad and I just want to tell you that it doesn't matter to me. I started say-ing What? But she'd already hung up. I can't tell you how long I held onto that receiver, just willing the portal to open again. Of course I couldn't have her here but when she's coming   I'll get a flat or   buy a house in case she wants   anyway   anyway   she's not coming yet. I was euphoric standing out there with her actual voice ringing in my ears. Soon as I came back in here though, that past started screaming in. All that feeling that had been put away for so long. The sheer desperation of the years after she was taken. I couldn't get it under control. I just wanted her to be coming here right away, fast forwarding into it then remembering she wasn't. Couldn't. For years yet. Go for a drink, I thought To settle yourself, and you know what happened after that. I should never have called. I should have known. I just didn't want to be alone. I could see myself telling you about her too, about how it had been and then I couldn't and it all got so fucked up instead. I'm sorry for that night, he says – resting his forehead to mine – And for everything. For taking so long to tell you so many things. It's just, that past is so unclean. So much of it lived without thinking I'd ever be different or survive long enough to want to be changed. I decided, years ago, not to inflict it on anyone again so I closed the door on the idea of being with someone and never thought about what it might mean or how I'd ever explain. And then you came and being with you's been like having a light shone into the back of my eye. All these months I've stumbling around half-blind and   I still don't know what to say. So whatever you want, to stay or go, I'll understand but   it's up to you now.

Then he sits down on the rug, looking up at me. Cigarette smoke rising, falling between. All this time gone by. The hours we've spent. Sleepy Song on the record player and his life run right through the room. And I am surprised I didn't know before. It's written all over him. All down his legs scars that must have been burns. I never asked but now I recognise them. Places discoloured that only show in the cold, where something hit him and hurt him long ago. Silvered nicks on his back that reflect the light. Were they cuts? And so many. I kneel down behind. Bless the place with my lips. His body all battle. Too thin, often sore. What he's done to himself and what he's had done. But this is the finish. The race is run. Lay my cheek on his shoulder and wrap my arms round. Just the soft of his breath then and weight of his life. We are long nights from the beginning. Come light years from the start. Now he waits, set for pain while I, it seems, hold the sword but I say All I want is you.

Really? Really. After everything you've heard? Even then. Are you sure? I'm sure. Then there's one last thing. No, no more, I say for we are in such fragile skin, so close to getting lost in the in-between. But out of darkness and into what's left of the night, he says I love you Eily and I've been wanting to tell you for nights, for weeks. I'm so in love with you I can't think of anything else. And those words shift through my body as he pulls me round. I love you too, I say What took you so long? Then I watch it shift through him. See him know I love him then. He smiles at me. I smile at him. And the fall that was coming has come here now. We welcome it. Leap down into it. Cannot wait to see how far.

Could I grow up in a night? Grow up in this day? Curled here with him on his small bed, in the cradle of our arms and wrap of our legs watching him deep in his deep dream, far the threat of what he's been while I lie here, in love. So much and sooner than I thought I'd be. Years off, I'd thought and not like this. But I have come into my kingdom where only pens and pencils were. Abrupt and all abrupt. No longer minnow in the darkness and the deep. Through the portholes and currents I've been. Going to the surface. Up into the sun. Touch my own throat.

His long arm. Shining like a body come fresh into the light. And she is in the centre of life. I am. I am her. Not unspun either, for what can it mean, more than how a life was lived? His breath gone peaceful in the tight and warm. Twin mine to his. Indifferent dreams, I hope. And list in their pooling through the dark, across books and wine glasses, over my bags, contenting us while across the world she lies, his girl, who is not me. Does she love him like I would if he were mine, that way? That other way I do not want? Tie up your long hair that the salt drops have wet. Being young you have not known the fool's triumph nor yet   nor yet love lost as soon as won. No. That's wrong. Only won here. Not lost at all. And dread? Won't any more. For bound to him is what's to bind and as for crying? For the wind.

Light falling all over, my legs ache awake. Kiss lips to his crepe lids and think Birthday cake! then cross his sleeping to do.

Outside this day is just as you'd want for the day when you are in love. Head up in clouds that aren't in the sky and clouds where my head should be now. In Sainsbury's I choose chocolate cake – Smarties and icing. Ridiculous perfect. Singing like a magpie all the way home, across the gutters, over the drains. But Where've you been? he says when I get in. To the shop, are you alright? I am I just   I thought you'd gone. Why would I? I say. Because because. I went to get you a birthday cake. Oh God, he says Sorry, and taking my face. It's alright. It's alright. And kiss him and we sit on the bed and I touch and   I really want to, he says But I don't think I can yet, do you mind if we leave it a while? It's fine, I say I'll make some tea. Shall we have your cake for breakfast? Yeah, that'd be lovely. Then he sits watching me and we are fine. We are fine, I think.

217

What do you want to do today then? I ask, over the cup. Don't know, he says What do you think? Well, maybe today's the day to lie on the Heath and drink cold beers and read books whose spines we will not spoil, remember? Good idea, he says Sandwiches as well.

So get the sandwiches at M&S. A few cold beers from the corner shop. In my bag, a book of his. The Anatomy of Melancholy. Are you fucking kidding? You'll be as old as me by the time you finish that and I only got it for research then barely read half. I like a challenge, I shrug. Yeah, I've noticed, he says and laughs and takes my hand.

Then we are revolting on the tube. Kiss all the way up to Belsize Park. Utmostly oblivious to ladies with their dog. Not really what you want to be in the proximity of, they loudly agree. Oh, but what you want to be at, I sigh. Him laughing Shhh you, hussy! and kissing me all the more.

Then lace we through backstreets down by the Royal Free. Holding hands. Being silly. Stopping to kiss, and touch, when others can't see. On into the parkland. Up Parliament Hill.

In the white wrenching view I ask How do you feel? Relieved, he says But I can't quite believe you're still here. I am though, I say. And even if I feel spaces opening between that neither seem to know how to fill, I know we will. I know I will once I've worked out the right distance again.

So on we go until we find a tree unoccupied by students busily out-clevering or pop stars playing pop stars or lonely people alone. He spreads his jacket on the roots and we lie on it. Kiss on it. Open our beers. Get out books. Do you ever see your brothers? From Sheffield? Sometimes, he says Mostly the younger one, John. The first time I saw him again, he just showed up at the door. I had Grace that night – so early eighties, probably. He stayed on my floor, drank a lot, got an ear-bashing from me for being drunk around her, then borrowed some money and disappeared. I think Gracie picked up a few choice words that weekend, which meant I got an ear-bashing from her mother about swearing. I didn't see him again for another five years when he just as suddenly reappeared. He'd been off to India, sorted himself out, become a psychotherapist – which made me laugh a bit – and he paid me back too. We get on pretty well now. I see him once or twice a year. We don't talk much about back then. I did once ask what happened, after I left. She went mental, he said but their father pulled her up pretty smart and I wasn't mentioned any more. When I asked if he was surprised I'd gone he said There were bite marks all down your arm, no one was surprised. He knew more than I'd realised about what had gone on as well, which means the other two must've had some idea also   maybe   who can say? He agrees with my theory though, that she starved herself to death. I doubt we'll ever know the truth but we both think there's something there. The other one, Peter, I don't know much. Lives in Sheffield with his second wife. Big Christian apparently. Found his faith when Jesus forgave him for gambling his house away. Last saw him at his father's funeral five or six years back, a real pious piece of work. Trying to convert me, complaining about John being gay. If he knew the fucking half of it he'd curl up and die of shame. Then he cracks open a beer, has a good long sup and stretches his lanky limbs out in the sun. And we roast a while, taking it on closed eyes. His at least. Mine are wide, tacking tales to his silhouette. His starved-feeling stomach breathing under my hand. Funny, after all my fancying, to find that I am loved and how much I love too. Come here. Sleepy kissed til there's leaves in my hair. Then mud-thumbed and grass-kneed

we find fits together but drowsy. Absolving. Estranging ourselves from the residue of last night's rendered hell. Asking
Tonight then? I trace his face Should I call him Mister? Just
Rafi, he says, snapping at my fingertips And you don't need
to worry, you don't have to impress, you're already the most
hoped-for woman in the world. Why's that then? They never
believed it when I said I was better off alone, kept telling me it
was time to take a chance and never believed when I said that
I was happy as I was. So humble pie for you tonight? True, he
laughs But oh it tastes so sweet.

And the day weights to dozing. I read as he sleeps, feeling as
though I got shook in the night and somehow forgot. It's not
me it all happened to   and yet. Now that I see how he wears
it I cannot forget or be back to before. This must be a getting
used to thing. Soon enough it'll probably lie down. For him
too. I know because here in the skin, where no strand seems
strange, this love insists upon itself. And we will be ourselves
again. It's only odd today. So watch the sun go right across the
sky, then nudge him. Wakey wakey, rise and shine, time to go
home and change.

What're you wearing? I ask back at his. This? he tugs. You
can't, it's filthy. Who cares, Raf won't be looking at me. Oh
don't, I say I'm so nervous already. Why? Because it's like meeting your dad. It's really not, he'd be chasing you round the table
in five minutes flat and I promise Rafi won't do that   the dad
was more David anyway. You miss him. I do. How long is he
dead? Two years. It happened pretty quick. Sore leg turned out
to be cancer of the pancreas but we were both with him at the
end. You know my dad died from that? I remember, it's a bad
way to go but his wasn't a bad death, if you know what I mean
and when I go   You're not though. No. How's your heart? It's

fine. Is it? Yes, I have a yearly check and   Eily   really   it's
okay. Promise me promise me. Hey love   hey   I promise, it's
fine   so what do you want me to wear? Have you a suit?
Mmmm, might have, he says. Well, I've never seen you in one,
will you wear it? Raf'll know I've lost my mind for sure but, for
you, anything. Okay then go get in the shower while I blow-dry
my hair.

I draw the line at a tie, he says buttoning his shirt and sitting to light a fag while I attempt make-up. Kneeling with my
hand mirror by the bed. Blue dress, old, but nicest I have. I
like having you here, he says Cluttering the place up with your
hairbrushes and that, all those little weird bottles and woman's
stuff. I roll my eyes. Fine, laugh, but it's nice watching you get
ready to go out for the night, with me, to my friend's, like any
couple might, anywhere in London on a Saturday night. I'm
just sitting here, watching you and   I can't believe my luck
– and his face goes full of feeling suddenly – I'm thirty-nine
today and, you know, I can't remember the last time I felt so
normal. That's you Eil, you've done that. You make me feel like
I'm a normal man with normal things going on and that's all
I've wanted, as far back as I can recall. I go sit by him then.
Kiss his crown, put my arms round his neck and be with him,
just for a bit, not for long. Until a clock somewhere downstairs
clangs time. Alright, he says putting his glasses on We should
be on our way.

Hand in hand we walk. Turning heads, I think. I'm so proud
to be with him. Look at us, he nods, into a shop window You're
so lovely and I clean up alright. And surveying ourselves now
we try to believe it. That we have come through that night, out
into these days. That we are in love and anyone can see, for isn't
it burning off us? Hey! Taxi! Come on Eily, get in.

Jesus, this is where he lives? Yeah, he gets the gate but I insist You go first, as the great door swings and whirl comes pouring through. Music. Booming Hello Hellos and that man from months ago, in knee-length shirt, grabbing hold and kissing him. Then back at arm's length Let me look at you! Tugging at his hair Rapunzel! and My God, a suit! Ah, he shrugs and Nice dress Raf, who laughs Especially for you, now introduce us. He steps aside and I   I am under eyes and suddenly palmed forward into yet more of his life Eily, this is Raf. Nice to meet you, I say, hand out but find myself crushed against exotic scents instead. Wonderful to meet you, darling girl, you're very welcome. Now come in! Come in! fussing my jacket off while I stare at the ceiling that closes miles above. And all the rest, just as he said. Books. Paintings. Beautiful universe that he is crossing into obliviously, already halfway down the hall saying Smells good Raf, and Where do you want this wine? In the fridge, champagne first, open it for me, would you? And the so much space takes him away, leaving me to finicket beneath my surveyal. Kindly meant though, I think. Glasses passed and Is it short for Eileen? No, I. I'm sorry, Irish names are It's alright, I say Everyone asks that, it's actually short for. Pop. Fuck! he says quick to the imprecise pour, laughing, licking it from his fingers. Clink it and Happy Birthday, Rafi says And to finally meeting you – then more quietly – David would've been so pleased. Well cheers, he says as I take his hand. Drink and hope it loosens my tongue. What's dinner? he asks, lighting up. Roast beef, just how you like – although really, why you English do is a mystery to me – and Eily you're a good influence, I see. Usually he arrives like he's been through the hedge. Well, there was some protesting, I say. Changed man Raf! Now if you can work on his smoking. No, there are limits, he laughs and amid it Rafi's eyes move over us and I feel seen as better than I can possibly be but then, maybe, he's only noticing that little hole in my dress. Lay the table, will you both? Dining room? But of course! Come on Eil, and I'm led in through beautiful rooms. Alright so far, love? I nod, but marvel at him at home in such realms and their photographs Look, it's you! Glass Menagerie, he says David directed, Rafi designed. And this? – him asleep on a crate, sword under his head. End of the tech, he says Henry V. And this one is David? Rafi, at the door, says It is. I put it down Sorry. No, no need, no need. Him – draping me – saying He'd have loved her, don't you think? Rafi pats my cheek I think he would. Where am I now? What is this world? I remember you from the National, Rafi continues He came back during that awful play. When I suggested a drink though he said he had a girl waiting. Oh, I said Unlucky for her. Not this one, he said. So, another long-lost sister? But no, apparently not. My goodness, I said Really? What's going on? I don't know, he said. But something is? Something, he said. I couldn't believe it. Would you really let yourself? I asked and he just smiled. That's why I came outside, to see if you were real. He kept warning me Not too close, like you were some exotic bird he didn't want to scare away. Sure enough though, there you were and now you're here, well well.

Off into the eating then. My manners, and Rafi's, are good but his   attentive though at every turn. Peas, love? Another yorkshire? More wine? while Rafi sporadically invokes David's view of this blessed night being long overdue. And I try to give smiles because they're all I have. Yet what remedy are they? Plain they both feel his loss but   happy tonight, happy too. And after eating Now, go open more wine and cut up that cheese, it's out on the counter, while I escort Eily into the sitting room.

It bleeds its description. Big and cold. Pasts slide by side as Rafi steers to a piano laid out with more photos in frames. Lots of him, with them, by himself. Some from productions. One with David, obviously ill, attempting to trap a last moment of normal but the smiles are too happy and the exhaustion plain. I have a few of those photos at home. Rafi offers another Ten years ago, France. Himself and David sat on a bench. Him, down front, smoking a cigarette. Younger and smiling but   not happy in himself. And this one I like, from later that same day. Him sat alone, cigarette again, apparently staring into the sun. So handsome, I say, then cringe. Rafi only laughs His blessing and curse. He has a good heart though. I'm sure you know that but   do you know about the nights he spent here? Well   I know he and David were   together. No no, I don't mean that. Sorry, I crucify. I meant, he smiles David was the saving kind, used to allow all sorts to stay here. God knows where he found them. It used to drive me crazy – although I must say I miss it now. But if it was   drugs or problems like that David would ask him to come over, whatever the time, even three a.m. I'd say He's rehearsing in the morning, but David still called and he always came. Sometimes spend hours talking them down. He's good at that. Very calm. Not afraid of what people might do to him. And I am surprised and not surprised to hear these things. So many worlds swim beneath his skin. I think David hoped it would help him forgive himself because that's all he really Ah now Raf, he interrupts Stop putting the weight of the world on her, I already have. Ignore his forgiveness spiel Eil, I'm fine as I am, and I get a quick kiss. Rafi raises his palms Not another word.

Sprung from then, we go into the late, drinking wine and

eating cheese – so much there'll be weird sleep. Talking about theatre. Talking about his script. His excitement detectable underneath the complaints of not knowing what he's at or how to write the end. And in their weft I lull, tracing his nails, lighting on every new lit bit of him until Time for bed, he yawns Alright to stay over Eil? Oh yes okay. Rafi kisses us Goodnight, once we've accompanied him to his door. Then I am led on up through this house in the dark.

At the very top, a room, white linen-laid. Bathroom through there, he points New toothbrushes under the sink. I've never stayed in a hotel but it must be like this. Little of everything. And brushing my teeth I watch him, in the mirror, undress. He folds his clothes. Hangs up his jacket and I know what I see is the routine of this room. Different, and who else has seen it I wonder? But before that thought has even moved, he says I don't think I've ever shared this room – maybe once, years ago – with anyone but Grace. Is it weird? No, nice, he says. And comes, stands behind. Kisses my neck. Then reaches over to start the brushing himself as I wander into the room. Undress. Get in the bed. Skylight above. Night and look into it. Black ways to heaven. He turns out the light and slides his long self in beside. It's a beautiful room, I say But it's like I don't know where we are. Somewhere else, he says, putting his mouth on mine. And. I lift to him. All of my body and inside the same. I love you. I love you. Play at just kissing until, soft, his fingers start to bring. Almost the whole way there but I want him. Tell him. And he is ready at last. So, in the quiet, don't we make love half the night – for surely now we must call it that? But make as though there's not enough time in the world to fill up with our pleasure and our delight. Bodies knowing the other's well from before but everything else running through now, making

225

it rare. Keeping quiet, for discretion, more. For hearing the secret of our secret thoughts falling between. And the desire that
follows, no matter what we do, cannot be spent up and does not
let go.

In the morning I wake much before. Still tired though, and
good way sore. But sit up, to look at him, lying there on his
front. Pale-skinned. Brown hair sleep-pressed forward. And his
life like a book lying open on my knee. I can reach down into
it, put my hand in it. Read everything. Even my own name is
written there now. But instead, stroke the hair back off his forehead. That's nice, he says Do it some more. For he loves a little
tenderness, I've come to know. And after a while he asks What
are you thinking about Eil? That you make me so happy. He
looks up. Smiles. That's a lovely thing to hear, and drapes an
arm over, itches his nose on me. You make me happy too. Then
closes his eyes and goes back to sleep.

Make tea! he says two hours later and once we're done. I
don't know this house, be a gentleman. Raf will be up, he's an
early bird, go on, I'll run a bath. So creep to the kitchen. Did
you sleep alright? Yes, and under the bathrobe feel so naked Yes
thank you you? Very well, he says smiling as if he knows what
we just did. Is he running a bath? Yes. So he's sent you for tea?
Yes. Then the tradition continues – between them the bath-
rooms were always full of dirty cups and covered in rings. His
voice gone all soft though for the man I'll never know, for David. And his smile at the memory barely covering his grief. You
must miss him, I say. Rafi touches his heart He's still very alive
in here for me but last night, I must say, has done me good. And
now that I know what love is, how is it possible to be left behind? I'd
like to show you something Eily, may I? and he passes a small
case. When I open, a photo. Seventies, I'd guess. Him. Mine.

Looking so young. Looking younger than me and Is that Grace he's holding? It is. And he seems just a boy really. Thin like he could snap. Skin barely covering the bones in his face and the vein in his forehead plain to see but the smile, for the child on his knee, is filled with happiness. He is completely absorbed. She is all there is in the world. Their long and small fingers curled round the other's. I can hardly bear to look because I know what's coming and that smile doesn't yet. You can see it, can't you? How much he loved her? I nod. That's important to know because it explains a great deal of what happened. And he watches to see if I know what that means. He told me, I say. Good, I'm glad he did but I imagine it was hard to hear. First time I heard it came as a shock, not something I expected of him but I understood even then – and better now – what that loss did to him inside. Eily, if you had seen him when she first took her   we didn't know for a week   he'd just been lying in that room in the dark and   he was so thin we thought he would die. It was terrible   those first years especially   watching him try to hide from the pain and being unable to help. David was so afraid. We begged him to move back here with us but   you know how he is   goes quiet and destroys himself. When those photos finally arrived he just broke apart, then told us. It was a very hard time, and thank God he survived, but all he's done these past twelve years is wait for her to come back. And maybe he'll always wait – I can't tell you how many times David said Why does that boy still not realise how lonely he is? I'm not lonely, he always says but he is the loneliest person I know and there's no need for it – but   if there's you, there's life and   I'm not upsetting you, am I? No no, I say. I only mean, Rafi explains on There's something very wonderful about him and despite everything that's happened, and all the years alone, nothing has ever changed that. But now, before I cause you to run out the door, here's your tea. Please tell Blanche DuBois we'll have breakfast in half an hour!

Wide high London. Finchley Road. Once we've kissed Rafi goodbye, walk to Swiss Cottage. He showed you, didn't he? The picture? He did. It's a beautiful picture. It breaks my heart so I keep it there and only look every couple of months, what did he say? That you're brilliant. Ah, gave you the sell. Not knowing I was already, and put my arm round his waist and think of his body, how it's so near. What you want to do today Eil? I don't know, cinema? We stand, look at the board. What do you think? I look up. Will I get that taxi? he says.

Then must remember we're still in one by Adelaide Road. Past the school, with Sunday rehearsers outside and on. Camden. His. Go get the door open Eil while I pay for this. And I'm jumping over dandelions all up his path. Opening up quick as I can. Him slamming the front door then behind me two stairs at a time – making me scream with thrill like a child. Making keys fumble. His mouth in my neck. Dress halfway to paradise and his hand in my God I could let him, almost, here in the hall. Come on key. Come on. Turn. Falling in. Falling over. Stumbling onto the rug. Me tugging his pants down and he my dress up and. Door kicked closed. Knickers pushed to the side he That's better, Christ! No, I say Stop. Stop to what? Doing it like this. Let's do it the way you once said you wouldn't, remember that? I remember, he says And do you remember the reason I gave? Because you didn't want to with a teenage girl. And how old are you now? Is that still how you see me? You know I don't. Well then, show me   or wouldn't you like to with me? Jesus, I want to do everything with you

Eily. So? Okay let me get you ready first.

He does it then, when he thinks I am. Just reaching into every next we can and everything he has to teach, I know I want to learn. So even though it hurts me, though it even makes me cry, I say Don't stop, when he asks if he should? For there's pleasure in hearing how much he has. More in the knowledge we transgress, and that he has done this himself only serves to heighten it. And after, he nurses me with his kisses and care. Wipes off my tears. Then whispers in through my hair I've never been closer to anyone than you and I've never loved anyone more.

Shower. Cheese on toast after that. Cups of tea. Marlboro Red. The still of his flat and both slightly scared at the weave we are utterly in. On the floor, in the shell of his arms, I shake. Alright love? I think so, did you like that? I did. And when you were me? Not as much. Does it always hurt? Not always and there're things you can do. Like what? Doesn't matter, that was a once-off. You mean Last Tango-ish? Oh God! he laughs That's all I'd need   how about a pint instead? Okay, I'll bring my lines along, you can be on the book.

So to the Prince Albert. There sit out in the sun. In an hour I've most of Juliet down. He says That RP's really coming along. But useless distracted by all this love I think of the mess we've both made of each other under our clothes. Scratches and bruises. Even the tenderness of mouths and look at him and Let's go home again.

And this night is a hot one. We must leave the windows wide. Fall asleep and stick with sweat and wake and laugh and Show me? What? Mmmmm. Have a think. How you do it by yourself. Kinky! Watch and. Give us a hand? So lazy! but do it with my tongue. Okay, no, that's going to make me come.

And I let him tonight, wherever he wants. Breasts or inside but Not my mouth. I know that Eil, I never would. I don't want to be that man to you. Do you miss it? No and I've news for you, a lot of women don't anyway. I know but I might've, if I'd got to choose. Well if it's any consolation, I never liked the taste much. Oh of course, what haven't you done? Until Friday night told anyone half of what I told you. God, you're good. That's what they say! Mouths elsewhere then and hands all ways, going further rounds until he complains I don't think I can again. So lie in together and kiss instead. Telling the stories of ourselves. Do you remember I cried the first night in this bed?   And you'd been so brassy back in the pub   Remember that girl after Christmas? I certainly do. She was because I'd spent that month just dying for you so I thought I'd run a mile instead. Aren't you lucky then I'm the forgiving kind! Yeah, you've made me a lucky man. Kiss for luck, and me. All this between and still more to say. I love you. I want you. I want you every day. Searching for some, any, words to explain but left following each other around this foreign place until we go under to a deeper sleep and let this day slip from what we live out into memory.

Morning.

I'm so relaxed but completely fucked, he says clicking and stretching. Too old now for all this sex? So much for empathy, he complains. It's the youth makes me callous. Yeah, among other things, now, go make us a tea. And he does look tired but so well to me. Lying there, smoking, watching me dress. Saying when I'm leaving Peace at last! I'm going to get at least five hours' sleep. And I sark – to evade any tears as I leave – Yeah well, lucky old you!

Then I am back in the world and must understand again how to cover my bones with my skin. Just London and traffic, with no night to hide in, and what I leave or bring with me from there. Walk. Know your way. See the here. Recall the place. Turn the corner. Make and make. But those histories related, settled like stun, open their eyes now. Unfurl their tongues. Begin to exhibit in different lights. They beat in me. Hammer at. Declaim Have your love but remember this All our houses are the same and there is no place now without us in. Off. Get off. What do I care what he did when I was two or four? Six. Eight. In that room you are the closest to life, the nearest you have ever been. He for you and you for him. Know you should know you might never feel this again and let it in. What it is. Let it be.

Well, who's been making the beast with two backs? What? You and, I'm guessing here, Montgomery Clift? What're you on about? So innocent, Flatmate laughs Yet carpet-burned to fuck. What? Elbows and knees. Oh   those   mind your business! Trying, he says Anyway, I changed the locks yesterday so here's your new key. We reckon, a month before they shut off everything. Might get to the end of the term, if we're lucky. Ta, I say But I'm staying at his. Well, if you need it, it's there.

    And on. My other life, first life swinging relentlessly back. So we'll start the Emotion Memory exercises next week. Everyone clear what these are about? Recreating a memory from the inside out. Every detail. Sound. Every smell. As though you were back there again. You never know what you'll find useful. It's a big one though. Sometimes people get upset so nothing that's happened less than two years ago, alright?

Can of soup and note on his desk. Sorry, got a call about a meeting last minute. Tell you all about it when I get in. Shouldn't be back too late. Love

And. Behind the soup. A photo, like I'm meant to look. Lots of black eyeliner. Tall and thin. On my birthday, written on it. Looking so pretty. Looking so like him. That's her then. I've seen. Behind that again, a birthday card. PS on the left saying Thanks for the programmes. It'll be an A for me now thanks to you. Signed with Hope you have a lovely day and don't feel too old now Dad, Grace x

In the dark I wait for him. Long for him to come home.

Still up? Thought you'd be fast asleep – such a late one last night, and kissing, he sniffs of wine and hums with good feeling. Tea? Yeah, good meeting? Great, he's pleased with the draft and making headway on the budget. Couple of grants came through too so   looks like we're on. Brilliant, I say I saw the photo. Oh right   she's beautiful, don't you think? She is. I just wanted you to see her   I didn't mean to freak you out. You didn't   do you love me? Of course I do, what's wrong? Nothing, she's just lucky to have you, is all. Yeah, I wouldn't say that. You're alive aren't you? Ah Eily, love. You'll always choose her, won't you? No, no more choosing for me. You will though, won't you? Hey, listen, all my fucking choosing is done. But I choose you, I say. Eily, he says Just miss him and come over here to me.

So time runs off with us. Days first. Then weeks. Happier, almost, than we know how to be in this overcrowded room. In the never quiet house. Gnawing Hula Hoops from fingertips. Sharing fags. Eating toast. And he helps me with Shakespeare for he knows his way right through. Now and then reads me bits of his script to check the dialogue's human. Some nights we walk to the end of legs and on the night bus home he shows me an older London, round the City, to the east. We are both, we are not from here but still it is for us. Whether luminous or its fathomless spans or its work to be a place. Then on his road another house sold. Not long now, he suspects. But cramped as we are, with my stuff everywhere, it's a wonderful life.

Then

Wait, he says Wait, I'm expecting a call. Don't make me wait, it's Saturday morning! That's it now, he hops up Don't move a muscle, I mean it, I'll be right back. But roll on my front to watch him go. Hear him in the hall pick up the phone half laughing Be quick Nick I   Oh, and the door goes bang. Muscles itching, I sit and wait. Five minutes later there's a door scrabble. Kick. When I open he's saying Ah ha, and I see, but indicating Cigarette, to me. I get, give and go back in.

   Who was that? for he's white as I've ever seen a man. That was   mmmm. Bring again of the phone. Fuck! He turns back round Hello? Yeah Nick, it's me. Five minutes of odds flow through my brain but those silent eyes are history meaning. Who was it? I ask, as he comes back in. Ahhh Nick   you know he's producing the film   we've got a meeting in   ah   Dublin. And the first call? That was, he says That was Gracie's mother. That was Marianne.

   Oh God   what did she want? Is Grace okay? His body sits down, lank over itself and hair hanging down. I kneel beside to touch it but I   am nowhere in this room. She's not sick   she definitely said that   there's nothing wrong with her   but that's the first time she's called me since they left   that's twelve years and   she wants to meet   whatever it is has to be done in   person apparently so 'in principle' would I agree? Did you? Yes, of course I did but   she'll call with a date once she's booked her flight. You never know, it might be something good? No no, whenever I've called that house every conversation has finished with I wish you were dead, so   whatever it is   it won't be good. Are you alright? You look terrible. Yeah I'm   it's just a shock   His face a picture of I don't know what, shifting into Ah fuck her, of course she'd do it like that. Like what? Not just fucking saying what it's about so now I'm left just   Left what? Just fucking wondering about what she's going to make me live without next. What can I do? I say. Nothing   nothing, love. Cup of tea? Breakfast? Actually   What? Anything. I could really   I could really use that fuck now.

So take him down into me on the bed. Give and offer what shelter I have. At first we are only people in love, reducing all life to the measure between us. But others pass into. Lives break through, making him go elsewhere and I become. For allaying. My body is. Made the most of. Worked into and twisted. And he says no funny or filthy things, just imitates himself like I'm a lesson well learned – Remember, she likes this, and this – so I might best facilitate his shutting off the view. Not on purpose, I know. This is the day. But it lasts until it hurts and I miss him and say Please come now, you're making me sore. And. He is irritated. Then he is Sorry   sorry   Eily love. Then does. Then lies down on top of me.

Strange day. And weather. And we are estranged. Standing on the Heath. Him looking away. Off to the left. I know his face but not what he's looking at or the expedient body, calming itself, that somehow appears to be mine.

Hey.

His eyes close.

Hey.

Open again.

Sorry   what were you saying?

Nothing, just, it's raining.

So it is   we should get in.

A pub. Pint me. Him soft drink. Why? Spot of Know Thyself probably won't go amiss. But at least he takes my hand.

While the shower clatters, I read. He smokes and   looks at the paper and   looks out the window and   time and   then I see something I've not seen before. Him. With a wandering eye. Tiny. Really. Very small but we are electrical so I get every volt. First, minute reactions to women walking by. The eyes lifting, barely. Soon though more. Soon every time. Then catching theirs and I go so quick inside

I wish you'd stop doing that. What?

You know. No, I don't.

I'm eighteen, not blind. I don't know what you're on about.

Yes you do. Eily, honestly, I'm not looking at anyone else.

So I ask about borrowing a book, to distract. Your copy of Doctor Faustus but there's a fine arse passing and Thomas Mann can't hold a candle to that. When I stop mid though he looks up swift Doctor Faustus Eil? Forget it, and I head to the toilet instead. Day, why are you being? Can you not just let us slide?

Of course, back there, the arse's owner's in my seat, pawing my pint glass, moulting in it.

Hello? Oh hi, just talking to your mate. He's not my mate, actually. We recognised each other Eil but can't quite place

235

from where. Oh really? It's true, sorry, is this your chair? Don't worry, he says as I say Yes. Just grab that one over there Eily, this is going to annoy us. Oh yeah, I bet it is.

So I grab the chair and sit by him and tune for this next hour into The Tron? Don't think so. Bristol Old Vic? Well that depends on. Apparently many things. Cue hilarious anecdotes of drink-sodden stints where paths surely must have crossed until they're so bedecked in actor banter I can't gauge what's afoot. But tire of him falling for every flash of her tits and not holding my eye when I catch him at it. Then how she makes me a paragon to cut me out Oh I'm sure you wouldn't be caught dead in a dive like that! You're clearly made of finer stuff than us. Play-slapping his arm, which I know he hates but does nothing to shift from. I look at her nails. Her talented claws. Would he like them in his back? Does he think I don't notice his ambiguity about what we are? Not holding my hand now. Not calling me love. Am I the unwanted hanger-on? Maybe. I know if I can smell the want off her he can smell it too. I still hurt from this morning, how he was. Has he already forgotten? But I'd let him do anything now, if only he'd send her away. So I look at him with all my love. Will him to see it and he does not. Just plays with her like he's someone else, who hardly knows my name. Not until, camel though she is, she finally gets up to the Ladies, I say Please stop, I don't like this game. What game? Please, you know what I mean. So you keep saying but, honestly, I'm getting a bit bored of your jealousy now. Won't look at me though, still won't look. Do you love me? Ah don't start that, it's been a long day. Do you? Come on, what am I supposed to say? That you love me and, hopefully, remember it yourself. Stop being so fucking childish, I haven't the energy for this. Fine, then I'll leave you and your fucking

236

friend to be grown-ups! I get up and. Eily don't, he says. Don't what? Don't go   please stay. Why? To compete? No, please Eily   don't leave me alone   not with her. But choking now in the weirdness and temper I go anyway. Eily, I'll see you later, alright? Eily? Eily? Back at the flat? I keep going though and don't turn around for fear of what I'd shout.

And I don't go back to the flat. I go to Kentish Town instead. Flatmate lying on the sofa like he's never left. Football on the telly. Wasn't expecting you tonight, paradise on the fritz? Yeah, something like that. Well, go grab yourself a beer, I'm expecting a couple of mates.

By midnight, langered. Wound up and hot. Chucking chips at the ceiling because Fuck the bank! And I'm laughing all over but when the phone rings insist I am not here. Hello? Oh mate, you're in the shit. No she doesn't want to talk. No, if I were you mate, I'd leave your grovelling until the a.m.

Knock knock.

She says go away, it's late. Tell her I want to see her and I won't leave without.

Go on, go out to him, Flatmate says But keep it down, the neighbours are dying to call the cops.

Like glint webs his grey eyes lift up to the light. Every part of him. Every part of him I What did you do? Eily I. Did you come here from her? Can I come in? No and did you? I walked her home. And? Something interesting in his face. Did you fuck her? No, can I come in, please? I go back to my room with no stuff in. Black Kentish Town where curtains should be and

Did you kiss her?

Eily.

Did you?

I did.

And then?

She asked me up.

And you went?

I went.

And then?

She   Eily

She what?

Eily

Tell me

She offered   she started to

Oh god oh god oh God

Eily   Eily I'm sorry   and he reaches   and his hands
look so thin and

Oh God how could you?

But Eily I didn't after a few minutes   I told her stop   then
I left   Eily

Get out.

Get out.

I didn't do it Eily. I stopped and

You're a bastard.

I know but   I didn't come I promise   I didn't even get close
          Too late for late manners. My body falls out of light.
Slips from its traces. Repeats

Get out!

Eily

Leave me alone!

Eily – grabbing hold of me – I didn't do it, do you understand?

But you kissed her and you put your dick in her mouth

It was nothing Eily, she was nothing to me

Is that what you used to say to Marianne?

Oh God   it is but   Eily I mean it now.

Get off me! Get off!

Eily, I could've and in the past I always have but this time I
didn't. Eily isn't that love? Eily?

But I slip him. Lie on the bed. Find what parts hate to cry
and nail them to my front. As if every vein though has come
undone the pain makes me anyway. Makes and forces. Almost
scream into the wall. Oh God don't cry, don't cry like that Eil
don't   don't   it's not worth that   I won't do it again   it
was an accident Eily   Eily? But I do not respond. I look into
the paint and its world beyond doing where all is white. Where
all is nothing and wish I was that. So it's a cold bed we make
tonight and lie awake hours upon.

In sleep too, damage. Dreams of dreams. Animals fighting
in my body. His, being obscene. Nightmare across to the early
waking and remembering what he's done.

Turn. His body lies half-naked and pearled. Inclining in towards mine. And further down, site of an old thrashing catching the sun. There is so much love. The eyelids flutter up and he
smiles before remembering. Then just looks at me. Somewhere
below though he finds my hand. Works his fingers in through
mine. But the hurt is so fine I must torture it for more. I look
at his mouth and imagine how he kissed her. She must've been
pleased. How he is when wants you. How that makes you feel.
Enough to get down in front of a stranger on her knees and
how hard was he then for her? I hate you, I say. You love me, he
says And I love you, and I did something bad but I swear I won't
do it again and I'm so fucking sorry. Get out of my bed. Eily.
Out of my room. Get out of my flat. Alright, and he stands into

the six o'clock. Puts on his shoes. Shirt. Coat. He says Eily, later, please come to the flat. I'll be waiting for you Eily. I say Then wait, and curl in on myself, leaving him only to leave.

Like rot it wrecks but, makes me ashamed. What he has spoiled. I wish her dead, or never been, with her well-done talents and creping cleavage. Warm bath moving round my head. Parts breaking surfaces by themselves as I play him between my legs. I wish we were back to that. And jog. And jog. And say his name. Wound and salve in the falling steam. Whatever my body wrings is for him, pitiless in its love.

Pointless. Pointless. The miss of him runs over everything else.

When I go into his room he is at his desk. Head on his hand. Smoking. At work. The sun making shapes, as he turns to look, all around what angles he is. I step into its castings. He unfolds himself and looks terrible, waiting for me. Are you staying? he says, and the pain shifts itself, even as I nod. I'm so sorry, he says. I know you are. Will you forgive me? I will. Don't cry Eily, don't. So I sit on his knee with my arms around his neck. I won't do that again Eily, do you believe me? I do. Oh God Eily, this has been a fucking awful day. I agree. And with no more to say put my mouth to his. There now. There it is. We kiss then til she is gone and we're turned back into lovers, freed from the monster. Saved from the abyss. Nunneries. Churchyards. Freezing lakes. Close shave. Day zero — we are at this, or it is what we choose.

And we are good to each other the rest of the night. Cautious around talk of her, or what happened. Trying just to be alright. To settle. Purge of the shock. Going to bed helps and, by the dark, we are almost as we were. But this is the start of the strange for us, of that long night's story doing its work in ways I now can see.

In the days after, we go calm and kind. Careful of each other around the mines of past, sex and To Be. It is the day's not awful price. But I wake often by myself. Him sitting, staring into space. And cigarette. And cold. Afraid of what's coming? Afraid how he was? That part of him caught us both off guard and maybe I'm not alone in the fear of his return – that man I didn't believe in, who now I sort of see. Although I can't quite fit him to the man I love, I still find myself at odd times panicking. That past he's had, what does it mean? Just passing an eye over frightens me. Not what his mother did, though her shape's right through his life. Not the drugs or the scars. Those are clear and sealed in time. It's the after. The losing her. All the women stripped back to their secret flesh and ate. Since my love's now proved such scant impediment paranoia picks up pace. Most evenings he's out now with his producer mate, revising dialogue or preparing their pitch and if I am not rehearsing late then I'm on my own at his. Now is the first I've felt young in this. Too young to know if his eyes are keeping secrets. And these hours away from each other, the conversations we do not have – was Marianne so minutely set aside? – makes hard work of life. So when he comes in I am all for him and he is always pleased but often Tired Eily. By weeks we're finding silences we didn't know we had. Stuttering into. Hiding behind. The safety of London getting very thin, hollow with what's going wrong and heavy, as it drags us down, like it were every truth. But nothing can put out all that light. The right joke or kiss and we're off for the night. Yet even in those lax-limbed darks the canker is my doubt.

Twentieth she says. What? That's the date. She called while you were out. So why he is pale. Are you alright? He nods. Did she do any more explaining? She did not. Well, two weeks and you'll find out. Yeah, can't fucking wait. Sorry, I. It's not you, he says Anyway   anyway   Dublin on Thursday. You and Nick? Ah ha. Why Ireland? Tax breaks or something and as we only need a roof   I wish you didn't have to go. Two nights, that's it and if we get them on board it'll solve a lot. So what'll you do with your evenings, you and Nick? Well neither of us have been before so I imagine, the pub   why? No reason. Eily? No, nothing just. Nothing what?   Nothing funny   when you're away   alright? Why're you saying that? No reason   just her calling and   you know. Yeah   okay   well   I've got to be somewhere so   I'll see you later on.

What unquiet imaginings do that? Make blame before thought? Then thoughts to back up? Until I said it I had not and now it swarms everywhere. But. In this regard, out on the tiles with the sea between, anything might   He might be anything and would I ever know? Back again at his I reread his note. Sorry, I'm going to be late. Now almost every night. Working at Nick's. Or. Choke strings tight. No. Why wouldn't he be? But   if Tired Eily, is that also of me? Why not? I inhabit such ordinary skin while he is   something more.

   Smoke. Sit on his desk. Watch him turn the corner and look up for the light. Then, because it isn't, check of his watch. Drop the fag. Front door. Stairs. Unlock. Hey, why're you sat here in the dark? Where were you tonight? Revising the draft, the end's still not right. Where though? Nick's, where else would I be? And I long for us lying on Hampstead Heath. Even as I turn aside from his kiss. Eily what's going on? Press my face to his shirt.

Cigarettes. Nothing. Eily? Undo his cuff. Then unbutton the
rest and taste his skin. I see, he smiles, lifting my chin but I
can't kiss him now. What is it? he says. Just fuck me. Okay   if
that's what you want. And he takes off my clothes. Backs me
onto the bed. Gets in me and fucks me and I climb myself despite his skin. All the past now collating instead of forgotten.
I suddenly misplace the best of myself, allowing a far worse in.
And there goes reason. There goes sense. Decency, and with
it, tenderness. So for everything that's happened and what its
mystery means I say You fuck really well. He doesn't respond
so I repeat it. Okay   why are you saying that? Because it's true.
Thanks   I suppose   you do too. Probably because you have
so much. What? Been with a lot of women   and men. And there's
the one goes under his skin. Don't say that to me Eil. It comes now
though, writhing, banging off my tongue It's only the truth,
you have fucked a lot of women. Jesus! Don't worry, it doesn't
matter to me   and all the prostitutes too, do you even know
how many? That's enough, what's wrong with you? Nothing
at all, I'm just saying   you can tell me anything   anything
you've done   it won't matter   it turns me on. Well it doesn't
turn me on, he says getting off the bed. Putting his clothes on.
I bet it does   a bit. You're just being disgusting. I am? Yeah
and I don't like it. Well poor you! Eily you know how I feel
about my past. Do you want me to say I'm ashamed? I am. I'd
do anything to take it back but you know I can't. Then how
could you? What? Go with that girl. For fuck's sake, she was
a slip on a bad day, let it go. Did you fuck her? Eily I told you
everything, I tell you everything, why would I lie? Just tell me
the truth, you came in her mouth. I didn't. You're lying. Well,
believe what you want, I'm going out, and he slams through
the door. But down from the window I shout To what? Go fuck

243

yourself Eily, he says nearly taking the gate from its hinge.

And I, inside, don't know what to do, tangling mishandled arguments he can't even hear now. Trying to   what? Just. Fuck. Fuck. Fucking hell. Fucking bastard. Fuck your stupid self and scream into his duvet until I am numb. I don't understand. How could you say those things to him? And now? And what? Turning so fucking scared. What if? Everything you've just done makes him and then   and what   what if he says I hate you, get out. Then that's you and what you deserve and. Go have a cigarette. Do and do. Until the room's all it. And my body hurts everywhere like kicked. I watch from his window. Into his street. Please come home. But he doesn't appear and that lasts so long eventually I must go down to sleep on my own.

Ride through dreams of falling and. Slamming and. Catch. Slipping and clawing. Shout. Stagger back into nothing through falling again Slit. Awake. Key in the door. 4.47 o'clock.

I lie like the dead. Watch him take off his coat. He does not look at the bed. Just strips off his clothes and gets a sleeping bag out of the wardrobe. Please don't do that, I say. He unrolls it, lays it anyway then sits in the armchair to smoke – hard, for no tomorrows. Where were you? No answer. Please tell me? King's Cross. Is that really true? No Eily, it's really not. Sorry. Silence. Stay put in the bed. For God's sake leave him to himself. But with his smell on the bedclothes driving me mad I get up and go kneel beside. Look up at him. He looks at me. Glitter of old marks near his knee that I lean down to kiss. Even the thought of them breaking me. The loneness of that life. What pain there must have been and now me saying stupid cruel things. I'm sorry, I say and am so ashamed. I hope he sees, but he makes no sign. Just watches as I start to cry. So I lay my head down on his knee. Feel his blood going under my skin. And neither say a thing into the deep silence we make.

In a while though he touches my hair. I'm sorry, I say For all that stuff I said. I didn't mean any of it. Please come to bed. He hesitates a little, but does. Then, God, the way we lie. Safe together just before the light and when I kiss him   he agrees to that. But we are so careful with each other now, like passing glass between our mouths, and gentlest way to be with hands. Bringing the other all the pleasure we can in this tiny breach of air. And he lets me say I love him. Says he loves me too. Fall asleep in that but when I wake he's on the floor and I'm alone.

There's a ceiling beyond my fingers. What have I what have I done? Why have I made him choose his own company over mine? Once I thought a man looking like him could never want someone like me. Now I'm hurting him all I can for being what he is. Dangle a finger. Stroke down his long back. He opens his eyes. Watch each other, then What's going on Eil? he says I know something is but I'm not sure what and   I'm really shit at this so   It's nothing, I say Just me being a bitch. He sits up, rubbing his face Look   I know what I did has fucked things between us and   there's a lot going on but   if we talked about it maybe? Isn't that what they say? Talking is good? But I'm far too ashamed to revisit last night. I'm really sorry for what I said, can we just leave it at that? All that stuff about my past though, what was that about? I don't know, I say Nothing, please, can we forget it now? Come on Eily, there's obviously something going on, can't we just have it out and be done. I said I was sorry, isn't that enough? Fine! he says getting up I'm having a shower then. And once he's out of the room, I get up too, but leave.

All day I am like smacked in the mouth. Even Flatmate says What the fuck's up? Nothing, and cannot face saying more. Cannot face anything. Him most of all. So that evening I go to Kentish Town. Spend it by the telly with the flatmate but wishing he'd ring. Persuade me back. He doesn't. Or Tuesday. Or Wednesday but Thursday lunchtime there's a note on the board saying Some guy says to call, he's going away and you have his number.

Hey, he says I'm off tonight so   you can stay at the flat   if you like and   I'm not going to be back until Sunday morning now. How come? Couple of possible locations to check and the evening flights were all booked up. So   what time are you getting the Stansted Express? Probably seven. Will I come wave you off? That would be nice. Okay, I'll see you then.

Plats shatter down as he waits for his to show. I call across the concourse. He swivels round. Looks to the clock, then to me. Cutting it fine. Got stuck on the Circle line, sorry, and I am – for this as well as all these days without him. Why did you leave like that Eily? Why haven't you been home? Sorry. Don't be sorry, just explain. I don't know, no good reason. Then why are we wasting our time? I don't know I. Oh fuck, he says That's me, platform nine. Don't go, I grab hold. I have to Eil, come on, let go. Do you still love me? Jesus fucking Christ, I do but Eily   do you still love me? I do   I love you more than anything. Good okay   then give me a kiss and   look   we'll sort it all out when I'm back, alright? But I can't let him go. Not yet. Kiss me again? So he does. A little. Not as much as I want, then slips me. Got to go love, I'll call you later, alright? I'll be waiting, I say Back at your flat. And break a bit as he walks away.

Silt air on the stair. Key in his door. Like aeons since I was here but it is days only. Nights, since I was last with him.

Weeks, since that night and we became   inside he's tidied. Bed made but not clean. Fit myself in the sag worn by lovers and him, and me, and Grace. And the smell of him, as always, turning everything simple, back to the rushing want. Before him I thought that when love came it would come perfectly. Not in a dingy room on dirty sheets and not caring at all about those things. It is the spell of him. Unconscious gift that if I told would make him laugh. I wish you were here with me now. Not the back-up note on your desk saying Eily, if not before, I'll see you Sunday night. This is the number of the hotel. Take care of yourself. And yet. Here it is. But you, alive in me. What're you at, this moment? Asleep, flying over the sea? Fancying a cigarette? Some lucky girl? Me? Don't. Inspect the fridge instead. One slice of ham and it could do with a scrub. Sink with my back to your boxes onto the rug. All your life in there. Turn on low. Transfigured Night. Remember then. And close my eyes. Stay awake. Below's music thumping up. But falling in I hear your voice and bring and bring. Wake up! Get up. Run into the hall. Hello? Did I wake you? I was just dozing, how was your flight? Okay. The hotel? It's fine. Well, good luck for tomorrow. Thanks, I'll try to call but. Don't worry, if you can't, you'll be busy I know and   I'll see you Sunday night. Okay Eil   sleep tight. You too. Bye then. Bye. Dead line. Dead. Deadening.

Up early. Today's the day. Wash dream from my eye. Sleep off my face. And my hair can dry in the sunshine that throws all around Prince of Wales Road. Second Years out on the steps in Jacobean rig. Jonson project or. Coming to the party tonight? Pub, upstairs? Might do, depends. Go on in, to the board. Double-check. It's me for the Emotion Memory later. And all morning it sits there. Then two. Three. Four o'clock. Now.

Nervous? *A little, yes.* Well, that's alright. Take a moment to settle yourself – could everyone else please settle themselves too. No going in and out during the exercise. Ready? *I think so.* Then, in your own time, tell us where you are.

I'm standing in the bath. How old are you? *Five.* Describe it. *Big. Enamel. White. Cold even with water in. One tap's dot's red. The other's gone.* What do you see beyond the bath? *Dun-coloured lino with an arc scoured in by the door. And a pink bathroom sink   with a mirror above   with those silver rings for glasses to put your tooth-brush in.* And are there glasses? *No   or   there are but   not there.* Be precise. *There are two on the shelf   to the left   with toothpaste and a nail scissors in as well. And a hairbrush that needs a clean.* Is that what you think in the moment, or what you're think-ing now? *Now.* Don't do that, recreate only what was. *There's a hairbrush with a lot of hair stuck in it.* Whose? *Mine.* How do you know? *Because it's long and blonde and my mother's hair is short and my father uses a comb so*   What else do you see? *A toilet. The old type, with a chain and a fluffy peach cover that matches the mat under the sink.* And what can you smell? *Coal tar shampoo.* Why does that make you smile? *It smells like my father.* Is he with you now? *No   I.* Is anyone there? *My mother is. She's washing me in the bath and singing The Spinning Wheel, but swapping Eileen for Eily.* Is she a good singer? *She is.* Describe the walls. *Green   Anaglypta I think   with a plasticky feel, peeling off under the window.* Can you see through the window? *Yes.* So looking through, what do you see? *Mountains, in the distance. They're heathery. Purple and rocks.* And closer? *A barn. Made of corrugated that's red with rust.* What else? *The farmhouse where my friends live. Then a blue car on the road and all the fields between.* And closer? *Horse chestnuts out our back. Blossoming.* Can you get closer again? *Fingerprints in Sadolin on the glass   my father's prints. He painted them and*

248

he wasn't very handy at stuff. Present tense. *He isn't very handy at things and a bit messy.* Do you know why that thought affects your voice? *Yes.* Why? *The future.* No, keep out of that. What time is it? *Morning.* How can you tell? *The radio's talking, that's morning.* Why does that make you smile? *I don't know.* Yes you do. *It's Gay Byrne   it's just so Irish.* Make a sound and let that feeling go into it. *Ahhhhhhh.* To a hundred people. *Ahhhhh.* Now what else do you hear? *Still my mother singing The Spinning Wheel.* And what's she doing? *Drying me off now.* Describe the towel. *Pink   with roses in white thread   rough.* Eily relax the tension round your mouth. Go on. *I want out but she's doing the talc. I pretend it's snow sprinkling on my back. I can hear it make the bubbles hiss.* Do you speak? *Yes, I ask What does it do? She says It helps you to dry.* What's affecting you? *I don't know.* Say the first thing that comes into your mind. *I want my father.* Why? *Because I know what's next.* No, stay in the moment, recreate the smell of talc and the sound of her voice, and once you've done that go on. *I   she asks   Have I missed anywhere? And I point down.* Point down where? *Between my legs.* Why? *Because I'm still damp there.* And what does she do? *She looks cross.* Why? *Because   I don't know yet.* Alright, what does she say? *She says she   I   I can't.* Eily, describe what she's wearing. *A blouse.* What colour? *Reddy brown   browny slacks   with a crooked crease because she's kneeling down and   I see a thumbtack stuck in the sole of her shoe.* Make a sound. *Ahhhhhh.* To a hundred people. *Ahhhhhhh.* Now – and remembering precisely – tell us what she says. *She says Don't you ever let anyone touch you there.* Make a sound. *Ahhhhhhh.* To a thousand people, Eily, trying not to hurt your voice. *Ahhhhhhhh.* Again. *Ahhhhhhhhhhh.* What's affecting you? *I'm   I'm ashamed.* Why? *Because   someone already has.* Make a sound. *Ahhhhhhhhhhhhhh* and it goes through the Church,

249

to the balcony, beyond, back to the girl in nineteen-eighty who, for the first time, knows she is alone with something she should not know at all. Describe a physical sensation. *I*   Eily, do it now. *I   Burning. My stomach is.* Why? *I'm afraid.* And what are you looking at? *My towel dangling in the suds.* And what do you hear? *Her asking Do you understand?* And do you answer? *I say I do.* You don't tell her? *I don't.* Why not? *Because I'm.* Because you're what? *Scared.* Because? *Because if she knew she would think I'm disgusting and not love me any more.*

Alright Eily, that was good work. What are you doing this evening? Rehearsing til eight. Well, make sure you go straight home afterwards, get some dinner, then some rest. The Emotion Memory opens doors it's important to shut again properly, do you understand? I do.

But there are two shades of light. First, the strip above my head. Second, the flashing Tell Tell. All these years of hiding in case she'd be upset when it's only what happened to you. Good. Good decision.

Wait until eight.

Phone in the canteen, now it's quiet. Go dial the O O Three Five Three Sevenone Eightfivefoureightone.

Hi Mammy. Yes. Yes I'm good. How are you? That's great but listen, I want to tell you something about, remember at Easter? Who we met in the street? Yeah. Him. Look, the reason I was offish was   No I didn't notice that. Really? You seemed fine with him I   Really? I always thought you two got along.   You were always so friendly when he dropped me off or whenever we went over to the farm. Okay   yes   I sort of remember that, you always keeping me on your knee when he was around. No, sure I was only five or six, how could I know it was to protect yourself? Really? Every time? Then that was

250

a good idea alright   no   I suppose that makes sense   He'd never try it on in front of a child.

Step back. Step back from the phone and fall into somewhere else. No. Stick pences in. Try. Dial again. Wait. The So and So hotel and can I have this room and please and thanks. Ring and ring. Please pick up. Ring and ring. Please be there. Ring and ring. Ring and ring. Ring and ring. No answer. Ring and Ring. Ring   off

Hey, you alright? Looking a bit peaky. I'm fine   I just   Coming down to this party? I did an Emotion Memory earlier, I'm supposed to go home. Nah, fuck that, no one ever does, besides our phone's cut off so you won't be able to speak to loverboy anyway, come on, come on! We'll have a laugh! And look   take that. I couldn't. You could, a little bit of something fast'll cheer you right up, you'll see. So rub my mascara and take the wrap. Thanks. No worries, go powder your nose and I'll see you down there, okay?

Look at her look at her look at you. What a fucking mess. All these years and little did you know, you were always by yourself. Snuff it then in the changing room. Tiptoe back out through Room One. Down the road, then giddy-up. Rubbed to the gums and, barely seconds along, I am running crystal clear.

I'll get them in, I say, heading up the stairs. Where music bangs full. Moving the bodies. Greetings Earthlings. Hang over the bar. Vodka. Double. Please. Going for it tonight? And I give the barman my best granule beam. Knock it back, hardly rasping. Another? Yes please. Another? Flatmate waving at me, dancing like a dick. So I get him a pint just as the blood lifts. And the eyes laugh. See you later. I hope so, he says. Then make through the crowd with today's poison hue getting killed off.

Pulled there, says the flatmate as I get beside. Look back to a smile from. Maybe I might have. But pushing with music. Bodies going around. Skirt life and flirt life. We are common enough now. Then steal forward to knowing what I've wondered in the past. She knew. Not exactly. But. She knew what he was like and gave you to him   and slip. Vodka quick licking in the midst of going up. Footing almost to the top. Waiting to. Waiting. To. And. Hear. The voice going Once a shagger. What? Loose every string. Go out in the smoke. Owl-eyed in this. In the junkyards and fuckyards of pick over prey. For some. For him, not me. Yet. Rest in their many arms. Twist my skin. Being young here because I am. Because all these days I have felt enough. And all this living hurts me so much. Get in behind my eyes. Colours of dark. In out of reason. Pull forward til I. Crave for him but the switch switches until, stretched and weepy, I see through my skin to the turquoise best of. A body overcome. I understand what he did. Magnificent, somehow. To give in. Wreck yourself so completely. The beauty of it. I can see past. Put my head in my noose. I want to kill myself or I want to go home. Enough of that! Flatmate steers gentswardly. Little Noseful. So, in my leeway, grant myself this. Then fall speckle-beaked down in through the night. My dominion. Reaching up through myself. Alight in this darkness. The lure of distress. I see it. I see. Him, standing somewhere with a stranger on her knees and. What part left person and what machine? I understand better now, amid this journey into what I am. Just the body of a woman looked at by the body of a man. And I catch the eyes. And I go over there. He'd sleep with me. This much I've learned. Forget that cunt, whispers the flatmate Come clubbing with us instead. But I stub out my cigarette and open myself to all that.

Alright Bright Eyes? Yeah, finished your shift at the bar?

Sure. Fox-brown eyes nip up me, and down. Join me, one on the house? Alright then. T-shirt riding as he reaches across. A line of hair to his navel that   I touch. Not shy then? Not any more. So we play at talking about how he talks. His American accent. How long he's been here. Where he's going tomorrow. Amsterdam. To do? Whatever, everything I can. I understand. And that I could fuck him. If I wanted. I might. For who's to say what really happened with that girl that night? And today's lesson is all pasts are adrift. So freckly and Irish, he says, dotting my dots, right the way down to where I could still stop. Anyway, I say I should go. No, you should definitely stay. Why's that? Because, I think, he says It's shagging time now, don't you?

Somewhere above we walk in the black. Below the pub, shutting itself. All the sirens of north London going off this Friday night. Up here they weep in through the brick. Good to know life still goes on without me in it. And so it is, in the dark I get kissed. For that is the point. Until the mouth aches. Until the eyes roll back in my head and I won't know it's not him or care who it is. There is no preferring. Shoes off. Falling over his bags. Pulling up my. Pulling down my. Tattoo I can't read and touch him and know how. Get on the bed. In by the nets and. Knickers right off and. Suffer his fingers. Breasts get what they get. All this familiar, already breeding contempt. Turn the eye elsewhere to make the body work right. Yet he pins me and in any man I wanted that. Is he thinking of me? Not of me doing this. Keep back from that. Make clean breaks. She knows how, at least. But the thought of him still gets me up towards off. You really are disgusting but you've come this far so   Go on through. Find the shape of the fuck. Put on the past if you have to. Who cares what happens? He can dig in me all he wants. Proper and large. Until he is not. Then kneeling up Give me your mouth. Which I don't but then   why not? It's the same all of it, when not with him. Why should I not be that again? Why did you even pretend to survive? Become yourself and hate yourself in the act. Gives what he wants for as long as he asks. When even that is not enough, watch him, above you, do it himself. Swearing things that make you laugh. Making ridiculous faces but   strange to know though   if this was him what would I not do to help, to bring him further on? This man I have no interest in. There'll be no investigating the pleasure of this one. Leave him to investigate it himself – which he does to between my breasts. Then comes, like someone spat. Rubbing it in – he likes that. Smears my face. Fuck's sake, get off. You love it, he says. Wipe my face on his blanket and know this cannot   ever   not be. Roll over. Watch his dirty feet. Hear the sound of piss and That was pretty good, wasn't it? I close my eyes. I wish I was home but I'm so wrecked. Then. From nowhere. Crash down or. Pass out. You might die, if you're lucky. Reviscerate, if you're not. Stay as far as you can though from waking up. It is all you have left of free.

And the night shifts through me. All the gears of sleep. Us lying together between the roots on the Heath, as though we have always been together under the sun. And touch a smear of butter off your lip. That smile you give me for it. Kissing my fingers. Inside my wrists and laughing. Reach through the dream of us. Going up, going just beyond the eye I breathe into your body. Run my hand down your side. And the smell of your neck which   is not right. Is. Fuck   is not you at all.

Back in the bright light and. Pull away. Well now, good morning. Slipping his hands onto my. Stop that. Come on, one for the road? No. Play fair, you've just got me hard. Take your hands off. Hey, don't be like that. Stop! You liked it enough last night. I didn't know what I was doing, I was wrecked. Gee thanks, he says letting me go. I get up Where're my clothes? What do I care? Knickers. Him lighting up. Too much I've had. Bra. Way too much of everything and I have done   what I have done   His legs swinging out now Hurry up and fuck off, I got to pack. Fuck you, I say. Yeah, you already did. And don't I regret it. Feeling filthy. On my T-shirt. Through my hair. Guilt and pull the skirt he's standing on now. Get off that. Why are you being such a fucking bitch? Oh poor you and your soft little dick. Hey, and I am pushed against the wall I can show you a hard dick if that's what you want. Get off me, I push back. No, him kissing at my neck and Clink through the byre floor, right through my head. Shift spit ert and push from and Get the fuck off! Don't you fucking claw me, and cigarette Jesus right on my arm. You're burning you're fucking burning me! Stop it or I'll scream and. He steps away I wasn't doing anything. You burned me. You fucking burned me! Did I? Must've been an accident. Keep my eyes steady on him. Feel around for my bag and, getting, back out spewing Fuck you's! Get out. Think Get out. Then

Air.

I see the hedge. And wall. It holds a roof up. There is litter. Life shows itself and my brain consterns with fright. Behind me. What he just and what I did. Blow ash from blister. Camden in front. Walk into it. Evaporate and I go to go, but. Where do you think you are going now? Kentish Town's to the left. And as for his   well   you can never go home again.

He did what? Fucking what? Repeat that? Flatmate says as he and the Missus and her boyfriend wait. Burned me with a cigarette. He did. Fucking cunt! I warned you not to, didn't I?

Yes. And now he's got to have his head kicked in. What? All because you couldn't keep your knickers up. We go? the Missus's boyfriend interrupts. Too fucking right, Flatmate says No fucker puts out fags on my mate.

The Missus brings me tea and toast. Thanks, I say I'm fine, so she resumes her packing, depressed, I think, by who I am. And I. Am much the same. Cannot bear to think of him. Or sit amid the lost teeth look of my room. Or consider last night. Or be anyone. So go sit out on the flat roof behind.

And the sun is its worst self, making a lovely day. Burning into my scalp. I should be washing myself. Cleaning him off. But I am too pointless for so much. Just turn aside. Turn aside. The awful shame. I might never move. Never rise from this spot again. Just eat bits of toast I wish would choke. And him. Where is he? What gifts I've prepared. Thanks for your love and here's your reward for the twelve years of waiting. It does not sit. And he does not even know our new obstacle yet. That in such short time I have gone so far. And it meant nothing to me. He meant nothing to me. At last I understand. This little. But lot. Too late.

What the fuck happened? Flatmate leant against the sitting-room door. Lilac-eyed. Missus's fella, having a smoke. We're barred. Was he still there? Oh yeah. What happened? I ask. I said to him I want a word. He said Make it quick. I hit him a slap and said You burned my mate. At which point he gets back behind the bar, going Not that bitch. So I says Yeah, her, and why should she get scarred because some little cunt like you has to take it too far. I didn't do anything, he says Not on purpose anyway. Well, I said Just in case, we're going to teach you a lesson about not hurting girls. Get out, he says Or

I'm calling the cops. So I punched him in the head. He kinda fell forward at first but came back with this. Then the fucking golem here drags him over the bar and gives him a couple of stamps. That's when the barmaid started screaming Get out! You're barred! so we left. But he's off on his travels with a black eye and a few cracked ribs. Thanks, I say. No worries, Flatmate says But you wouldn't get us some ice would you please?

Into the bath once the Missus leaves and scrub myself to pain. No matter though, I'm still myself and probably not his long road home. Leave the water in, would you? It's the last. Okay. Go lie on my mattress. White nightie. Passersby. My Walkman. The view. Go into the music and as the songs spool let them be me instead. There's not much respite so, as sleep comes, sink into it until the world goes blank and blind.

Banging. What? Banging glass. Eily! Wake up! Open my eyes. Wake up love. And he is right outside. What? Hey there, sleepy head, will you let me in? I've been knocking for ages. Come up I, chaotic, to life then. It's him and all I see is that.

Locks and pull and   there he is. Offering a six-pack of Taytos For the Irish contingent. And I leap him. Fling both arms around his neck. Now that's the welcome I was hoping for, he laughs, squeezing me almost to feet off the floor. How come you're here? I didn't like how we left things so – already backing me back to the room – I hung around at Dublin airport for a return. Crisps crunching now as I'm slung on the bed. I missed you, and kiss him. I missed you, he says. Guilt flooding up but that feeling between. I hide in it. Go to it. Tell him I love him and I want him inside. One minute, he says And I'll be happy to oblige, then nips to toilet while I scrabble my knickers off but Contrary to what you might think mate, I really don't want to see your knob. Sorry, didn't know you were in here, he laughs What're you doing lying here in the dark anyway, having a little cry? Think I nodded off, Flatmate says Pass me that towel? This one? Ta. Then flush and bathroom light and Fuck, what happened to your eye? Not the bailiffs again? Nah, fucking chivalry that. What happened? Nothing, bit of a scrap is all, anyway I'm freezing my bollocks off so see you in the matin mate.

Did he get in a fight? Sort of, I say as he lies back down. What happened? Who cares? I try but the morning falling in on me like slate. Eily what is it? I hide my face. Did something happen while I was away? I I do not reply. Look at me love. I do not. Eil did something happen to you? And I Sort of, then. Did someone hurt you? Sort of. Eily what does Sort of mean? If I look at him now though I know he'll see and I Keep this second. Hold in this place where he loves me. Then. Eily please tell me. And I raise my head. Oh, he says No it isn't that tell me anything else Eil and I'll believe you, alright? But I can't lie or speak so he is left to ask Did you sleep with someone while I was away? Pulse and Pulse. He can already see. I'm sorry. Oh God, through his teeth, getting right off the bed. Who? Who was it? Was it him? and grabs me up. Catching the burn though so I scream Let go! Was it him again? It wasn't. Was it? No I swear. Then who? You don't know him. What the fuck? he says Two fucking days and you couldn't wait? Let go of me, you're hurting me. Who the fuck was he, tell me? Just a barman! A what? Barman from a pub. You just picked some fucking barman up? Yes. Why? I I was off my head and What the fuck? shaking me so hard the pain in my arm haywires everything else. Please let go I was upset you didn't answer the phone So you fucked someone else? You're hurting me. Hey in there! Flatmate banging the door then opens it Take it easy on her. Mind your own fucking business, he shouts. Mate, I know what she did but   Get out, or do you think I don't know it's you filling her up with that shit? Just calm down mate. Don't fucking tell me to calm down. Flatmate turns on the light Look at her arm mate. He did that. He did what? Fucking burned her with a cigarette. What the fuck? and the silence coming down. Slow then, him pulling up my sleeve. Slow turning my elbow to see. His eyes then slow travelling up me He did this to you? I nod. Jesus, he says dropping his head like not knowing what to do. Don't worry, Flatmate says We sorted him out, me and the Missus's bloke. So where is he now? A & E or   Amsterdam. Right, he says Right thanks for that   I   I'll take it from here. Already closing the door. But go easy on her, okay? Yeah, he says Yeah   of course.

Alone beneath the bulb, I am all seen and I have done this, made his eyes full of disbelief. When did it happen? This morning. So   did you spend the night with him? I did. Did he make you Eil? Shake my head. That's   good, he nods relieved but killed. I'm so sorry, I say It was a mistake, I didn't even enjoy it. Well that's a relief! I mean it   I was wasted and   you were away. What's that supposed to mean? Nothing   I just I didn't know if   No! I didn't do anything Eily, you did! I know please forgive me? and wind my arms around his waist. Let go of me. But I will not. So for a half-blasted moment we half-blasted stand. Close together yet ghosts by our reflections back. And everything passes over. Everything passes through. Then his body decides to leave. Don't leave me! No   I'm going home and – unlocking my arms – you should probably lie down. Don't go, you can't go, please, I'm scared. Of what?   That I'll never see you again, and the tears come down. Jesus Christ!

he says, still the anger, though conflicting, across his face. You know how it is to do something terrible, I say Please don't leave me alone with it. Like balancing the many then, his eyes take mine. I cannot see into what he thinks but he says Alright. He doesn't want to be here though, rebels at the hurt. And as we strip off I can tell he has already left. He is halfway home in his mind.

Put out the light and, in its absence, lie side by side. Where miracles were, prayers only now. When I touch his hand though, he lets me. Shifts an arm to take me in. But the memory of myself here against him slowly gets to agony. Then because neither of us know what to do with any feeling, except be together in it, we do. Him taking me under. Letting me hide. The sadness making want but, that it might be the last time, has me cry almost the whole way through. Please stop, he says I hate hearing you cry. I can't though, and when we kiss, the pain crosses our mouths so he stops that and won't try again. Wipes off my tears instead. Puts his lips to the burn. And he is so quiet, like sound might break whatever he's brokered inside to spend this night with me. At odd moments the anger takes him though, has him pin me down. I'd like him to hurt me but he doesn't, much. He mostly holds onto it, as I hold onto him. And after, lying in his arms, I dream this is another time. That first night when I also cried. The night he told me he loved me. The Rafi white night. So many nights and days we've had. Those things we have done. All we have said. But he lets go of me then, turns to face the wall, reminding my heart that it's breaking down. And there'll be no sleep. There'll be no rest. Just dread of the morning to come.

Slow the awful dawn pursues the night above my bed. Tongues of it on the ceiling glow in from far off but I have him still. Still I clutch. Only after hours he is asleep. I watch though because I know when I close my eyes he will get up and leave. What I have done, does it have to mean this? Is there no way back?

Blasted by daylight come to torture me. I think of the long veins in his arms and   know, before turning, there'll be no one there. Did I just dream him stepping over? Putting on trousers. Putting on his shirt. Sitting near me to do his laces up? Running his hand down my cheek saying Don't wake up love, I'm off. So was I not asleep? Where was I? All I know is he was here beside me and isn't any more.

Flatmate looks up. Where is he? Gone. When? Just now, just a moment ago. I fling open the window to hang myself out. And see him. The back of him. Tall and straight. Come back, I shout Please don't leave. I can see him hear me. Know he almost turns his head but chooses not to and keeps walking away. Don't do that, Flatmate says Get in. You'll fall. But still I'm calling Don't go! although he already has. Please turn round! Please come back! Flatmate's pulling me in Calm down. If I run I could catch him. Don't, he's gone and he doesn't want to talk to you. But I'm kicking and pulling until we're both on the lino. Calm down. Christ. You're going to hurt yourself. But the grief is wild. I cannot tolerate it. To have lost him. To have lost him. There is no worse than this. I can't contain the panic so Flatmate pins me until I exhaust it. But the will is strong and it takes some time. Come on, let's go into the sitting room. Christ, I've never seen anything like that. He left me. I gathered as much. He left, I say again, to test for truth. I know, he says, and so it is. If it's any consolation, he looked a right fucking state. And it is, I think it is.

And lie long on the sofa. Flatmate in and out. But I am there

261

forever. Why have I done this to myself? Couldn't have timed a betrayal better. Could scarcely have hurt him more. I attempt his silence but get wrecked by my own. I think I'm going to lie down.

Destruction only though in my room. Traces of sex with the man who is gone. And the big bag of crisps. I lift, open them. Tongue swelling to the salt. Cheese and onion comfort and pangs innocent. I eat the packet. Another one too. Then another. Nother to long past full. But I'm not running across schoolyards. Their magic's outgrown. Go so, adult, and puke them again then come hide in your dirty sheets. Under there I have so many dreams but none of them of anything. Just all the doors in London. Going through. Into blank. One more. One after. No faces behind and I'm not even lost. I am futility. I am nothing at all.

Wake later, but don't think to get up. Lie in the lack of air and discomfort. Instead return to the crisps. Eat more. Many as I can fit to wall myself behind full, but useless body will not collude. It wants to throw up and forces me to. Choking over the toilet to bile and cramp. Then's when tears. Shivering and slime. And the flatmate says Let's watch a film and don't worry, he'll be back. He's mad about you. Anyone can see that. Just give him a few days, then a call.

The night's all race with that, the thought. And because I do sleep, then feel better for it, hope begins to show. Perhaps it's not all as bad as I think. He still loves me I know so might remember the things I have forgiven him. I did try to forgive him things.

Monday. Early. I almost run in. Only zealous other First Years about at this time. Ma May Me May Ma Mo Moo-ing and, more essentially, not queuing for the phone.

Ring.

Rings for a bit.

Normal.

Like we are in bed and he leaves it for next door to get. Only when next door won't, he does. Bathrobe in winter. Summer not. Goes out to but always barefoot. Getting at last to Hello? And I am sprung open by hearing his voice. The miss of him Jesus. Hello? he repeats. It's me I just. I'm busy, he says and hangs up.

Alright love? says the cook. Can I have a tea? I go outside. Have a fag and watch the day with an enemy's eye. The cup burning a hole in my palm. Alright? she says, coming up the steps You look like shit. Thanks, I say. What's wrong? I tell her everything. At the end of it, she says Shouldn't have taken that stuff off that dick. I know but. Anyway, let's go to Voice.

And today drags the more for owing nothing to me. Store the pain in some switched-off place, which is becoming every-where it seems. Only later on do I get back my brain and by rehearsal I am on the knife. I understand everything I need to do. Excused of myself by the in out of words. Such a small space between me and her – girl about to lose her love. But we are not the same. She loves truly, doesn't she? Was pure and steadfast in ways I could not be. She was intact though and I cannot help thinking he was always knocking on a broken door so when the gale came there I was, useless and letting it in. But I understand something of her strangle at the light so bring it along for her now. Much better, the Director says at the end You've not wasted your weekend. No, I suppose I've not.

On the tread back though I try him again. Breathing hot phone box piss and getting his neighbour who shouts in Phone for you mate, yet again! He opens up. I know that creak. Cheers for that, and because of tiredness his accent's gone all strong Hello? It's me, please don't hang up. Eily, he says. Yes. And silence and   You didn't say goodbye. You were asleep   thought it was as well to leave you be. Right   so   have you had a busy day? Yeah   bit of follow-up and that. Well that   sounds like   Listen Eily, I want you to come and get your stuff. Oh no   I   Or I can bring it over if you want? Wait   I. And I've been thinking, he says If you need money for a deposit or anything, you know you only have to say. And I and I cannot. He has organised this thought. He has been considering this today. I don't need money. Well, think about it anyway, I don't want you to be struggling on top of   so how will we do this then? Do what? Move your things   I've   packed them up. Do you want me to throw them in a cab or   No   I'll come. Already arranged and done. Shall I come down now? No   it's late. Well   I'm not rehearsing tomorrow? No   I'm not here how does Thursday suit? That's fine   are you going away? No just dubbing on that stupid film and it always puts me in such a foul mood. I say I know you hate dubbing, as indication of I know you, but he does not pick up on it. Right, Thursday then, around six? Fine, I say and and and It's nice to hear your voice. Yours too, he says Are you alright, Eily? Not really, are you? No, not really either. So at least there are two of us in it. Night then, he says. Night, I say.

Switch the kettle on when I get in but the Flatmate says I wouldn't bother, the electricity's gone.

The next two evenings I hang around the school. Might as well do extra work with the lads on my scene. But the fucking around in the canteen does my head in now. I can't find it in me to care about the Agents' Showing and the bitching Third

Years because some slippery fucker's wedged herself into three scenes. Even Second Years foaming over their end-of-term purge elicit no pity, for all the world's an empty stage if he's not standing in it. And even to sleep, no fucking perchance to dream. Just nightmares of leavings to be.

The Camden Road at five to six, dusty with summer and leavings of itself. Litter in hedges. Sweet wrappers and chips. Roadwork gravel filled with neighbourly dog shit as cyclists and buses go by. And his street, more under the reach of trees, much the same as it was. Front door though splintered and broken-locked. TVs from everywhere giving out chat, or rolls of News music, as I go up. Hesitate but   knock. Hang on a sec, he opens then Come in.

Walks well away though, before I am. The beginnings of Transfigured Night but switched off then. I'm not too early? No no. But he won't show his face and fake sorts at papers on his desk – his tidying belied by the state of the place, worse than I've seen for months. Sit down if you want – vague wave to behind. I shift books from the bed Where'll I? Anywhere, anywhere, dump them on the floor. So how was the dubbing? Oh you know, and rubs behind his glasses. Tired? A bit. What happened your front door? Someone kicked it in, we'll be waiting years now to get it fixed. Yeah   I know how useless your landlord is. Trip back to silence. Then. Cigarette? No thanks. He tries lighting his but Fucking thing! Shakes away at it until, sparks later, it does. Then smokes and examines a hole in his jeans and, only once he's organised, looks right at me So   how are things? Not great, and you? He shrugs, surveying me but with eyes gone quiet. Eating much? for he's gotten thin. Enough, he smiles Your burn's calming down. I touch my arm but, mercifully he moves on to End of term next week, is that right? Yes. Well good luck with the showing. Thanks   you still meeting Marianne that Thursday? Yes. I'm sure it'll be fine. I'm sure it will, he agrees, re-attempting a smile but the weird decorum cracking it. I'm sorry, I rush out. Don't worry, he says – up on his feet though – Anyway, you're here for your stuff. I just   I stuck it all in your bags. Oh right. And everything suddenly manics. He's hauling them out. Shedding fag ash. Knocking over books There were quite a few bits and pieces, you might want to have a quick look   Wait, I say. He does not Your purple case has a rip so I used some gaffer tape and   Please, I say. No, let's just get this done. Will I carry these bags down to the station or   All the flurry making panic. Far too quick to keep up. Five minutes of tidy to clear out of our life. Does it really have to be over? It really does. Really? as though disbelief might alter it somehow. Yes, he says. But why? Why do you fucking think? Please, I'm so sorry, I really am. I know you are, now get up. Won't you forgive me? I do Eily, but that doesn't change anything. Why? He drops the bags What do you mean? You know yourself why we're here. But I love you, I say, pulling at every seal. And what did that matter last Friday night? Don't be cruel, I made a mistake. I know, he says – more gently – Far better than most. God knows I've done enough fucking around to have no right to judge or ask for anything as far as fidelity's concerned – least of all from an eighteen-year-old girl. But that's the problem, you're eighteen and you shouldn't have to feel bad about wanting your freedom. No, I say Don't do that. It wasn't about wanting freedom. It was just being fucked up, all those things we've said, I meant them and I know you did. I did, he agrees But I should never have said them to a girl your age. And I hate this voice he's suddenly made for her. Pat on the

266

head. Now run along. It was just a stupid fucking mistake, I shout I was upset and with everything else going on with us. And what the fuck was going on with us? his own voice shouts back You wouldn't say what the fucking problem was and   I couldn't work it out and   You went after someone else right in front of me, I say You went home with her and   whatever you did or didn't do   it frightened me   you were so unlike yourself then. He covers his face and sits down beside I'm sorry, he says That was very bad and, you know what's worse? I was so proud of not having gone through with it. The fucking life I've had Eily, the way I've lived, I've no reason to expect you to be alright with it   or recognise some stupid fucking difference that no woman would, or could, never mind a girl your age. All those things I told you would've been best kept to myself   I just thought   never mind   what does it matter anyway. Don't be sorry, I say I'm the one who really fucked up. No, these things happen Eily, don't feel bad about it and besides if you were with someone else, someone better than me, that stuff would prob- ably get easier for you. And so quickly he is closing me out. A logic working far beyond where I thought. His life arranging itself around the idea I'd be better off without. But I don't see that and I don't agree. For Friday night has also shown me how he works, under the skin, and I want to say Come up from your dead life again, retell me your secrets my love, and this time I will be more. Too late though. He won't believe me now and just strokes my back like I am a child. But I'm not and I feel the pain in him – bad in this moment as it's ever been – so put my arms around him. At least we can have that. You just came into my life so unexpectedly, he says I never thought this would hap- pen to me but, right from the start, I knew I could love you. I tried not to but   I did anyway and   then there was no more calm. You just brought me to life in ways I haven't been in years. I've fucking loved it Eily, you and me together, but it was a mistake. How could it not be when you're so young and I'm so fucking incapable? It wasn't, I say It's how things should be. He doesn't object, but he doesn't agree. Come on, I say resting against his cheek. And he seems so fragile. Does not protest even when I kiss him then. Allows me to and gets tempted into kissing back. Lips parting just enough to kiss how we've always liked. Secretly. Intimately. Bitter and fine. Touch his face and his Stop, he says We're not doing that any more. I want to, I say And so do you. I know, he stands up I'd fucking love to but I'm not going to Eil. Why not? Because, he says All those years before we met were mostly quiet inside for me. Long as I kept things in order I've been almost fine. Do a job. Smoke. Go for a pint. Lie here and read a book of a night or bring someone back, should the opportunity arise. Then write my letters and think of Grace. Dream about her being old enough to visit. And it got to suit me Eily. It's kept me very calm. This is how I've learned to fix my life. I don't have to touch the walls. I can rattle around inside. It's like looking down through water and seeing to when I'm old. I know exactly how I'll get there if I stay on course. And that would be an alright life Eily. It would do for me and I was resigned to it, content with it even but   then you came along and   I loved you much more than I wanted, far more than I thought I could. But with you all this other stuff began to return. The life I wanted when I still had the right to want anything. It was there inside me all this time, asleep, but it's wide awake now. And the problem is   after all the people I've slept with and the things I've done, I'm so ready to try to be with someone but   you're eighteen and   that's not right. You don't want to get married or have children and why should you either? I certainly didn't at your age. And, much as I could wait, by the time you're ready you won't want to with someone like me because   as you've seen   nothing comes easy to me. So I have to stop this now and get rid of all these things that you never meant to bring. But at least with what's happened, I'm thinking straight. And I know to come up out of that old life, to this, to you, isn't what I want. Please, I say Can't we try? Can't we just see what happens? He shakes his head. But why? Because this isn't how normal people are when they're in love. They know how to be happy, and you need someone who knows that, who can do that for you. I thought, for a while there, maybe I could but   I don't think I can and   that's hardly a surprise. But you love me, I say. I do, he agrees I really fucking love you and right now it feels like I always will but I don't want to any more so   we're going to have to let this go. And I can tell he means it. This is what we won't come through. The implacable logic of a well-built wall that I cannot see around or get through and he will not help. You're a liar, I say And that's all bullshit. I slept with someone and hurt you, just admit it, just shout at me and then forgive me and then let's get on with our life. I'm not hurt, he says. Yes you are, I can see it, that's why you won't even give me a chance, you fucking hypocrite, how many things have I forgiven you? All the anger stretching out between as I stand up to start pulling my bags free. Let me help you, he says. No, get off, I don't want anything from you any more. Eily, let me help. No! I shout. He steps back Alright, if that's how you want it. It's not how I fucking want it but apparently this is how it is. Then bang open his door and toss out my bags. Eily, he says Let's not part like this. But I'm crying with frustration and don't care for polite. I don't care how he's planned his formaldehyde life and hope he feels every bit as bad as I do now. Please love, he says, trying to take my hand. Get off me, I'm going, just like you wanted. And as I'm about to Eily, he says. What now? Fucking flesh as well? No, he stretches his hand out Keys. Jesus, I say How can you bear to do this? But his face's gone back to December. And before. Impassive grey eyes content to wait while I rummage. There! I slap them into his palm. Thank you, he says long fingers closing. Then I just go. Before the door shuts though, hear them thumped across the room. A little satisfaction. Where did they land? Behind the desk? On his armchair? Stop. You are not going back there any more. And the great abyss of the loss of him opens up inside.

Out into seven. Quarter past at most. The dandelions turned to clocks as I straggle down his path. Bundle through the old gate. Wretchedness making its meal of me. But if I look back I know I'll see him and, because I won't spare myself one hurt, I do. And there he is. Cigarette smoke and light rebounding all across his pane as he looks down at me. So I wipe my nose on my wrist and turn away. But I know he'll watch until the end, until I am completely gone. Then all on his own, in that room without me, begin his life again.

God tortures me with morning, scourging eyelids red. Flatmate nerring Imagine in the bathroom. Fuck him anyway. And me. My brain drilled through. How much did we even drink? Stomach sore from? Oh. Puking. Pink like blood but just vermouth. Bags. Still out in the hall. Arms. Still in their sockets. What have I to do today? Get up and be alive.

Better find somewhere, Flatmate says wet at the door. Won't be long until the water's off then it'll be rank in here. Have you somewhere? Yeah, going to bunk with a mate, suppose you thought you'd   I did but fuck that. Maybe I'll leave my stuff at school and after the summer have a look. Now I have it. I've a plan. See, my brain still works.

But a hard day to night

Draw the blankets round but that's not him. That's cigarettes and burning skin. And under it? No. Don't look for him. Put your head down to sleep. But when it starts, the brain sets off. Going with the thought of   so many much   before what I did. Straightened out on his bed, naked and laughing with him. One of the two in that good oxygen, taking it hard down into the lung and so glad of each other then. Think of It's alright to be shy with me. Everything was alright with him. I could do no wrong until   Now I'd like to wake up but the dream keeps going. In through the red and onto cutting off my fingertips. Shearing to the bone. Laughing too. Presenting as My gift to you, my love. Who'd not want me? And when I do wake I'm still all aberrant eyes. So sure he was just here. No. Fingers still attached, more's the pity. Some stranger at the glass and hide under the duvet because these nights will be too long.

Go instead to the rich imperfect days. One week to the end of term. Cold water showers jagging my back. See the sun shine and walk my way in it through the bowers of Kentish Town. Intent in each moment. Do not think. And in my Juliet bed gown let the words do the work. Come, gentle night, come loving, black-brow'd night, Give me my no it makes me sick. Now only stand and forget the text. His keeping still, the very best paralysis. Okay stop, the Director says What the fuck's wrong with you tonight? But I am another girl and beyond

271

caring about fucking my own self up. This is a stupid play, I say then walk out. And I don't even care if they make me stay that way. Chalk Farm is poisoned for and to me. Go sit out on the bench and watch little boys from the estate behind making cheek with some Third Year lads I could fucking have you, and you, and maybe you. Then roaring as they're chased off down the road. I would laugh if I cared. I don't though. Or want to be here. Or see the point. Go to get my things. Hey, the Director appears I want a fucking word with you, what was that in aid of? Nothing, leave me alone. Oh no, and I'm shoved into the study room. You don't behave like that in my rehearsal room so you better make this good. With no will to lie then, or for disaster more, I dwindle a sullen I split up with my boyfriend. What trite that sounds, for it contains no trace of what he was to me or how it is to lose someone again. Well you're a fucking disgrace, the Director says. Don't ever bring your personal life to rehearsal again, do you hear me? Work. That's what this life means. If your leg's amputated halfway down Wherefore art thou fucking Romeo, you keep going, do you understand? And there is a thread. Pull it. Pull. If he knew what you'd done he'd kick you up the arse as well. But further beyond. Remember yourself. All you came here for. So I go back inside. And some sense starts up again.

Moving out tomorrow, Flatmate says You shouldn't stay here by yourself, it might get weird. Why don't you bed down at a mate's? No, I'll stay. It's not much longer now.

A candle is mine in this vigil of night. Smoke and now can't be burns enough. Even not alone, yet too quiet. City creepy below. Passers on the walkway. Faces at the window. Just sit inside in the electric-less dark and try at keep trying to breathe. Touch the places where he slept. Who is he thinking of tonight? Marianne, I suppose, and that's right. She was first anyway. She's probably also somewhere in London tonight thinking of him or that misbegotten life. The idea of it going suddenly square in my brain, like seeing into them. All the years gone since they spent that week in bed. Since they made their daughter and became he the devil, and her, for years, only what she stole. Bone picked and bleached clean of what they once felt. And now will that become me as well? Remembered, lying on his bed with some new girl, as too young to be serious about? I missed her of course but now I know she only blew off the dust for you. Am I already gone to the past? Gotten off his body by someone else? So many years to be apart ahead. But maybe one day we'll cross paths in a Safeway's. This is my wife, he'll say And this is our son. And I'll look at the little boy whose hand he holds tight and see him in there but none of myself. Hear him telling his wife Eily and I went out for a bit, way   back   when. Then it'll be off with them, back to the life I'm not in. How have I so easily gotten so much wrong? But whistling down from the blue night it comes: I had not grasped that the sun still rose after I love you. Maybe he missed that also. So neither of us was careful enough and broke it before we'd understood. But as he thinks of her tonight I hope he also does of me. Sees beyond the hames, the screaming and the keys to my imperfect love that was meant utterly. And he was right, that was the wrong way to finish. Tomorrow I will be myself again.

Kwik Save boxes. I help pack. Bit sad to leave, Flatmate offering his spliff. No thanks, how's your eye? Nearly healed, shame too, it would've looked great for the Agents' Showing. I was all prepared. 'I coulda had class. I coulda been a contender. I could been somebody. Instead of a bum, which is what I am.' Not a bad Brando as Brandos go but there's a horn blowing down on Patshull Road. That's me, he says, slinging his hook. The next few minutes in and out. Lugging his telly and what he'll nick. His mate helps with the sofa – That's for the fucking bailiffs, you'll be alright without it, won't you? And when he's done gives me a hug. It was a good laugh living here, here's my mate's number if there's trouble. His mate shouting Come on man. I'm double parked! Better go. See you Friday. Okay then. I go back to the kitchen and watch them pull around. Salute to his and watch until he is gone. His future Tufnell Park. Turn the tap. Water runs. Good. So turn it off again.

Pleasant after sunshine, Camden getting towards night. Carrier bag sweat on me and his front door still broke. Quieter than usual. No telly blares. I go on in but, top of the stairs, sounds trickle out from his room. Voices. A man's. A girl's? Listen but too low to   company or something else? You have come this far. But if it is? Just knock anyway. Quiet. What? he shouts and when I don't respond What do you want? I knock again. Who the fuck is it? I   it's Hi   it's me. And the silence it goes into. Has he heard? It's me, I say again. Then hear him cross but he only opens a crack. Look, not tonight. Just for a minute, I say I haven't come for a fight. A struggling moment of   Please? Fine, he says Come in, but you can't stay long.

Already going when he opens my heart stops with shock. Thinner I'd thought of but not starving almost. Worse than I knew you could get in a week. His grey eyes gone black back. Skin dry and white. The shirt hanging off him. Jesus you look awful. Why did I say that? Thanks, he smiles at the floor. I close

274

the door behind and the next awful is the state of in here. All the boxes open or turned out on the bed. Desk. Armchair. Ripped and emptied. Everywhere. Everything. Curl-cornered scripts. Tapes and clothes I've never seen. Even the video that's always packed. Records. Postcards. New old photographs. Frittered with fag ash and blanched in splashed tea. Dirty cups all about. Only his suit, freshly cleaned, looms in its plastic on the back of the door. Oh my God what happened in here? He looks around dully and lights a cigarette. Ah, just wanted to go through some stuff. His eyes, behind his glasses surveying the wrack, sodden with tiredness So what can I do for you? Did you leave something here? Might be difficult to locate right now but if you tell me   No   I didn't come for that   Jesus   you look terrible, how long since you ate? Eily, he says What do you want? Sorry, sorry, the reason I'm here was just   to bring you these, and offer the carrier bag. What's in there? Minstrels and some bread and some eggs. He smiles a little then sits on the bed, starts unpacking it Thank you – just looking at them – That's very thoughtful of you. Well, I know Marianne's tomorrow and   I know what you're like and   I thought you might want some company tonight, actually, when I was outside, I thought I heard someone in here. What, some girl? No I don't know. Well there's no one but me. Then we look at each other through the misery of the place. Hard to believe a month ago this was where we were happiest. Thanks for the offer Eily but really, I'm fine. The state of him though Please, I don't like the thought of you being alone, or what about Rafi? He's away look, I'm fine. Thank you for bringing these and taking the time but   if you could just go – and standing again – Maybe we can have a drink later in the summer   once everything's calmed down. But his slowness is so unnerving I don't want to leave. Let me make you some toast? Put the kettle on at least. Ah no Eily, come on I'm busy and I'd rather be by myself. So for it. Go for it. Nothing left but to say Are you having a relapse? Having a what? I look at the video player A relapse with you know. He looks from me to it, understands, then starts to laugh. What's funny? He keeps going. Getting it all out. The anger in it. So much, until he's laughed himself still. Why were you laughing? Because I've only now realised there's not one thing I've managed to accomplish in my life with dignity. What do you mean? He laughs some more. It's just embarrassing, dis-gusting really, to think you know that about me feel you have to ask but fuck it is funny. Don't say that, I didn't mean it that way. No, I know, he says Apparently I'm just clinically incapable of not humiliating myself. He stops then and gives a strange sort of smile Don't worry though I'm not having a relapse but thank you for asking anyway. What are you doing then? And the smile wipes off. He leans over a cassette player then presses. Hiss pours, with nothing until a man says Gracie, give us a song? I say That's you? He nods. Sing for Daddy. That's it. Into the mic. Into there. Good girl, and a little voice Baa baa black sheeps. Sometimes he joins in. Very good Gracie. Can you sing another song? No! Not one more? No! she shouts. Jack and Jill? Do you know that one, Grace? No! laughing at her own boldness with him. Some laa-ing close to the mic, then further off. No Gracie, give me that. Give that to Daddy love. That's Daddy's work. Squealing now like she's running. And the look on his face. There's an Ooop! He turns to me She slipped on a cassette. Then crying and Did you hurt your hand? Wiggle it love. Like this. That's it. I think it's alright chick. And the tape clicks off.

I'm sorry, I say. Don't worry, he shrugs It wasn't an

unreasonable conclusion, this place is a mess, then drops himself back on the bed. Did you just come across them? I was
looking them out, hence the crap everywhere. I sit down beside
Why? In case   to remind myself if there's any funny business
tomorrow   if she wants the letters to stop   I need to remember what I've already lost and   not give in. Covering his face
then, he suddenly goes down. What's wrong? He sinks further
so I stroke his arm. I'm just a bit down tonight, he says Tomorrow I'll be fine, I'll be fine again but tonight   is pretty hard.
And I can't bear this. I hate it. The desolation in him, spread out
across this filthy room. My part in it. His own. Let me stay with
you, I say. He shakes his head I couldn't do that. Just as your
friend, just for tonight and we won't talk about what happened.
I won't try to change your mind. I'll leave first thing and   if
you let me stay with you   Stephen I promise I will let you go.
But if you stay Eil, how will I ever get rid of this? he says. Rid
of what? I ask. All this fucking love, and at this his voice goes
out from under and tears start falling down. Quick he heels
them off but there's only more so he hides behind his hands to
damp their noise. Then tries to sit himself up and be right. But
he cannot yet. And I've never seen him cry. He looks so young
in it. I can almost see the child he was with the busted lip and
not knowing there would be worse. Or that half-destroyed boy,
two years younger than me. Or the young man with his daughter on his knee not realising how short that time would be. All
here in this man who tried to offer me the very best he had. I
climb onto the bed and wrap my arms around him. Oh Stephen,
oh my love, and he lets me take him. Awkwardly we hold onto
each other then, tight. His skin and bones showing the other
side of love we've arrived at. Not hate. I see it now, and so clearly tonight, that the opposite of love is despair.

In a while he sits up. Wipes his face on his sleeve Sorry about that. You alright? He nods, blows his nose, embarrassed I think, but says Listen Eily, if you really don't mind, some company would be good. Great – I get up – Something to eat? Yeah, I'm fucking ravenous, you wouldn't make scrambled eggs, would you? I would. And already he's closing himself up neat but that's fine now he won't be alone.

You shouldn't say that, you know. What? he asks opening the Minstrels and vaguely tidying up. All that stuff about your-self. But he's busy shovelling the sweets in and just shrugs. What about work? Plenty of actors would be delighted with half of what you've achieved. Fucking work, he says – chewing a massive amount of chocolate – I'm so sick of it Eil. What do you mean? Sometimes I think it's just bled me dry. You know, I started rehearsing 'Tis Pity the week after David died. Some-one dropped out and the director was a mate and   I needed to be doing something so I agreed. But after David   it was like someone had taken a hammer to me. For months I felt like that. Sometimes still. But I went straight into it and worked like a dog. It gave me somewhere to hide, I suppose, but that play every night   what it's about   by the time the run was over I was at the end of myself. And I realised all those years of trying to keep myself still, keep myself well, I'd just been ripping out of my insides which was fine except there'd been nothing going back in. I knew something needed to change or I'd just stop and then what would I do with myself? So I decid-ed maybe it was time for the script. I'd been thinking about it, on and off, for months. Nick said he was interested so I start-ed it and within a week there you were. Apparently I thought I'd let love in. He laughs a little now and picks chocolate shell from his teeth. But anyway. Anyway. Well, the eggs are ready and when I serve up he eats away like a wolf. These are great Eil. There's more in the pan. Aren't you having? I already ate and you clearly need it Stephen. I know, it's ridiculous, he says I can't believe I still do it myself. Christ, when I was a child I'd have done anything not to go hungry but now   food's the first thing that goes.

I pick about his room while he eats more. Put that tape on, would you Eily? You don't mind me hearing them? No, what difference does it make now? Look at each other then but blank it out for the only way we will get through this night is to for-get we are apart.

This time he reads to her. Questions and chat. But why did he blow down the house? Him doing the voices. Tickling, I think, when he huffs and puffs because she screams with ex-citement. He just sits, fork mid-air, listening like they're both in here. Amazing, it feels like no time's passed. You sound dif-ferent though. Your accent. Your voice. That'll be the forty a day, he says. You shouldn't smoke so much. Oh well, all the shagging keeps me fit. I catch his eye. Sorry Eil – like he's just heard himself – I didn't mean that. Oh yes you did! And then, broke as we are, we both laugh.

Later, when it's black and I've drawn the curtains tight, he liberates some photos from an ancient Keats. These are some pictures for Grace. I asked John for them a while back then couldn't face sending them on so that's her   my mother, I mean   if you want to see. And I do.

Black and white. Tattered tan. By a low brick wall a young woman stands. Slight. Long dark hair. Serious-eyed but in such a pretty dress and   I am surprised She really looks   I know, like me and Grace. I didn't look like my father. I never did. Look at this one. A younger. Her family. Two little girls, bows in their hair. Looking so Irish from back then. Parents stern and the family resemblance goes their father's way. I don't suppose I'll ever know what happened there, he says But I could probably guess, if I tried.

Sit together then, slowly finding the other's hand. Silence coming in on us but right it should now. No more to tell. Nothing to explain. For the rest of the night we scarcely say a thing. Sometimes he smokes. Sometimes I make tea but, anywhere we are in this room, he keeps touch with me. Long fingers through my fingers, or his head on my knee, or letting me doze on his chest. All night I wait and watch with him. Sleep, and don't, but we see the dawn come. And morning. By half six I'm awake, stretching and looking at him, looking better already. Just sitting, staring out at the sun. Palming my ankle. Thumbing my new burns. I'm fine now, he says I'm fine again. So I break the tie and get up. Good luck today, and kiss his cheek. You too, he says With your Juliet, then as I get my coat on. Eily? Yes? Thank you. You're welcome, I say and keep my promise to go.

Out into the cold sun of morning. I am tired but I am still. That shake of losing him settling itself, becoming what it is. I do not rebel. I have given love its due. Put kindness where it should be. Now we may part in this good memory. I hope he will be happy, that today will not be bad. But now my own clock ticks and turns inside. Go on. Get on. Let your own Juliet in.

Walk round the College of North London to the Prince of Wales Road. Anglers Lane. The Church of Christ. Grafton Road. Under the bridge at Kentish Town West. Harmwood studios up on the right. Talacre Gardens. Dalby Street. Malden Road. Across to the Fiddler's Elbow. Up by the Crown. In there,

St Silas. Wide blue skies as I go on up the stone steps. Earlier even than pigeons at infernal coo. Second last day of term now. Second last of this year. Touch the grey door. Tap the code in. Open. Strange in its stillness and. Some new thing in me which, if followed, who knows where will lead? When I first came here I wanted the world to look at me and now I might prefer to be the eye instead.

But fall back in. Romeo and Juliet. All other life switched off. Get her going in myself and feel that life of hers inside. Her precious heart and all things of her moving round, readying themselves, until their time. How she walks and how she speaks. What she does. The way she thinks. Making her particular. Setting her free. Just the right way. Find the right way to show her through me. All that tuning. No more today. Time to be ready. Time to turn on the light.

Afterwards, cross-legged, in the Church. The Principal drums deep into us all we're not worth. I get one nice nod though so am reprieved. Interviews later for the less fortunate. But for the first year, that's it. See you all in here early for the Agents' Showing run-through, he says Watch and learn boys and girls. Off you go.

Hello? I say. But no one's in. Try the taps in the bathroom sink. Nothing. So we've reached that final stage. I have reached and I accept it. Calm too in here now, though cool. All bare in the Missus's room. In Danny's, an empty can of Coke. Crumbs on the sideboard, I won't bother to wipe. Pizza boxes crammed in the bin – I'll never empty it – and white bread run to mould on the fridge. Sitting room then. Carpet all stain and nicked-sofa imprinted. On the window sill still an ashtray. I think I'll leave it as memorial to the laughs we had. Make my way back to the toilet. Empty a bottle into the tank. So this is how it will be, last night in our flat. Tomorrow there'll be a party. I'll sleep on someone's couch. Later I'll take the Stansted Express. Get a plane to Ireland. Waves come over as I sit on my mattress. Quiet and deserted. Summer's come. The absent men. Desolation in this moment and where the future is, blind. But after I have cried, lie back and close my eyes. Stick my Walkman on. Batteries clinging to life. Perhaps I'll sleep right through this night. I'm tired enough. Try. I try. And soon I am rolling on through it. Dreamless, mercifully, and whenever I almost wake, seem to persuade myself to go back down again. All the distant sounds of city though still managing to get in so Wake!

Hours is it, I've been asleep? Maybe. No. Barely after six. Twelve to go. How shall I cross this? Will I be scared in the dark? Bang a loud knock. Up I sit. Bailiffs? Killers? Flashers? Oh fuck, oh fuck it. Knock again. Peer round the bedroom door. Yes? and gruffer, like I am of the world Who's there? Eily, it's Stephen, he says Any chance I can come in? And such a surprise I hardly know what to do. Just go and open. All tall there in his suit, shirt tails hanging out. Little dishevelled but lovely. Am I disturbing you? No, I say Come in.

My blood makes terrible noises as he follows me in. No furniture left so   let's go to my room. Where's everyone else? Already moved, this is my last night here. I see   isn't that a bit creepy for you? A bit, and I lean back on the wall So   Actually, he interrupts I couldn't have a glass of water, could I? Sorry, the water's off. Already? Fuck that's rough   then do you mind if I sit? No no, go ahead. He takes the end of the mattress and evening sun on his face. And he is different somehow although I can't quite   Well look, he says – looking himself like not knowing where to start. So he lights up before trying again

– So look, I saw Marianne   well   you know that   anyway I thought I'd come over because   after all the drama it caused I thought you might want to know   but I mean, if not, just say I do, I say Of course I want to know.

Okay – his fingers making churches that press to his lips – So   I went to the restaurant for one, as agreed. I could already see her in the window from Bow Street, swirling a glass of wine. I wasn't expecting that – I thought it'd be more of a strong coffee and sharp knives sort of thing. There she was though, looking much the same. Maybe a little older, though no signs of grey, touching by the temple for his own. But nervous as I was Eil, I could see she was worse, which helped me get over the doorstep. Anyway, she stood up when I came in. I wasn't sure of the etiquette but she shook my hand, thanked me for coming, offered a seat and was – naturally – too well-bred to get straight to the point. So there was summoning a bottle of whatever she had and hoping I didn't mind she'd chosen a red. Should we order first? Then during that carry-on, all the How's your health? And Is Rafi well? and I hear you're working on a script? In the end I just said Mari, what's all this about? – and I was surprised I called her that but   there you go. And what did she say Stephen? She said It's about Grace, and would I please hear her out first? She was pretty hesitant to start with but then it all came out. The general gist being that, apparently, Grace has been running riot. Skipping school, difficult at home, disappearing off without saying where's she's going then arriving in late reeking of drink. She got suspended from school for smoking a joint and, soon as she came back, did it again. So it was in the balance for a while about being expelled. It's sorted now but this was all news to me and, to be honest, I didn't know what to say. Then Marianne said, you know, I don't

283

want her going down that road. I couldn't bear to watch that happen to her too. I'm sure you're concerned Marianne, I said But a couple of rebellious spliffs doesn't make an addict, I had a lot of other contributing factors. She only said I know, but   I could tell there was more and, sure enough That's the other subject we need to talk about. She wouldn't look at me then and I got this wave of dread. Mari, I said Has something happened to Grace? She just looked at her nails so I pressed Marianne, has someone hurt her? I mean Eily, you know what was on my mind. No, I said something to her, she said Something I shouldn't have, about you, and I very much regret. About when I was using? I asked – I couldn't think of anything else. He gets up and. I told her about your mother, she said. I knew she couldn't know   so I asked what she meant? She said I guessed there'd been violence from flippant comments you'd make but, later on, I discovered there was something else   something sexual, is that right? I was pretty taken aback. Fucking horrified actually. I said How could you possibly know that? Even wasted I would never have told. So it is true? It is, I said But how do you know? When you were in Intensive Care, she said I went through your things and found a letter from your mother in an old notebook. She sounded eager to hear from you so I wrote asking her to contact me. A few days later, your stepfather did – that's when he told me she was dead. I explained who I was and why I had gotten in touch. I was diplomatic about the details but he understood and seemed concerned so I invited him to visit – I thought seeing family might help – but he refused so adamantly I was shocked. I promised his mother I'd leave that boy be, he said And, truth be told the sight of me would probably do more harm than good. He wouldn't expand but asked me to keep in touch. After that I had a few thoughts of my own. He, obviously, sounded quite rough on the phone and, presumably, there were valid reasons you weren't in contact any more but he did seem sincere so once a week I called. He was always pleased to hear you were improving and I began to ask about the rift. He was evasive but gave me to understand that more than I'd previously realised had gone on. We kept it relatively formal though, until the nursing staff caught you picking your leg open. That's when I finally broke down. Told him everything. What you'd done. That I was pregnant and couldn't understand why you were doing this to me. There's a lot in that boy's past, he said And it's not the kind of thing I like telling a girl like yourself but, perhaps, if it would help, he probably owed you that.

When my wife was dying I wanted to contact Stephen, he said They hadn't seen each other for a few years by then. I thought he'd want to know and have a chance to put things right. He'd always been a gentle sort of lad and what son wouldn't want to do that before his mother died? But when I brought it up, she was completely against it, wouldn't have me even mention his name. I thought it was because he'd run off and she couldn't forgive him, which seemed hard but then she was a strong-willed woman. So that's how it stayed, right up until it was clear to everyone, including herself, that the end wasn't far off. That's when she started to talk about him. Just a little at first but, soon enough, all the time. And not rambling, it was clear she was in her own mind. They were things I'd never really heard her say. About his father leaving her high and dry. Her family expecting her to give the baby up because that was the way. But, when she first held him, she said she knew she never could. I met her a few months later, on a bus. She said she was a widow, that her husband had been killed in a car accident. If I'm honest, I didn't believe her even then and over the years that story changed many times but she was so young and pretty I didn't really mind, or about the boy.

She seemed to remember him most fondly as a little boy, running round the yard, picking dandelions for her. How he'd spend hours on his stomach playing with his car. Or when he couldn't stop kicking his ball against the back door – I remembered that myself, three times I changed that glass. And once she'd started all these memories came flowing out. The holiday when she was pregnant with our first and Stephen was just above her knee. The two of them in the rock pools, eating ice creams. She said While I was watching him I realised I didn't love his father any more and that he was a fool for not caring about his son. But I understood how lucky I was, she said And that Stephen would always be who I loved most. She repeated that story frequently, like it was her last good memory. A few months later our son arrived and she had a very bad collapse. She was never really well again. But we all found it hard to hear her remember Stephen because of how long it had been.

So one night You've been talking a lot about Stephen, I said Let me contact that school of his, maybe they have an address. She refused and when I asked why she said Because I made life hard for him. I said It wasn't that bad. No, she said You don't understand. Something was broken, then once I got sick, it just opened up and I stopped being able to keep it inside. But I know now and I have to leave Stephen be. He's a good boy, despite what I did. I knew she'd always been rough on him so I said He won't hold the odd thrashing against you now. No, she said It wasn't that. It was worse than I could think and she wished she'd cut her own throat before she'd done it. I was shocked to hear her talk that way. But she went on and what she told me then I'll never get over for as long as I live.

From the start she knew she could never be without him and the fear of him being taken never left. People told her once she'd had more that would die down but our sons came and made no difference, didn't even feel like her own. All the feeling she had was for him and they understood each other in ways no one else ever did. Even when she had to beat him he knew it was for his own sake. As he got older though, the worse the fear of losing him became. It grew out of proportion. It went over the edge. It ran everywhere. He was a young man by then and starting, she knew, to think of things that might take him away. She dreamt it first, only that. And it shocked her, the idea, but   held onto her too. Then climbed into her and followed her, laid itself on the fear. Showed her how to find itself in the ways he looked at her. Like whispering and screaming it was with her all the time, convincing that, although unnatural, it would be natural for them. So one night, as a kindness, she took the step and afterwards knew he had also wanted it. She said I was careful to not hurt him that way, that was the difference, I thought. But sometimes she could see he wasn't happy, as though he didn't understand, then she'd have to beat him for tempting her. She'd swear it was the last time, they'd go back to a life without it in but she could never contain anything around Stephen so it always began again. Building up until she didn't know how to not. Then she'd let herself and tell herself it was alright because he was just a part of her really, another part of her own body. He belonged to her, after all.

He takes his glasses off, sets them down on the bed and sits rubbing his eyes with the heels of his hands. I say nothing to break the silence but watch a tear run down his cheek. Are you alright? He just nods and I know to leave him to calm himself.

Tic and tic and he sniffs it up, then wipes off his face.

I couldn't speak Eily, hearing all that, coming from Marianne but up out of that different world. Like going back in time. Still being there. Feeling what was happening but looking at my mother and then off into the patch of fucking damp on the wall. And the dread of it, Eily   you know   like you'll never escape.

Anyway   Marianne said my stepfather became very upset but said he was glad to be rid of the burden at last. He said your mother told him you were right to get away. That you deserved a life of your own but when you left the fear went everywhere. She tried to kill herself. She wanted to die but kept vomiting the pills and only in time understood why. Staying alive was the first part of the penance, she said. Years of rising to the surface, into the realisation of what she'd done. Years of living with the guilt but still hoping you'd return. She'd have forgone even forgiveness just to see your face again. But it crept into her, the knowledge that neither would happen and all life had become without you. Acceptance, and its attendant despair, was the second part of the penance for her. Its merciful third was her absence from the world, it could be her only amends. She finally understood how to encourage death to come. Let the years of starving take their toll. And she hoped, wherever you were now, you had made your life your own. He said she never spoke again after that. He thought she may have been waiting to confess because she deteriorated so rapidly afterwards and died the following night, alone. And he decided to leave you be. He thought she'd been right about that at least and didn't think he could face you anyway.

He stops again and takes a breath. Lights another cigarette. Apparently he'd never told anyone before Marianne – I can't imagine he ever told anyone after. He said after she died he got rid of every trace because he couldn't bear to think of what she'd done, on his watch. That he should have known and, when he thought about it, wondered if perhaps he had but it was easier to hang it on my difficult age and her just being a bit mad.

When I heard that story I was appalled, Marianne said And all I could think of was the night in the hospital when I told you your mother was dead. I don't remember, what about it? I said. She said Stephen, as soon as I told you, you started to cry and you cried a long time for her. Of course I saw nothing strange in it then but later, when I knew   I wondered what it meant. Because I still wanted to be with you though, I chose to forget. I never called your stepfather again. I didn't tell you or even remember until I began needing excuses for doing what I did. And I let what happened to you get so twisted in me. It's suited me to consider it one more awful thing. Another example of what I was protecting Grace from and I've never had cause to revise that opinion until   I told her.

Christ, Eily, when she said that I felt sick. What did you tell her for? I said You had no right. I never wanted Gracie to know. I hadn't planned to, she said But she arrived home one night very drunk and very late. When I confronted her, she just kept asking why you weren't allowed to visit? She said she knew it wasn't your choice, she could tell it was me. How she was going to move to London to get to know you properly and what was wrong with that? I had to say something Stephen. I couldn't just concede. I thought if she knew how it had been she'd realise she was being unfair. So I told her the worst of how you were back then. I didn't even have to embellish Stephen, the truth was bad enough. I told her about all the arguing and the sleepless nights. The brawling and the passing out. Junkies dossing around the flat. Picking my way through their sick, even when I was pregnant. People kicking in the door looking for you. Waking up alone and not knowing what you were up to. Every penny we had thrown away on it and all we had to do without. Food. Heat. Rent. Freezing in the winter because we couldn't afford coats. And what it was like, at four months pregnant, to get the call you'd collapsed. I'd been trying so hard to persuade myself that you were staying clean. You wouldn't jeopardise this because you'd waited so long for the break but, all the same, there it was: We don't know if he'll pull through so you should get here fast. It was a miracle I didn't miscarry then and there. And the shame of it Stephen, in front of the doctors. Then days of watching you in that bed. Not knowing, even if you came out of it, what would be left? Those weeks of waiting when you finally did. Having to leave the room because you'd get so upset and not knowing what I'd done. I didn't know anything except you were a mess and I was alone. My parents were awful – they enjoyed not being surprised – and by the time I got you home I was so angry. I know that probably wasn't very helpful but I still loved you and I hoped. All I wanted was a normal life Stephen. I wasn't asking very much. And you were so apologetic, so remorseful that I believed you would change. Then the money began to go missing again. I kept explaining it away because the truth just made no sense. You knew your body wasn't able, that it couldn't. Then the day I had my check-up, I'd arranged to visit a friend but I couldn't wait to tell you that the baby was well. It was the first good news in months so I came home instead. She was really kicking and I wanted you to feel it. But when I came in there you were, passed out on our bed. You and that asshole and a needle half pushed down the side like you thought I was stupid and might think you were asleep. But I thought you were dead and as I checked for a pulse, I finally realised that you didn't care. Not only about me or the baby but whether you were alive or dead. That's when I knew I had to leave. I couldn't take the fear of it any more, and the endless lies. So there was the humiliation of asking my parents if I could move back. Then the rest of the pregnancy I just waited for the call. I was actually relieved when you wound up in Friern. At least you were safe there even if everything else was destroyed.

God Eily, the things she said. I think I'd just blanked out what it was like inside. In my memory it's always heading off somewhere, nodding out on someone else's stairs or fucking about off my head. But I suddenly remembered what she was talking about. And it only got worse from there. She told Grace about the sleeping around. How I'd cheated on her every chance I had. Fucked her best friend in the toilet when we were on a night out. Given her the clap then accused her of giving it to me. About walking in on me with some girl in our bed and so wasted I didn't notice until she hit me with a record. More often knowing I had been, smelling it off me, but I'd just lie right to her face. I did that all the time, I know I did. Everything she said was true Eily and horrible to hear, to really remember how I'd treated her and then think of Grace knowing too. She said she asked her, what kind of man does that Grace? I've given you the best of everything in life, how can you choose him over me? But Grace just kept asking why she had to choose between? That you'd been clean so long, how could you not be different? Your letters proved you were. I couldn't have it Stephen, she said You being defended by her. I told her she knew nothing and I was sick of this childish romance about you she'd invented. You don't know what that man's capable of, I said. He's not fit to be your father. He isn't safe. You said what? I said and she said, I said Grace, I've gone out of my way to protect you from this but that man   he and his mother   they were far more than mother and son and if you think I'd ever risk him doing the same to you, you are very much mistaken.

Jesus Eily, to hear her say that. To know she'd said it to Grace. I just got up saying Oh God, how could you? I know, she said But   But Eily, I thought I was going to fucking kill her. I started shouting How dare you? How dare you say that about me? Whatever fucked-up things I've done I could never hurt Gracie. Marianne just kept saying Please Stephen, please sit down. But I couldn't and it just   All these years, I shouted When will you have enough? All these years of punishing me and now this. To try to frighten her   your own fucking child, for fuck's sake, how could you do that to her? Everyone in the restaurant was staring and I just   couldn't believe it. It's the worst thing I could imagine being said about me and then said to my little girl. Eventually the waiter said If you don't sit down you'll have to leave. I nearly hit him and Marianne kept going Please Stephen, please. I wanted to walk out but   I couldn't. I had to know what Grace said. Marianne was crying I think, by this stage and I was beside myself but   I did sit back down. And we sat. I was so fucking stunned it took a few minutes to ask What happened then, Marianne? She said I know that was awful, a terrible thing to say, and not true, I know you would never have hurt Grace. Marianne, I said I don't really fucking care what you know, what does Gracie think? She said Grace asked what I meant? And you said? When he was growing up there was   some kind of sexual activity with his mother. Even as I said it I realised what I'd done but it was too late by then. She wanted to know everything I knew and how I did. I tried to back-pedal but she was insistent, so I told her what I've just told you and   How did she react? I said. Stephen, she said She saw right through. She understood immediately and better than I ever had. I know he left home at sixteen, she said So what you're saying is that   when my father was a child   his mother did something   molested him? He was younger than I am now so isn't that what that means? Grace, I said. No, she said You're telling me my father was reared by a woman who did that to him? His own mother, the same way you're mine? My grandmother. Grace, I said. And you've known this all my life? Every time I've asked about him and you've said what a liar he was, what a strung-out mess, you knew that had hap-pened but you kept it to yourself? You didn't think it would help to explain? I didn't want to upset you Grace. But now you're telling me, she said So I'll be afraid of him. That's the only reason you're telling me, isn't it? Jesus Christ Mum   he's my father and something awful happened   what's the matter with you? And she was right Stephen, I saw it so clearly then, what the anger's done to me and how I've excused myself. All because I somehow had to win and seeing Grace see it made me very ashamed.

I know she called you the next day. I suppose that must have been a surprise. I don't know what she said but obviously not what I had. To be frank, we've hardly spoken since. The only reason she hasn't appeared on your doorstep is that I have her passport. I've tried to talk to her, to explain. She won't have it. All she'll say is that there has to be a change. So that's why I called you. That's why we're here. I know you'll find it rich of me to start asking for your help but I'm not asking entirely for myself. I'm asking because this is what Grace wants, even needs, and I've lost all right to refuse. So what exactly are you

asking Marianne? I said. And she said If you would be willing
to come to Vancouver, Stephen, to start spending some time
with her?

Oh Stephen! I say. He just nods. What did you say to her?
Well, I'd sort of calmed down once I'd heard what Grace's reac-
tion was and   it's not as if I was ever going to refuse, so I said
Yes of course I will, and Marianne said Thank you.

We just sat there then. It was a lot to take in. Realising your
worst secret isn't a secret is a very odd sensation. I didn't really
know what to think. I couldn't decide whether it was a relief
or I still wanted to kill Marianne. But far beyond all of those
things, those locked doors between Gracie and me were suddenly open. After so many years of waiting and wishing for
only that. I had to keep turning away to wipe my eyes. I felt a
bit useless actually Eil. And then the fucking food arrived.

He sits himself up and starts to smile. Oh bollocks, I thought
and, like she read my mind, Marianne said Well, we might as
well eat. Turned out I was hungry though, so I began wolfing it. We each had another glass of wine. Talked a little more
about Grace and what had been going on. When would be a
good time for me to come. Then we ordered another bottle of
wine – I suppose we weren't feeling so civilised any more. But,
in spite of everything that had just been said, I felt suddenly
pleased to be sat in that restaurant with Grace's name passing
back and forth between us. After so many years, and all that
went wrong, it was right to sit with Marianne and talk about
our girl. And, I don't know if it was the wine or what, but I
realised now was my chance to ask what I never thought I'd
have the opportunity to. Can I ask you something Marianne? I
said. Just as we're getting along so swimmingly! she groaned
Go on. Why did you take her the way you did? Just after she

was born it would have made sense but we'd been getting on pretty well for years – at least that's how it seemed to me – and the way you left   it was such a shock. Why did you do it like that? I can't believe you don't know, she said. No, I said I don't. I did it because I was still in love with you, she said And after everything we'd been through, when you finally cleaned up, you never asked me to come back. Not once Stephen and I would have too, right up to the moment when I got on that plane with her. Maybe you just didn't love me any more, or maybe you were ashamed, but I loved you so much my only option was to hurt you in the end. I thought it was so obvious, especially to you. I'm surprised you didn't realise. That never crossed my mind, I said No.

Remember those visits at David's? she said When I started to show you how to do little things for Grace and we'd laugh together like we were just normal new parents? Yeah, I said Of course I do. Well on one of those days I looked at you – being hopeless, I think, with her babygro – and I suddenly knew all that love was still there, which was ridiculous, frankly, after everything, but true nonetheless. Too proud to show it, of course. I had to keep punishing you. I wanted you to come grovelling and chase me around like when we first met. I'd get my chance to recriminate but still take you back. So I waited for you to give me that look which would mean The Start. And I waited. And waited. And then realised you were with David. He and I were in the kitchen, having a chat. I mentioned something about us reconciling. You should talk to Stephen, he said but   the look on his face. I just knew. And after The Seagull, everyone did. That was so bloody typical of you. Real salt in the wound. But even when you and he finished I think I still hoped. Then one night, collecting Grace, I asked what had caused it and you said you'd had a fling with Eleanor what's-her-name. That's when I knew I was wasting my time because you didn't see me as anything other than Grace's mother now. And you were always friendly, even warm, but you didn't notice me any more. Not when I wore short skirts, or low tops, or told you I'd slept with someone else. Good for you, was all you said and never got that look in your eye again. God that look made me put up with so much. It made me feel like the most beautiful woman in London, but it was gone and only Grace mattered to you. All that struggle, trying to help, trying to persuade you to clean up and the moment Grace arrived, it all just vanished. I think I was jealous of how you felt about her, what you were willing to do for her, that's terrible, isn't it? Marianne, it wasn't as straightforward as that, I said It's not like I hadn't given myself a good run for my money after you left. I know, she said But that's how it seemed to me then. So when I met Phil, and we decided to move away, I saw a chance to make you think about me again. I pretended, even to myself, that it was about protecting Grace but I waited to tell you until the very last minute so it would be as bad as it could possibly be. I never doubted I'd shame you into agreeing. I could still read you pretty well and you were always so sorry, so ashamed. I knew what it would do to you, losing Grace. I did it so it would. But you looked at me, Stephen, really looked at me that night and I'd finally done something to you.

By the time you showed up in Vancouver though, you weren't looking again. It was stupid of me to be upset, for God's sake, I was a happily married woman but   some things never go away. I might have been more amenable if you'd made a pass and I'd gotten to refuse. Except I probably wouldn't have, even then. If you'd only just left it Stephen, I might've come around on my own. It was your desperation for her that drove me mad so, every time you'd ask, you were just tightening the noose around your own neck. When we left England I'd decided I'd never make contact again. For those two years I worked constantly to make her forget. Never mentioned you. Called Phil her dad and tried so hard to make him that. But she'd never say it, even at four. She remembered you and asked for you. I never thought she would then, out of the blue, she'd ask When's Daddy coming round? Or run, calling for you, after some tall man in the street and I'd know I shouldn't be putting her through it but   I couldn't help myself. The bitterness was so bad. Her first memory though, is of you. Of you showing her the sea. I hate it when she tells that story. Why do you get to have that with her? Anyway, what does it matter. Daddy's who you've always been to Grace and, you probably won't believe this, but it was my parents insisting 'This isn't right. You have to tell that boy where his daughter is' that finally persuaded me to contact you again.

Eily, when I heard all that, he says I wanted to fucking kill her again. For the first time in over sixteen years I stopped feeling guilty and not because I thought she'd deserved it but because I realised I hadn't, not all of it anyway.

Jesus Marianne, I said All that rancour over all these years and I never knew that's how you felt about me. I used to wish there was some way you'd forgive me, I would have done any-thing for that. But I never asked you back because you said you never would. And by the time I got out of Friern Barnet there was nothing left of me for playing games. I could barely cope with getting out of bed and I'm sure it was humiliating, what happened with David, but he was all I had. At least until you let me see Grace and she gave me a reason to live, something to work towards and I did get there with her. I made a new life and

I know it didn't look like much but it was a lot for me. It was everything. And when you took her away I nearly died. Losing her is by far the worst thing I've ever had to survive. And now you're telling me, when it's years too late, that it all could have been different? I could have been part of my daughter's life and got to watch her growing up, if I'd made you feel pretty, if I'd chased you around? If I'd only realised there was still a fucking game going on? Jesus Christ. I would rather believe it was because you hated my guts than this stupid, vain, completely fucking ridiculous bullshit. At least hate has some blood in it. At least there's some human feeling in that, but to have done this to me because I didn't guess you shagging someone was supposed to make me jealous? Because I loved my daughter more than you? Then try to make her think I'm some kind of fucking pervert so you'd feel you'd somehow won? When did you not fucking win Marianne? You and your lovely life and your big fucking mansion that contains all the memories of my daughter I'll never have. I don't know what you thought the prize was but, whatever it was, you fucking won it. Well done! Jesus, if it wasn't for Gracie, I'd wish I'd never laid eyes on you.

So   that was that and we just sat there in the aftermath. I didn't know what else to say. I was completely fucking blind with rage. She was crying at first, then Stephen, she said I've behaved so badly, but I didn't have the energy for it. Leave it Marianne, I said There's nothing else to say. But No, she said Everything you've said is true and I've thought about it many times in recent months. And what, Marianne, I said Did you think? She said I think, how could I not have forgiven you by now, Stephen? I should have long ago because, the truth is, I've never been sorry I laid eyes on you. You gave her to me and I love her and, God, she looks so like you too. I sometimes think that's my punishment for taking her away, having to look at you in her every day. I think I should have gotten over myself years ago. On balance the time with you was difficult, yes, but you didn't ruin my life. As it turns out, those few years were a rough patch in what's been a fairly calm sea. By and large my parents took care of me. Expensive education. I never wanted materially, and when everything went to pieces with you I still had a home to run to. Soon after you I met Philip and I've been happy with him. I have three children I love – even if one is intent on driving me insane. I've had all those things I wanted in life. Big house. Nice car. A career which, if not stellar, is enough. And even though I know it's not for me, here you are after all I did, still willing to help with Grace. I think I've been pretty lucky in life, very, in comparison to you. Stephen, I feel terrible about what I said to Grace and I know it's far too late but I am very ashamed of having cut you out of her life. I can never make that up to you but I do apologise, sincerely apologise, and hope you'll forgive me one day.

I just looked at her Eily. That was pretty fucking unexpected, you know? I wanted to give her an earful then I thought Oh God, I'm so tired of all this and what it's done to every part of my life. I'm going to see Grace again, that's what counts, and if nothing else I understand the weight of a past you deeply regret. So I said I will forgive you Marianne but only if you'll finally do the same? I can't very well not now, she said Shall we try again, for Grace? Yes, I said I think we should. It got a bit quiet again so, to help finish off, I asked after her boys. She talked a little about them, which eased things up – that and the wine. We drifted on to people we'd known, who I was still in touch with and who was still working? I made some daft remark about being the last man standing and she started to laugh, which then set me off. We were both pretty hysterical I think, as well as a little drunk. But all that primness sliding off her was kind of   irresistible. I began to see her again, what had made me so wild about her back then. You look exactly like you did at twenty-one, I said. I wish that was true, she laughed I've often wondered how it would be to see you again, if you'd feel like a stranger? And do I? Not really, more solemn perhaps – and whose fault is that? – but mostly the same. Not too much I hope, I said. It was a compliment Stephen, take it! The first year we had together was pretty wonderful don't you think? It was, I said and, you know Eily, the way she looked at me, I suddenly stopped being angry. I suppose I never thought I'd see her smile at me again. We should do this more often, I said Although, perhaps, without the yelling first. I'm sure we will, she said Now Miss Grace has had her way. We finished up about then. I got the bill and paid – I owed her for her grand-mother's wedding ring, if nothing else.

When we came out she said Walk me as far as Charing Cross? So we strolled across Covent Garden. She scabbed a fag and I said I do remember I got you a coat Marianne, that time you were talking about. You stole me a coat Stephen, she said Which is not the same and a few months later one of your cronies stole it again. Then I got stuck in a bus queue in the rain and caught a cold and that's how Grace came to be. Really? Oh yes, I was quite sick and you were very sweet, kept bringing me bowls of soup and tea. You were always very attentive when I was ill, quite endearing actually. So I was just getting better, and you were in my good books for a change, and we ended up having a go. You kept saying how warm I was and should have a tem-perature more often, do you remember? And, funnily enough, I actually did but I said I never realised that was the moment.

Soon as I woke up the next morning, she said I had the feeling something had changed. I remember looking over at you, fast asleep beside, just starting to run a temperature yourself, and I thought Well Stephen, nothing will ever be the same again. For some reason I put an arm round her then. And she let me. We were both so wrecked. It was like the walking fucking wounded. But nice to be there, in that moment and sunlight, walking down the Strand.

When we got to Charing Cross, I hailed her a cab. Before she got in, we said our goodbyes and I went to kiss her cheek but she kissed me on the mouth, properly, you know? I was kind of off guard so I kissed her back. He looks over at me, but how can I react? Just pretend to nod calmly until he looks away. It was strange to kiss her, he says Because it was the same and, naturally, the old troublesome part of me started thinking Well, that might be fun. Old times' sake et cetera and then   I thought of you   and it was a pretty tired kiss after that, between two people who are really done. When we stopped she said That was nice. I thought Shit! and said Look Marianne. Only checking, she laughed Mind still on other things, eh Stephen? I didn't answer but, as she got in, she said So there is someone? I just shrugged. That was not a conversation I wanted to have with her. Never mind, I'm married, she said And I already know you shouldn't be my type, so I'll see you in Canada. See you soon, I said, shutting the door. Then they pulled out into the traffic and that was that.

Fuck Stephen, I say looking at him, only realising now what's different. His whole body. It's filled with light. He just doesn't know it yet and holds himself, because it's strange, very tightly down. So we look at each other with quiet eyes until he, too overcome even to smile, lights another cigarette. Stephen, you're going to see Grace. I'm so happy for you. I can't really believe it, he says I went into the first travel agent I passed and booked my ticket, second week of August, just over two weeks. Then I called her. Not for long – I'd only two pound coins – but she picked up and said Dad I knew it would be you. So I told her I was coming, that I'd see her soon. That things would be better with her mother from now on. That I loved her. She said it too. I asked if I could call for longer tomorrow? She said Yes, as my money ran out. And he covers his face because, maybe, he'll cry? Then shakes his head, to be rid instead, and looks up outside. I can see he thinks of something so far off from here. The purpling sky of Kentish Town isn't it. Who am I in the middle of this? Thank you for coming here to tell me, I say, expecting him to get up now and start making to leave but when he does how will I keep the promise I made? He doesn't move though. He says I decided I'd walk back, to clear my head, but the further I did the harder it became. Because, despite everything that had just occurred, I started dreading the hours ahead of sitting in that empty room. And I kept remembering last night, how it was before you came. Then how pointless it felt to kiss Marianne. How I know – and I do – that'll be the same with any woman who isn't you. And we are suddenly in the ocean. It is almost over our heads. But he stands up then, quick then, chucks out his cigarette. So I thought I better come see you, he says. Why? I ask, with the heart going awful in my chest. Because I am a fucking hypocrite, he says But I'm so tired of it and I don't want to make myself learn to live without you. So what do you think about getting on with our life together, whatever that will be like? Stephen, do you mean it? He pulls me up to my feet. I do, he says Will you have me back? I will, I say. Come on then, he smiles Let's you and me go home.

We stand outside a moment and be the faces beyond the glass surveying our old world. Empty flat. Goodbye that life, then pass on down the steps and drop my key in a drain. And so we go down through Kentish Town. Warmer out than in. Battered and happy. Quiet though, because soon enough the night will come. On into Camden. Up the Camden Road. Right onto his much For Sale street – not his though. Just dandelion leaves trod all down his path with this going away and the coming back. Some great ending it feels like. For now though, just go through his broke door.

His room a bit tidier. Boxes pushed a bit back. Warm from the day and cigarettes smoked. And all in through, the smell of him. Drop the duvet. Close the door behind while he shoulders off my heavy bag, turning in the dusty light. Pulling up his window to let the evening in. Some car then roaring down to Camden and after it, in waves, the Thursday traffic reams by. Soothes like balm. Calms the mind, and we, in here, are very calm, knowing now for the first time precisely where we are.

And he comes to me across the room to put his long arms around. Leaning down to be held and hold so well. Moving until we find the right place, where I fit with him. Sealing together. Closing every gap. Breathing each other like an ocean we have thought a long time of, and missed. I push his jacket off first. Shirt then. Tugging down where he must help, smiling at me, shaking cuffs from his wrists. Laughing when I kiss his warm armpit and, as he slides his glasses off, I touch his smooth shoulders with my mouth. There where they curve into collarbone. There, in the deep, as they round to his arms. Long and lean and strong I think. Just starting to turn brown. And kiss his chest in amongst the dark hairs. Smiling up to, arms around his waist. Opening, slipping off trousers and belt. He, obedient, stepping out, only stopping to kiss. Pulling now at his underwear, touching just a little and careful. Smiling to the grey eyes smiling at me. Catching me up to stroke my cheek. Then stepping back to watch me undress. Slipping clothes off and showing him myself. His warm hand laid on my breast. Thumb moving my nipple a touch. Happy together but so silent we are that a clock two floors up is more, that pigeons in the tree beyond make more noise than we two need to. And my turn to lead him back across the room. Sitting him on his armchair. Kneeling down between but up to kiss. To take his long fingers through my hair. Find his mouth with mine. His tongue with my tongue. His hands running my body but I'm sliding down. All his old scars. Each country of him. I know them like the world. The good smell of his chest, the lean stomach as well. Hold where he is hard, then bend to press against my lips. Shiver through him as I let it in. Past my teeth and onto my tongue. Deep into my mouth and he goes smooth in. Like warm stone. Soft skin. Moving him. Feeling all the filling veins fill until it must be almost sore. But the more I do, the more it goes. Down his legs. Up his torso. Travelling into the balls grown tight in my palm. Of all his body, the tenderest part, so I put my mouth there too. In through the folds and tickling beneath until he laughs and catches at my hand to stop, but taking all the pleasure that I have to give. Loving to. Rising up a little against when he goes back into my mouth. Tasting all of him there. Taking in far as I can. Going quicker until lips bruise. Then the long of my tongue does the work instead. Holding gently to keep him straight. Licking the little wet off the tip. Sticky of it on my lips. Going down again. And the excitement roams over. Up his back. Across his chest. In the bob of his throat, and as he puts his head back, I see where it's begun hazing out sight. His whole long body giving to each movement I make. The only sound is my mouth creasing with wet and his deep increasing breath until he's brought – in case I don't know – to saying Eily I'm really close. But I ignore this, because I can. Just keep him there, hard as he's ever been. But in a moment he says again Eily, I'm really close now. So I take him out, to say So come then. He just looks at me, tortured with want and full of feeling. I can't do that to you, he says. I want you to, I say Let's just be us today. Then take him back into my mouth, on the very verge of go. So he grips my hand. So he strokes my hair. So and then, he lets himself. And I can feel the pleasure roll across him, to and from my mouth. The swell of his body as it goes through. Then the first drops from the first wave spring to the back of my tongue, coming up from inside him and out into me. And I able for it, the warmth and taste of him. For the more of it and more. Him hardly controlling, even pushing a bit. His whole body alive and hot in my mouth. I shift back just enough to make more room, then swallow, swallow it down. Swallowing until he is done and. Breathes as if he can't quite catch the air while I, to complete, lick him clean. Still hard though he's finished, but fragile in it. Kiss the gentle head and rest myself in the crease, down by the dark pubic hair and breathe him in. Open as I have ever been. The wind could rush right through without touching my skin so at peace with it, and in love with him, that I could stay here for years. But he leans himself forward and says Come up here to me. I reach my arms round his neck to be pulled onto his knee. Two months Eily, he says Or two years or twenty, whatever you'll give me, I'll take.

In the close night I wake alone in bed but, across the dark, he is at his desk. Streetlight filleting the bones in his back. Cigarette, of course. So I get up and go put my arms around him. What are you doing, my love? Just thinking, he says And looking at this picture of my mother again. I can just about remember her looking like this. Who could've imagined what would come next? Or guessed the girl in this photograph would starve herself to death? Or that on hearing it all I'd be able to think of was   how much I loved her   when I was a little boy. In our quiet warm world we think on that. Then he drops the photo. Stubs out his cigarette. Says Come on, and takes me back to bed. We make ourselves comfortable in each other's arms there, then go to sleep.

LAST DAY

Friday 21 July 1995

Strings of sunlight all through my hair as I make on up Haverstock Hill. Quick, for he almost has me late. Shit! Nearly ten! Run down Prince of Wales Road. Front steps bereft of the usual herd, all up on the balcony now. In I too and up the stairs. Just beginning, as I get there. Wedge myself in amid the costume rails. Poor fuckers, she whispers friendly-like and budging up. Hey Alison, yeah, I don't envy them this. Everything resting on it. Get a job. Get an agent. What's Danny doing? Miss Julie, I say. She rolls her eyes Of course he is, he doesn't half fancy himself!

Straight after the run-through First Years disperse for the readying. My job's a spot of foyer sweeping. Making sure the Spotlight pictures are neat. Telling Danny, as he wanders past Break a leg! and Me and Stephen are back together again! Good work, he says Any chance of asking his agent to keep an eye out for me?

Soon enough the afternoon showing begins. First and Second Years – banned from sound – cram ourselves into the canteen. Hear casting directors and agents come in. Glasses clink and Hello darling! Third Years cracking the side door open, waiting for their cues. Then disappearing off into the Church. Afterwards whispering That went well, or I fucked up, or I really can't tell, suppose I'll have to wait and see. But time goes round and soon he'll come which makes me somewhat insensible to their suffering.

Tap polite claps through the door, then a hum up of standing. I go out into the loiter of Third Years waiting, making interesting, looking thin. Teachers sympathising or saying Well done. Hey Danny, happy? Reasonably, he says Just got to hope now I get a bite, but there's someone waiting for you outside. So I follow on out to the brim of day. And leant against the pillar, there he is. Talking to some small man – or who by comparison, seems. The lightness still all about him, right through his long frame. Fag in his mouth. Loot under his arm. Saying No he is, I saw him last term and I'm actually thinking of getting him to read. Then he sees me Hey Eil! – taps the little man's arm – Hang on a sec, this is her. And reaches through the mayhem for me. Been waiting long? Few minutes, he says So let me introduce you. This is my girlfriend Eily, this is my agent. Hello. Shake and Is that short for Eileen? Éilís, Stephen says Hey Danny, over here, there's someone I want you to meet.

Fancy a walk Eil, before we head home? So we See you later, the others and off we go. He unfolds the Loot as we cross to Crogsland Road. I'm thinking it's time to move. I'll soon need the extra space, what with an office and a room for Grace and fancy moving in properly? My mother will probably kill me, I say But I don't care so yes! Then stop to kiss on the kerb between the Enterprise and, now closed down, Fortune Village Chinese. Whereabouts do you fancy? Camden forever, I say. I thought you might say that, so how about this one then? Three bedrooms up off Delancey Street? Yeah that looks great. Okay, then I'll give them a call, as we cross over the Chalk Farm Road. Up onto Regent's Park Road. Across the bridge. Taking the heat of the afternoon on our heads. Arms around each other, we go past shops and the Russian tearoom on the right. All the way up to the phone boxes by the park gates. I'll just nip in and make that call then, he says. I rock back on my heels as he does. Watch a plane passing over. The white it brings.

A perfect sky cut but of this world, like me and him. In it. Ready now.

What are you smiling about? he asks. Just am. Well we can see it at six and, if we like, we could move in next week. Then quick catch hold of each other, wide-eyed. Ready for the plunge? Long past Eil, you? I am. Good, come on.

So through the shade of sycamores we climb Primrose Hill. Grass crisped by July. Dogs barking below. Some lads from my year making the most of a football. To me! No, to me! I said You dick!

At the top we stretch out on the scrub and kiss a little and admire the smog. Easy together so fall to some catching up. We got the final green light for the film. Congratulations! I say Does that mean you've solved the end? God I hope so, he says I just realised after all these months of thinking about him again, even with all his fuck-ups and the state he was in, I was actually kind of fond of him. I wanted to give him something better than what happened to me. Besides which, it's not autobiography. I can finish it any way I want. So how did you? Well, he says Now he's up there on the roof, end of the night. Losing it. Waiting for God to come back. Slowly the sun starts to rise so he watches as the sky turns white. Quiet everywhere. Then he sees a girl making her way down the street. Maybe still a little drunk from the night but beautiful, with her hair catching all the light. Almost mesmerised, he keeps watching her, his ungodly sign, until the sun is up and she has gone from sight. Then the camera pulls back gradually from the roof, the street and away across all he can see until he's no more than a fragment of the city, until even he can't be seen any more. It's beautiful, I say. I hope so Eil, there should be some, even in that life. And he kisses me then, so we kiss. Then for a while we're the kissing idiots on top of Primrose Hill teaching all of London what happiness is, for lying there together, we already know.

Standing up later we pick grass and daisies from our hair. Linger for a moment over the city arrayed. Come on, he says, arm around my waist It's time to go. One minute more, Stephen? So he stays to look with me through its towers and bridges. Across its shops and along its streets. At Londoners getting ready for their Friday nights. Somewhere below trains go in underground while above buses find to all the different towns that have become London now. But even its tumult is peace for me. He walks down the hill a little before turning to call Eily, Eily, stretching out his hand. Come on my love, he says We haven't got much time. I take one last look at him there against the evening sky then go naked to him, open to him, full of life.

Acknowledgements

Firstly, I would like to gratefully acknowledge the support of the Arts Council of England and the cool heads of Tracy Bohan, Hannah Griffiths, Rachel Alexander and Mitzi Angel.

Then, many thanks for so many things to my mother Gerardine, my brother Fergal, Marietta Smith, the great Henry Layte, Phoebe Harkins, Ross MacFarlane and Damian Nicolaou.

For all the reading and forbearance – as well as everything else – I thank my husband and daughter, William and Éadaoin Galinsky.

And finally, and fondly, thanks to all of Group 33.